Praise for
William P. Wood

"No one writes a better police procedural than Bill ·Wood, and *Sudden Impact* is his best one to date—lucid prose, meticulous legal detail, and unforgettable characters struggling in various moral quandaries. Terrific, unputdownable stuff."
>—John Lescroart, *New York Times* bestselling author of *The Thirteenth Juror* and *The Hunt Club*

"William Wood is a master of suspense. *Sudden Impact* is Wood at the peak of his powers, tense and eloquent, with characters and a story of political intrigue and riveting tragedy."
>—Steve Martini, bestselling author of *Compelling Evidence*

"Wood clearly knows the inner workings of the judicial system."
>—*Publishers Weekly*

"A feeling of truth permeates this book . . . one of the better courtroom dramas of recent years."
>—*New York Times,* for *Rampage*

"The story never cools down and never plays tricks."
>—*Kirkus Reviews*

"The nonstop action and relentless pace will satisfy fans of the hard-boiled thriller genre."
>—*Publishers Weekly,* for *Gangland*

"A spellbinding tale about the men and women who dispence justice from the bench."
>—*Associated Press,* for *Broken Trust*

"William P. Wood . . . knows the intricacies and ironies of the legal system. He also knows how to employ them to weave a compelling story."
>—*San Diego Union,* for *Stay of Execution*

Also by William P. Wood

SUDDEN IMPACT

WILLIAM P. WOOD

SUDDEN IMPACT

A NOVEL

TURNER

Turner Publishing Company

424 Church Street • Suite 2240 • Nashville, Tennessee 37219
445 Park Avenue • 9th Floor • New York, New York 10022
www.turnerpublishing.com

SUDDEN IMPACT

Cover design: Maxwell Roth
Book design: Glen Edelstein

Library of Congress Catalog-in-Publishing Data

Wood, William P.
  Sudden impact / William P. Wood.
    pages cm
  ISBN 978-1-62045-466-4 (pbk.)
  1. Murder--Investigation--Fiction. 2. Legal stories. I. Title.
  PS3573.O599S83 2014
  813'.54--dc23
                           2013025220

Printed in the United States of America
14 15 16 17 18 19 0 9 8 7 6 5 4 3 2 1

For my mother, Eleanor, and my father, Preston,
with more love, admiration, and gratitude than I can
express

SUDDEN IMPACT

ONE

OFFICER BOB QUINTANA did not see the car that hit his partner Tommy Ensor.

It was one thirty in the morning, now Thursday, and the rain had gotten heavier in the last fifteen minutes. When he looked down the dark, rain-sheeted Capitol Mall, he could just make out the lighted white front of the ornate State Capitol three blocks away. He was bored and cold on the N Street side of the large construction site so he went to see what Ensor was doing at the front of the new building.

He found Ensor standing outside the foreman's trailer, sheltered by twenty stories of partially finished red steel girders and flooring for the new Wells Fargo Bank headquarters. Ensor wore a black Sacramento Police Department raincoat, his uniform hat in protective plastic, and he carried a large flashlight. He swung the flashlight around the gaping, unfinished lobby, where the plastic sheeting covering machinery and scaffolding crackled in the storm's wind.

"So what the hell did you get me into?" Quintana asked.

"Forty an hour plus," Ensor said. He grinned. He was tall and angular and ten years older than Quintana. "Maybe in September

3

I can swing us to work security at the State Fair. That's maybe a hundred an hour."

"I can take the heat. This weather's killing me."

"Only about five hours to go." Ensor strolled to the raw concrete edge of the lobby and Quintana followed him. Rain pooled in the dirt outside around large trucks and digging equipment glistening. "Speaking of, you still coming with me to Clear Lake on Saturday?"

"Hell, yeah. I got guys in Auto Burg begging, *begging* for some of the smoked trout I brought back a couple months ago."

"Okay. We're on. I plan on pulling out around four. I'll bring the peppermint schnapps. You bring the cigars, I don't care what kind." He looked over at Quintana. "You asked Beth about taking off for the weekend?"

Quintana shook his head. "I don't have to ask. She's okay and we're not married yet."

"Oh, Bob, Bob," Ensor said slowly, "listen to me. This is the perfect time for you to ask about stuff like this, before you get married. Get a routine going. It saves a lot of road wear down the line, believe me. Sixteen years now and I tell Janey when I'm going on a beer run, for Christ sake. You get trust going early."

"Beth's fine," Quintana said. "She's talking about something else."

"So she's talking about kids."

"Oh, yeah. Like right away. Like we didn't agree we'd wait a year, two maybe."

"Talk all you want, do whatever you have to do," Ensor said, moving his flashlight beam among the dark, bulky machines. "You still get surprised. My second kid, Marty, he was a total surprise, but it works out, believe me. My four—two were on the schedule and two weren't, and it's all great."

"Shit. Four," Quintana said. He cursed into the rain and dark. "I need to rethink my options." He laughed and so did Ensor.

"Hey, you got any coffee left?" Ensor asked.

"I got a Thermos full in my car."

"Bring that sucker out here. It is too goddamn cold." He stamped his feet, clicked off the flashlight and put it in his raincoat pocket. A sudden rush of wind pelted them with rain even in the shelter of the unfinished lobby. They both darted further back.

Quintana pulled his uniform hat down so he would not get rain flying right into his face. "Hey, Tommy, some asshole knocked over the cones out in front. I saw them just now as I was coming by. I'll get the coffee while you put them back up." He grinned.

"I'm senior tonight," Ensor said, "so you should go get your ass soaked." He grumbled and pulled his own hat down. "Yeah, yeah, meet you back here in a couple."

Quintana watched him, hunched over in the rain and wind, heading for Capitol Mall which the grand new structure faced. Half of the block had been cordoned off partly with chain-link fence and orange traffic cones for the men and machines to use during the day. Quintana realized that Ensor, like him, had taken off his orange, reflective vest sometime during their dull, lonely vigil. People emptied out of the heart of California's capital after five. After midnight there was no traffic, either. Just extra off-duty pay.

He turned and headed back through the lobby that reeked of damp cement and upturned earth. His flashlight beam bouncing around the man-made cavern made spectral shadows and fantastic monsters.

Suddenly Quintana heard a crunching—almost gelatinous—thud and a speeding engine's whine fading swiftly with distance. The sounds came from behind him. They were the sounds of an impact. Between them it seemed like a great deal of time passed, even though he realized it was a second, a fraction of a second perhaps.

He yanked out his handie-talkie from his raincoat and at a lope started back to the front of the construction site. "Tommy? What's up? Tommy, you there? What's going on?" he said rapidly.

His harsh questions to Ensor were met with silence. He snapped off his flashlight in case someone was waiting in the darkness and picked up his pace as he now raced toward the entrance.

Quintana splashed through the pooled rain and mud outside the building, past the trucks and cranes. He got to Capitol Mall, rain swept and deserted. He looked up and down the street and saw no one and he kept calling for Ensor on the handie-talkie, then he lifted his head and shouted aloud.

He snapped his flashlight back on and sent its beam sparkling with raindrops dancing into the street, past the link fence and the ragged line of overturned orange plastic cones. Then he spotted a bunched black shape in the middle of Capitol Mall.

As he ran toward it, Quintana wondered why everything was so dark; then an observant, detached part of his mind noted that several of the high overhead streetlights had blown out at some point during the storm.

When he got to the middle of the street, he instantly recoiled. Ensor had been thrown onto his back, his uniform hat farther down in the lane. His right arm was bent across his body, white bone sticking up jaggedly, and his legs were tangled impossibly with each other so that he seemed to have two left feet. Quintana got down on his knees and quickly checked for a pulse. He found it in Ensor's neck, and checked his breathing. He then saw that the left side of Ensor's head, the prematurely gray-white streaked hair, was red, and, through a ragged hole, Quintana could see the pale gray of Tommy Ensor's brain.

"Tommy? Can you hear me? Tommy? Tommy?" Quintana said loudly as a red sheet spread across Ensor's face, blood and rain obscuring his unseeing eyes.

Quintana knew he should not move Ensor, but he could not leave him in the middle of the street. Any car or truck would not make out either of them until it was too late.

He got his hands under Ensor's armpits and awkwardly dragged him the six feet across one lane of Capitol Mall to the grassy median where he carefully laid him down. Then Ensor stopped breathing.

Quintana swore, the rain running down his face, making it hard to see. He started chest compressions, blowing air alternately into Ensor's mouth. He fumbled, dropped the handie-talkie in the grass, found it, and, between brutally pushing down on Ensor's chest, and trying to will Tommy to live with each forced breath he gave him, he yelled a call for help.

"Officer down! I got an officer down! I need immediate medical assistance! Immediate medical assistance!" and he heard a hoarse, strange voice obscenely, frantically giving out the address, his name, and Ensor's name, as if there were some way to turn back the last forty seconds.

TWO

"JESUS, WHAT THE HELL WAS THAT?" the passenger exclaimed to the driver.

"Just something in the road, Eli," the driver answered, his face fixed forward looking through the windshield.

"Felt like something, Frank," the older man said stubbornly. "Could you see?"

"No, I couldn't."

"Maybe we should stop and take a look."

"It was just something in the road. Tree branch maybe," the driver repeated slowly, tautly. "You were half asleep."

"Well, it sure as hell felt like we hit something back there."

The driver licked his lips. He was younger than his passenger and he wore a dark blue tailored suit with an ivory shirt and a neatly knotted burgundy silk tie. The heavy trees and streetlights alternately splashed shadows and lights on their faces as they passed.

The older man yawned. He had a small, round face and half-glasses partway down his nose. His silk tie was loosened and he rubbed his cheek. "Felt like an elk, Frank. When Vee's mother and I lived in New Hampshire for a while, I hit this elk. It just came out of nowhere, out of some trees and it felt just like that. Bang."

"I don't think there are any elks in the state capital, Eli."

"I guess not." The older man chuckled. "Gave me a shock just now."

"I've almost got you home."

"So I see."

They fell into silence. The driver breathed heavily and the trail of shadows and lights over his face showed an abrupt light film of sweat.

"Damn," the older man said softly. "I still miss her, Vee's mother. She was a fine lady, Frank."

"Yes, she was."

"Two years she's been gone and it seems like two thousand or two seconds." Eli blew out a breath. "The whole damn thing is so damn strange. That's the one thing I know. The older you get, really older like me, the stranger the whole damn thing is."

"Almost home. You had a lot to drink tonight, Eli."

"I suppose I did. Standard practice lately." Eli glanced over at Frank. "But it's in a good cause tonight. You watch. People at the thing tonight, they'll help us get you on the Court of Appeal."

"Sure they will."

"Leave it to me. This is the kind of business I know. Making people feel right about doing the right thing."

"I appreciate it, Eli."

"Nothing to appreciate. Just my nature. My one natural gift. Good at parties, good at handing out the drinks, good at slapping backs and kissing the right asses." He chortled to himself and his voice grew softer and then faded as he talked.

Frank didn't look over but he thought Eli had gone to sleep again.

Only a couple of blocks to his father-in-law's house and then he could go home himself, Frank thought. But that wasn't all he thought about, the empty streets stretched ahead, the cold rainy night everywhere around him.

Eli stirred beside him in the car. "I wonder what the hell we hit."

THREE

ASSISTANT CHIEF OF POLICE JERRY NISHIMOTO got the call ten minutes later on one of the two cell phones he kept charged on his teak bedside table. He could hear the wind whine through the Chinese elms and Monterrey pines around the house. The hardwood floor was cold on his bare feet when he threw off the covers and sat on the side of the bed.

He automatically noted the time and knew that this was not the call telling him he and Lisa were going to Nassau all expenses paid or that they had won the Mega Millions lottery prize of seventy-five million dollars. But even after twenty-three years as a cop, he still reveled in the jolt, the instant rush of brightness that lit up his mind and all his senses at a moment like this. He willingly paid for it with having high blood pressure, weighing too much, and being short-tempered.

He found the pen and pad he kept near the phones. Caller ID showed him that it was Guitierrez.

"Go ahead. This is Nishimoto."

"Jerry, one of our patrol guys got into a hit-and-run just a little while ago." The chief of police, Nishimoto's boss, friend,

9

and sometime adversary, spoke a little breathlessly with a slight Spanish inflection.

"His fault?" Nishimoto's first commandment was to make sure the Sacramento Police Department's bulwarks were not in danger.

"No. He and another off-duty were working a security job at the Wells Fargo construction site and somebody came like a bat out of hell and nailed him." Chief Gutierrez's tone was both angry and sad.

"Who's the cop, Javier?"

"Ensor, Thomas Ensor."

"Shit. Shit," Nishimoto said involuntarily. Lisa stirred beside him, turned on her table light, and sat up in bed. She brushed long brown hair off her eyes, glanced at Nishimoto, and then looked ahead.

"Damn right this shits. I gave Ensor the Medal of Valor six months ago and now he's at Sutter ER, and that's where I'm going to be in exactly eight minutes."

"How bad is he?"

"It was a fucking major hit-and-run," Gutierrez swore uncharacteristically, "the report I got is very bad."

"I'll pull a team together, Javier. We'll get you some good data on what happened very fast."

"Very fast. I'm calling Ensor's wife as soon as I hang up and I want to have something to tell her and the mayor this morning, Jerry. In the next couple of hours would be ideal." He spoke coldly. They had talked about who would succeed the urbane and popular chief when he retired in the next year or so. Nishimoto knew he was Javier's choice between the two assistant chiefs, but that could change. A hero cop's hit-and-run could change everything in a split second.

Maybe it already has, he thought. Lisa got out of bed and went into the bathroom. He heard the clattering of the clothes hanger behind the door where she hung her green robe.

"I'll get down to the barn," Nishimoto said, meaning the police department downtown, "and set up a tactical headquarters. We'll run communications and investigations out of the fourth floor."

"Jerry, just get some bodies out at the scene right now. I want that place wall-to-wall with our guys. Okay?"

"It's done, boss."

"I want someone damn good riding things. Damn good, all right?"

"I'll put the best I got."

"Call me on my cell as soon as you have a name, a license plate, some goddamn thing." He hung up.

Nishimoto got out of bed, flipped on the bedroom lights, and took out his freshly dry-cleaned uniform, the gold tabs sparkling on the collar. He moved without haste, but very deliberately. He was thinking who he needed right away and who could wait until things were set up. He ran through lists of equipment that would be brought to the largest conference room on the department's fourth floor. He was, he admitted, relieved that the chief, and not him, was notifying Ensor's wife. Although he had done his share of delivering bad news, like the time Oscar Negron dropped dead at his desk of an undetected aneurysm and his wife tried to grab Nishimoto's gun when he told her, he had no talent for real personal empathy. It was a gaping defect that he would have to work hard to correct when he became chief.

Then it came to him suddenly who he should send to lead the investigation. Someone with a proven track record of quickly closing cases, a long history with the department, and, best of all, a known irritant, a major source of annoyance to his rival for appointment as chief.

Terry Nye, Nishimoto concluded silently. He'll get results and he'll drive Altlander crazy doing it. Thrown off balance, always keeping an eye on Nye and me, Assistant Chief Altlander could easily stumble. So would end Altlander's pursuit of being chief.

For a moment, Nishimoto regretted that a tragic opportunity like this one had to be seized. But it was an opportunity nonetheless.

He saw Lisa come out of the bathroom in her robe as he dressed.

"You don't have to get up." He struggled to close his belt.

"What else am I supposed to do? The phone rings. You're up."

"It sure as hell isn't the first time. Go back to bed."

"I can't just go back to sleep."

"There's nothing you can do. I got to get out of here." He fumbled trying to tie his black tie.

"What exploded? Who died? Who's been shot? What's the crisis this time?"

Lisa shoved her slender hands into the pockets of the robe. She was taller than him, narrow faced, her mouth pressed thin lately. Or maybe he only started noticing how bitter she seemed lately. He got his service gun out of the locked safe on the top shelf of the clothes closet. He remembered hiding the safe so cleverly until the afternoon he found his eldest child, six-year-old Michael, wobbling on a chair, trying to reach it. What he said to Michael, and how he said it, was the only time he deliberately terrified his son to tears. Lisa did not talk to him for a week afterward.

Now Michael and his brother, Cooper, were in college in Oregon, and their sister, Jana, was already working for a movie company in Los Angeles. The strange, unanticipated emptiness around the house seeped corrosively into both him and Lisa.

He buckled his gun into its holster and put on his well-shined black shoes and repeated what the chief had said about Ensor.

"I feel sorry for his wife," Lisa said. "She's not the smartest person on earth, but we had a good time at the dinner when he got the medal. She's pregnant again."

"Ensor's not the smartest guy on earth either. Five kids at his pay grade is crazy." Nishimoto stopped and checked himself quickly in the full-length mirror on the closet door. He was no longer pleased with what he saw. The college track star and top of his class at the Academy was unrecognizable. Somebody balding, paunchy, and stone-faced had secretly taken his place.

Lisa headed for the kitchen, turning on lights as she went. Nishimoto finished dressing, remembered to grab his raincoat and cell phone. He could not find the car keys.

He followed her into the kitchen. Branches of a Chinese elm outside scraped against the window over the sink. Lisa watched the coffeemaker at the granite counter they had put in a few years earlier.

"Where are the car keys?" he said.

"I must've put them down somewhere," she said, glancing around the cluttered countertop, cereal boxes, jars, scraps of notes. Lisa worked as a manager at a company that ran condominiums around the city and she left reminders to herself everywhere in the house. "Here they are." She uncovered them from beneath a pile of notes and handed them to him.

He said, "My car won't be out of the shop until tomorrow. You're okay to get to work?"

"Elaine can pick me up again. Maybe I won't go in."

He paused. "I don't have time for coffee."

"I thought just in case." She didn't offer more.

"I'll try calling later," he said going to the door that led into the garage. The rain clattered loudly for a moment and fell off as suddenly, as if exhausted.

Lisa followed him a few steps. "Is he going to die, Jerry?"

"Maybe. I don't know. Maybe."

"It's not supposed to be the way a cop who got a medal goes out, is it? Cops don't fall off ladders or get run over. Cops don't die like everybody else."

"Sure they do. There's nothing special about being a cop when it comes to that. Cops die in every stupid, ugly, shitty way just like everybody else," he flared. He didn't know why he was angry.

Lisa stared at him as if she did not realize how crucial this investigation about what had happened to Thomas Ensor, starting at that instant, was to both of them. How they lived the rest of their lives depended on it, and Nishimoto was convinced she was thinking of something else, which could not matter as much. Nothing could.

As he went into the garage, his wife said, "Jesus. Jesus Christ," like she was about to cry.

"I'll try calling soon as I can," he said when he started the car.

FOUR

TWO BLOCKS BEFORE HE GOT TO HIS OWN house on the eight hundred block of South Land Park Drive in Sacramento, Judge Frank Stevenson switched off the headlights of his black late-model SUV. He had just dropped off his father-in-law Eli Holder at the big old house in the Fabulous Forties neighborhood. Cheery good nights, Eli wobbling a little into his darkened mansion.

Now the rain spattered noisily on the SUV's roof, the windshield wipers purred almost silently, and there were no other sounds as he stared ahead.

He fought the impulse to punch the accelerator and rush home. Instead, he managed to keep exactly at the speed limit. Sometimes passing the old Art Deco Tower Theater, he spotted Sacramento cops lurking in a patrol car, waiting to pounce on drivers speeding around the turn off of Broadway onto South Land Park Drive.

Judge Stevenson thought it unlikely any cops were waiting there now at one forty in the morning, but he did not want to be stopped.

What the hell happened? he thought again. *Did anything happen?*

It was clear Eli was too drunk and tired to know what happened.

Stevenson himself was having a very hard time picturing the

last ten minutes, as if a thick translucent curtain had drawn over his sight and hearing.

All he knew with complete and unfettered clarity was that something significant had just occurred, and he had to get home without anyone seeing him.

The older, well-maintained homes along the street, fronted by tall oaks and elms, were dark and quiet so early in the morning. Only the garish purple and yellow neon piping around the theater's spire, receding behind him, splashed color in the night world.

Stevenson felt his heart pounding heavily and, although he was forty-two and in splendid shape, he was afraid he was going have a heart attack. He clutched the steering wheel so hard his knuckles cracked, and he took deep breaths.

What happened? What happened? What happened? flooded his mind like a bell ringing incessantly.

When he glanced ahead, he saw a break in the dark, opaque clouds over the city, revealing a momentary vista of the night sky. He saw stars distantly and a fractured marble white moon overhead and then the clouds rolled over it all again.

He turned left when he got to the eight hundred block, passing the houses of his neighbors, everything in its place and familiar. But merely seeing his own house come into view, flanked by the redwood tree and the elms, the lawn trim, a two-story white colonial on a street of other colonials, Spanish and modern homes, unchanged, safe, gave him sharp physical pain. He slowed the SUV in the middle of the street because he did not trust himself to turn up his own driveway.

He squeezed his eyes shut, trying to stop the pain, which he recognized was not a heart attack or really physical at all. It came from an unidentifiable place and he was at its mercy and it terrified him. He made inchoate groans. The rain, softer and likely to last longer, started again. The windshield wipers flicked back and forth across his unfocused eyes.

I can't just sit here, he thought. *I've got to get home. I've got to put the car away so no one sees it.*

He tried to forget Eli had even been with him. It was too much now to sort out what having sweet, weak, unreliable old Eli with him would mean.

Who might remember, maybe, fragments, something.

It's his fault. I wanted to get him home. I could see he was getting tired and his small heart attack was only a year ago. I was trying to help him for God sake . . .

Not now, not now, Stevenson yelled inwardly.

Stevenson eased forward a little jerkily, as if he had just learned to drive. From long habit, he reversed the SUV so he could back into garage. He liked to be able to drive the SUV straight out into the street in the morning. But suddenly a thought struck him. He rolled back to the street again, turned once more so the SUV was facing into the garage. He hit the door opener and the white door swung up.

Can't let anyone see the front of the car, he thought. *Close call. Got to watch every step.* He drove ahead and stopped.

He sat for a few moments in the garage inside the SUV, the engine running quietly. He turned it off and fell into the silence. He hit the garage door opener again and the door swung closed. He was in complete darkness except for the dim, watery streetlight leaking through the sole decorative window in the garage.

Okay, now what? he thought and his legs started shaking involuntarily, like the last three thousand feet when he, two other judges, and a surgeon climbed Mount Whitney. He roughly grabbed the door handle and got out of the SUV, bending over abruptly as a spasm shot through his gut. He thought he might vomit, but the moment passed.

Stevenson went to the front of the SUV, on the driver side. Veronica's black Lexus was parked alongside it.

He knew he had to be quiet. That was key. Veronica and Haley were asleep in the house. Everyone on the block was asleep. If he could just see what had happened, sort it out in his mind, undisturbed while they slept, he might be able to manage the situation.

Stevenson studied the crumpled front fender, shattered outer headlight, the deep ragged dent in the hood, and the spidery lines along his side of the windshield. *No wonder the moon looked broken,* he thought. He ran his hand over the crushed metal, like he could smooth it out or grasp its significance by touching it.

There's no way to hide damage like this, he realized. It was open, raw, and revelatory. It announced its meaning instantaneously to whoever saw it.

I've had an accident. I've hit something, he thought. *Everybody will know.*

The force of that realization sent him stumbling frantically around the front of both the SUV and the Lexus, to the door leading into the laundry room. He yanked at the handle, almost yelling, then jammed his hand into his pocket for the house keys. They were on the key ring still in the SUV. Stevenson clambered back, got the keys, and worked intensely to control his rising panic. He gently opened the door and stepped into the laundry room. It smelled of lilac and bleach. He did not turn on a light and loudly bumped against the washing machine. "Fuck," he hissed aloud.

He moved into the dark kitchen. It was a new, strange place; familiar objects were different, even dangerous. As he hurried to the roll of paper towels by the microwave oven, he managed to hit the side of his head on the sharp edge of the copper hood over the stove. The pain was like lightning. He swore again.

A pinprick by comparison, he thought with immediate recognition. *Nothing like a couple-ton SUV hitting a human body.*

He yanked the whole roll of paper towels off the counter and shoved it under the faucet in the sink. His thoughts were a cascade of impressions and certainties and he had to jerk them back to the important, essential task at hand. He grabbed a sponge and a bottle of dishwashing soap, too.

With the soaking roll of paper towels, sponge, and soap, Stevenson carefully and quickly went back into the garage. He made his way to the driver's side of the SUV again. By the dim light, he pulled off a yard of towel, dropped the roll on the garage floor, and bent over the crumpled fender. He started working very methodically and slowly, rubbing the metal, black paint chips coming off in the towel. But in a matter of moments, his movements became abrupt, spastic, and he was moving more wet paper towel over the ruined front side of the SUV. Clean it, clean it, he thought, and, when he glanced at the towel, he saw bits of gray hair and felt small, knobbly hardness.

He switched to the sponge, dousing it with dishwashing soap. He rubbed harder, more scraps of paint coming off. He peered at the sponge. Embedded in it were irregular white bits. *Bone,* he thought. *That's bone.* He felt the spasm of nausea seize him, but went back to the windshield. This time he wiped away a smear of pale redness.

He stopped, panting a little. The garage smelled of lemons from the dishwashing soap. Stevenson gathered the sponge and used paper towels and took them into the kitchen, shoving them into the garbage under the sink, burying them beneath food scraps and discarded mail.

He remembered an expensive cover he had bought for the SUV but rarely used because it was so much trouble to tug and pull on. He opened the SUV's trunk, managed to jerk out the bulky tan cover. Working in the semidarkness, he found it even harder to get it in place. It was heavy and awkward and, as soon as he got part of it over the ruined fender and headlight, it slid off the roof. Stevenson felt an uncontrollable, impossible laugh forming in his center. It was a joke. The whole thing, whatever had happened just now, was a horrible, unjust prank played at his expense. Here was inescapable proof, this absurd performance dancing around the SUV with a formless, recalcitrant car cover fighting him every inch.

Finally, he got it crudely over the SUV so the whole vehicle was concealed in a tan rumpled skin. No sign of damage.

Stevenson slowly went back into the kitchen and washed his hands several times at the sink. The little black and white TV beside the sink made him think of Veronica when she did the dishes, half paying attention to the news or an old movie. *What am I going to tell her?* he thought. *What do I say?*

He remembered the brushed steel refrigerator and opened it. Haley's latest dietary experiment, tofu and soy milk, took up one side, alongside what he and Veronica ate. Haley was very particular that there be no mingling. There were four chilled bottles of fine champagne in the lower rack, and a bottle of expensive vintage chardonnay he and Veronica had tried at dinner the night before last. It seemed remote and indescribably ideal.

I want to be back there, he thought. *I'd give anything to be there.*

Stevenson stood in the glare of the open refrigerator, tossing the cork from the bottle, drinking greedily, as he did with water or Gatorade after a good morning run.

Need something stronger than this, he thought calmly. *White wine doesn't quite cut it right now.*

He had a goal. He left the empty wine bottle on the kitchen counter and walked into the dining room. A copper-lined dry sink stood against one wall, the row of bottles in it inviting and comforting.

That's more like it, Stevenson thought, his eyes adjusting to the dark, his hand going for the single malt Scotch he savored sparingly or offered to good friends sometimes. Like the chardonnay, he simply twisted off the top and tilted the bottle down his throat. The liquor stung, but it was strong and exactly the right thing.

He paused, swallowed, and coughed harshly. *Okay, I can't drive the SUV in the morning,* he realized clearly. *Can't even let it out of the garage.* He imagined the SUV as a wild animal that had to be kept caged for everyone's safety.

Stevenson drank again and the enormity of what was coming started to rise to the surface, like a vast black shape from the depths of the deepest ocean moving inexorably upward.

He was shaking again. He did not know what to do or say. He had no idea how to get into bed with Veronica in a few minutes, how to act. He was lost.

Stevenson almost dropped the bottle of Scotch in shock when the dining room light snapped on.

FIVE

THE EARLY MORNING RAIN was light but persistent and it carried a penetrating cold with it when Detective Terry Nye arrived at the Wells Fargo Bank construction site. He parked on the 4th Street side of the site. He wished he had remembered to bring his umbrella or something besides his old raincoat.

He was pleased to see that barricades, and the cops manning them, were up on the streets around the site. He hunched his head low in a futile attempt to keep the maddening cold wetness off his head or from going down his shirt collar.

Cops shouted back and forth, and three large portable industrial lights were trundling into position on westbound Capitol Mall on the construction site side, which had also been blocked off. The lights flashed on, bathing the rainy block in an unforgiving white blaze. The dozen cops in their black raincoats looked like busy elves. Highway flares were set off and dropped in the streets, guttering scarlet and smoke in the night. Video and still camera lights bobbed along the street, capturing everything.

Nye found Sergeant Willy Obergon directing a crime scene van into a parking place within the cordoned off block.

"Bad morning, ain't it?" Nye said as he and Obergon found shelter from the rain just inside the unfinished bank building.

"Lousy. I don't look for it to get any better." Obergon was fifty, a little younger than Nye, and they had worked together for years, back when Nye was the oldest and longest-serving traffic officer in the Sacramento Police Department. Obergon was short, stocky, with a brown, lined face. "CHP is on its way with their accident reconstruction crew. I've got the area sealed, my guys are making sure nothing important gets washed down into the drains."

"Yeah, you better get hold of the city water people. See what they can do about trapping any runoff for a while. Get the construction company on the line too. Tell them they're shut down on this part of the site until we're done."

"They'll love it." Obergon spat. "Any word on Ensor?"

"When Nishimoto gave me the call he says the latest is they've got him in the ER. I talked to a couple of guys at Sutter Emergency and they said he looks . . ." Nye stopped and stared out into the street and the purposeful men and women working to make sense of what had happened. Obergon finished his thought.

"Fuck whoever did it, Terry. Fuck. Them. How come Tommy Ensor gets nailed?

Where's the justice in that?"

"Not a whole lot. So. Nish's orders are, I take over now and get him answers like an hour ago."

"Great fucking way for a short-timer like you to go out," Obergon said sourly. "You still punching out in two weeks?"

"Thirteen days," Nye corrected. "Thirty-one years. I sure as hell wouldn't have picked this for my last detail."

"Everybody's going to give this one hundred ten percent, Terry."

Nye felt a surge of emotion that he had not had for a long time, when the days, and even longer nights as a detective, had devolved into routine, repetition, and emptiness. He patted Obergon on the shoulder. "Sure they will," he said quietly. "You seen Rose yet?" he asked of his relatively new, and now last, partner in Major Crimes, Rose Tafoya.

"No, she hasn't checked in," Obergon said.

"She better get here soon. Nish's bird-dogging this one by the minute, and I've got to give him an update"—he looked at his watch—"in ten. I got to tell him everybody's here."

"I see some more cars over there," Obergon pointed to the left where four cars, two patrol and two unmarked, pulled up, the barricades were briefly opened for them and then closed again. "You worked with Ensor, didn't you? Couple years back?"

"More than a couple. Ten at least. He's a good guy." Nye did not say that Tommy Ensor, his former partner by then, had tracked him down, more than once, to bars in West Sacramento or Broderick and taken him home after he and Marceen divorced. Nye had a lot of friends in the department, but no one except Ensor reached down to pull him up. He did a lot of things like that for a lot of people. Everyone knew there was only one Tommy Ensor in the department.

"Where's his partner?" Nye asked, pulling up his raincoat collar and heading toward the cars that just arrived.

"I've got him stashed in my wagon, Terry. He's been around for only maybe three years. He's really rocky. He looks up to Ensor."

"So he can join the parade. Look, I want to talk to him before IA shows up, okay?" Nye intended to find out what had happened from Ensor's partner before the required Internal Affairs inquiry started. It was mandatory in situations where an officer was injured or killed, whether on duty or not.

"Fine by me," Obergon said. He watched an attractive young woman holding a maroon umbrella stride toward them. "Tommy Ensor wasn't screwing around when he took these off-duty security deals. He just needs the money."

"I'm not worried about Tommy," Nye said low to Obergon. "I don't know his partner. I want to see what we got here and what kind of guy he is before IA lands on him."

"That's why it's no problem for me," Obergon said. "All I want is to seriously fuck up whoever did this."

"I would like that," Nye agreed. He jerked his hand back toward Obergon when the young woman joined them. "Rosie, this is Willy Obergon. He's an asshole."

Rose Tafoya, thirty-four and athletic, her neat black hair pinned back, shook hands with Obergon. Even at that hour and in the rain, she was impeccably dressed, as if to meet the chief of police or the mayor. "Bad morning, ain't it," she said to Obergon.

"Christ, how long you been hanging around Nye?" Obergon said in mock alarm.

"Long enough to hear every one of his old war stories," Rose said, and Nye broke in.

"The clock's running. Nish's impatient so let's get rolling. We got rush-hour traffic coming down this street in a couple of hours and we don't have a goddamn idea what happened."

Rose pointed. "CHP's here." Two more bulky vans belonging to the California Highway Patrol slowly came through the barricades.

"Okay, Willy, you go take care of getting them set up. Rose and I are going to talk to Ensor's partner. I want you to put a lot of these people out beating the bushes for witnesses."

"This place is a ghost town," Obergon said. "We'll be lucky if another driver saw anything."

"Let's hope we get lucky. Come on, Rosie."

They walked in silence for a few moments, skirting around the construction site to the 5th Street side where the police vehicles were parked in a row. Three cops in raincoats stood at Obergon's car. The youngest one shook a little. He was crying.

Rose said, "Rush hour comes, Ter, all that traffic, all those people and they'll go right over where Ensor got hit and none of them will know it or care."

"Yeah, but we will. We're going to massacre the motherfucker who left Ensor in the street."

SIX

STEVENSON TOOK A BREATH and steadied his voice. "Haley, what are you doing up?"

His daughter, eleven years old, gray eyes and brown hair, stood in the kitchen door. "I heard a noise downstairs, Dad."

"I'm sorry I woke you, button."

"What are you doing?"

"Nothing. Just something quick before bed." He put the cap back on the Scotch carefully. He was afraid his hand might shake.

"Don't you want a glass?"

"No, I'm done," He almost laughed. Leave it to Hurricane Haley to notice something like that. The fearless daughter he wished he knew better. "You shouldn't be up. It's late. School's coming faster than you think." He wondered where the false jollity in his voice came from. "Let's go back to bed."

Haley seemed to study him for a moment, as if making up her mind about something. It was not that long ago, maybe a year Stevenson reckoned, that she had come in to see him and Veronica and announced she was now too old to call them Mommy and Daddy.

25

It would be Mom and Dad from now on, direct and adult, and certainly for the rest of their lives. Hurricane never changed her mind once she made it up.

"It's late," Haley agreed, turning off the dining room light that had so startled him. "You don't usually come home this late."

"Tonight's special," he said with a pang as they walked together into the living room and started up the stairs.

"Why?"

"Grandpa's helping me get onto the Court of Appeal. We had to see some people tonight who can help me do that," he said, truthful in part. The unspoken duplicity slipped into place so cleanly he did not have to think about it. *Can't tell her something happened, he thought. Can't tell her I hit something.*

Hit somebody.

Jesus, maybe I've killed somebody.

Haley did not see his stricken expression in the dimness of the hallway upstairs. Stevenson could not breathe for a moment but he kept walking into her dark room.

No, I didn't kill anybody. Maybe somebody got hurt. Maybe. I wasn't going that fast, goddamn it to hell, I was not going fast enough to really hurt someone.

Haley got into bed. Around her, on shelves he had put up, was her collection of small stuffed pandas. She no longer carried a favorite black-and-white panda everywhere; that, too, was left with the childhood she was outrunning so swiftly. She still however kept them all near, a rank of accusing glass eyes Stevenson impulsively wanted to suddenly smash.

"I like coming to see you in court," Haley said. "It was cool when you let me sit where you do. I thought you liked being a regular judge. You always say you do."

"Well, it's a promotion, button. That's a good thing. I also think I'd be a better judge on the next level up, figuring out legal issues, hearing arguments, and making decisions." He momentarily forgot his present situation, and natural vanity and ambition asserted themselves. Since he was a kid, he was constantly told that he would advance further and further, inevitably, and without interruption. He was one of the special ones. Stevenson looked away from the dead eyes around him. "Hey, we can talk about it in the morning on the way to school. It's Thursday, I'm taking you to school."

"I've got soccer practice so I'll be done by five."

"I remember," he said, although he could barely hear her. "Good night, button," he said.

"Good night," she whispered. He turned and heard her covers rustle as she rolled over.

Stevenson went back downstairs. He had forgotten that it was his day to take Haley to school and pick her up. *I can't use the SUV. She'll wonder why we're not going to school in my car. Got to take Veronica's. Got to have a reason for leaving my SUV in the garage.*

Got to figure out what to do.

He trembled with the enormity of things that had to be fixed, explained, concealed. There were always so many details about life that never drew attention or raised concern. They simply went on like breathing. But change one little thing, like taking your eyes off a rainy, badly lit street early in the morning for even a second, one fucking moment, and all those mundane details saw their chance and became huge obstacles, each threatening and dangerous.

Stevenson almost ran back downstairs and into the study off the living room that he and Veronica shared. They had adjacent, blond-wood desks, elegant and spare. She worked on her cases and he worked on his.

He closed the door gently. Flipping on the light, he sat at his desk and impatiently waited for his computer to come on, then started scanning local news sites, searching for a mention of an accident, breaking news, anything.

He clicked and clicked again, story after story. Nothing. A parade of civic problems from levee repairs along the American River, a big retirement for a powerful state senator, a fire in a derelict rice warehouse downtown. Stevenson glanced at the time on the computer. Of course there was no mention of any accident. It was too early.

He sat back, mouth tight. Maybe there was nothing to report. It had all happened so quickly, he could easily have imagined a more serious accident. Certainly. Even Eli didn't see anything. It doesn't matter if he was his usual three sheets to the wind. Eli would still have seen something big if there was anything to see.

I may have brushed someone, Stevenson thought, *somebody who had no business being out in the middle of the street, and they got up and went home.*

Maybe, he thought excitedly, *they did go to a hospital but they knew it was their fault. They made up a story about where they were and what happened.*

Stevenson turned off his computer. Veronica had left a stack of files from her law firm on her desk. She was a partner and did not have to work this hard, but she relished long hours, the challenges.

He went back upstairs, feeling a little relieved. The damage to the SUV looked bad, but that did not necessarily equate to severe injuries. People got knocked around and got up and walked away from all kinds of things, like the window washer a few weeks ago who fell three hundred feet and only had a broken leg. People were resilient.

I didn't actually see anyone, just a half-formed impression, Stevenson thought, *a black shape crossing his vision for a split second, and the SUV rocking, and that was it. Probably only a few broken bones. If that.*

Maybe it was even only a big dog.

The wash of relief was short but intense. There was blood on the SUV and he'd found bone fragments. They came from a human being. He knew that inside.

I did not kill anybody. He raged impotently.

It wasn't my fault, goddamn it.

He found his wife asleep in the bedroom, the lights still on. Two thick, buff-colored file folders lay on the floor beside her. There was a half-full glass and a bottle of pinot grigio perched on the folders.

As he changed, she groaned. "Oh. Frank. What time?"

"I don't know. Too late."

She yawned and smiled at him. "I've discovered the sovereign cure for insomnia. Nobody can work on stock valuations for a merger and stay awake. We'll make a million marketing it."

He sat down on the bed beside her. "Vee," he started, and then he could not say anything else. She looked at him.

"I was feeling sorry for myself, alone tonight," she said. "How did Dad's little shindig for you go?"

"Great. Good turnout. He's got one hell of a network in this town."

"He's a sweetheart. Everyone loves my dad. They always have." She leaned and kissed him. "They'll love you, too, now. *Mr. Justice Stevenson.*" She said it archly but with pleasure.

The Scotch and wine had barely touched what was lurking just beneath his awareness. He finished her glass of pinot grigio, refilled it, and offered it to her. She took a swallow.

"What's up?" she said more somberly. "There's something."

"I just felt like sharing a glass with my lady," he said.

"That's not it, Frank."

"Now you're insulting me," and he forced feigned hurt into his voice. He took the glass from her.

"Well, look, it's late and if you don't want to tell me whatever it is," and she stopped because he kissed her hard. He was seized with frantic desire, almost enraged, and his roughness, and how strange it was, startled both of them. Several times she moaned and muttered that they had to make less noise, the noise they were making was going to wake Haley. He did not stop.

Afterward, Veronica turned off the light and lay close to him, and he pulled her closer. "Hooray for the Court of Appeal," she whispered sleepily.

Stevenson felt something shifting inside him, a foundation piece that anchored so many things. He was more horrified and frightened than he could remember ever being in his life. Even lying next to his wife, he was alone in the farthest place in the universe.

I didn't stop, he thought in the early morning blackness. *I kept going.*

SEVEN

NYE AND ROSE TOOK QUINTANA into what was going to be an office off the unfinished bank lobby. Stacks of boxes and bare girders did not provide much privacy for their makeshift interview room, but at least they were not out in the open where all of the other cops could see and hear them.

Rose had out a small digital recorder. Nye used a plain notepad he pulled from his suit coat. Quintana would not look at either of them. He hunched his shoulders and moved his hand over his face.

"Okay, Bob, I want to get an idea what happened, what you saw," Nye said.

"I didn't see anything," Quintana replied fiercely. "That's the whole fucking problem."

"Okay," Nye said, "what time did you and Ensor get here?"

"Ten. On the dot. It's a ten-to-six shift. The construction outfit's got somebody they keep around after they shut down and then we take over until they start up again the next day." He coughed, looked down, and shook slightly.

"You come together or in two cars?"

"We both drove. Parked on the N Street side." He rattled off the makes and license numbers.

Rose said, "You better stay away from your car or Officer Ensor's until IA clears you to go. We're going to process both cars."

Quintana glared at her. "There's nothing to find."

Rose glanced at Nye. She was not moved or impressed by Quintana's reactions. Although he and Rose had only worked as partners in Major Crimes for six months, Nye appreciated her intelligence and detachment. She was easily the best of his partners and he would miss her. He was having trouble talking to the young cop. She knew to take the lead.

"What happened from ten until the accident?" Rose asked, clipped and unemotional.

"Nothing, nothing. Nothing. That's what I'm saying," Quintana snapped.

"Hey, settle down," Nye said.

"Look," Quintana rocked back and forth, preoccupied, starting to fade on them. Nye could tell. "Is this official? I need my union rep?"

Rose came closer to him, hand on his arm. It was both to quiet him and let him know who was in charge. "It's official, officer. IA's going to ask the same things, probably not so friendly. But my partner and I aren't IA. We're just like you and Officer Ensor. We're going after whoever did it. Not you. "

Quintana's eyes were unfocused, wide. "I don't give a fuck if I get fired. I messed up and Tommy's dead."

"He isn't dead," Nye said gruffly. "Now, fucking settle down, okay? Nobody's saying you messed up."

"They will. I did."

Rose discreetly pointed to her wrist, reminding Nye that they owed Nishimoto his status call very soon. He nodded.

"So walk us through from ten until the accident, Quintana," he said.

The young cop's hands clenched, his face froze and drooped. Nye could see he was coming apart very quickly. "Come on," he said more quietly.

Quintana blinked. "Okay. Okay. Tommy and I agreed on breaks every half hour. We split up the building. He took the front, Capitol

Mall side and 4th Street. I took N and 5th. We met in the lobby, had some coffee."

"Anybody come by?" Rose asked.

"I had a couple of pedestrians maybe around midnight, couple girls maybe from an office around here. I couldn't hear what they were saying."

Nye said to Rose, "I want to go through the buildings nearby, talk to the night crews if they got them. Find out who was working late tonight." She made a note.

"What about cars? Any traffic you noticed?" Rose asked.

"Yeah, yeah, I guess. Couple cars on N heading for the freeway, midnight maybe. Just cars. Nothing unusual."

Nye said to Rose, "Rain started around midnight." He turned to Quintana. "I bet you and Ensor stayed inside here after that."

"No. We did what they hired us to do. We walked the place. That's how Tommy did things. He's a straight shooter."

Rose said, "Did either of you talk to anyone between ten and the accident? Did you get any calls, personal? Anything?"

Nye could not watch Quintana anymore. He felt the waves of pain rolling off the young cop and it hurt. This was the big reason he decided to pull the plug. After three decades, he simply could not take the pain that came at him anymore. *No matter what you tried or how you steeled yourself against it,* Nye thought, *like water, it always found a crack, a little crevice and started dripping in and then the whole damn ocean flooded after it.*

And I've got my share plus of cracks for it to get in, he thought with brutal candor. He took a breath and walked across the dusty concrete floor.

Quintana shook his head. "Tommy didn't mention anyone. We didn't get any calls from the construction company. I called my fiancée." He slumped. "Told her how boring it was out here."

"Who lined this job up?" Nye called back to Quintana. His voice echoed dully in the cold, dim space.

"Tommy did. That's the kind of guy he is. He knows I'm getting married, a couple extra bucks is going to help. He's got friends all over the city and he heard about this deal and signed us up."

Rose asked, "How long have you and Office Ensor worked together?"

Nye walked back and faced Quintana. The young cop ran his hand over his face as if he did not know the answer. Nye remembered those pauses when the mind reaches for memories, something to get you away from wherever you are that precise moment.

"About five months. We're on patrol in the North Area. I thought I was a lucky bastard to get assigned to Tommy. I mean, Medal of Valor. Jesus. He's a terrific guy, but the Medal, I mean that made me wonder what I'd do if I was in the same situation he was. This sounds like I'm bragging, but I figured I got myself ready. I'd be ready if something happened. It's an honor to work with him. That's it."

Rose gave Nye one of their cues. Like good teams of interrogators, they had choreography to their tandem questioning. Nye was impressed how quickly she slipped into the back and forth with him.

"I think that's about it, Officer Quintana. We've got just a couple more questions."

Nye said, "Tell me about the accident."

Quintana relayed it flatly and quickly, but his hands balled into fists and he paced away and then back as he spoke. "So the bottom line, I didn't see the car. I didn't catch a make or license. I didn't see anyone around. My fucking report's maybe three lines long."

"No horn? No sound like someone hitting the brakes?"

"All I heard was the sound of Tommy getting hit," he choked. "Jesus."

Rose nodded slightly to Nye. He nodded to her.

"Officer Quintana," she said, "you and Officer Ensor took a couple of coffee breaks, right?"

"Yeah."

"You drinking anything else to keep warm?"

"What do you mean?" He looked at her puzzled, wary.

Nye drove it home. "It's a boring, cold job. You, Ensor, both of you brought some beers, I don't know what else. Tell me. Who brought the booze?"

"Nobody. Just coffee." Nye watched Quintana's growing guilt and grief reforming into targeted anger. "What the hell are you saying?"

"This is an off-duty job." Rose said, "It wouldn't be the first time a couple of cops had a couple of pops to pass the time."

Nye came closer to Quintana. "They're doing a tox screen on Ensor at the hospital for sure, Quintana. He's got any alcohol in his system, it's going to show up loud and clear."

Quintana looked like he was about to cry again. "Fuck you. Tommy wasn't drinking. Like it was *his* fault he got hit by some fucker?"

"That's one way," Nye said flatly. "You tell me the other one."

Rose moved to Quintana's side. She had her eyes on him.

The young cop breathed hard and his neck bulged. He was part of the new generation that worked out and ate energy power bars and drank bottled vitamin water—and when he swung, Nye flinched instinctively because the blow would have been terrific.

Rose deftly grabbed Quintana's arm in mid-swing, twisted it back in a control hold, and had him bent low in a fraction of a second. Quintana struggled, cursing. "Give me a fucking blood test! Check my goddamn BAC! I wasn't loaded. There wasn't anything I could do. Jesus Christ, there wasn't anything."

Nye watched his futile rage run down swiftly, like a spring giving up its tension. Rose released his arm. "Officer Quintana, don't try that again. One warning. Okay?"

"Go on back and wait for IA," Nye said.

Quintana nodded, attempted to straighten up. He moved stiffly out of the lobby, heading for the cars where Nye and Rose had found him.

Nye's cell buzzed and he answered it. Rose made a final note and put away her recorder. Nye said, "CHP needs us outside. They're with our guys. They found the point of impact."

He and Rose left the unfinished lobby. A night wind, the follower of the storm, blew coolly and cleanly around them and the silent city. Only the street in front of them was bright, a little smoky from the flares, and bustling with people and equipment.

Rose said, "I believe him, Ter. I feel sorry for the poor guy."

Nye approached the cluster of CHP and SPD technicians, with clipboards and infrared measuring devices, gathered on the glistening black street. "I hope there's nothing in his car or Ensor's and I sure as hell hope the kid doesn't try to toss anything if there is. You don't remember Cole Barrett," Nye grinned emptily at Rose, "way before your time. Just an average guy. Clocks in, clocks out. Nothing to write home about. Never going to get out of Patrol."

"Not like some people," she grinned back at Nye. They stopped a few feet from the technicians.

"Modesty keeps me from crowing about my own accomplishment. So, Barrett gets busted one afternoon, his day off. Blasted to hell, drunk as a skunk. He gets popped in the county when the Sacramento sheriff and us are having one of our usual little lover's fights about some turf thing, who remembers? Sac sheriff ain't about to let a bombed city cop walk away. Anyway, the deputy gets Barrett out of his car, professional courtesy doesn't cuff him, and then he checks the car, routine. He spots this toolbox half open in the backseat and sticking out of it are a couple hundred dollars. The deputy asks, What's this? Barrett shrugs and, when the deputy goes to look at the toolbox, Barrett's doing the quarter mile sprint across Greenback and four lanes of oncoming traffic."

"Sounds dangerous."

"The Sac sheriff chasing him thought so and let everybody know it in triplicate afterward. He tackled Barrett and cuffed him this time. So, turns out Barrett's been holding up supermarkets across the line in Yolo County as a way to supplement his not-so-impressive patrol-cop salary."

"I don't see Quintana having a problem like that." Rose sighed. "I think he's in for a lot of other grief unless he pulls himself together fast."

"That's right on the money, Rosie. IA will eat him for lunch if they need a scapegoat for whatever happened out here."

"So you don't want to give IA a report of our interview with him, I guess." She leveled a sharp look at Nye. Rose did not like straying from clear procedures and protocol.

"Let's give him a chance to get calm down. I'm big on second chances. Okay?"

"Okay, old man," Rose said, not entirely at ease.

"Rosie, think of all the stories you'll be able to tell when we're done. I envy you."

The CHP accident investigation and reconstruction team consisted of five officers and two technicians. The SPD contingent added another three. They moved in a straggling bunch from spot to spot, the guided tour of a hit-and-run, under the white blaze of the lights.

The floodlit, bony white State Capitol rose at the end of Capitol Mall, icily indifferent, Nye thought, to what they were doing.

Nye had his radio open to the newly established tactical command post in the Sacramento Police Department. "Okay, guys, downtown's listening and they'd like to know what's going on."

A stocky, older CHP officer in glasses and a brown uniform and transparent raincoat nodded and crouched down, pointing. He spoke loudly, sweeping his right arm as he spoke. "We're in the middle of the westbound right hand lane of Capitol Mall, eight feet from the median and four feet from the curb. This is the point of impact."

"Why do you think so?" Rose asked, arms folded. She was grim.

"We've got an impact tire transfer here in the roadway. The vehicle was coming westbound on Capitol Mall and hit the victim. The driver might've seen him just before impact or maybe not, the transfer is so short, it could just be the effect of the collision."

"The bastard didn't slow down or put on his brakes?" Nye asked.

The CHP officer stood up. "Can't say. We can do some analysis and maybe come up with a time, but it's short. Possible guess is the driver just didn't see the victim until he was right on him."

"Okay," Nye said sourly, "next?"

A wiry SPD tech with a reedy voice took over. "The victim went approximately twenty-three feet down the lane on impact."

"The vehicle must have been barreling down the street." Rose said, her eyes traveling along the invisible trajectory of the collision.

"We're working on possible speeds," the SPD tech agreed. "We've got to find out the frictional properties of the street here, what it's made of, average daily traffic, any vertical or horizontal curvature."

The CHP officer interrupted, "Before we can do a speed estimate, detective, we need to know the road factors cold. And build in the effect of the rain. It was coming down like a shitstorm." He remembered who was listening. "Excuse me," he said.

Nye strode down to where Ensor had been thrown, the pack of techs and officers trailing him. "How much does Ensor weigh?" he called out.

"We're getting that," the SPD tech said. "It's a basic number for the impact evaluation and speed determination. Lots of kinetic energy in a collision."

"Yeah, and it all comes from a guy getting smashed by a car racing down the street," Nye said. Techs were working on the street where Ensor lay.

Nye stared down, Rose beside him. "So I can see you've got some paint fragments left in the street. What kind?"

"Black. We'll be able to get more to match from the victim's clothes, too." The CHP officer bent down, pointing. "We've got glass fragments here and back at the point of impact so it looks like the victim hit the windshield, driver's side's a good guess."

"Are you going to be able to figure out what kind of vehicle we're dealing with?" Rose asked.

The SPD tech nodded emphatically. "You bet. The database's got all kinds of cross-matches for paints. We can trace it back to the manufacturer, over to the carmaker, maybe to the region where it got used and the vehicle was sold."

"Same for the tire transfer at the point of impact, detective. It's a wide tread and we should be able to match the width and the tire composition to a vehicle."

"Any ballpark right now for what we should be keeping an eye out for?" Nye said bluntly.

The CHP officer nodded, adjusted his glasses, his transparent raincoat crinkling and crackling. "Big vehicle. Black. Truck. RV. Could be an SUV."

"Soon as we get a look at the victim's injuries, we can do speed calculations," added the SPD tech.

Rose blew out an angry breath. She pointed at the orange traffic cones scattered like bowling pins along part of the collision trail in the street. "How about them? Were they up or down when Officer Ensor got hit?"

"Unknown," said the SPD tech.

Nye looked around and up. "I count three streetlights out. We need to find out when they went down. We got to check it out with the city."

Rose nodded, made a note. Nye headed over to Obergon beside a crime scene van. "Thanks," he said to the assembled techs and he turned to leave. "Let me know right away what you come up with on the paint and the tires."

Rose and he paused in the cordoned-off street, the night clear and fresh, an oasis of human activity in a dark landscape. "I think I see the problem," she said.

"Yeah. Down there," he pointed back along Capitol Mall to the mustard gold arches of the Tower Bridge over the black river, "is a straight shot from the freeway and West Sacramento, the Port of Sacramento, every big truck on earth."

"I-5 South's got an off-ramp about a third of a mile away, too."

Nye summed it up. "Don't worry. I signed out of the peanut gallery getting the briefing. This is just you and me trying to figure out how we're going to narrow a search for a big something, maybe car, maybe a truck. Maybe a goddamn Oscar Mayer Weiner Wagon. All we've got is a street with access points to the biggest freeway in the state and truckers and cars from north and south all around."

Rose said, "Hey, cheer up, Ter. We know it's black."

"Swell. And it's got tires. We practically got it in the bag." He called out, "Hey, Obergon, let's get into these buildings. It'd be nice to find a witness."

Nishimoto leaned forward after Nye and the techs finished and switched off the conference call telephone in the center of the large metal table. The phone was gray and splayed flat like a drying baby squid, something he used to see his mother hang outside their house on a clothesline for dinner. He stared at the phone for a moment. He had not thought of her for a long time. He was acutely conscious of Altlander coldly appraising him at the conference table.

"All right, ladies and gentlemen," he said steadily, using a mask of stern command to get the instant attention of the five other people and to banish his own stale reveries, "let's get back to first things. We need our one eight hundred tip line on every TV and radio station in Northern California, in the papers. Short announcement that anyone on the road around midnight to two A.M. in the vicinity of the State Capitol, who may have seen anything, call us." He pointed down the conference table. "Alex, you have that ready to shoot out in the next half hour."

A woman halfway down the conference table, with a cobalt blue travel mug of coffee and thick makeup over old acne scars, scribbled in a tattered steno pad. She was not in uniform, unlike everyone else. "Any reward?"

"There will be. I need to work on that with the chief and Ensor's family this morning. For now let's get the word out that we want people to come forward."

"I could talk to the Governor's office, Jerry," offered Altlander at his left, upright, tall, self-assured. "They'd go in for at least fifty thousand. My old buddy the cabinet secretary could make it happen before noon."

It was stated blandly, without being an obvious boast, like getting a spare part for a broken motor. But Nishimoto knew exactly what his rival was doing. *Arrogant asshole,* Nishimoto seethed. *This is my investigation and it's going to stay mine.*

Got to wrap it up tight and fast. Make an arrest. Don't leave Altlander any time or room to grab it, he thought furiously. When he spoke, he was cool.

"Thanks for the suggestion, Lou. That may be exactly what we'll do."

Altlander nodded solemnly and made a short note on the topmost legal pad before him. Nishimoto felt insult in the very gesture.

He turned back to the woman down the conference table. "Next, I want to get out a department notification. Alex, you're going to make sure every shift is read a statement about Ensor's condition, expressing the chief's sadness and prayers for his recovery. I think we should put it up on the department's homepage by zero five thirty, too."

"Definitely. I'll put together a statement for the media from the chief. I've got Jilli at the hospital with the chief," she said, referring to her assistant in SPD's communication office. "So far no media have shown up, but that's going to change as soon as they know who got hurt."

"I want to see that statement before it goes anywhere."

"Absolutely," she nodded.

He caught Altlander making more notes and glancing carefully at the other men and women, all senior staff in the department. He suddenly didn't know who he could count on. It was a shocking and unexpected realization. Nishimoto felt a wave of giddiness, like he was hanging over an immense deep chasm.

He wouldn't let Altlander or any of them know his unrest.

He gave steady sounding orders. "I want to reach out to the various groups Ensor works with, let them know what's happened, how they can be supportive. Talk to the Police Athletic League parents, Sky Cottage and the parents and kids there, Camp New Horizon, too."

"I've got one of Tommy's at risk kids from Camp New Horizon," said a jowled, white-haired officer shaking his head in sorrow. "Sonofabitch, I bet couple dozen cops around here helped out Tommy's wannabe gangbangers just because he made it so damn important."

"That's why I want all his organizations and people to hear from us," Nishimoto said, "Ensor's touched people all over the city. We're all going to be together pulling for him to make it."

He saw the nods, the formal acknowledgments around the table, and heard murmured curses at Ensor's assailant. *I don't inspire,* Nishimoto thought sadly, *I can't make them feel like Ensor or Altlander do. Like they're part of great things. Like they can do great things. I only give clerk's orders.*

"Wouldn't it be a good idea to get the family he saved, the one got the medal for, on board, Jerry? Media's bound to go to them right away, aren't they, Alex?" It was Altlander again, and Nishimoto was annoyed to see Alex from Communications nod emphatically.

"I was coming to them," he said snappishly. "Yes, give the family a heads-up right after this meeting, Alex." He could sense events being jerked away from him. *Goddamn, I need an arrest.* He hoped to hell Nye would bring him what he needed fast.

Nishimoto turned to the slight, gray-haired man at his right. "What's Ensor's status right now, Joe?"

The old cop stared around the table. "Five minutes ago, the Sutter docs have him in surgery. He's got major head injuries, broken right leg, broken left leg, right arm's compound fractured. Pelvis broken, and the docs are really worried about the tear in his aorta from the crash. They've been trying to make sure he doesn't bleed to death for the last hour."

"Jesus," Altlander made the word stretch into three syllables. "Jerry, this is a cop killing. The chief's got to get the city behind an all-out manhunt." Altlander stood up, as if he had a crowd, but the effect did not seem false, even in the small group. He was the center of attention. "We've got a hero police officer fighting for his life because some coward struck him down in the dark and left him to die in the street. Remember the testimonials at Ensor's Medal of Valor ceremony? We had an overflow crowd of people this officer's helped. Kids who won't end up in Juvenile Hall. Moms and dads who got a chance at decent work. And, yeah, cops like the cynical bastards at this table, and I'm proud to say I'm one of them, who mentored a kid who was about to go off the tracks because Officer Ensor shamed us into doing it. So I'm putting myself on record that the department must make finding Tommy Ensor's attacker our first priority, our second priority, our third priority," and he struck the table each time.

Nishimoto saw that by the third bang on the metal, heads were nodding. Joe and someone else were hitting the table in time with Altlander, like it was a drum, and the message was reverberating out.

Without thinking, Nishimoto jumped to his feet, and the contrast between him and Altlander was instantly obvious and bad. But when he realized it, it was too late. He said, "We are going to find the driver who hit Tommy Ensor. The chief wants it badly and so do I. But we've also got a city that isn't shutting down and people counting on us to maintain public protection."

He stuttered slightly. The faces around him were puzzled or cold. He ploughed ahead to a ludicrous finish, "I think we all know Ensor would want the department to keep," he stuttered, and lamely ended, "doing its job even now."

"Not good enough, Jerry," Altlander delivered a pronouncement. "This investigation is the department's job. So we've got to put our best on it, and Nye isn't our best. I know he's your guy, Major Crimes is your division, but Terry Nye's too old, he's out the door in a couple of weeks. This is too important for him."

Nishimoto shook his head, regained his mask of command. He said aloud what he fervently hungered for. "Terry Nye's got a bulletproof record. He's going to bring in the driver who hit Ensor."

"So you'll put him on a short leash?" Altlander swiftly demanded.

Nishimoto saw the trap too late and knew it had been sprung because of his own carelessness. "What do you recommend?"

"Three days."

Nishimoto saw the nods around the conference table. The chief would undoubtedly concur. He had his own imperatives.

"All right. Seventy-two hours," Nishimoto said, without emotion.

EIGHT

STEVENSON WAS AWAKE THE NEXT MORNING just before the alarm went off at six thirty, as if an internal clock was tracking time and wanted him up before Veronica.

He quietly went downstairs into the study and turned on his computer. A promising bright dawn was breaking outside the curtains, already lightening the room. He shivered a little because it was still cold and he only had on an undershirt and his pajama bottoms. His feet were bare. He was not tired and somewhat surprised at how deeply and dreamlessly he had slept. The horror and dread he felt the night before had gone into hiding someplace.

He quickly punched up the news running on local TV and his jaw clenched.

HERO POLICE OFFICER GRAVELY INJURED IN HIT-AND-RUN was the top story. He read it, finding more on every news site he checked in California. It was a great, tortured effort to connect this tragic event to himself. *What the hell was a cop doing in the middle of the street,* he nearly shouted out loud. He heard Haley stirring upstairs, the sounds of the hall bathroom door closing.

The feeling from last night while he lay in bed rushed back. It was as if he was being crushed between implacable rocks, heavier than imagination. Frantic fear seized him. He read the news stories over and over, searching for the slightest hint that the mysterious driver or the vehicle had been seen. *No witness,* Stevenson thought with scant relief, eyes locked on the computer. *They don't have a description. Nobody saw it. Just Eli and him. Only the two of them knew and Eli apparently didn't know much.*

Stevenson got up, pacing the study. He had struck and badly hurt a cop, a cop everyone apparently admired. The cop was fighting for his life, that was the phrase used mindlessly over and over in every news story. He had a family, four kids. Stevenson formed an inward prayer that the cop would live.

Do I know him? Stevenson wondered. He could not recall ever having seen Officer Ensor in his courtroom, but he had rarely had people from law enforcement as witnesses in his courtroom. *I get white-collar, long cause trials. Class action environmental trials, homeowners screwed by greedy builders. Great headlines no matter how they go,* he thought, *the youngest judge in the courthouse with the brightest future.*

He stared vacantly. He felt like he had been punched; the enormity of what was happening was a physical blow.

The room was light enough for him to make out, on the wall and in the bookcases, the ranks of plaques he had earned for his pro bono work he did when in private practice. There was a framed newspaper article about how he'd saved two elderly couples' homes from seizure by the city. Another article included a photo of a man wrongly convicted and sentenced to life in prison, crying on his lawyer Frank Stevenson's shoulder when he was finally released from Folsom County Prison. And the picture of the happy couple in Elk Grove with their new baby from China, an adoption Stevenson had arranged after much difficulty and diplomacy. All kinds of cases he did for no money and got no accolades. *I didn't do them for the glory. I'm not a bad guy,* he argued. *I try to do some good in the world.*

But I don't know what to do now, Stevenson thought in panic. He looked back at the glowing computer screen's live news feed. *Time,* he realized, pulling his eyes from the faintly flickering words, *I've got to get some time to think this through.*

He switched off the computer. He saw another framed photograph on the wall, taken at the start of a summit attempt on Mount Whitney three years ago. Two fellow judges from out of state and a thoracic surgeon from UC Davis Medical Center joined him in the expedition. The galvanizing excitement caught in the photo never left them but was magnified by the intense fear joined that set in two thousand feet below the summit. They thought they might not get off the mountain. The other judges had fallen ill in camp, freezing and suffering from altitude sickness, but Stevenson and the surgeon were determined to push on to the summit. They barely made it before a storm drove them off. For that brief moment, poised at the top between success and possible death, he felt exhilaration unlike anything before or since. It was a strange mingling of invincibility and mortality.

As he went upstairs, he felt the same exhilaration he had at the summit.

Nobody saw it happen last night. Not even Eli. There's no witness. Except maybe one.

Without much change, Stevenson convulsively formed a new, second and darker prayer about the cop fighting for his life. And, if his second prayer were answered, there would still be no witness.

While Veronica finished dressing and Haley came into the kitchen, Stevenson made breakfast. He scrambled eggs, made toast, and brewed coffee for Veronica and him and put out blueberry yogurt and an apple for Haley. She ate solemnly and carefully. She was already dressed in her mandatory school uniform of dark blue sweater and skirt and white blouse.

"What's up, button?" he asked, dumping the skillet into the sink and running water. He was surprised at his own ordinariness.

"I don't want to go to school."

"I don't blame you. School's no fun sometimes." He sat down but did not eat. "Do you feel okay?"

"Yes." She looked at him again, gray eyes that seemed to see everything, and always had, from the first moment he held her at the hospital and she stopped crying and gazed up at him in silent regard.

"Something going on at school you want to tell me about?" He worried, and so did Veronica, that Haley was too solitary. She had friends, and weekends lately seemed to be a run of birthday parties for a phalanx of Dylans, Mollys, or Evas, mixed in with the occasional sleepover. But she still seemed alone.

"Oh, school. I can manage," and she nodded to him. Then Haley said, "I wish you were happy."

It stabbed him because it was part plea and observation. *She sees something,* he thought. He forced jollity to cover his apprehension.

"I am happy. I'm happy about you. I'm happy about Mom. I'm happy about today. The sun's out, you're going to a stimulating and educational day at St. Francis, Mom's going to work, and I'm off to court."

"Don't make fun of me."

"Well, you sound so serious." He put his hand on hers and for a split second almost gave in to a passionate wish to tell her everything. It was nearly overwhelming in its intensity. He fought it down.

"I'm against things that don't make us happy." Haley finished her breakfast and cleared her place.

"You're a philosopher." He smiled too much. "Make sure you're ready to go. We'll be leaving in ten minutes."

As she passed him, Stevenson impulsively reached out and hugged her and she wiggled free. "Come on, I've got to go," she protested. He wondered if the time would come soon when she could not bear even to be near him.

Veronica came in. She wore her own uniform, a pearl gray suit with a gold dolphin pin and slim sunglasses on her head, as if she were ready to enter a race. "Did I tell you Anson wants to take the Lenard twins out for a drink after work?" She meant the senior partner in her law firm.

He got up. "Nope."

"Well, he says we've got to get our biggest clients well lubricated tonight. They're not going to like my bill for their land deal out by Arco Arena. So, it's going to be you and Hurricane for a while tonight. Believe me, this is one I'd like to skip."

"I was going to break a little early today anyway," he said, making a sudden decision. "I can pick Haley up and we'll figure something out for dinner."

Veronica gulped down a cup of coffee and bit off some toast. "Dad getting you down with his campaign for the appointment?"

"No at all. What do you mean?"

"You know he can get intense when he gets a cause," she touched him gently, "and you are his cause right now. He drove Mom and me crazy when he got his enthusiasms. Making homemade apple jelly, sailing, stargazing." She rolled her eyes.

Stevenson had known from the start of his relationship with Vee that she idolized her father. He was the cheerful and secure center of her growing up. It did not hurt that they were very well off and that Eli could indulge his transient enthusiasms because he had no real work to do at the bank.

"He's fine. He's setting up a lot of introductions for me," Stevenson said. "I just don't want him to do too much."

"I wish I could have come with you last night. But the merger valuations had to get done," she finished her coffee. "Keep an eye on him, Frank. He'll push himself too far if you don't."

"I'll take care of him," he said. After last night, there was no alternative. They were indissolubly tied together even if Eli did not really realize it.

Vee had been frantic when he had the heart attack last year. The death of her mother, along with Eli's old age and increased drinking, made her sharply sensitive and protective whenever her father's well-being was concerned.

"Ugh. The twins. Two sets of poached eggs eyeing me." She remembered her chore for the day.

Stevenson put his arms around her. She smelled of lavender soap and coffee. "It's their idea of a compliment. Let me know if they say anything or Anson tries anything and I'll have my bailiff pick them up. I might take care of them myself."

Veronica kissed him, and then reached over and turned on the small TV on the counter.

"Leave the TV off!" Stevenson said too loudly. He grabbed for it and she swatted his hand away.

"Hey, I need to find out what the market's doing," she said. The brief good mood had broken abruptly. "You're not the only one with a lot on his mind around here."

He didn't answer. The first thing on the TV was a shot outside

Sutter General Hospital. A young woman reporter described the immediate outpouring of community support for Officer Thomas Ensor. Kids from soccer and boxing clubs that Officer Ensor coached were shown crowding into Sutter General Hospital's entrance.

"I wonder what happened," Veronica said with faint interest and then, to Stevenson's relief, she flipped to CNN and MSNBC.

"I'm sorry, Vee," he said while she took in the stock figures running on the screen. "I didn't mean to snap like that."

She nodded, looking at him a little puzzled, absentmindedly twisting her wedding ring. She sighed. "Dodged a bullet on the commodity markets. Anson will be floating all morning."

"Listen, Vee," he started, again half fearful he would blurt everything out. She flipped the TV channels back to the local news, turning up the volume as the young woman reporter concluded, "So the Sacramento Police Department urgently requests anybody who was driving in downtown Sacramento last night in the area around the Capitol between midnight and two A.M. and may have seen anything that will help them solve the hit-and-run of Officer Ensor to call them on this toll-free hotline." The number flashed on the screen. Stevenson turned the TV off.

"You were out last night, Frank," Veronica said. "Maybe you should call the police."

"I wasn't anywhere near there."

"I know. I'm kidding." She frowned again at the odd sharpness in his voice.

"Listen, I said I was going to get out early this afternoon."

"You're the judge. It's your courtroom."

"I'm going to go see Eli. Strategize about this appointment." Her father had been instrumental in procuring Stevenson's appointment to the superior court six years earlier.

"Say hi. Tell him I'll call tonight when I get in, maybe late. He likes the gruesome details about my land deals." Her grin faded. "Something's wrong, Frank."

"Nothing," he said blithely.

"You don't want to tell me."

"There's nothing to tell."

"Okay, I'm not going to twist your arm," she said, hurt that he was being untruthful. Stevenson knew she grasped that much.

He tried evasion. "Your dad's going to spend most of the time pumping me about what Hurricane's doing in school."

"Who's asking about me and school?" Haley appeared with her small bright backpack.

"Your grandpa. Who else?" Veronica said, checking to make sure Haley had everything for the day. She glanced at Stevenson, then away.

Stevenson was relieved at the distraction. He knew he had to go on with his daily routine, change as little as possible, wear a camouflage of normality until he could find a way out of the perilous course he was navigating.

"We're right on time," Veronica said to Haley, "Your father holds the land speed record for getting dressed."

"I'm on my mark," he said and then added casually on his way out, "Vee, I need to take your car today. The SUV started making funny noises yesterday and I barely got home. I can drop you at work and then take Haley to St. Francis."

"That's kind of awkward, Frank. I planned on having my car to get around today," she said, peeved. "What kind of noises?"

"Hell if I know. Noises. Ones it shouldn't."

"I can call for a tow," she reached for her cell phone.

"I'll take care of it," he said angrily. "Don't call anybody, all right? I'll get it fixed, but for right now, this minute, I need to use your car, all right?"

Veronica shrugged and put away her phone. Haley went to the vast stainless-steel refrigerator and got out a cold apple, stowing it in her backpack. *She hears everything,* Stevenson knew, *she takes it all in.*

He was afraid of his daughter suddenly.

"Okay, Frank, don't make a production out of it. I'll bum rides or take a cab."

"Thank you," he said curtly and, as he went upstairs, he heard Veronica and Haley chuckling about Eli's consuming interest in her activities. He had plainly set out to spoil his granddaughter. Stevenson thought it would be wonderful to have that as the sole topic of the day.

He shaved clumsily, nicking himself, and took a quick shower, running icy water to shock himself, as if he could wake up from a very bad dream. He put on a charcoal gray suit, striped shirt, blue silk tie, and black shoes. He looked vacantly back at his image in the bathroom mirror. He was forty-two, his face angular, hard, and handsome. But there was something furtive and hesitant in his eyes. It had always been there, and now it had coherence. *You didn't stop,* staring at himself he thought as he had the night before, *you just kept going.*

"All you had to do was put your foot on the brake and stop. Open the SUV door and get out and that's it. Now it's too late."

He spoke the words to engrave them, like he did from the bench when he made orders or argued with lawyers or instructed a jury. Speaking them aloud gave them weight and effect. There was no court reporter to memorialize what he said now but they were as solid and real as anything he put on the official record.

"You hit a cop. He may live or he may die, but you hit a cop and you didn't stop."

Stevenson made a wordless, wrenching gasp, eyes shut. It was not about him alone. He did not know what would happen to Veronica or Haley. They were trapped with him. So was his soft, good-natured father-in-law.

He swept change into his pocket, put his wallet and courthouse identification badge in his suit, hung his BlackBerry on his belt. He looked, outwardly, almost the way he did every day.

His thoughts churned when he went downstairs, ready to apologize to his wife and daughter, keep up the pretense of normality.

They were not in the kitchen or the living room. Stevenson called out impatiently, nervously.

He went back into the kitchen, and through the window he saw Veronica use the garage door opener, the door sweeping up gracefully, with Haley at her side.

Stevenson raced out.

NINE

"THREE DAYS?" ROSE EXCLAIMED when Nye got off the phone with Nishimoto. "What if it takes longer than that?"

"What if it only takes to lunch today? Look on the bright side, Rosie. Maybe we deal this one out in the next three hours," Nye said lightly. He had been as incredulous as Rose when informed of the deadline for their investigation.

"I want this puke as badly as anybody, but didn't you tell Nishimoto it's kind of thin on the ground right now? We don't have much yet?"

"I told him."

"What'd he say?"

"He said, seventy-two hours, Nye. So it's set in concrete."

"If I stay with the department as long as you," Rose said solemnly, "I will never get as laid back as you, Ter. Nothing gets you."

"I'm on fire now," he said with a grin. His trademark was a laconic outer shell. He was actually furious at the undoubted tug-of-war inside the upper reaches of the department that was deforming the investigation into Ensor's hit-and-run even as it had barely gotten underway.

"Sure you are. Burn, baby, burn," Rose said.

Nye and Rose spent a frustrating early morning methodically checking the office buildings up and down Capitol Mall from the Wells Fargo construction site. Although they had a half dozen uniformed cops going through the buildings, too, they were able to only get through some of them before dawn. Few of the offices had twenty-four hour security on the premises and it took time to get permission to enter the buildings. Nye figured it should go more quickly after everyone was open for business at eight or nine and when the news about the hit-and-run had gotten around. So far they had not found anyone in the offices much after the close of business the day before.

There was one bright moment that made Nye think they were lucky. They talked to the operator of the Tower Bridge, a four-lane Depression-era vertical lift bridge over the Sacramento River. He could have seen traffic along Capitol Mall from his control room, but said he did not see anything. He was busy keeping an eye on the dark river for any stray boats that would have required him to raise the bridge. Rose spotted the thick pillow beside his desk and the plastic dinner carton with the remains of enchiladas. Rose told Nye outside that the guy was probably asleep and could not admit it. He agreed. They moved on. Nearest the Tower Bridge was One Capitol Mall, a newer glass-and-stone office building which straddled the restored tourist area of Old Sacramento and the new face of the city being erected down the street. Inside, on the sixth floor, Nye and Rose located a lobbying firm, Wells and Rocker, whose offices had an expansive, unobstructed view down Capitol Mall to the construction site. Two young associates had been working very late preparing for a Senate committee hearing that morning. But they had been in the firm's inner conference room and did not even know it was dawn until Rose told them. Nye's momentary hope of finding any kind of witness quickly collapsed.

"Six thirty, Ter," she said. "How about a breakfast break?"

"Why not? This is a damn long shot anyway."

They went back to the site. Quintana had left with IA several hours earlier. Nye did not like presenting Rose with the unpleasant choice she had to make about not telling IA how Quintana reacted during their questioning. But he wanted to give the young cop a chance. He watched Rose, capable, efficient, seemingly always in charge, and knew she had her own problems, mostly at home with her husband. *She's got to understand about holding out a hand sometimes,* Nye thought.

They helped Obergon open up the street for the morning rush hour traffic that started roaring by. By a little after seven, people and steady lines of cars pulsed into downtown Sacramento, passing the filigreed white State Capitol situated within a park of pines, lemon and orange trees, and flowers from every part of the state. TV camera trucks arrived and reporters set up as close to the construction site as they could. Overhead, a TV station's helicopter whirred loudly. A few people paused on the sidewalk, pointing at the street. Fewer still stopped and lowered their heads. One woman came over and shook Nye's hand tightly, telling him it was awful, awful, and she hoped they would find the undoubtedly drunk driver who did it.

"How long do you want us to stay, Terry?" Obergon asked. He was still in his raincoat even though the sky had come up brilliant blue and clear. He bounced a now unnecessary heavy flashlight in his hand.

"We're done. The techs got what they need. Keep a couple guys here in case some citizen feels like telling us what happened." He said to Rose, "First thing we get back to the barn, we need to set up a search pattern for about five, six blocks around the accident. Nish'll go for the manpower to check the whole area."

Obergon scowled. "Right. Somebody saw something. I got to believe that."

"Keep that good thought," Nye said.

He and Rose drove a couple of blocks to the Pot Belly Pig Deli, one of the many small diners that served breakfast and lunch to the mob of state workers in the sprawling agencies surrounding the Capitol. It was crowded. They sat down a little wearily and ordered.

Rose leaned back and rubbed her eyes. "I didn't want to ask before, Ter, but what about our others cases? What do we do with them?"

"You heard Nish. We don't have any other cases. We got all eyes on us, Rosie, and this is the one for the next three days."

"I just don't want to put everything else on the back burner." She sat forward, intense.

"Trust me. You can drop the ball on every other case and, if we clean this one up, Nish won't mind. The chief won't mind. We'll be on TV. You'll get a letter for your jacket," which meant a recommendation.

"It's not about snagging a damn attaboy, Ter," she said angrily. "Like our dumpster gal, what about her? Or my leg case? They're still about two days old. They'll get pretty stale if I don't work them even for a couple days."

Nye watched the Vietnamese waitress put down their food. He understood Rose's worry. They had gotten two tough homicides. The day before, someone put a woman, Caucasian, unknown age, into a dumpster off of Royal Oaks Boulevard not far from the Main Post Office, and set her afire. The heat was so intense that the victim was stuck to the dumpster and had to be pried out like a burned hamburger from a skillet. Rose attended the autopsy. Nye declined because he stopped going to autopsies years earlier. The pictures in this case were bad enough, tiny white teeth like candy gum stuck in a hairless, earless, blackened melted face. What made it all perfect, in Nye's opinion, was the pathologist's report that there were soot deposits in the dead woman's nose and throat. She had been burned alive. No facial identification was possible because of the burning, fingerprints were gone, and the few teeth left probably would not provide enough for a dental record match.

Their leg case was painless by comparison. One leg was found by a fisherman on the American River. It was a right leg, weighted down with a twenty-pound railroad cleat tied to it with copper wire. Rose had gotten police divers into the river and, shortly afterward, they found a left leg, also weighted with a railroad cleat. Both legs looked like they came from the same black man, but it would take DNA tests to prove it. At the moment, neither he nor Rose could even be sure of the dead man's height. Because of the body's site of the amputations, he could have been anything from five feet eight inches to six feet four inches tall.

Until that morning, Nye assumed these two cases would be his last in the department and the truth was that the solution to one or both of them would not cause no more than a ripple in the city's attention nor drastically change the department's murder stats.

And both cases, in addition to the three others they carried,

would take a lot of work to close. Like food left out in the open, they would not improve with age.

"What can I tell you, Rosie?" he said, eating mechanically, head down. "Everybody's got priorities and we just got ours."

"So maybe we end up kissing off the two new ones?"

"Maybe."

"How about—" she started to say, picking at a bulbous blue-berry muffin.

"Don't bother," Nye spoke and chewed. "If we aren't working Ensor twenty-four-seven for next seventy-two, we'll get beat up. You don't need that just getting started in the bureau," he meant Major Crimes, "and I sure don't coming out the other end. I don't want to go out screwing up a hero cop's hit-and-run."

Rose didn't say anything, and he could see she was mad, con-flicted, and resigned all at once. She finally said, "Okay, Ter. I get it." She looked at him for a moment. "If my kid ate like you, I'd make her go to her room."

"I might've done the same with my kids," he agreed. "Living like I do, you kind of lose some of the finer points of etiquette." He raised a pinky to show his refinement. He tried to make it a joke, but the truth was he hated living alone, eating alone most of the time, except when he was on duty with Rose, and worst, sleeping alone. He was, he acknowledged with some bewilderment, a little unclear how he had come to this point.

They finished breakfast and spent a few minutes going over their next moves. Both of them had noted which buildings around the crime scene were covered by surveillance cameras. It was possible that a camera picked up traffic on Capitol Mall.

"You ever seen the security setup at the Capitol?" Nye asked.

"Never got the tour."

"It's pretty sweet. They got cameras covering every inch of the building, the park, the approach streets. They don't want another guy in a milk truck bombing the place." A deranged trucker late one night not long before crashed his tanker truck into the Capitol's eastside and set it ablaze, killing himself. If the truck had contained anything more dangerous than condensed milk, the destruction would have been catastrophic.

"So they've got at least a full one hundred eighty looking down

Capitol Mall?" Rose asked eagerly. "They must've gotten our driver on camera."

"Could be. The streetlights were out. Heavy rain. I don't want to get too excited yet."

"I like it so far. You know anybody at the Capitol who'll give us the video?"

"Yeah, couple old bums still hang around," he shook his head. "But for this one, Rosie, we need to get warrants for any video. I want to play it very conservative when we get to court, everything in black and white."

"So we're looking at doing a half dozen search warrants today."

"Yeah."

They agreed that the hunt for witnesses had to be coordinated and set in high gear. Any tips coming in through the telephone hotline had to be sifted, checked. They needed to keep on the crime lab to get some quick matches on the paint fragments and tire tracks at the scene. But the major chore was to make sure a be-on-the-lookout notification went to all of the auto repair shops in California.

"Someone's got to see a black whatever-the-hell-it-is with major damage. Friend, neighbor, family, somebody's going to notice. It goes in to get fixed, somebody's going to see it," Nye said.

"A lot of car shops aren't on our list," Rose said. "Chop shops. Wrecking yards. Guy who fixes cars in his garage."

"If the asshole moves this vehicle, tries to hide what he did, he'll get spotted."

"How about if he locks the damn thing in his garage?"

Nye grinned wolfishly. "Name how many people you know can afford to let their car or truck or SUV gather dust in their garage. Ain't likely. People need their wheels."

"What if he just dumps it? Calls it in stolen?"

"We put every stolen vehicle report that comes in under the microscope, Rosie."

Nye paid since it was his turn, and they walked to their car. A blue, white, and yellow Light Rail train, bell clanging as it crossed streets, rumbled past them, carrying blank-faced state workers and a smattering of young adults. Nobody looked happy, certainly. It used to be, sometime in the dimming past, that Nye never saw a train or bus go by like that without being grateful for what he did for a living. On his worst days, and there had been a considerable and unanticipated number since Marceen left him and their kids moved away, he still felt connected to the pulse of the world. He still believed that what he did, even if he was inept sometimes or failed, mattered in the long run.

Without his noticing at first, all of the mistakes he had made started to gang up on him, until it was a daily parade of reminders about people he let down or careless mistakes that tainted evidence, even if it happened years before. And there was the great grinning gargoyle of a screwup that he had managed, with effort and success, to tuck down below his recollection until it, too, started bobbing up to the surface. At that point, he knew it was time to go.

Rose got behind the wheel of their unmarked police car. Nye still liked this moment, when they were going somewhere, the frustrations and confusions were not besetting, and frankly, just being with her because it made the world seem less chaotic. He would miss this moment.

"Before we go back to the barn," Rose said, "we should swing by Sutter General and see how Ensor's doing. Check in."

"I don't know," he replied, "it's going to be a zoo. Cops, cameras, just a lot of citizens, too."

"I know you hate hospitals, Ter," she said. "But if Ensor doesn't make it, we should've been there."

"Nothing good happens in a goddamn hospital. You ever see anybody happy there? Even the ones doing okay? Go to a bakery, everybody's got a smile. Hospital, it's like going to county jail or doing a visit to the joint, you walk out the door and that's when you feel great because you're the one getting away."

"Don't give me attitude, old man. Your kids were born at Sutter General."

"Right. Case closed. Makes my point."

Rose grinned. "You are such a lying fool, Nye. All I heard from you since we partnered is what great kids you have."

Nye did not answer. His daughter lived in Nevada, his son in Arizona, each with a family. His daughter was due with her first child in July. He told her he would move near her soon after his retirement and he had to admit the notion apparently did not sit well with her or her husband. Nye felt for the first time recently that some milestone had been reached, a dividing line, and he had much less left to him than he realized. It was melancholy and sobering and it made him restless. He was unsettled at the prospect of the void facing him when he left the department.

He glanced at Rose. Where was she going? Thirty-four and quietly ambitious, a little self-conscious around people she thought smarter or better brought up. Rose had a six-year-old daughter, and her husband Luis could not hold a job. He was currently managing a local hip-hop band. She had a lot of family back in Cebu City in the Philippines. Nye thought she could go farther than he had. He was sorry there would not be time enough to help her.

"Okay," he relented. "Let's go to Sutter."

"I was taking us there anyway."

All the plausible, sound reasons he repeated daily to himself about the merits of retirement—full, dreamless sleep, no fears of relapsing into the happy haze of uncounted drinks, no more feeling sorry for himself, eating better, being near his daughter and his first grandchild, and the others he concocted, discarded, trotted out to speed the remaining days on—did not seem so solid for a moment.

He wondered why.

Nye swore and shook his head, but it was all right. Working with Rose at the very end of his career was like the bittersweet vision of his second chance. Maybe he couldn't go back and do things over again, but he could try to do them better from now on. Starting right now he had a couple of days left and this critical investigation and, in that time, he could redeem himself and show Rose mistakes to avoid. He had his own private religion going, he realized with an inward grimace and amusement. The Church of the Second Chance.

Altlander closed his office door and motioned to the shorter, more compact man in shirtsleeves to sit down. He remained standing. His face was tight and breathed heavily, as if from running.

"Christ Almighty. *Nye*. He puts that old drunk on the case."

"Terry Nye wouldn't be my first, second, or third choice." The other man had deepset black eyes and a fringe of balding hair. "Too old, too slow, too unreliable."

"Too damn right. So what the hell is Nishimoto thinking? What if this decrepit boozer falls off the wagon now?" Altlander swung away, shaking his head. "For everybody's sake, the department, Ensor's, everyone, Nye has got to get off this investigation."

The other man looked steadily at Altlander. "How can I help?"

"You can start by letting him know Internal Affairs is looking at him, I mean, looking up his asshole. Let him know every screwup he's made is going to get another going over."

The other man stood up, arms folded. He stuttered slightly, but he had worked since childhood to correct the impediment, so it was barely noticeable except in times of tension. His words wobbled a little now. "He's getting out of the department in a couple of weeks. Maybe nature should just run its course."

Altlander picked up a pen and tapped it loudly on his desk. "Think so? When he could compromise the investigation into a cop like Ensor's hit-and-run? A cop worth ten of him? You know, Johnny, I'm starting to question your judgment. It may be when I'm chief, I will need a new head of IA."

The other man raised his head. He stuttered more obviously. "I don't see Nye as lead on this case."

"Make something happen. Fast."

"Nishimoto's going to look pretty bad when I turn the heat on Nye."

Altlander grinned toothily. He dropped the pen with a clunk to his battered mahogany desk. "You reap what you sow."

The other man turned to the office door as Altlander grabbed the ringing telephone on his desk. Every light flashed. Altlander waved him to get out.

TEN

"STAY OUT OF THE GARAGE!" Stevenson called loudly. Both Veronica and Haley turned suddenly in surprise.

"We were just going to get in the car," Veronica said.

"I'll back it out so you don't have to climb all over to get in," he said, a little breathless.

"Fine. Thanks," she said, herding Haley to one side. "You covered up the SUV," she pointed at the tan rectangular shape beside her car.

Stevenson got into the driver's side of her black Lexus. "Yeah, the rain, the noises it's making. I don't know when I'll take it out again."

Veronica and Haley got in, buckled up. "Well, then let me get it fixed, Frank. You're tied up in court. I can come home and be here when the tow truck shows up."

"No." He spoke slowly, as though talking to a dim child. It irritated Veronica and he knew it, but he could not help himself. He had contradictory impulses to keep her distant and close at the same time. "I said I would take care of the damn SUV. Thank you for offering, though. But no thank you."

"Look, do not take whatever you've got on your mind on me. Or Haley," she snapped.

"It's not something on my mind. I thought I was pretty clear about the SUV. I'll handle it."

Stevenson noticed that Veronica did not answer him. She shook her head in annoyance and turned to Haley in the backseat. "We're not fighting, honey."

"You could've fooled me." Haley stared out the window as they drove.

He wanted to grab Veronica and make her listen, tell her what was happening to him, and now because of him, to them all. It burned inside him that he had no idea how she would react if he told her everything. *The same goes for Haley,* Stevenson thought. He felt as though he was riding with two strangers.

The rest of the drive to St. Francis School was in silence. The school was adjacent to a bulky Mission-style church set incongruously in a reclaimed neighborhood of old Victorian homes spruced up to hold lobbying firms and law offices, across the street from a large bicycle emporium that featured titanium racing bikes. He pulled up to the curb as other parents were dropping off their kids at the dun-colored Spanish building. Haley joined the stream of kids going inside, two or three clustering around her.

"Meredith Klein," Veronica said as they pulled away.

"What?"

"The little blonde girl with Hurricane. Meredith's mother is deputy chief in the Legislative Analyst's Office. Her stepfather's George Myrrdin, the governor's Legal Appointments Secretary."

"I never made the connection." He took a breath, "You're your father's daughter, all right."

Veronica checked her briefcase to make sure she had everything. He knew it was her way of tamping down frustration and anger, directed at him. "He said you should never go anyplace in this town without making at least one new contact, getting one new phone number. I always make it a point to spend some time with Meredith's mom at soccer games. Nothing very obvious, just parent talk about our kids, how they're doing, and then a couple well-timed remarks about what you're doing, how well everyone at the courthouse thinks of you. It gets back to Myrrdin. When you make the move for a spot on the Third, he'll remember all the good things he's heard when he's going through your papers."

"I didn't know you were doing that, Vee."

"All part of the service." She snapped the briefcase shut. She said brightly. "Well, I hope your day gets better. Mine sure won't." She paused, "And I hope whatever you've got on your mind, you feel like telling me later."

"I shouldn't take it out on you or Hurricane."

"No. You should not," she scolded with exaggeration. "Last night was nice," Veronica smiled and kissed him. "I'm not complaining if that goes a little longer."

"All part of the service," he said, imitating her usual lightness. He could not say anything more.

He dropped her off outside her law firm on a deeply tree-shaded street five blocks from the Capitol. It was a small elegant new building that only held the California Central Water Project and a high-flying energy company. Rexroad, Keelor, and Stevenson, LLC occupied the top two floors. He gamely wished her luck with the Lenard twins that evening and anyone passing them would have heard nothing more than husband and wife banter about the day's upcoming tribulations.

Stevenson drove away, his heart pounding again as it had the night before. *I've got to survive,* he thought. *I've got to make it for everyone's sake. It's my family I've got to protect not just myself. I'm doing everything for Vee and Haley.*

He slowed going into the underground garage beneath the white, sharply angled bulk of the Sacramento County Courthouse to let a bus from the Rio Consumnes Correctional Center carefully navigate the sloping entrance as the heavy steel mesh gate rattled up. Through the barred rear window of the bus two Hispanic inmates stared at him, then laughed.

Plans. I've got to make plans, he thought, the laughing faces drawing away as the jail bus rolled ahead. I need a structure right away, things to do or it's all going to hell.

Stevenson pulled forward. He was preoccupied. He fished for his ID badge and Smitty, the attendant at the gate waved him forward.

"Come on in, Judge," he said. He was past retirement, a former deputy sheriff wounded during a robbery. "Got a full house today.

They brought over the batch from the main jail a couple minutes ago. Now we got a load from RCCC."

Stevenson managed a smile. "I'm using my wife's car today, Smitty. The SUV's making noises."

"Sure, no problem, Judge. You put her car on the list for parking down here. I won't tow you," he chuckled.

"Thanks," Stevenson said. He wanted to make sure Vee's car would not raise a red flag. Parking spaces in the garage were allotted to judges and other personnel, and only the vehicles on the application were permitted. He remembered when an older judge, now dead, had parked his son's VW in his space and found it gone when he came down to go home. He was furious that the courthouse garage staff towed it without calling him first. But the presiding judge backed the staff. Security came first in a courthouse that was once targeted by radicals during the sixties and now, on any given day, filled with defendants in custody for everything from drug trafficking to murder. And each defendant had friends and family who might try to help them. Stevenson was not going to risk having Vee's car taken away and then have many people noticing that he was not driving the SUV without his cover story being spread around.

"I hope it won't cost you an arm and a leg to fix," Smitty said, eager as usual to talk. "But Jesus, you try fixing a car today yourself? Take a look under the hood, Judge. I don't even recognize what most of the stuff in the engine is anymore."

Another car pulled behind Stevenson and honked its horn for Smitty to raise the gate. Stevenson took the opening to break away, waved, and drove to his assigned parking space.

His courtroom, Department 34, was on the fourth floor of the courthouse. He rode up in an elevator packed with sullen, frightened, subdued people, women with babies, men in work clothes. Two burly Sacramento sheriff's deputies who worked as bailiffs sharply watched everyone in the elevator.

He got out, the corridor thick with milling people, and used the rear access doors to go down the hallway that ran behind the courtrooms. Boxes of court files were stacked almost up to the wide windows that went the length of the courthouse. Stevenson saw the brick cathedrals of the Southern Pacific rail yard a mile away, the looming tower of the county jail, and the canopy of trees that covered the old downtown heart of the city. It was a view he barely noticed over the last two years since he had been assigned to Department 34 and now, passing it, he thought he had never seen it before. It would be magnificent, he yearned fleetingly, to get lost in the web of tracks and sidelined locomotives in the vast rail yard.

Clarence Yardley, the oldest black judge in California, called out a phlegmy greeting from the backdoor to Department 32 as he passed.

Keep moving, keep moving, Stevenson thought as he bustled into his own department. His clerk, Joan, was putting bulky files into the steel cabinets in her office just outside his chambers. She followed him in. His bailiff, Audie, surreptitiously working a small plug of chewing tobacco, came with her.

"Master Calendar sent us anything yet, Joan?" he asked, avoiding looking at them. He didn't know if she'd spot something different in his face. He went to his heavy mahogany desk, rummaging through papers.

"Just got this, Judge. A three defendant, multiple count trial," she handed him the thick yellow official court file.

"Criminal case?" he asked in surprise. He had not been assigned one for nearly a year.

"Every department's pitching in," she said. "Nothing pled out yesterday."

Stevenson took off his coat and hung it behind his chair. It was an ancient axiom of the judicial branch. On the day every criminal defendant decides to go to trial, the grand justice system comes to a screeching halt. "Well, it'll make a pleasant change of pace. Makes you happy, Audie, I assume. Let me know when the lawyers get here."

She nodded and as she turned to go he said without emphasis, "I'm going to break early this afternoon. I've got some personal business to take care of."

"Is everything all right? Anything wrong with the family?" she asked. Joan was fifty, short, and dark haired. She wore thick sweaters all year and efficiently managed the department, especially during the paper torrents of his civil trials. She remembered birthdays, appointments, and anniversaries and she had been with him ever since he was appointed to the bench. *It would be tough to hide anything from her,* he knew with a stab.

"No, no. Everybody's in the pink. It's tax stuff I need to talk over with my father-in-law," he said with sudden inspiration.

Audie said, "You'll love this trial, Judge. We're going to need *three* Spanish interpreters. The three bad boys are all in custody, too." He grinned at Joan who nodded. With interpreters and the additional chores of defendants who were in county jail, the trial would be a logistical tangle. Of course Audie was cheerful. He was a big young man who had been in the Sacramento Sheriff's Department for five years. He played football at Chico State. Both he and Joan were intensely loyal to him.

Stevenson sat down. Audie ploughed on, "You see what happened to a city cop? He got run over near the Capitol."

"Horrible thing," Joan said.

"No, I missed it," Stevenson said. "That's terrible. What happened, Audie?" He wanted to hear how the night before was being talked about around the courthouse. He crossed his arms.

"The cop was working an off-duty security job at the Wells Fargo building and somebody hit him when he was in the street. Knocked him couple dozen feet and did a real job on him." Audie hand his hands on his hips and he shook his head. "Good guy, too. Couple deputies here know him."

"Any description of the driver or the car?" Stevenson asked. He watched Audie's angry expression. The informal cop network would have recycled every tidbit of rumor or information by now.

"Nah. But there will be."

"Why?"

"Because it's probably some drunk coming over from West Sac, hitting the bars, going too fast, probably had his lights off. Guys like that turn up pretty quick or somebody turns them in. You hit a cop and drive away, you're going to be really scared."

Joan said, "I hope it's resolved fast. I can just imagine how the poor man's family must feel right now."

Stevenson swallowed hard. He had forgotten the cop's family. Of course the man had one and they must be going through hell. He realized that both Joan and Audie were looking at him, awaiting some response. He blurted out, "Maybe you're right, Audie. I wasn't there."

For another moment they continued to look at him and Stevenson had the helpless falling sensation of someone who has let go of a rope. Then Joan nodded, "I see what you mean, Judge. We don't know what happened. I wasn't there either. We should wait until there's more information."

"Right," Stevenson said with relief, "and hope the officer recovers completely."

"I don't think so," Audie said. "He's looking at early retirement and one hundred percent disability, it sounds like. He got nailed bad." Audie left to check on the courtroom. It was likely spectators would show up for a trial with three defendants.

Stevenson couldn't even focus on the list of charges haphazardly jotted on the court file.

Stevenson closed the door after they left. He stared vacantly around his chambers. *Plan,* he thought again, *I must plan what to cover and then make sure all of the exposed liabilities from last night are removed. I can't afford to make things up on the fly. I can't let Eli be questioned about last night. He's not strong.*

So I can't become a suspect. Period.

His silver framed photographs of Vee and Haley taken on vacations in the Bahamas and up at Lake Tahoe, sun and sand and sun and snow, were scattered around his chambers. He was in very few because he took the pictures. He felt as if he were a million miles from those places and that happiness.

Stevenson closed his eyes for a moment. His chambers were more than usually cluttered with boxes of evidence from recent trials that didn't fit in Joan's locked evidence closet. Gilt-edged volumes of cases settled by the state appellate courts and the California Supreme Court filled the bookshelves. His award plaques and diplomas hung on the wall behind his desk.

Even though he had lived and worked here, took the familiarity of the mint-green sofa and chairs and everything else in the room for granted, Stevenson had the very strange feeling of never being here before. He looked around. This morning, after the long night, he was like a castaway on a new, unexplored desert island. There were unseen dangers everywhere.

On the credenza behind his desk was a TV. He turned it on, bracing himself because he needed to find out the latest news about the injured police officer.

He stared, sweating a little, at the picture of the growing crowd around the hospital. Weeping children, weeping men and women. Not many but a few. In the back of his mind, a scornful comment formed. *Of course the damn TV news picks out the most melodramatic images and makes it seem like that's the whole story. Manipulative sonsofbitches.*

He did not think about the cop's family. He could not.

He was planning as he watched.

ELEVEN

WALKING INTO SUTTER GENERAL HOSPITAL, Nye and Rose dodged camera crews and stray reporters sprinkled among the mass of people clogging the lobby, spilling out into the parking lot.

She muttered to him, "Turn it off, okay? You been snarling like you haven't gotten your dog food in a week."

Nye sharply glared at her, then softened. "Sorry. I got something on my mind." Like a cowardly threat just delivered from John Guthrie, the too-righteous head of Internal Affairs. What made it sting was that Guthrie had the temerity to throw the net over Rose as well. *Okay, so this is another distraction I don't want Rosie dealing with right now.* He would handle it alone and protect her.

"Remind me never to get really banged up or shot," he murmured to Rose, wordlessly pushing aside a cameraman, equipment perched on his shoulder like a wild growth, and reporter interviewing a stern-faced woman.

"Like anybody'd come out for you," Rose said. "Face it, Ter, I won't get this kind of turnout and you sure won't."

"No, guess not," he said with unexpected regret. "But maybe I might. I got a lot of assholes who'd like to see me go for a dirt nap.

Hey, there's Nish." They headed for the assistant chief, standing off to one side of the shiny broad lobby with several other cops.

It was not quite seven thirty in the morning and the number of people flocking to the hospital was startling, Nye admitted. He intended to check up on Ensor's various activities but he assumed that some well-dressed kids were from sports teams Ensor worked with, and the rougher contingent was his dropout gangbangers. There was a constant murmuring, low and insistent, like a church service in a strange language. It amazed Nye that a fellow cop, someone he had partnered with briefly, had time enough for so many activities, touching so many different kinds of people. In his own life, even now and definitely when he had a wife and growing kids, he thought each day was a deliberate obstacle course: never enough time, never enough juice left to do everything.

But it wasn't just having the time, he recognized. If he had all the free days in the world he still wouldn't have done what Ensor was doing. There was a mystery. What made Ensor go that extra distance to help so many other people? It wasn't like he was perfect. Nye remembered Tommy Ensor after they took breaks for lunch or dinner. The belching started and went on for an hour, even when Nye told him to cut it out. Tommy got a kick out of doing it and needling him. Tommy liked his dirty jokes, too, telling them with great glee, and then repeating the same ones a few days later. Nye remembered how much Tommy merrily mugged telling the one about the one-eyed hooker and the john who begged to know what the exotic sexual service she offered could be. When they couldn't come to terms over price, she popped her glass eye into her hand. "I'll be keeping an eye out for you," she told the unsatisfied john.

The truth was, even though they rode together for a while, and Ensor gave him a desperately needed lifeline when he was crawling through every bar and strip joint in a ten-mile radius and about to throw his career away, he didn't know the guy. Not at all. And so there was the mystery.

He and Rose got bad news coming over. The city water department had been unable to do anything about trapping possible material from the accident washed into the drains. It had been a long shot, but he didn't like starting off with failure.

"Nye, Tafoya," Nishimoto said formally when they got to him.

"You just caught me. I'm heading back to the department. Give me something good."

Rose quickly briefed him on their plans for the remainder of the morning.

"Wouldn't that be ideal, the bastard's on a surveillance tape?" Nishimoto nodded. "Get those search warrants done ASAP. If we can get a decent image off of a tape, I want to put this bastard on every TV station in California today."

Nye greeted the cops near Nishimoto, guys he didn't see as often these days. Solemn, subdued, each of them. *They know,* Nye thought. The wisdom of the streets. Not conscious, not even articulable, but real and undeniable anyway. Ensor was down and their experience told them he was unlikely to make it. *They know,* Nye thought again.

Rose asked before he did. "How's Officer Ensor doing, Chief?"

"There's a medical briefing in a couple of minutes. He's been in surgery for the last four hours. His minister got here a little while ago. It's very bad."

"We thought we should see how his family's holding up," Nye muttered.

"I've got Janey and the kids in a room. Keeps them away from the media," Nishimoto gestured around them. "I'll take you down."

They headed along a bright antiseptic corridor, passing gurneys and nurses, Nye noting that Nishimoto kept his own bodyguard of cops close to prevent the reporters from getting near him. Rose walked stiffly. She was, he knew, feeling very nervous about doing or saying something wrong. But she was the one who insisted they had to come. Nye admired her guts.

Nishimoto said low to him, "Listen, there are some people who want you and Tafoya replaced, Nye. Not in three days. Now. I've gone to bat for you particularly because you'll do a fucking great job. Don't make me a chump, okay?"

Nye nodded. He assumed the IA threat had been liberally spread around. "I want to personally shake hands with whoever did this to Tommy."

Nishimoto glanced at him quickly, uncertain about the icy cold sarcasm. Then his face hardened. "I forgot you and Ensor were partners for a while."

"There's that," Nye admitted.

"I'm glad you appreciate where we both stand."

They reached a portion of the corridor guarded by two more uniformed officers. Rose glanced at him. They both knew the next part wouldn't be easy. She went in ahead as Nishimoto held Nye back by his arm.

"Last point," Nishimoto said, his face red, his voice a little higher and raspier, "anything you get, you and Tafoya come up with, I want it, right? Nobody else hears it before me, right?"

"Sure, boss," Nye said. "Anybody in particular I should avoid?"

"I think you know."

"Altlander maybe."

"Just make sure your partner knows the drill, Nye."

"I'll talk to her." He went for broke. "Three days is too short, boss."

"Don't even think about a minute longer," Nishimoto barked at him.

Nye was only a little surprised at the intensity of Nishimoto's response. The assistant chief looked like he was about to have stroke. He could be mercurial, swinging from social conversation to ferocious attack in a second sometimes.

Nye understood more things with a short-timer's perspective. Nishimoto had been one of his few champions on the fourth floor although he had the highest investigation clearance rate in Major Crimes and his long years on patrol had given him a unique body of experience about the city and its subterranean players. He was too out of step, by some measurable distance, too quiet or too exuberant when he had been drinking. Nye had always needed Nishimoto.

Now the assistant chief, for the next three days anyway, needed him a great deal more. Perhaps he was Nishimoto's lifeline if other parts of the department like IA were being aimed at him through Nye. *No margin for mistakes. No excuses. No time.*

Nishimoto left him, taking the other cops. If the contest between Nishimoto and Altlander was going to be fought over this investigation, Nye knew the assistant chief would want to be close to the chief. His unflattering nickname at the department was "The Shadow" because he never got too far from the chief's side.

Nye braced himself and went inside. A small group clustered at the room's solitary picture window that overlooked the big Metro bus terminal across the street where all of the buses started and ended each day.

Jane Ensor and her two oldest children, both teenage boys, stood around Quintana. The young cop suddenly bent his head to the woman's shoulder and put his arms around her. Nye heard him say, "I'm sorry. I'm sorry," again and again.

Nye felt incredibly awkward and embarrassed. There was no way to gracefully back out of the room. Rose was also caught near the tableau. He tightened his jaw and she raised her eyebrows in resignation.

"Hello, Janey. I don't want to bother you," he said reluctantly.

She looked up. She patted Quintana. "Okay, Bob, okay, thank you. Thank you. I'll see you later." Her face was opaque, her movements mechanical. She gently pushed him away.

Quintana squeezed her hand and gave a bleak look to Nye and Rose as he left.

Nye said to Ensor's wife, "This is my partner—"

"We had a chance to get introduced, Terry," she interrupted, displaying a thin smile as if it struggled from a far place. "I like your name," she said to Rose, like they shared a private joke. "It's been quite awhile since we saw you," she said to Nye.

"My fault. I kind of let things get away. How are you, Janey?"

She shrugged. "Like a ton of bricks fell on me, honestly I'm not quite here, if you know what I mean." She looked around. "I've got to sit down." She settled in a slightly worn blue plush chair. The two boys stayed at the window, adolescents in shock, wanting to hold on to their mother and unsure how to do it now. *Quintana's behavior must have confused them tremendously,* Nye thought. "You remember Marty and Jack, don't you, Terry? Little older now than when you saw them."

"You've both grown a lot," he said to them, both of them with Jane's broad features and Tommy's dark black hair. "Your dad and I are old friends. Lot of people probably been saying that this morning, but take it from me, if you need something, just let me know, okay? I owe your dad a lot."

The boys barely nodded and went back to the window, talking low to each other. They were hastily dressed, mismatched shirts and pants, dress shoes, evidence of the fear and chaos that caught their lives up in the moments after the call from the department. *Probably the chief,* Nye thought.

Rose pulled up another chair beside Ensor's wife. "What Terry said obviously goes double for you. We're going to put everything into finding out who did this to your husband. It's a personal pledge from me and Terry." She glanced at Nye. "This is our only investigation until we get whoever it is."

Jane Ensor vaguely nodded. Nye noted the pile of used Kleenex on the small table by the chair, the thoughtfully laid-out box of tissues, carafe of water. There were empty coffee cups, crushed candy wrappers. The signposts of fear and uncertainty. "I've got Jimmy and his sister with my mother, so they're okay for now," she said. "I was pretty rocky there for a while this morning, but I'm coping right now."

Nye got down on one knee. It was uncomfortable and he knew it had the staged appearance of a proposal. He didn't care. He remembered the nights Ensor brought him to the small duplex in East Sacramento, sat with him in the trim kitchen, took him outside into the neat backyard when he heaved up whatever he'd been drinking for the last hours, and Jane coming in, making coffee, talking to him in whispers so none of the kids would wake up. What came through his dark haze of self-pity and self-love, what Nye heard was Ensor and his wife holding onto him.

"Janey, it's going to be all right. Tommy's a tough strong guy, you know that. He's got a hell of a lot of people thinking of him," and Nye detested the easy roll of the clichés. Nothing else seemed to come into his mind because just behind the platitudes was an intense hatred of Ensor's assailant that he couldn't acknowledge without giving up his usefulness as an investigator. "So, I'm going to keep figuring that Tommy's fighting and you're fighting, too, and your kids are, too."

She stroked his head. This close to her, the atrocity of the timing of Ensor's hit-and-run gave him a hollow feeling.

"I'm scared, Terry," Jane bent to his ear. "What am I going to do without him? I don't even want to think about it. What do I do? I am so scared right now of being so scared," and she sat back because the door to the room opened and a doctor in spotless white, steel-rim glasses and a brush mustache came in. She stiffened.

"We'll stay," Nye said, getting to his feet. The two boys moved to their mother.

"No, go on, we'll be fine. Go find out what happened," she said with a brusque wave. "Just one thing, Terry. I know there are a lot of people who like Tommy, he's got a lot of friends. But maybe he's got one enemy. It only takes one enemy, doesn't it?"

"We'll check everything, Janey. Count on it."

He and Rose got back to the hospital lobby as the crowd surged around a podium set up near two brushed-steel doors. Another doctor, young and brisk, stood at the podium, camera lights whitening him even more. Rose paused and they listened.

"Officer Ensor is out of surgery," the doctor said. "He sustained major trauma to his pelvis, left leg, left arm, and significant internal injuries including a ruptured spleen, kidney damage, and a partly dissected aorta. He's been stabilized but he will require multiple additional surgeries to deal with these injuries. We were most immediately concerned about the tear in his aorta, that's the main artery going to the heart, and fortunately the surgeons were able to repair that damage."

Rose bent her head at the weight of the things done to Ensor. Nye knew there was something more. *Nice touch,* he thought, *to let Ensor's wife know at the same time so she didn't hear it over the TV and could stay secluded with her kids.*

The young doctor's briskness covered his unease at not being wholly in control of what was happening. "Finally, Officer Ensor sustained severe head trauma during the accident. We've undertaken a number of procedures to minimize the damage, but we're going to be watching him very closely for the next twenty-four to forty-eight hours. He is in very critical condition."

Driving out, the day ripely blue and clear, Rose didn't say anything for a long while. Nye watched the city around them, everything mundane, delivery trucks and mail carriers, joggers diligently improving themselves, a skateboarder or two, school buses rolling up to the Sutter's Fort Museum and children pouring out, Caltrans guys in orange helmets digging up part of I Street, and city utility workers in elevated buckets deftly chainsawing limbs off the too-luxuriant trees. It was a normal, busy, fretful day in the state's capital. *Nice to pretend that's all it was,* he thought.

"Ensor's going to be messed up even if he makes it," Rose said, eyes ahead on the street.

"He's not going square dancing."

"Jesus. Think of his wife and kids. It just hit me as we were leaving," she said. "Their whole life is going to be different. No matter what."

"Yeah."

"Jesus," she said prayerfully and he suspected she was thinking of her own family, Anorina and feckless Luis, and wishing she could hold them both at that moment.

He needed to bring her back to what they had to do. "Look, Rosie, we can't get conned by that crowd back at the hospital. Ensor's wife's right. Tommy had enemies because he's been a cop for a while so we need to start with open minds about last night."

"Maybe it wasn't a vanilla hit-and-run. I agree." She made a left turn, passing old midtown office buildings being energetically converted into high-priced condominiums. "I swear, Ter, I don't know what makes it worse, if Ensor got in the way of a plain old drunk driver, standard issue hit-and-run, or someone tried to take him out deliberately."

"I'll make some calls to a couple old pals," Nye said sardonically. "See what's the topic of conversation this morning among the elite."

He did not want to answer Rose about Ensor's fate. From their perspective, his assailant had to be hunted down regardless of whether he hit Ensor accidentally or sought him out to kill. Right now it was equivocal: Quintana's statement and the physical evidence meant it could be either.

Nye glanced sympathetically at Rose as they neared the department on its tree-shaded street downtown. If Ensor was the target of a killer because of something he did as a cop, that at least gave his terrible ordeal meaning, a purpose, even made it a noble sacrifice. It might not leaven his family's agony, but they would have the consolation of a father and husband taken down in the line of duty.

The other way, struck down by a random driver in a blind accident, was truly horrific.

Nye looked out again at the bustling, oblivious, and arrogant city. The idea that it was all meaningless frightened him as much as it did Rose.

"Yeah, I'll make some calls and let's get those search warrants cranked out," he snapped to her. He heard the same desperate briskness in his voice as the doctor back at the hospital. The same as Nishimoto.

Whoever hit Tommy Ensor had hit them, too.

TWELVE

"OBJECTION, YOUR HONOR! You can't allow the prosecution to put those inflammatory photographs in front of the jury! Your Honor?"

Repair or get rid of the SUV.

Of course, that was the first thing. The SUV was the centerpiece of it all.

Stevenson stared at the list he had made in chambers and carried out onto the bench as the assembled lawyers for his criminal trial began the tedious wrestling over evidence and motions even before a jury panel was brought in for initial questioning. He didn't hear the attorney gesturing and talking to him from the counsel table.

But how the hell do I get the SUV fixed? Or how can I get rid of it? I can't just drive it into the river. Someone would find it. There were Vehicle Identification Numbers scattered all throughout the SUV, not to mention the license plate and other kinds of specific identification that would quickly trace it back to me.

So what am I supposed to do? he thought raggedly. *Take the damn thing apart piece by piece and drop it around town in dumpsters or trashcans?*

Then he remembered the story about a man who ate his car, bit by bit, over two years and got himself into the Guinness Book of World Records or some other accounting of human foolishness. *Sure,* he thought. *I'll eat the SUV. Fender hors d'ouevres and dashboard entree. Only takes a few years.*

He also knew with complete clarity that he could not report the SUV stolen. If he did, there would be questions about where it had been taken, who drove it last, who had access to it, and then when did he drive it last. *Were you with anyone, Judge Stevenson?*

Eli would be questioned and Stevenson had no confidence his father-in-law, aware of the horrific situation, confronted even by friendly police, could maintain the lies that would ensure safety.

But no matter what he decided, Stevenson he didn't have much time at all.

People were going to notice he wasn't driving the SUV anymore. Very soon.

Stevenson sat back, unblinking eyes on the rear of the dimly lit courtroom, over the heads of the sprinkling of people in the audience section and the attorneys bleating in front of him. The three defendants, Hispanic young men, sat glumly with deputy sheriffs as big as Audie in chairs behind each of them, ready to spring forward if they moved at all. So the defendants simply sat with the fatalistic blankness of patients awaiting an unpleasant medical procedure.

The real problem with the SUV wasn't people like Smitty down in the courthouse garage, Stevenson reasoned. It was much closer to him. What about Veronica and Haley? Vee was on notice that the SUV needed to be fixed. She'd start asking about it and become annoyed if he went on using her car.

Stevenson almost groaned aloud in frustration.

"Your Honor? Can we please get a ruling on my objection, please?" the attorney, a man from the Indigent Criminal Defense Panel, which handled overflow when the public defender could not take a case, demanded querulously. He had a gray ponytail tied with a small ribbon.

Stevenson was jolted back to the trial. He sat forward, looking bland but stern. "Mr. Wallace, you don't need to keep repeating yourself. Objection overruled."

"But, Your Honor, the only reason the People want to put those pictures before the jury is to inflame them against my client." He gestured at the youngest defendant in the middle, who sighed. The interpreters sat beside each defendant along with their attorneys. It made a very crowded counsel table for the defense.

"Mr. Wallace, the People say it's important for the jury to see the specific inquiries your client is charged with inflicting on the four victims. Isn't that so, Ms. Piersal?"

A young woman with dark glasses shot to her feet. "It's essential, Your Honor. The victims were all savagely beaten by these defendants," and Stevenson waved her down.

"I got it the first time. The jury should see the pictures, because the probative value of the pictures outweighs their prejudicial effect. But just a selection, Ms. Piersal, not the whole album you've got."

Another defense attorney sprang up. "Judge Stevenson, that is exactly the point. What the State is planning is to racially prejudice the jury against these young Hispanic men."

Stevenson did not have to see the deputy district attorney leap up. It was not a subtle or complex case. The defense would have to trot out any angle to avoid the inevitable. It was vicious and sad story, if true. Three young Hispanics attacked four victims during a daylong crime spree that ran from Stockton up to Sacramento, robbing two women, a gas station attendant, and a man walking his dog. They wrecked their stolen pickup truck.

He studied the young men. It would be ideal if one of them had stolen his SUV. Left his dozens of fingerprints all over it like they did the pickup truck.

But that was another problem with reporting the SUV stolen. There would be no evidence of a third, unknown person in it. Stevenson had no idea how to contrive the appearance of a mythical car thief that would deceive trained detectives.

Audie and Joan moving discreetly near the bench seemed like ghosts or shadows. Every part of his courtroom was in dim and in funereal gloom, even the empty jury box. Only a single wide cone of light illuminated the judge on the bench, like a deity on display, a bronze replica of the Great Seal of California hanging behind him, flanked by the state flag and flag of the United States.

The deputy district attorney was saying something sharp, loud in reply to the defense attorney's blunt accusation.

Stevenson didn't hear her. He looked down at the next item on his list.

Cover story. Account for every minute from close of business yesterday.

This was essential, too, he thought. He left the courthouse promptly at five thirty, then picked Eli up for dinner at Dawson's over in the Hyatt Hotel. Around seven they were at Ricci's, a bar downtown lawyers and a lot of judges frequented, where Eli had assembled an impressive collection of possible donors and influential people for cocktails. It was a long night after that, making conversation, but mostly listening to whatever pet peeve or dreary commentary for which someone wanted a captive audience. Stevenson duly listened noncommittally. He envied Eli's easy progress around the large banquet room, the jokes and friendly chatter, the handshakes, small kisses to women, shoulders patted for the men. Eli freely helped himself throughout the evening to the no host bar and Stevenson contented himself with tonic water.

People saw me, he thought. *They'll know where I was. I didn't drink, but they'll put me in a downtown bar before the accident.*

Next item on the list: Who saw me last night?

He needed to find out what people remembered and what they might connect at some point with him and last night. It had to be done very carefully, with great skill so he didn't defeat the whole purpose by arousing suspicions, inviting questions.

"Your Honor, the People do not intend to refer to the defendants' ethnicity," said the young deputy district attorney. Before she could say more, Wallace, the ponytailed defense lawyer, was up again.

"Well, if that's true, Your Honor, we are making a motion *in limine* now to prohibit the district attorney from making any comments or references during the trial to our clients' ethnic background."

Stevenson was distantly aware that the young woman representing the District Attorney of Sacramento County had raised her voice. He looked at the next item on his list. *Evidence. Where? What?*

Aside from the SUV itself, there might be physical evidence that could connect him to the accident. He stared into the shadowy courtroom again, the stirring, and the burning eyes of the few spectators in the dimness like lurking predators in the jungle gauging their prey.

What other evidence? He tried to concentrate on it. *Phone records, restaurant bills, something that uniquely tied him to a time and place downtown last night?*

I'm forgetting something. Missing a link, he thought angrily.

Stevenson felt sweaty. *So much at stake.* He looked at his clerk, marking documents for the attorneys and Audie, giving everyone his practiced thousand-yard stare to show he was in physical control of Department 34 as much as his judge was its overlord.

"Your Honor? Your Honor? With the greatest respect, I must ask you for a ruling. On the record. Shall I repeat my motion?" Wallace asked with thinly veiled insult.

"Judge, you haven't ruled on my objection to their motion *in limine* yet," complained the deputy district attorney.

Stevenson sat up, his back damp, and a sheen of sweat on his face as if he had been running. The strange, inappropriate exhilaration he had felt the night before returned, as if some part of him wanted to be cornered like this, escape blocked, hungry predators closing in.

I can turn this around, like I've done all my life, and beat the bastards.

"You want a ruling, Mr. Wallace? I can do that. Motion denied. If the ethnicity of the defendants comes up in the course of the trial, you can renew your motion."

"Thank you, Your Honor."

"Ms. Piersal, I expect you to alert the Court before you introduce testimony or evidence of the defendant's ethnicity. I'm going to expect a showing of relevance."

"Of course, Your Honor."

Yes, Your Honor. Of course, Your Honor. Thank you, Your Honor. The daily deference Stevenson had grown used to, in fact now felt entitled to expect. It seemed ludicrous given his situation now.

He had to get to a telephone.

"Your Honor, I have the defense's joint proposed *voir dire* questions for the jury," and Wallace passed a thick sheaf of papers to Joan, who handed them to Stevenson.

"Has the prosecution seen these?"

"I'm giving them to the People right now," Wallace smirked and handed a copy of the questions the defense attorneys wanted to ask each potential juror.

"We'll take a half-hour recess," Stevenson announced abruptly, glad he had an excuse to get off the bench, "to review the defense questions and then I'll hear any objections."

He got up quickly and Audie barked with well-trained timing, "Court's in recess." Stevenson saw the deputy sheriffs behind each defendant move closer to take them to the holding cells for the recess.

He clutched his list. There was so much to do.

Stevenson closed the door to his chambers and called his father-in-law. He was quickly connected to Eli's executive assistant. "Why, Judge, this is turning into a real treat," Georgina drawled excitedly. "It's like the old days when we used to see you every day. Are we seeing you again?"

Stevenson, before he met and married Vee, had done legal work for Eli's bank.

"I'll remember to bring your candy today. Is he free?"

"I'll plug you right in. Half a pound of soft centers would be very nice."

"Well, maybe that and a little more." Georgina giggled.

A moment later, Eli came on. "You can still read my mind. I was going to give you a call, Frank."

Stevenson froze. "About what?"

"Another little get-together like last night. Maybe for this weekend?"

"Sure." He said with relief. "Let me check with Vee, but that should be great. Can you set it up that fast?"

"Fastest Rolodex in the capital. People are used to getting calls like this from me by now," he chuckled. "And the booze is always flowing."

Stevenson's mind raced. Eli hadn't mentioned either the incident last night or the news reports about the cop. *He must have forgotten what little he saw.*

"Look, do you have a couple minutes this afternoon?" Stevenson said with forced casualness.

"I can make time. For what?"

"Nothing so much," Stevenson grabbed for the first thing and felt soiled for doing it. "It's about Haley, Eli. I'd like to talk to you about your offer to get her into a better school."

"Then come out here," Eli said. "I'll be waiting around two thirty. It's about time you and Veronica let me pitch in."

"Thanks. I'll see you then."

Stevenson carefully hung up the phone and swung his chair around. The computer on his desk glowed. Mechanically he tapped out the latest California news and saw the cop's story staying high. The headlines were still of a piece but different from earlier that morning: HERO COP FIGHTS FOR HIS LIFE.

Instantly he thought sharply, *What about me? What about my life?*

And regretted it instantly. *Oh, Christ, I wish I could wipe it all out, do it over.*

But that moment had passed. He was committed irrevocably now to a different course. There was no going back.

Stevenson got up, checked his watch. Twenty minutes until he had to bring the trial into session again. Just about three hours before he could see Eli. Between now and then he had to figure out how to deal with his father-in-law. An idea was forming in his mind. It was risky but much less so than anything else he had considered.

Stevenson was so restless he went out the back door of his chambers into the gleaming, yellowed linoleum covered hallway behind each courtroom. He headed down the short walk to Department 32. Yardley usually had fresh courthouse gossip, who was sleeping with his clerk or who, like a former judge, had been caught screwing a female deputy sheriff on his desk late one night.

Judges normally barged in on each other without either calling ahead or letting the clerk know. When Stevenson turned into Yardley's department through the clerk's office door he spotted Yardley hunched over his desk, coughing, signing papers, while two others hovered near.

"He's got people with him," Yardley's thin black female clerk confided unnecessarily. "Police officers. Search warrants."

A few moments later, the two cops, a young athletic woman, and her older, lanky partner with a vaguely military-style haircut and deeply lined face, came out talking animatedly to each other. The young woman put a sheaf of papers into her thin brown briefcase and the two of them brushed by Stevenson and left through the darkened Department 32.

"You just signed your life away, didn't you, Clarence?" Stevenson said.

"If I had anything left to sign away," Yardley said throatily. He groaned looking at his watch. "I'm rationing my cigarettes today and I've another hour to go."

They strolled out into the hallway, idly watching an orange-suited county jail inmate, shackled and in a belly chain, being half hop-skipped and shuffled between three bulky deputy sheriffs to Department 29. Stevenson tensed, trying to sort out what he should be doing. He only half listened to Yardley recounting how another judge was probably going to abruptly announce soon that he was heading off to Micronesia for two years to essentially be their supreme court.

"Like he thinks nobody will talk about what he and that kid were doing in the front seat of his car the other night over on South Broadway. Crap, my bailiff knows all about it. It's no damn secret." He chuckled thickly and coughed.

He's dying, Stevenson thought. *Retired, sitting by assignment as a judge and pulling in two salaries, he's still dying in front of my eyes. Why doesn't he just smoke as many damn cigarettes as he wants? How is it going to matter if he cuts down? He's trapped.*

He suddenly felt closer to Clarence Yardley than almost any other human being.

Except I'm going to make it, he thought furiously.

Yardley went on, "Those two cops just now, they're going after whoever ran down that cop last night. Search warrants for all the surveillance cameras you know, on all the buildings down on Capitol Mall where it happened? The Age of Big Brother. Somebody figures we get our pictures taken maybe a few hundred times every day now."

"They think they've got pictures of the accident?"

"Pretty certain they do. It's like these cell phones and computers and I can't even figure out how to get my damn TiVo to work," he coughed. "It's amazing."

"Where would we be without technology," Stevenson said, his mind working frantically. He thought he had a few more days, maybe through the weekend.

But he knew he didn't have any time at all now.

THIRTEEN

WHEN THEY GOT TO THE SACRAMENTO POLICE Department earlier that morning, Nye and Rose went first to their own office on the third floor to gather up any messages and whatever else they needed and then cart it over to the command post Nishimoto had set up. They would run the investigation from there.

The mood inside the old gray granite building was grim, tense with anger. Every cop they met coming in or heading out said something about Ensor and offered to help.

They did not bother with the slow, geriatric elevators on the ground floor but took the worn marble stairs, passing the faded formal pictures of ancient chiefs of police lining the walls, and detectives and uniformed cops escorting willing or unwilling citizens to rendezvous with their particular destinies.

Nye and Rose took over two desks near a rusty, barred window looking down on the tree-lined street. Opposite them, four other detectives, two from Major Crimes and two from Robbery, worked on the hotline tips and the canvass of the buildings surrounding Capitol Mall. Even though the command center was crowded with desks, a conference table, computers, it was still comparatively more spacious than the jammed offices the detectives shared with each other and all of the aging boxes and cabinets of records. Nye impressed Parkes and Vu from Major Crimes to help Rose with the seven search warrants they would need to get signed for surveillance camera videos around the crime scene. He checked to see who the on-duty warrant judge was that week at the courthouse and grunted with satisfaction. Yardley. Nice and dependable. No one could recall Judge Yardley ever rejecting a search warrant and he would not start with this batch.

"Anything interesting at all come in, guys?" Rose asked the other two detectives, Talman and Pesce.

"Nothing much so far," Pesce said, tie loosened. "TV just kicked in so they're starting to pick up." He pointed to a stack of hotline tip forms. "Mostly wrong time and wrong street. A guy called, though, says his ex-wife probably did it. She doesn't drive a black truck or SUV or anything. But she tried to run him down once, so he's sure it's her."

There was a cold chuckle around the room. Three TV sets were on low, all on news programs. The overhead exposed pipes hissed faintly with steam going through the old building. Nye said, "Bring me whatever you got every half hour. I want to just look through them myself."

"You don't trust us, Ter?" Talman asked sarcastically.

"Don't even go there."

"I don't trust you," Rose said.

"Forget about me picking up your lunch again, Tafoya," Talman said.

Nye let them blow off for a few minutes and then stood in the middle of the tightly cluttered room. "Okay, here's the routine. Rose, Parkes, Vu, you guys will put together the search warrant packages. I need them ready to take over to the judge before noon. I want to get hold of those surveillance tapes and go through them as soon as we can this afternoon."

Rose, as always, made notes of everything. The others listened. No one moved when a small dark rat skittered across the floor and vanished onto a hole. It was a common sight.

"Talman, Pesce, keep current on the hotline. I want you to get out whatever description we have on the vehicle to body shops, repair shops, everyplace we can. Work through the AG," he meant the California Attorney General, "and use their network to get the description out to every sheriff and police department, too. We'll update as soon as we get anything. I want you guys to keep on top of any stolen vehicle reports, too. The chump might decide to try that one."

He paused, braced one hand on his desk. "This stays here, just for us, okay? We've got three days."

"You're shitting me," Vu said instantly.

"Rosie?"

"For once he's not pulling your chain," she said.

Nye hardened his face. "So we will get this done and get whoever hit Tommy Ensor."

Nye saw Parkes look stunned and then astounded then he accepted it. Like they all had to.

Nye went on, "Don't talk to the press people or your friends. Rose and I discussed checking out Ensor's enemies list. Got to be done. So we'll need his last assignments, his last partners before Quintana. Get any reports he filed in the last six months."

"How do we do that, Ter, without tipping the whole world what we're looking at?" Pesce asked quietly.

"I think you say to anybody outside of this room and outside of the building that it's all routine, standard procedure when an officer's injured. Low key it. For anybody outside this room inside the building, tell them to mind their own business and shut the hell up," Rose said calmly.

Nye almost grinned. "There's your answer," he said to Pesce. "Work your snitches hard, too. See what they're hearing. All we need is a whiff, some goddamn hint that someone's acting funny, bragging, going all shy and quiet, hiding out, beating up the wife or girlfriend or boyfriend, doing anything out of character suddenly. Obergon's getting the word out to the patrol guys, too."

Vu, the youngest in the room, but as sharp as anyone, leaned back in his chair. "How realistic is it that Ensor was deliberately attacked, Terry?"

"You tell me after you talk to your snitches and we plough through his reports," Nye said.

"I just want to go on record that I think Ensor's clean."

"Nobody's says he isn't."

"We start checking around, they will." Vu was belligerent.

Nye caught Rose's eye. The other detectives abruptly looked confrontational, waiting to see how the scene played. She stood up.

"I'm just going to say it, because everybody's thinking it. We're all upset. Officer Ensor's a good guy and it hurts like hell when something like this happens. But we won't do him any service if don't bring in whoever did this to him. We've got to find whoever it is. So," she paused, "we all know that means we may have to go places we don't like or find things we'd rather not. It's better we find out what happened than the flipping TV or IA."

She sat down. Talman blew out a breath and nodded. Nye could feel the tension ease as quickly as Vu had ratcheted it up. They started working on the search warrant packages while Pesce went on answering the phones and logging information into his computer as people called in. Out of all the garbage there might be one gem.

After about a half hour, Rose got up and went over to Nye. He had just finished calling an old contact at the Capitol who worked in the CHP's security and dignitary protection detail. Even without a formal search warrant, their video surveillance tapes would be made available. Everyone wanted to help.

"Hey, Ter," she said quietly to him, "suppose we do turn up something about Ensor? You know, something bad."

Nye knew as well as she did that a criminal investigation often yielded unexpected and embarrassing or even appalling secrets about both victim and perpetrator. It was unavoidable. Crimes ripped apart the shelter of people's lives and exposed everything to the world. "We'll cross that bridge if we have to," he said carefully. "I don't want anything else to hurt Janey or their kids." He suspected she was also still bothered by his request to conceal Quintana's interview from IA and didn't like the idea he would ask her to do something like that again.

"Okay, I see where you're going," Rose said. "You're scared of finding another Cole Barrett, right?"

"Yeah, scared shitless," Nye conceded.

Nye used his cell phone to make his eighth call that morning to another number from a small notebook he kept in his jacket. He didn't put any of the numbers in the notebook on his computer contacts or anyplace else. Nearby Rose was quickly and surely pushing her way through writing the search warrant affidavits with the other detectives and a constant low chatter of conversation filled the crowded room. It was nearly ten thirty.

He got an answer on the fourth ring. He said, "Happy trails, Deirdre."

"You're a voice from the past, Nye. You haven't come by or called in months." Deirdre Gammon wasn't annoyed. Nye pictured her half smiling at him as always, late forties, heavily made up, well preserved.

"I didn't think you missed me."

"I do. Every day, honey. Are you taping this?"

"Wouldn't think of it."

"I bet," and he definitely knew she was smiling at the other end of the line. "Well, you want me to put you down for a session today? I've got a space at three. An out-of-towner just canceled."

"I'm tempted," he began but she broke in with a throaty laugh.

"Bullshit, Nye. You are still a consummate bullshitter."

"Maybe. This is serious, Deirdre."

"Tell Mamma," she ordered in the stern, commanding voice her clients yearned for.

"You see the news about the cop who got hit last night? His name's Ensor, just a patrol cop, family, lots of off-duty charity-type work."

"And? I don't know him. I haven't heard anything either."

"I want you to let me know if anybody's talking about Ensor. One of your regulars maybe hears something. Or even better," he spoke back to her in an equally commanding tone, "you make some calls, check out what's floating around. I want something, okay? I want it today."

"Oh, Nye, this is what makes me sad. We could've been a great team. We still could, as soon as you get out of your joke job. Lots of the customers would love an older man, older woman three-way."

"I mean it. I want you to get me something today."

"Oh," she sighed theatrically. "For what?"

"Same arrangement. I'll keep Vice off your back."

"So I guess you really aren't taping this. Well, that's all well and good, but I assume you're hot to trot. What kind of money are we talking about?"

Nye was growing annoyed with the banter of an aging hooker. "For starters about twenty-five thousand dollars. There'll probably be more." He had heard a little earlier that the board of directors of SPOA, the Sacramento Police Officers Association, was meeting at that hour to approve putting up a reward of twenty-five thousand dollars for information leading to the arrest of Officer Ensor's assailant.

"All right then. Let me get to work and see what I can find out."

"Call me on my cell."

"I've got it."

"Because you haven't been keeping up, Deirdre. Our relationship needs nurturing, right? You need to reach out a lot more and let me know what's coming through your door. I'm not feeling the love." He spoke harshly. Snitches needed threats as much as coddling.

"Please don't hurt me," she said and he knew she was smiling again.

He hung up. Rose came over and put the first three search warrant packages in front of him. Pesce had dropped off five possible leads from the hotline, too. Nye started checking through the warrants. He thought about Deirdre. Years ago she had been a sixth-grade elementary school teacher, arrested for having sex with a student, fired, and then started what she euphemistically called a dungeon in the basement of her Carmichael home, complete with red-brick wallpaper and cheap stocks and whips. A great parade of men, and a few women, went into her dungeon and unwittingly left behind tips about crimes about to be committed or crimes in the past.

Nye, loaned out to Vice and jokingly tagged the oldest under-cover vice cop in California, had helped arrest her during a sweep of prostitutes in Sacramento.

He managed to get her a reduced sentence and she became one of his best snitches. But she was also the saddest to him. She was intelligent and could have been a wonderful teacher. She could have been anything.

Whenever he thought he understood people, even a little, Deirdre Gammon and what she was pulled him up short.

The command center had a stream of visitors, all unwelcome. Nishimoto stopped by almost every hour for face-to-face updates from Nye. The chief, looking tired and sad, came in alone. He cheered up a little when he saw the purposeful activity being directed through the command center. Then Rose was called out and she came back studiedly blank about whoever wanted to see her and whatever it was about. Nye's cell rang and a text message popped up for him to see Guthrie in IA.

He took the stairs down to the first floor, across the lobby busy with unhappy people and cops, to Internal Affairs set off in a short side hallway. The four detectives in IA glanced knowingly at him as he strode in, feeling a little like he imagined civilians did when they saw a cop car behind them. The pang of guilt.

Guthrie's balding head was down when Nye came in to his spare office. Guthrie had no family pictures on his walls, just certificates and diplomas framed in plain black metal. The file cabinets had thick metal locking bars and combination locks.

"What's up, Guth?" Nye asked casually, the door ajar.

"Close it."

He did and waited. The prescribed charade was to make the object of IA wait and sweat, even if for a minute or two, even if it was not a formal session, just a courtesy call. Nye, over the years had come to regard these time wasters, and IA itself, as he did bats and snakes, necessary evils.

Finally, Guthrie looked up and put his hands behind his head. "What the fuck are you doing, Nye?"

"'Splain yourself, Lucy."

"You're almost out the door, free as a bird, and you jeopardize all of it on this investigation. I mean, crap, can't you just sit at your desk and eighty-six the shit you've accumulated in the last couple of years so the next guy doesn't have to get it steam-cleaned?"

Nye felt a grin helplessly form. "You care, Guth. You really care."

"I don't want to see Ensor's hit-and-run messed up. You will mess it up." He leaned forward, scowling. "You know it, too. Right? Deep down?"

"Well, if that's all, I better get back upstairs," Nye said, his momentary grin turned to cold fury.

"This is for your own good, Nye. You're a short-timer, I'm

happy for you. So act like you're a short-timer. Burn your time, walk out clean."

"Assistant Chief Nishimoto assigned me."

"Well, you've still got a choice. Tell him you can't work on the investigation. You can say you need to get things in order."

"I'm not kicking the bucket."

Guthrie lowered his voice, a smaller man, an accountant by appearance, who had once been in Burglary, but found he needed a mission and official corruption was ideal. Nye didn't think he had ever heard the humorless idealist laugh. "It's going to feel a hell of lot like it. Trust me. You get off this investigation now."

"Because why?"

"Every screwup you've made, every bad call, every bad write-up is getting resurrected, Nye." He gestured at the files spread over his desk. "There's a lot here. Some of it I remember. You were soaking it up pretty good once upon. Drunk on duty." He poked at a thick file. "Then there's the really serious shit, like this clusterfuck you engineered, that family?"

Nye cut him off. He wasn't going to let this naked department power play draw him in. He wondered who was calling the shots, probably Altlander, but even Nishimoto could have a byzantine reason for doing this. Hang around long enough and nothing seems crazy, he thought.

"You won't go there, Guth," he said quietly. "Tommy covered for me and you start going after me for drinking, you'll have to hang him out, too. That's not going to happen and we both know it. My jacket's no secret around here or around town. Knock yourself out. I'm staying on this one."

Guthrie looked pained, even human. "Christ, Nye. Think of your pension—you can still lose it. You could walk away with nothing."

Nye opened the door. Guthrie said, "Maybe you don't care about your own future, but your partner's just getting started. You go down and she goes, too. That sound right to you?"

"I'll take care of Tafoya," he said finally.

But Guthrie slipped in the last word, "What's she say about this clusterfuck? She okay with what you did?"

Nye did not answer. He had not told Rose. He had not yet figured how he could tell her without losing her respect.

Near eleven, Rose, Parkes, and Vu finished the search warrants and Nye thought they would tightly cover the surveillance tapes, maintenance logs about maintaining the video equipment, and logs about whoever operated the cameras. Nothing retrieved through these warrants would be thrown out when Ensor's assailant went to trial. Now they just needed to be signed over at the courthouse.

"I'll drive," Rose said. "You're starting to yawn, old man."

"My jaws are tired from warning you not to screw up," he said as they left the building. "I'm one hundred percent right now."

Rose grinned. "You sound like my kid. She starts yawning and wants to stay up another half hour and then falls asleep. You don't fool me."

"Twenty bucks says I do," he yawned again. "Yeah, you drive, hotshot."

They left Pesce and Talman to check out four hotline tips that looked interesting while Vu and Parkes stayed to run the command center. Vu had instructions to call the crime lab where the paint chips, tire imprints, and other physical evidence was being examined. The results of the canvass so far had been disappointing. There was no witness to the hit-and-run in the buildings around Capitol Mall. A lot depended on the surveillance camera videos, Rose agreed with Nye.

They drove to the Sacramento County Courthouse in a few minutes, calling ahead to make sure Judge Yardley was available.

Nye thought it was likely that Rose, although she never said so, found accompanying him through the courthouse was a chore. In the lobby, then the elevator, heading to Yardley's department, he was stopped by deputy sheriffs, other city cops, a bail bondsman or two, and a gaggle of lawyers, both defense and deputy DAs. Nearly everyone was friendly. And then everyone wanted to talk about Ensor and hoped he would recover.

"Who don't you know?" Rose asked as they got off the elevator on the fourth floor.

"Look, Rosie, you hang around this place for as long as I have and you'll get every chump around here coming up to you, too."

"I don't think so. You're like a politician, Ter. Everybody had their hand out. Like you could get it for them. They all want something."

"Everybody wants something."

"But that's not our job."

"A lot of it is," he said. "Give a little to get something."

"Give what? To who?"

"You play it by ear."

"I don't think I want to hear anymore."

He glanced at her. She had to know how much real, as opposed to ideal or textbook, police work depended on trades and back-scratching. It was such second nature for him, Nye never considered it until that moment when he saw Rose's disapproval. She was now looking straight ahead, and she was no longer joking with him. The undercurrent of unease was back, as if she didn't know how far he would go or how much she could trust him.

Nye liked Rose but could not change himself even for her, but, if it would help, he would pull in the spikes for the next two weeks. He could play the genial older mentor and perhaps she wouldn't have to see anything else.

Who knows, he thought, maybe Rosie's the exception to the rule. She could be successful in the job without his mistakes or depthless cynicism. Maybe she can get along without helping somebody's kid avoid a petty shoplift or buying a drink for some lawyer whose guts you hate. Or the more serious chores that sometimes had to be done like Deirdre.

He was, he recognized, being sentimental about her. She had worked hard to get into Major Crimes and undoubtedly made her own share of bad calls and rough deals.

But he liked to think she was still unmarked. The maggot that bored into him and every other cop he knew would pass her by.

His only real regret now about impending retirement was being unable to show her the traps ahead and all the little tricks he had learned to avoid them or ignore the pain when the trap sprang and caught you.

It took little time to present the search warrant packages to Judge Yardley, who was more than willing to accommodate them and made jokes about how many warrants he had signed for Nye over the years.

"A couple were so thin you could see the sun through them if you held them up to the light," Yardley coughed. "But this guy's always come through, haven't you?"

"I try, Judge."

"Yeah, well, I hope this is my little contribution to your case. It's a sad world where a fine person like Officer Ensor gets run down."

"So it is," Rose added.

They left the courthouse and went back to SPD, dropping off the signed warrants for Parkes to serve. They would all review the surveillance tapes after lunch on the TVs in the command center.

Rose had put together a list of Ensor's three partners before Quintana, going back four years. Nye would have been well beyond that arbitrary marker. They decided any grudge or payback directed at Ensor must be more recent rather than older.

In the car again, heading south on I-5, Nye suggested they see Walt Maslow, Ensor's partner when he got the Medal of Valor.

"Why him?" she asked.

"I'm open if you got a better idea. The clock's running. We got no wits so far, the physical evidence is still being cooked over at the crime lab. The tips are, per usual, mostly a waste. Let's start shaking Ensor's tree and see if anything interesting falls out. Ensor was big news when he got the medal. Maybe that ticked somebody off. "

"Okay, fine with me. You have his address?"

"He lives in a trailer park in the South Area off Florin. He retired." Nye chuckled without humor. Most of the homicides in Sacramento came from neighborhoods around either Oak Park or Florin Boulevard.

"Great. Just where I want to end up when my tour's over."

"So stay on 5 and then I'll direct you."

"Of course you know this guy."

"Of course I do."

"Got any more you want to give me before we drop in on him? Like something I should avoid or go after, Ter?" she prodded.

"I don't want to spoil your first impressions," he said.

"That bad?"

"Let's just say that Maslow and Ensor weren't an ideal couple."

FOURTEEN

IT TOOK EVEN ROSE, with her usually superb sense of direction, a few wrong turns to find Walt Maslow's home in the rabbit warren of narrow streets that made up the New Horizons Mobile Home Park.

They pulled up and parked on the street. An older brown sedan occupied the single carport decorated with bright plastic pennants flapping in the slight breeze outside. Maslow's mobile home was a beige rectangle sitting on a concrete foundation and looked as though it would only be mobile in a six- or seven-point earthquake. They could hear the bells and squeals from a TV game show coming from inside, but similar sounds seemed to be coming from all of the other mobile homes nearby.

"You do the honors," Nye said when they went to the metal door.

"What's the gag, Ter? This guy mad at you? You're mad at him?"

"Cripes, Rosie, it's no big deal. He'll enjoy seeing you more than me, that's all."

She sighed and rang the bell. It wasn't until the fourth ring, which she held, that the door slammed open.

"What the hell do you want?" demanded the large black man

sitting in a wheelchair made gaudy with colored streamers and a small American flag sticking up from its rear.

"SPD, Mr. Maslow," Rose held her ground. "I'm Detective Tafoya and this is—"

The man in the wheelchair interrupted as she gestured toward Nye, who wore a cool smile. "I know who that puke is," he said in a deep, gravelly voice. "Hey, Nye, hiding behind your partner again?"

"Hi, Walt," Nye said calmly, "you got a minute?"

"For what?" he demanded.

"Tommy Ensor."

Nye and Rose felt the abrupt silence, then it was filled with the excited squeals of the unseen TV contestants. The man in the wheelchair hunched forward slightly, staring balefully at both of them. Rose didn't take her eyes off of him.

"I guess I've got time for that," he said, a strange hardness in his deep voice. "It's kind of my whole life, making time for Tommy. Come on in."

Maslow's home was neat, a surprisingly large living room with sofa, chairs, and lamps, and a bedroom glimpsed just behind it. A gray-haired black woman in blue jeans poked her head through a sliding partition from the kitchenette, said nothing, and closed the partition again.

Maslow hit the mute on the TV remote and the antic figures capering around went quiet. Nye noted Rose taking in the birdcage near the curtained window, where two parakeets chirped wildly to each other.

Maslow spoke to her but he watched Nye. "They're Fayard and Nicholas, couple of big-time tap dancers years ago. Cute, right? I hate them. Hate birds. Wanted a dog, but the wife hates dogs, so we got the two happy birds."

"Mr. Maslow, thanks for seeing us," Rose said with a smile. "I assume you've heard—"

"Yeah, birds, what the hell do you do with a fucking bird? Am I right?" Maslow spoke to Nye suddenly. Then he said to Rose, "This guy tell you I had a great dog when I was in the Canine Unit? Macho was his name. Big, mean lab-shepherd fucker. I loved that dog, I tell you. So, here I am, parked for fucking life," he gestured emphatically at his wheelchair, "no dog, the wife," he raised his voice on the last two words and dropped it again, "likes to party in Vegas, leave me here with some fucking caretaker."

"Caregiver," Nye said.

"So, what do I have?" he demanded without acknowledging Nye, talking again to Rose as if she was his only audience. "So, like go ahead and just shoot me now. I mean it. No kidding. Shoot me now." His face was stony.

"Mr. Maslow, you may be able to help us determine what happened to Officer Ensor," Rose said glancing at Nye to see if this was unusual. Nye pretended to watch the parakeets.

"So, you going to shoot me?" Maslow demanded again.

"No, sir. I am not going to shoot you."

The stony face split widely with a smile. "Got you, right? Got her, right, Nye?"

"You got her, Walt," Nye said turning from the birds and sitting down on the plaid sofa. "We need to find out about the time you spent with Ensor."

Maslow wheeled the chair merrily in a half turn. "Hey, did this puke tell you how he used his partner as a fucking shield in a two-eleven on Meadowview? I bet he didn't."

"No," Rose said carefully, her eyes on Nye again. "He's never mentioned it. I heard about it."

"I bet, I bet," Maslow cackled. "Okay, shoot me now," his voice was hard and insistent.

"Can we cut the jokes, sir?" Rose had her PDA out to take notes. Nye figured she would ask him about Maslow's slur sometime soon. He wasn't surprised she knew about it, only that she had not come to ask him. Like many incidents in the police department, it was old and grown simple with age and mostly forgotten except by veteran cops and embittered ones. He was ready to tell her his side of what happened and let her judge whether he had done the right thing. He hoped it wouldn't lower her opinion of him. There was one other thing, of course, he could never tell her. He had no doubt what she would think of him if she heard it. Guthrie would always taunt him about it. Her good opinion of him had come to mean a lot to him in the last few months. He did not want to leave the department with it extinguished.

"Nobody's going to shoot you, Walt," Nye said, "unless you keep acting like an asshole. Ensor's in the shit and we don't know what happened."

"Yeah, yeah, and he's probably going to die. I heard all of that on the news," Maslow waved a big hand, hunched forward again, "so what the fuck, Nye? You think Tommy checking out means one damn thing to me?"

"In fact, I do," Nye said mildly. "So, tell us about the time you two rode together? Who's got a hard-on for you or Tommy?"

The kitchenette partition opened and Maslow's wife brought in a metal tray table with a plate of fruit salad and a tuna sandwich. She set it down beside him. She turned her back on Rose and Nye wordlessly.

"Quacks say I got to eat on a real rigid schedule," Maslow said, starting to take large bites from the sandwich without offering either of them anything. Nye's stomach rumbled faintly and he realized that he was hungry again. Rose waited for his cue. She had picked up quickly that there was some sort of duet playing itself out between her partner and Maslow.

When Maslow didn't speak for a few moments, Nye prompted, "Okay, you and Ensor were partners for about two years down in the South Area. Then you went your separate ways a little over a year ago. Who'd you piss off while you were riding together?"

Maslow swallowed hard. "Hey, I could use something to drink out here, it isn't too much trouble, please?" he called out to his wife. "Look, you knew Ensor, Nye. It came to taking care of business, I had to take care of it most of the time. So, anybody got pissed, it wasn't at him, it was me. I got to bounce some heads, some fucking banger's giving me a hard time or some puke's pulling something and I got to put him down, I was the one taking the weight, not Tommy."

"You're saying Officer Ensor made no enemies you can think of while you two were partners?" Rose asked. She sat down on a chair opposite Nye so that Maslow was between them.

"How the hell do I know if he made any enemies? I had trouble keeping track of the ones coming after me," he made a gargling laugh and almost spit out a piece of half-chewed sandwich.

"You got names, Walt?" Nye asked.

"How about the Segura brothers? I shot one of them. Maybe Robert or Richard was it, Wainright? I had to hit that one up one side and down the other with my baton. Had to hold his scalp on when we took him to the hospital before booking him. I sure wish I had Macho with me that time." He waved his sandwich. He rattled off three other names and Rose diligently wrote them down.

"Tommy ever say anything to you about any of these deals?"

"He was always saying something," Maslow spat, "what the fuck was I going so rough for, what the fuck was that last kick for, shit like that. Like it wasn't his ass I was looking out for, too."

Rose remained impassive but Nye figured she had noted how Maslow's anger built and his speech became more profane talking about his former partner. She said calmly, "Did Officer Ensor ever do anything more about any of those incidents?"

"Like run to the watch commander or fucking IAD?" Maslow snorted and swallowed the last of the sandwich like a starving predator. "Hell, no. That's not Tommy's style, right, Nye? He just needled you about shit until you wanted to push his face through the fucking car window."

"He never reported you? You never got written up because of him?"

Maslow smiled icily. "Right. Never got written up because of Tommy Ensor. I got written up, I got fucking SPOA representing me twice on bogus undue force claims pukes made, but not from Tommy." He glared at Nye, then Rose. "What the fuck are you asking me?"

Rose shifted in her chair. Probably wondering what Maslow's wife's making of all this, Nye thought. He let her ask the next inevitable question.

Rose said, "Where were you last night, Mr. Maslow?"

"Oh, my fucking God," Maslow roared suddenly with an explosive laugh. "Tafoya? You are learning fast from this dumb shit," he pointed at Nye. "You think I went after Ensor? Ran him over because I was so consumed with my resentment?" He mugged grandly.

"Something like that," Nye said. He waited.

"Man, the department's got a real bad case of shit for brains if you two are in Major Crimes. Look at me," he said, wheeling around slowly as if on display at a fashion show, "I am in a wheelchair. Wheelchair. I cannot move my legs. At all."

"Paraplegics still drive. You have a car outside. We saw it as we came in," Rose said.

"Well, this crippled shithead does not drive because he cannot drive. The car's the Vegas Express. The wife takes it every weekend, whenever she feels like it, and leaves me sitting here with a bowl of food like a dog." He breathed huskily, hunched forward.

Rose looked at Nye. He raised his eyebrows slightly. Time to move on.

"Mr. Maslow, you and Officer Ensor took the call that led to his getting the Medal of Valor. I'd like to hear about it." She made it sound like a request from an eager, attentive student. A young cop wishing to learn from her elders.

"Me, too, Walt. I never heard your side of what happened."

"I made my report. Wrote it up just like it was, no bullshit. My report got Tommy his fucking medal." He ran a tongue inside his mouth as if holding back a powerful emotion. Then he said carefully, "See, thing is, I could've done the same thing he did, okay? Could've been me getting the medal. Maybe Tommy, too, but me for sure."

"But you didn't get it and he did." Rose said it kindly.

"What does that tell you about how fucked up the world is?" he demanded. "Split second, change one little fucking thing and I got the Medal of Valor and I'm not in this wheelchair."

It was the last part that startled and intrigued Nye. He had never imagined before that there was a connection.

And it was connections, seen and unseen, that solved investigations.

Late October, Halloween around the corner, eighteen months earlier, Walt Maslow and Tommy Ensor were three hours into their regular patrol shift at about ten on a gray, cold morning, coming along 65th Avenue when a large dump truck barreled along in front of them, took the right hand turn far too fast, flipped over, and slammed into oncoming traffic.

Even as Maslow, who was driving, headed for the dump truck, it slid into a mass of cars and burst into flames. Ensor was barking into their radio.

The good news was that the accident happened in a heavily industrial section of the city so there were no homes nearby. The bad news was that it was on a busy street, packed with cars and, as the dump truck careened into one after the other, it set afire ruptured gas tanks so that the whole street lit up in orange and black and filled with a thick, choking smoke.

Before Maslow had even brought their patrol car to a stop close to the first burning vehicle, a white minivan, Ensor jumped out and started running. Maslow took over the radio, giving instructions and descriptions of the large accident to the dispatcher. He had a perfect vantage point to see what Ensor was doing.

Ensor got to the flaming minivan. It lay on the passenger side. There were four young children and a woman trapped as fire and smoke started to fill the interior. Over the shouts of other people, the rumble of exploding tanks and wreckage shifting, Maslow clearly heard the screams from inside the minivan. High-pitched, terrified, the sounds like frightened birds in a cage.

Ensor ripped off his uniform jacket, wrapped it around his left arm, and tried to batter through the windshield with his baton. The driver's door was hopelessly crushed and wouldn't open. The faces of the children, the woman with blood covering her face, were pressed frantically against the windshield as Ensor shouted at them to move back. He switched to kicking at the windshield. Again. Again. Finally it shattered, waving hands and a brown-haired little girl pushed through the jagged hole, mouth open in hysterical pain-filled screams.

The flames were brighter, greedier, moving to engulf the minivan. Maslow debated running over to help, but there were people rushing around everywhere, traffic screeching to a stop when it hit the huge tangled accident. Someone had to direct traffic, clear a path for the emergency vehicles hurrying to the scene. So he moved the patrol car to block 65th, and stayed on the radio. He could still see Ensor.

Ensor pulled two children from the minivan, their clothes on fire. He got the flames out, dragging them to the parking lot of a commercial printing plant. He ran back to the minivan, which was now almost completely on fire, the remaining children trapped in their seatbelts like the woman driver, who was unconscious now.

Ensor disappeared back into the minivan, disappearing into a burst of black smoke. Maslow nearly left his post, but he stayed because it was vital to keep more cars from getting caught in the spreading fire, the chaos of scared and injured people blindly darting around in the street.

The seconds went by, the red and orange flames from the minivan arched higher. Maslow kept talking into his radio, standing in the street, cursing the emergency crews, fire and cops, who were so slow in arriving. But it couldn't have been more than three or four minutes since the dump truck ignited the street.

Where the hell was Ensor, Maslow wondered fearfully? He paused in his nonstop diatribe going out over the police channel. He pushed a screaming man away from him so he wouldn't lose sight of where his partner had vanished.

Just when he was going to abandon traffic control and go to assist Ensor, he saw Ensor reappear in the minivan's smashed windshield, backing out, dragging the bleeding woman with one arm around her inert body, the other arm clutching a limp little boy. The back of Ensor's uniform was smoking and on fire.

Sirens, like a chorus, grew in intensity. Maslow knew the fire department and cops were finally showing up. He decided to stand his ground.

Ensor was roughly tugging at the woman. He let the little boy down to the ground, his uniform now dotted with islands of flame. The woman was tangled in her seatbelt. Ensor scrabbled into his pants pocket, oblivious to the fire burning him, and found a carpet knife. They had confiscated it about an hour earlier from a wino lurking outside a 7-Eleven. He slashed at the seatbelt with the knife, moving in a blur. The woman tumbled free and Ensor yanked her roughly backward, away from the minivan, along with the little boy.

Maslow ran forward, pulling the boy and the woman away, off to the sidewalk where other people lay or stood in shock, burned and stunned. Ensor was gone again in that split second.

As four fire trucks, paramedics, and a half dozen cop cars showed up, helmeted men and women rushing into the smoke and twisted mass of cars and the fiercely burning dump truck, Maslow pulled Ensor back by his belt. In his arms, Ensor clutched the remaining child from the minivan. Maslow pushed him to the asphalt and beat out the flames

on him. The minivan made an unearthly groan and exploded in gouts
of smoke and tongues of angry, frustrated orange and red flames.

"Tommy had first- and second-degree burns," Maslow said, the parakeets chirping behind him. "First thing he says to me, we're in one of the paramedic trucks, he says, he thought he saw his kids in the minivan. His own kids."

Rose stopped making notes. "He was pretty brave."

"And fucking lucky. We didn't stop to see what this fifty-one-fifty," using the shorthand in the Welfare and Institutions Code for a crazy man, "was doing that morning at the 7-Eleven, Tommy wouldn't have had anything to cut that lady free with. See, what I mean? It's all a roll of the dice. I was driving so he bailed out first when we saw the thing go down with the truck. I couldn't. I was the driver," Maslow looked hard at Nye for confirmation. "So he gets the medal. I get a big pat on the back like everyone else there that morning."

"You did the right thing, Walt," Nye said. He stood up. "You and Tommy were a good team."

Maslow looked down, one hand quivering with rage or sorrow.

Rose saw that the interview was over. She also stood up. "I'm sorry, Mr. Maslow, but I missed something. I assumed you were injured that day."

"You thought I got this," he slapped the wheelchair solidly, "on that deal? Fuck no. I got this one all by myself eight months ago."

Nye nodded to her, "Thanks, Walt. We got to go. Give me a call if can think of anybody else you or Ensor might've pissed off."

"What did happen, Mr. Maslow?" Rose asked.

Maslow's hand hadn't stopped quivering and he cracked a wintry smile for her. "Okay, I got a new partner. He's out with the flu or his kid has the measles, some damn thing. I'm riding solo. I get a call, possible four fifty-nine," meaning a burglary, "going down at this mattress warehouse on Power Inn Road. It's like ten at night. I roll on it," he sighed heavily, "long story, I find this puke and he's some kind of fucking jackrabbit and he starts running, goes up the roof, I go after him. He takes a jump from the warehouse roof, goes onto another building. I take the jump. I didn't make it. Twenty feet down to the alley, land on my back on some fucking city recycling bin. Just like that. Just fucking like that."

"I'm sorry," Rose said sincerely. "That stinks."

"Don't it? Last couple months I been back home, with my spousal unit," he smiled coldly again, "thinking about all kinds of things. What I figured out is, I must've thought I was another Tommy Ensor. He did it. I could do it."

"I'm sorry," Rose said again.

Nye gave Maslow a half salute with two fingers and they went outside. There it was, he thought, out in the open, the unseen connection between Ensor's heroics and Maslow's wheelchair. Nye hoped Rose saw it, too, because she would be a good investigator if she did. It was the secret links to places in the heart that often solved cases. As they were getting into their car, the cheery game show once more loudly pouring out from the mobile home, Maslow's wife surprised Nye. She had come quickly out the door behind them.

"You done?" she asked. She had wide, furious eyes.

"Yes, ma'am, we are," Rose said.

"He's got no one to beat up anymore," Maslow's wife said.

"Sorry if we disturbed you," Nye said, hating what he saw in the woman's eyes.

"Is there something we can do for you?" Rose asked.

"Yes, there is. I wish you would shoot him."

Nye let Rose drive again while he used his cell phone to update Nishimoto on the search warrants and the interview with Maslow. He checked with Vu about the tips and the canvass. They were still having no luck in finding a witness. But three possible hits from anonymous tipsters gave locations for newly damaged pickups and a semitractor. Nye jotted down their names. He detailed Pesce and Talman to check them out. He read off the names of possible assailants Ensor's former partner had just given them and told Vu to track down where they were. He liked the way things were moving after the stale, bitter session with Walt Maslow.

"Warrants are all out. We'll have the tapes to look at after lunch," he said. "We're going to close this one down. I know it."

Rose didn't answer and he assumed she was annoyed with him for some reason. He yawned involuntarily. "Probably got to take a break soon here, Rosie. I can't do straight back-to-back shifts like I used to. Maybe coffee would help."

She had changed lanes onto Business 80, passing the sprawling Department of Motor Vehicles complex off Broadway, heading them downtown.

"Okay," Nye said, slumping in his seat, "what's up?"

Rose still didn't answer for a moment, pausing to respond to their radio. Then she said, glancing at Nye, "I was just thinking, Ter. I got Annorina's lunch menus all written out for the week. I stick it on the fridge with a magnet so Luis can make one up. Which he never does," she shrugged, "but I still go through the little game. I make up dinners for the week, put them in foil or baggies, yeah? Annorina gets a decent dinner even if Luis won't make one. He gets it, too."

"Nice. Thoughtful," Nye said, wondering where she was going with the domestic details, which he didn't entirely want to know.

"So, I'm a pretty organized person, okay? You think so?"

"Definitely."

"But what if it doesn't matter? Maslow back there and even Ensor. Maybe all of it's a scam. Luck. Dice toss."

"I have no idea, Rosie. I think you just have to do what's right and then the rest of it falls where it does."

She lowered her window, resting one arm. The cool breeze in the car revived Nye a little but he admitted he was tired after a long night and morning.

She said, "You know someone's going to get a call to go back out there to Maslow's place. Soon, I bet. We'll be lucky if it's only a two forty-five," she meant a significant assault.

Or maybe a one eighty-seven, Nye thought, *because either Maslow or his wife's dead and we catch the call.* "You can't change the world and I know I sure as hell can't," he said.

"Yeah, Ter," Rose answered, looking at him sideways for a moment. "You were planning on telling me about the Meadowview deal, yeah? So I didn't just hear about it around the building?"

Because she's got to trust me, just like I've got to trust her, at a level beyond thinking about it or rationalizing it, even if it's only for a few weeks. It's got to be an instinctive part of working together or the whole thing falls apart. "Any time you want, Rosie," he said soberly.

"How about now?" she said.

He started without preamble. "Six years ago, I'm with Roger Penley. He's chief of police in some little city down in L.A. County now. Hates black widow spiders. Tried Macing one once. Blew back in his face and mine," and Nye caught her disapproving frown. "So," he went on hastily, "we got a call to a possible two eleven at Valley Liquors on Meadowview. We get there, all looks quiet, nobody even around. Penley's out first, hand on his gun. I'm right behind him when he freezes. We both see this bozo with a big weapon, turned out to be a .357, drawing down on Penley from inside the liquor store. What Penley didn't see was a second bozo starting to come out of a parked car to my right. Another half tick and the two of them would have us both in a cross fire out there in the parking lot."

"You picked the guy in the store."

"Penley was between me and the store, but he was slower and he hadn't seen the second bozo. I fired past him into the liquor store, four shots, yelled we had a second guy on my right. Penley put him down him with one shot."

"That's not a bad call," Rose said with a trace of surprise. "Not like the versions I heard."

"Penley and me both walked away from it and nobody in the department complained. But it makes a better war story for guys like Maslow if I hid behind my partner."

She glanced at him sideways again for an instant. "I believe you, Ter."

He was pleased, deeply. He had discovered that Rose seldom spoke for effect. When she said something, she meant it.

She turned onto heavily tree shaded X Street, heading up it toward the center of downtown Sacramento. Nye said, "I know what might pick me up. How about a quick detour to Vallejo's on J Street? Best goat plate in town."

"I could go for that," she agreed. She started to say, "I've been thinking what the bad guy's probably up to this morning," when Nye's cell phone went off and he held up a hand to her while he answered. The caller ID had immediately caught his attention.

It was Deirdre Gammon. He listened and said a few words. He closed the phone and he was wide awake.

"No goat plate for now, Rosie," he said. "We need to get to this location," and he rattled off directions to Deirdre's homey dungeon, "like now."

"What's up?" Rose asked, swinging to the right to take them back to the freeway.

"We have got a real live witness tied up and waiting for us."

FIFTEEN

STEVENSON BROKE HIS TRIAL for lunch promptly at twelve. He was tense and still had not completely worked out what he needed to do when he saw Eli later that afternoon.

He invited another judge, Carlos Montoya, to the Jade Garden on J Street that was within walking distance from the courthouse. They both served on the Resources Committee the presiding judge set up to examine the shrinking space within the crowded court-house. Montoya kept a set of weights in his chambers and worked out over lunch or in the morning. They talked over Mongolian beef, tofu, and brown rice about keeping in shape while spending most days sitting down. Stevenson regaled Montoya with tales of climbing two mountains or training for long races. They ran into several attorneys and chatted about county bar association business, who was likely to go after a seat on the delegation to the State Bar. Everyone wanted to talk to Stevenson because his father-in-law had access to people with checkbooks and was worth a jolly word on a sunny afternoon.

Stevenson, though, wanted to be seen and seen as he had been the day before: a judge handling the dozens of details of running a trial department. He wanted impeccable witnesses to his unchanged behavior.

He was surprised at his own unsuspected capacity for duplicity and deviousness. He was even disgusted by it. He hadn't realized he had the ability to so easily pretend to be someone he was not. The fact that it was a life-and-death situation made it all the more startling to him. He was sure Montoya and everyone he saw so far thought he was no different from yesterday.

But Stevenson also admitted he felt that strange exhilaration again, like he reveled in getting away with what he had done. Flaunting it except that no one knew it. He wondered if that was how the defendants in his courtroom now or any criminal felt after their crimes.

"You're in a good mood, Frank," Montoya said as they walked back to the courthouse through the late lunch strollers, passing the blocky utilitarian County Administration Building, the towering jail just beyond it. "Good news from the Governor's Office?" Everyone knew Stevenson was making a move for an appointment to the appellate bench.

"Far too early. I just started an interesting trial." He tried the lie and it floated naturally, effortlessly.

"I wish I could trade with you," Montoya sighed, "my armed robbery's going south. I can see it. The jury's not looking at the DA anymore. Probably his deaf witness swearing he overheard a conversation did it. This kid has hearing aids in both ears the size of dinner plates."

Stevenson laughed and tapped Montoya's meaty shoulder. "You can keep it, Carlos."

Then Stevenson realized why he appeared to be cheerful. Through lunch, running into other people, now walking back to the courthouse, there had not been a single mention from anyone about the unresolved drama of the badly injured cop.

His upbeat mood gave way to frustration and then fear again soon after he got back to his chambers. Joan and Audie insisted on telling him the latest news about the cop, the dire medical bulletins, the reward offered by the police association, more reward money being put up by the city council.

"Guys around here think he's got maybe a forty-sixty chance of making it," Audie said with the casual brutality cops cultivated or feigned.

"He's got to be getting the best medical treatment," Stevenson said. "His odds are much better than that."

"I hope so, Judge," Joan said sadly. "I can't stop thinking about his family. They keep showing his wife and children on the news." She shook her head.

"He dies," Audie went on with his own thought, "we're talking to SPOA, maybe having the city and county law enforcement guys make sure the DA goes after first-degree murder."

"It looks like it was an accident," Stevenson said. "That means vehicular manslaughter, not murder."

"Yeah, well, the DA needs both police unions next election."

Stevenson closed the door to his chambers and sat down heavily. He felt the great brute forces arrayed against him marshaling for attack, even if he was still unknown and invisible.

He had to stay that way. No one could know, not Vee or Haley. Not them especially. Above all, he wanted to keep them ignorant of what he had done.

So I've got to make Eli help me. He'll do anything to protect Haley and Vee if I make him, Stevenson thought grimly. *There has to be a way to keep Eli unknown, too. That's the only way to protect us all.*

He had twenty minutes before the jury was due to come back. Stevenson made a list of people, eight or so, he had spent time with the night before. He needed to create some firewalls, precautions in case things went wrong and questions did get asked about where he had been at a certain time last night. He started calling. With his newly uncovered talent, he made the calls seem innocuous, trivial.

"Hi, Mel," he said to a spry older woman named Melanie Chastain, who was on the city council, and whom he and Vee saw socially every so often. "What time did you get out of Ricci's last night?" His hand clutched the telephone.

"Too late, Frank," she said. "I've been paying for it all day. You and Eli did the right thing, bailing out early."

"I was asleep by ten," he said. "Trial work is a young man's game. Takes too much out of me."

She chuckled melodically. "Sure, Frank. You're in better shape than anyone I know. I thought you hung around with our merry band until midnight."

"Not me," he said, hoping fervently that the lie was accepted casually, "I had to get Eli home. He's still a little fragile after last year. Anyway, I had trial first thing this morning."

"I could be wrong. I was a little, how shall we say, a wee bit indisposed last night. What can I do for you? We're having a lousy day," her jocular tone vanished, "keeping up with this injured police officer. Really rotten."

"I heard about it this morning. It's all over the courthouse."

"Blink of an eye, Frank and it's thee or me. So, what's doing?"

Stevenson had thought up an invitation to a small dinner party the following week. He would tell Vee about it tonight, but it made a convenient excuse to check in with some of the people on his list. Melanie Chastain said she and her husband could probably make it.

He sat back. That had gone fairly well. At last one person now could say he and his father-in-law had left early or at least be uncertain when he had left the bar at Ricci's.

His next three calls were less successful. Two attorneys and an old classmate from McClatchy High he rarely saw actually were insistent that he was still at Ricci's after midnight. He gave up trying to plant the notion of an earlier departure because the more he brought it up, the more he could tell he was cementing their recollection of the true time he left the place.

Joan knocked on his chambers door and stuck her head in, "The lawyers are all here, Judge."

Stevenson still hung onto the telephone like a lifeline after his last failed call. It took him a moment to come back to where he was. "Thanks. Tell Audie I'll be out in five minutes."

"Stop the frowning," she wagged a finger at him as she closed the door.

He hung up the telephone, got up, went to the small closet near his private bathroom, and took down his black robe. He slipped it on, automatically closing the Velcro snaps, his mind fearful and empty. The exhilaration was gone. He felt like he was in a small, leaky boat being forced farther from shore by unforgiving ocean currents, out into a trackless and depthless sea.

Stevenson gathered up his trial notes, the idle ones he jotted down rather than commit to the computer on the bench during the trial.

He had an almost irresistible and awful premonition that he was going to be caught, no matter what he did.

He grabbed the door to his chambers and jerked it open.

No, he thought savagely, *that's unacceptable. Not me. It happens to other people, the stupid, frightened, unlucky ones I see the cops drag through the courthouse every day.*

But it won't happen to me.

It was a vow as deep and significant as the one had made to Vee or the love he felt for Haley.

SIXTEEN

"HE'S REALLY A STATE SENATOR?" Rose repeated with a little surprise. She had been a cop long enough not to be wholly startled anymore by anything people did to themselves or others. But it was still possible to catch her a trifle off guard.

"Yep. District's down in Kern County."

"What's with these guys? Are they nuts?"

"They think they're invisible. Laws don't apply to them."

Rose shook her head. They sat in the car in front of Deirdre Gammon's house in Carmichael, on a quiet residential street at the end of a cul-de-sac. "I don't even know who my senator is," she said a little sheepishly because it was something she thought she should know. "Like it matters. Okay, Ter, are we taking him here or someplace else?"

Nye thoughtfully chewed on a sunflower seed from a small package he had found in the glove box. Rose's contribution to good health, something left over from a school lunch. On the way over they had debated whether to go after Deirdre's purported witness now or follow him back to his office or home. There were pros and cons either way.

"My vote is we bag him here," Nye said, spitting shells out the window, taking another seed and cracking it with his fingernails. "He goes back to the Capitol, he's on his own turf and he's going to feel safe. Then we got to deal with the sergeant-at-arms, state police if we want to talk to him or take him in. Lot of hassle."

"Better reason to grab him there. He'll be shook up."

"We want him to talk to us."

"We're going to pop him for solicitation, right?" Rose asked.

"We could."

"Okay, we hold it over him," Rose said, popping sunflower seeds for herself, expertly crunching it all, shell and seed, and spitting the residue out her window. "Let's get him here then. It'll scare the hell out of him more. He's got to be feeling pretty secure."

"I imagine so," Nye agreed, thinking about how Deirdre told him she had her customer cinched to a mattress. "You mind taking the lead? He might open up to a woman faster."

"Jesus, Ter," Rose said with mock disgust, getting out of the car.

State Senator Niles Clarke's hands shook so badly he had trouble fastening his belt. He sat in a chair in his suit pants, blue dress shirt half buttoned, his white feet bare. He was in his midfifties, bald and flushed. He kept telling Rose and Nye he owned the largest auto mall in the Central Valley. They had just handed him back his wallet after verifying his identification.

"I was just doing this for laughs," he said again.

They were in the small living room. Rose and Nye stood in front of him. Deirdre Gammon was sent to make coffee. She had protested loudly and obscenely initially when Rose and Nye pushed her down-stairs into the basement dungeon, the false cardboard brick peeling, undercutting the required suspension of disbelief that this was a realm of doom and despair. The room stank of Lysol and sweat. On the way back upstairs, Rose leading Clarke, Deirdre Gammon gave Nye a wink.

"Be quiet for a second, okay?" Rose now said to him sharply.

Clarke stopped in midcommercial for the latest model Toyotas he could get them at a special law enforcement discount. He nodded dumbly.

"Here's the situation, sir," Rose went on, moving a little closer to him, "you are in a brothel. You are engaged in sexual activity. This is a crime, sir."

"We were only role playing," Clarke said with false assurance.

"We found you naked, tied with plastic chains to a mattress downstairs while a woman in black leather pretended to whip you. What do you think it looks like?"

Nye bit his inner lip so he didn't laugh.

"It's therapy." Clark sat up a little straighter, the same attitude he used effectively when chairing the Senate Budget Committee. "It is purely consensual and therapeutic."

"You have a doctor's prescription, sir?" Rose asked.

"I can get one," he said, starting to stand up.

"Sit down," Rose said. He sat.

"Whose pool did I piss in? Somebody's ticked at me for something because cops don't come out to a private home midday for no reason," he said to Rose and then Nye, bluff defiance in his voice suddenly.

"A neighbor complained," Nye said.

"You can't hold me here unless I'm under arrest. Am I under arrest?"

Rose came much closer to him, reducing his personal zone to a mere inch. "Listen to me carefully, sir, you have been caught in an act of prostitution. It's not the crime of the century but you can go to jail for up to a year. It would be a major news story for your hometown papers and TV."

Nye liked the way she neatly sidestepped answering his question. Rose had good form when it came to handling questioning. He heard Deirdre rattling around in the kitchen. They had worked it out that she would stay clear of the room until they were finished.

"I want you to think about your situation sir," Rose went on while Clarke stared at her with a mix of anger and fear. "My partner and I are going to ask you some questions and your answers will determine what happens to you after that."

"What's the catch?" Clarke asked warily. "I've been in politics long enough to hear a sideswipe coming."

Rose shook her head. "There's no catch. You need to answer these questions completely and truthfully, that's all."

Nye watched Clarke, ready for any sudden moves. You never knew what someone would do in sex cases. Nye was caught off guard by a meek auditor in the Franchise Tax Board who charged four armed SPD cops when Vice caught him in a sting with two underage prostitutes. The auditor broke one cop's arm and gave Nye a black eye before he was pinned to the ground.

"All right," Clarke said evenly, his trembling hands clutching his knees, "go ahead. I'll answer anything. You know I don't pay her," he jerked his head raggedly toward the kitchen where Deirdre could be heard, "this isn't whatever she said to you, officer. There's no prostitution if I don't pay her."

"He pays," Deirdre called out. "He's got an account."

Clarke's eye jerked back and forth and Nye silently cursed Deirdre for breaking the rhythm of the questions and letting Clarke know she was eavesdropping. They needed to wind this session up quickly before Clarke got his emotional armor up again.

Rose stepped away slightly, cuing Nye that it was his turn.

"We have information that you were on Capitol Mall last night," Nye said coldly, "around one in the morning and you saw something. What did you see?"

Clarke stared for a moment, then swallowed hard. "Okay, now I know what this is all about. There wasn't any neighbor complaining. She called you, didn't she? Because I was talking to her about last night," he jerked his head toward the kitchen. "She told you I said something about the accident and the police officer who was hit, didn't she?"

"You tell us," Nye said.

"I've heard about the accident. It's awful. Terrible. But I can't help you. I didn't see anything. I don't know anything about it. I was only kind of bragging to her that I knew something about what happened last night." He started to stand up, hands holding his pants waist as if to keep them from falling down. "Now, I've got important committee business coming up at the Capitol, but you can call me if you have any other questions."

Rose moved in again. "You're under arrest for a violation for section one forty-seven B of the Penal Code," she turned him around, snapping plastic handcuffs on him.

"Wait a second! Wait. Wait!" Clarke cried.

She recited his Miranda warning and Clarke kept interrupting until she was finished. He twisted futilely. "Do you wish to give up your right to an attorney and talk to us, sir?"

"Yes! I mean, no. I don't want to give up anything! What the hell do you think you're doing?" He shouted at her and Nye. "I'm a member of the California Legislature, you bastards. I will make goddamn sure your stupid little careers are over if you don't let me go."

"You're threatening us, sir," Rose said, Nye taking out his little notepad and starting to write. "That's a separate offense."

"Just a second, just a goddamn second, you bastards," Clarke tried to pull from Rose's implacable grip on his shoulder.

"It's your choice, Senator," Nye said coolly. "Because right now we're all going out to our car, driving downtown, and booking you into the main jail. I figure it will take all of ten, maybe fifteen minutes for someone to pick up that you're in the tank and have the place staked out with cameras."

Clarke sat down, Rose holding him there for a moment.

"I have a family," he said slowly and furiously. "I have a record of doing goddamn good work for the people of this state. You bastards are going to destroy everything."

"Then my recommendation sir," Rose said calmly, "is that you answer our questions and we will leave you."

Clarke stared up at her, Nye for confirmation. "You've got to keep my name off your reports," he said desperately. "Okay? I'm anonymous."

"We can't make any promises," Nye said. "But we'll try to independently corroborate anything you tell us. We'll keep your name out of the investigation if that works out."

"No. Not good enough," Clarke said, shaking his head. "Look, I know a little about trading," he smiled falsely at both of them. "My name's got to stay out of the investigation period. I did see something."

"What did you see?" Nye asked sharply.

"Do we have a deal?"

"Yes, we do," Rose answered without waiting for Nye.

"What about her?" Clarke said it low, nodding toward the kitchen.

"I'll take care of her," Nye promised. He could keep Deirdre quiet with the reward dangling in front of her. If the time came to settle with her, he could write a report omitting Senator Clarke. She would understand that if she tried to peddle his involvement she would lose her money. It was one of the trades Rose probably wouldn't approve of entirely. "Were you around Capitol Mall at one o'clock yesterday morning?"

"Yes, I was."

"Where were you going?"

"I've got a condo downtown on 8th Street, I use it when the Legislature's in session. I was going home after a party." He grinned slyly. "Well, not really after the party. The Timber Association had their annual dinner at the Sheraton last night and I was leaving," he smiled at Rose and Nye, "a little after-dinner entertainment I met at the bar. Great bar at the Sheraton."

"What's her name?" Rose asked.

He shook his head. "She's not part of the deal and she wasn't in my car with me. She went back to her roost in the bar."

Nye felt a tickle of wonderment at this middle-aged public servant's energy. State Senator, running a major committee in the legislature responsible for billions of dollars, family in Kern County, large business, and a round of hookers. As if it were all part of simply going through life, the daily checklist of activities. It was a little like his astonishment at how much Tommy Ensor managed to accomplish. Nye frankly did not see how they could do so much in a day that was no longer for them than it was for him.

"All right, you're on your way home," Nye picked up the questions quickly, "and you got to Capitol Mall. Did you see an accident?"

"No. I didn't. Believe me, I would have stopped to help."

"Did you see any vehicle, car, truck, something you could describe?"

He shook his head. "No. I made a turn off Capitol Mall to go home and that's when I saw something."

"What was that, sir?" Rose asked gently.

"As I came off Capitol Mall, I saw this kind of, well, kind of shelter made out of a cardboard box and some cloth, to keep the rain out, I guess. It was so odd, a little makeshift camp right there on Capitol Mall. There was a little lantern or some kind of light on the ground just inside the shelter."

"Did you see anyone?" Nye tensed and he knew Rose's calm demeanor masked taut expectancy about what Clarke would say.

"There was a figure crouched in front of the shelter as I came around the turn, so I could see him for a few seconds and then I was too far away. It was a man, a homeless guy in a kind of poncho. He stood up just as I drove by and he waved at me." Clarke said with puzzlement. "Like this," and he moved his handcuffed arms up and down in slow motion, almost like semaphore signals. "I thought he was nuts."

"I want you to describe him. Very carefully," Nye said, writing as Clarke went on talking.

SEVENTEEN

THE EARLY AFTERNOON TURNED OUT to be a warmer Thursday than predicted as Stevenson drove north out of downtown Sacramento in Vee's car, heading up I-5 toward his father-in-law's office complex. Last night's rain left thick white clouds hanging brightly over the city.

He recessed the trial in a burst of loud recriminations from the opposing attorneys, each accusing the other side of preparing subterfuges to contaminate the jurors, who still had not been chosen or even brought into the courtroom. Each side demanded he rule immediately. Stevenson struggled to pay attention, told them he would rule on their various objections in the morning, and quickly left the bench.

He was still torn about how much he should reveal to Vee's father. It was a tightrope. He needed Eli's help but even more he had to ensure that the older man didn't inadvertently bring everything down by blurting out to someone point that he vaguely remembered hitting something. Twice driving out onto the freeway Stevenson was so preoccupied he drifted into other lanes and got angry cars honking at him.

Traveling over the river, he watched the lazy houseboats and slow power craft along the wide swath of brown-green water between banks choked with trees and brush. He would have traded places in an instant with anyone on one of the boats, even the decrepit hulk chugging down river, its shirtless master waving gaily to the other people.

He met Vee at a party along the river, held at the Sacramento Yacht Club, when he was a junior associate in his law firm, assigned to menial chores connected to the business of Eli's investment bank. It was the bank's annual summer party and Vee's attendance was a surprise. She was supposed to be sailing the Maine coast but decided to attend at the last minute. Stevenson first saw her set against the green lawn, framed beside the river and the pleasure craft berthed at the club, wearing a white-and-blue dress, and thought instantly that she was the most beautiful and desirable woman he had ever encountered. She still was.

He got to know Eli and Lurene, Vee's late mother, a woman who never seemed to frown and filled her days with charity and kind words. When she died two years ago, they all took it very badly, Haley and Vee and Stevenson, too. But Eli had come unmoored entirely; the drinking that was always a job requirement became a refuge. He was drifting away. Only this pursuit of the Third District Court of Appeal appointment had grounded him again and he given him purpose.

That first summer Stevenson and Vee dated often and came back to the river for swimming or picnics. She taught him to dance. He took her bike riding along the sinuous trail that wound around parks and the river for miles.

It seemed so long ago. It seemed so far away.

Stevenson rolled into the parking lot of River City Financial, got a ticket from an attendant, and parked. He walked into the airy lobby of the sprawling single story complex and gave his name to the young receptionist expertly juggling a stream of incoming calls and people arriving for appointments with the bank's impressive staff.

Eli's father had started the bank, swelling its portfolio and clients over four decades. During that time it became painfully clear that his only son was not fitted for management or bare-knuckle negotiation or even simple bookkeeping. Eli's gifts were personal and limited. He was charming and he charmed. He soothed clients. He was the happy face that started or ended the tough negotiations others carried out. When the bank moved from its first offices downtown out here along the river, it split into investments and banking. Eli retained the title of vice president for strategic investments but his duties stayed the same. He kept the booze flowing, as he told Stevenson earlier that day.

Stevenson had enjoyed working with him. Eli was a genuinely decent man.

Stevenson chatted briefly and emptily with several secretaries and fund managers as he went to his father-in-law's suite at the far end of the building.

Georgina greeted him with a hug in the outer office. "Well, where's my tribute, sunshine?"

"I forgot to bring it," Stevenson admitted.

"I guess I'm insulted." She pretended to pout.

"Why should I help you spoil a perfect figure?" he said with false anger.

"You are forgiven, as usual." Georgina smiled. "He's got somebody, but I'll let him know you're here."

Stevenson stood by one of the leather sofas, taking it all in again. Fresh flowers, colorful abstract oil paintings, light cheery coffee tables, and Georgina presiding over the carpeted reception area. Nothing had changed here anyway. Here at least the world was still moored, secure. He checked his own watch. He had to pick Haley up after school, Vee wouldn't be home for hours after that, which still gave him some time to figure out what to do with the SUV. He had to solve that part of the puzzle first because he had seen the two cops getting their search warrants in Yardley's court. His relentless hunters were on the move.

He wanted to be in control again, like when he sat on the bench this morning, looking out at the lawyers and defendants. When he looked out on the courtroom and spoke, no one in the world could touch him.

I'm a judge, he thought, I decide what the law is.

He desperately clung to that hope from his old life.

The tall, pale-wood doors to his father-in-law's office opened and Eli and another man momentarily stood in it, shaking hands. "Don't worry," Eli said with genial assurance, "by this time next week, you won't even remember the names of the tax guys."

The man left and Eli motioned Stevenson, "Frank. Come on in."

Stevenson followed the shorter man into his inner office, the doors closed discreetly behind them by Georgina. "I expected the last customer to kiss your ring."

Eli smiled at the compliment. "I try to bestow my blessings freely."

Stevenson immediately noted the half-empty bottle of vodka on Eli's desk amid the multiple framed pictures of Vee, Haley, and him. Eli sat down and so did he.

"Little freshener, Frank?" Eli indicated the bottle. "I've got everything. You know that."

"No. Nothing," Stevenson said. He struggled inwardly.

"Well, maybe I better keep my streak going," and Eli poured a large measure into a cut crystal glass. "So, which school are you thinking about for Haley? I've got a couple of suggestions, old friends . . ."

"I'm not here about Haley."

Eli's smooth faced wreathed in mild surprise. He took a drink. "I guess I got it mixed up."

"No, you didn't. I wasn't telling the truth when I said I needed to talk to you, Eli."

"Well, here you are. Here I am. What's on your mind?"

"Do you remember anything about me driving you home last night?" Stevenson held the arms of the chair tightly.

"Not really, Frank. We had a good event, I remember that. I remember it was raining," he frowned and drank again. "Something else maybe. I was asleep pretty fast when you dropped me off."

"Is that all, Eli?"

"Christ, sure. What else is there? Jeepers, you've got a look on you, Frank."

"I'm in serious trouble."

"What is it? I can help."

Stevenson sweated even in the air-conditioned office. "There's no going back once I tell you. For either of us." Stevenson's pulse quickened, poised for the rush of adrenaline as if he stared down a great height.

"It sounds like a warning," Eli said, puzzled. "But I want to help. You know that."

"Yes, I do. I'm counting on it because I need your help and I wish I didn't."

"Bet you want a drink now."

Stevenson knew he was going to hurt Eli and there was no way to avoid it. But he was certain he could spare the older man the greater anguish of being questioned, the relentless interrogations. Fearing what he would be asked. *They would hurt him much more,* Stevenson thought. *I'm going to make sure he's protected.* It was an absurdly self-serving justification, and Stevenson knew it.

"I better do this stone cold," he said.

So Stevenson told Eli everything that had happened from the accident the night before to his sad effort to conceal the SUV from Vee and Haley that morning, all the way to his fumbling phone calls a few hours earlier to give himself cover.

It only took about six minutes and, halfway through, Eli wasn't smiling anymore.

"I don't believe you," Eli said at the end. He put a thick hand across his face for a moment.

"It's what happened."

"It can't be. I know you," Eli said, standing up, a small smile. "I do not believe you would leave a man in the street, Frank. That is not you."

"I did it, though."

Eli stared at him, his mouth pursed. "No. I do not accept it. There's a mistake. You only think you hit this cop. Somebody else did. You hit a dog or something else."

Stevenson recognized that Eli, for kind and good reasons, was frantically searching for some crack or crevice or flaw in the plain facts he had just heard and which he knew, even underneath the haze of fatigue and liquor, was the truth.

At that moment, Stevenson could not have said why he kept going last night. The whole trajectory of his life to that second, working his way through college and law school, competitive in track and swimming, then mountain climbing, reaching for a judgeship and now the Court of Appeal, described ambition and maybe arrogance and compulsions, like all people, that even he did not recognize.

But nothing in his life or work or loves answered the question. *It happened,* he thought. *I didn't stop.*

That was all he knew with unalterable certainty.

Stevenson got up. "This police officer may make it. He may not and it sounds like he's just hanging on." Stevenson oddly felt much calmer, reciting the devastating facts like he was laying out someone else's case. "It doesn't change things for me much. I checked the codes this morning. I'm potentially looking at something between a low end felony with up to three years in state prison if the DA charges it as a hit-and-run under the Vehicle Code. Or vehicular manslaughter under the Penal Code if the cop dies. In which case the possible upper term is six years in state prison."

Stevenson stopped pacing in front of Eli's desk. "No matter what happens, if he lives or dies, I'll be removed from the bench. Disbarred. Spend some time in jail or state prison."

Eli looked up. "Poor son of a bitch."

"I didn't mean to hit him. It was dark and he was just there," Stevenson gestured as if Ensor were before him again in the room, "and he shouldn't have been there."

"I didn't mean the cop."

"I'm worried about Vee and Haley. What happened was something I did and I don't want them to suffer for it."

"Right, right. No question," Eli said slowly. He got up and opened an old-fashioned chrome bar behind a false set of leather-bound books. He poured two large glasses of Scotch, gave one to Stevenson. "Bad idea, mixing your drinks," he said with a bleak smile and drained the glass. He poured another.

Stevenson took a large gulp of his own, surprising himself.

"I need your help to protect them," Stevenson said, putting the glass on the desk. "I need it right now."

The other man sat down, slumping in his expensive handcrafted leather chair. "You sure as hell do," and he looked much older, sadder for a moment, drank as quickly as Stevenson, and straightened. "It's a goddamn accident, Frank. Nobody's going to see it as anything except a tragic, unavoidable accident." He reached for the telephone.

Stevenson stood over him. "I didn't stop. I left."

"Doesn't change anything. It was still an accident, and I bet if we look a little closely at what this cop was doing last night, he was the major cause. Right," Eli nodded, convincing himself, "I bet we will find that this cop violated a whole raft of police department policies about after-hours work, failure to wear some kind of goddamn gear so he's visible at night," he started dialing.

Stevenson watched his father-in-law talking himself into a hermetic, perfect solution. He knew he could stop him in a moment even as Eli finished dialing.

"The crime was complete when I kept going," Stevenson said.

"So what? There could be any number of good reasons you didn't stop last night. You didn't know you'd hit anybody," Eli tossed it out with enthusiasm. "Christ, I didn't know we'd hit anyone. But now you're prepared to come forward. You're not hiding anything."

"I didn't stop," Stevenson said again. "Coming forward now doesn't change anything. The time to do that was last night or even this morning. It's too late now."

"I don't buy that. Listen, I'm calling a friend, old friend," he emphasized, "in the Department of Justice. He can give me a ballpark read of your liabilities and minefields here, Frank. As a *personal* favor."

"Hang up," Stevenson said evenly.

"Let me handle this for you. You're all tied up, I can see that. Christ, who wouldn't be?" He shook his head.

Behind Eli's desk, Stevenson looked out a wide gauzily curtained window onto a small park with stone benches in a stand of linden and elm trees. Two secretaries sat on the benches talking and eating their late lunches.

"Hang up, Eli, unless you're going to tell this friend my name and everything I've told you. I've committed several additional crimes since last night. I've destroyed evidence. I've tried to give myself an alibi," he blew out a breath. "Not very well."

As he spoke, Eli's eyes seemed to cloud and he hung up slowly. Stevenson knew the situation had at last come into unmistakable focus.

"I was with you. I'd be committing a crime if I didn't tell him your name," Eli said carefully.

"That's right. Right now, your only choice is whether or not to call the Sacramento County DA or the cops."

"I guess they could say I was guilty, too."

"I warned you."

"Hell, yes you did. Anybody else, I would have had my guard up, known where the attack was coming. But not when it came from you." His face sagged again.

"It's me and our family or we all go down," Stevenson said, the image now adamantine crystal in his mind. "It's your choice. Give us both to the police or work with me to protect Haley and Vee."

Stevenson detachedly watched Eli stare at him. He knew exactly what was going through the other man's mind, running faster and faster and finally realizing there was no escape.

Eli said, "The cops you ran into, the ones getting those warrants. What are their names?"

"How does that matter?"

"We should know who's coming after us."

Stevenson understood he had succeeded in forcing his father-in-law to choose sides. Angrily he thought again, *It's your fault. I was trying to help you, get you home because your daughter and I worry about you.* All he said was, "I can get their names from the judge who signed the warrants."

"Yeah, do that. Maybe you can slow them down, point them somewhere else if they get close."

"Thanks, Eli."

"This is killing me, Frank."

"I'm sorry. I am truly, deeply sorry and if I could undo everything I would do it, no matter what it cost." Stevenson said, the other man's tortured face across the desk from him. "But there's no other way now."

He stood up, glancing at his watch. "I think we've got a couple of hours to figure out what to do with the SUV. I've got the beginning of an idea."

EIGHTEEN

NYE AND ROSE GOT THE DESCRIPTION Senator Clarke had given them worked up into a bulletin and it went out from the department before three in the afternoon. A statewide be-on-the-lookout hit all law enforcement agencies and news outlets: white male, approximately six feet tall, about one hundred and fifty pounds, unshaven, long dark hair, between thirty and fifty years old.

"Jesus, can you get it any looser?" Vu demanded when Nye handed him the write-up. "This fits a million guys."

"We didn't have anything a couple hours ago," Nye said bluntly. "Now we got a body to look for. So shut the hell up. Please."

"He's the guy? He hit Ensor?"

"He saw who hit Tommy," Nye said. "If we're goddamn lucky."

Vu grumbled and Parkes and Talman went on answering the telephones now ringing incessantly with tips from the public. The flood of tips was nearly overwhelming, and farming out the halfway decent ones occupied two dozen patrol cops already. Pesce was out collecting the video surveillance records and would be back soon.

Rose took Nye aside. "Ter, I got to tell you something."

"Make it fast, Rosie. I am running out of gas. I figure I can make it through a check of the videos to see if we got anything at all, and then I'm down."

He was a little surprised that she didn't bite on his last submissive note. Rose normally never let him get away with any whine or complaint.

"Altlander pulled me out awhile ago," she said worriedly, voice low so the others wouldn't hear her. "He says I've got to give him anything we come up with. Before Nish gets it."

"Because you're a good cop?"

"Because I'm a good cop who wants to be on the winning side."

There were already distinct factions forming within the department about which assistant chief would be chosen to succeed Gutierrez and some alarm about the rivalries inhibiting how the cops, from patrol to detective, did their daily jobs. Nye hated department politics but it was like bugs in summer, impossible to avoid.

"Nish had the same come-to-Jesus with me at the hospital," Nye admitted.

"You were going to tell me sometime?"

"I forgot. I'm sorry." Then a thought struck him. "Nish wanted me to make sure you knew he got first crack at what we turned up. Sounds like Altlander left me out."

"Yeah," Rose said solemnly, "he did."

Nye went on, "Guth in IA told me to sit this one out. I figure Altlander's pulling his strings."

"What'd you say?" She looked angry.

"Unprintable."

"Fuck him."

"Something like that."

"He bring me in to it?"

"Not so much," Nye began but Rose cut him off.

"I can take care of myself with those jackasses." She was breathing sparks.

"No question. Seriously, Rosie, this means we don't have any friends. Just us."

She calmed a little and pretended to shiver at the idea. "So, what's your bright idea, old man?"

Nye grinned coldly. His own future lay plainly before him. But

Rose had to weigh her own and he could help her there. He detested the idea of demeaning Tommy Ensor's investigation by making it a part of the power struggle between those two egomaniacs.

"How about this? You go tell Altlander we got a lead on the driver about five minutes after I let Nish know. You make sure to let Altlander know I'm telling Nish exactly the same thing he's hearing."

"It'll frost him big time."

"And Nish, too," Nye agreed. "Let the bastards fight it out and leave us alone."

Rose smiled at him. "I am going to have so many great war stories after a tour with you."

"That's what I've been telling you." He made a show of checking his watch. "On your mark," he said. He had his phone in hand.

"Get set," Rose added evenly. She reached for her cell phone.

A whoop from Vu brought all of them together at his desk about twenty minutes later.

"I got the crime lab," he announced. "They've got some great news."

"Put it on speaker," Nye said.

"Hey, Cummins, you're on speaker with the gang," Vu said, arms folded.

"Who's in the room?" Josie Cummins, the soft-spoken director of the Sacramento County Forensics Laboratory asked curtly.

Nye quickly recited everybody grouped anxiously around the telephone on Vu's desk. "We're ready for some good news, Jo," he said. "Give."

"Well, we've moved the ball down the field, as you guys like to say," Cummins said sarcastically, "but we're not at the goal line yet. The tire imprints and rubber we found at your crime scene come from an SUV, late model, probably sold within the last six months or year at the most."

"How do you get that, Jo?" Rose asked, swiftly making notes on a legal pad.

"Factory installed. The SUV, and I'll get to that part in a second, rolled off the assembly line and these were the tires put on it by the auto manufacturer."

"What are we looking for?" Nye asked.

"Hold on a second. My peeps have been working flat out since this happened, let me savor the moment, please."

Nye glared at Vu and Parkes. Talman and Rose frowned at the telephone as if it were responsible for the painful delay. "Time's up," Nye said.

"Indeed," Cummins said, then went on unperturbed. "We also matched the glass fragments found at the scene and the glass fragments recovered from the victim at the hospital. Safety glass, also manufacturer installed at the time of assembly. Same model and year SUV. The paint fragments line up, too, Nye. I could go into court and swear to the make, model, and year of the SUV with one hundred percent certainty."

"Okay, so open the envelope, please Josie, and let us all in on the deal."

"You're going to look for a 2013 black Cadillac Escalade sports utility vehicle. We're narrowing down the dealerships now, but it's probably going to be someplace within a twenty-mile radius of Sacramento. I should have the dealerships for you before close of business."

"Josie," Rose broke in, "are you talking about dealerships around here that sold that model SUV in 2013?"

"Exactly, Ms. Tafoya," Cummins said her with her exaggerated politeness reserved for people she didn't know well, "we've been checking it out with the auto manufacturer and we're getting a list of dealerships," and Nye broke in this time.

"Hold it, Josie," he looked around at the other detectives, "you're getting way ahead here. Can you nail down the physical evidence and link it up to a particular batch of this SUV?"

"No," Josie said slowly, "I'm just making a reasonable assumption that the vehicle was probably purchased in Northern California."

"No good," Nye said with a sigh, "we can't assume that. You've done a great job and thank your folks, but we're going to have to look at every dealership around the country if we can't narrow down the SUVs to a particular batch."

Vu let out a slow breath and Nye could see the other detectives were unhappy, but they understood his caution. Because of the location of the crime, adjacent to a major freeway artery, there was no responsible way to eliminate other geographical areas from which the vehicle could have come. California was a driver's dream state. Roads and freeways led everywhere easily. The SUV could have been bought anyplace and driven through Sacramento.

Nye hung up after Cummins promised a written report would be faxed over within the hour and the detectives didn't move for a moment. He chewed his lip thoughtfully. Rose stared at her notes.

Finally, she said, "Well, this is a big improvement on where we were right after the crime."

"But it leaves us with a hell of a lot of checking to do," Nye finished.

"We're talking about a nationwide search of dealerships, Terry," Vu said bitterly. "It could take weeks."

"We'll get cooperation from every law enforcement agency. It won't be that bad," Nye said without quite believing it. The chore of tracking a specific SUV model year, compiling a list of buyers, running through them, could certainly take weeks. "Jesus, if the bastard had only gotten custom tires or a custom paint job," he said angrily. Either one would have given them a clean shot at the owner of the SUV. As it was, the vehicle was a needle in a very large haystack.

He straightened up. He could see the morale of the other men and Rose sinking after the first burst of hope and euphoria and he was not going to let that happen.

"Okay, we're way ahead," Nye said for their benefit as much as his own, "we've got a vehicle description and we're going to put that out right now. We get the public hunting for it with us and the other agencies. We can start thinning out this shitload, excuse me," he said with feigned remorse, "of hotline tips. Eliminate the ones that don't involve our suspect vehicle. Focus on the ones that talk about an SUV or better still, our model SUV." He pointed at Talman and Parkes.

"I can shitcan," Vu said with equally feigned remorse, "about three quarters of this garbage right now then." He gestured at the forms he and Parkes had been generating after each phone tip.

The ringing phones, shifting computer displays, and constant murmuring from the TVs obscured the disappointment they all felt. If nothing else, the command center pulsed with energy and Nye was determined to ensure that energy was purposeful and productive.

He and Rose stepped into the starkly lit hallway a few moments later, other detectives and civilians eddying by them, some giving them a thumbs-up, others calling out encouragement.

"I thought we had it just now," Rose admitted. "I know I shouldn't jump the gun, but I couldn't help it."

"We're closing in, Rosie. That's the important thing. We're taking big steps and we're getting nearer to this fucker."

"I've been thinking about that for a while now." Her even features were drawn with concentration. "So, I'm the bad guy and I'm seeing all this going on, TV announcements to the public, bulletins about Ensor's condition, people swarming all over the hospital because Ensor's a guy they love, what am I thinking right now? I know what I've done."

"Trust me, whoever it is doesn't give a shit about Tommy or his family. All he's thinking about is himself and how he can get out of this. Period. He's not thinking about the pain he's caused."

"Yeah," Rose said, "he's trying to figure out how to cover it up, get clear. Maybe the driver's not a guy."

"Man or woman, we're talking about a selfish, cold-blooded sonofabitch."

"We don't know, Ter. Maybe he's hurting. He could still turn himself in."

"Anybody with an ounce of decency would've been on the phone or shown up on our doorstep a long time ago. I am looking forward to dancing on this heartless asshole."

A few feet away, the elevator door opened jerkily and Nye saw Pesce, laden with a cardboard box held in both arms, come toward them.

"You got the videos?" Nye asked, his surge of raw anger talking to Rose about the hit-and-run driver making it sound like an accusation.

"I do," Pesce said with an uncertain smile, wondering why Nye was snapping at him. "Everybody produced. No holdouts or twists."

Nye beckoned him forward impatiently, the three of them heading back into the command center. "Okay, let's get the TV going. It's matinee time."

NINETEEN

STEVENSON LET ELI RAMBLE for a few minutes after they parked Vee's car. His awkward ragged prayers to set the clock back fifteen hours were lost among the park's trees, carried over the river indifferently swirling a few yards away around the empty concrete boat ramp jutting into the dull-colored water.

Discovery Park was close and it seemed a better place to talk about what needed to be done than Eli's busy office with the constant threat that Georgina or someone else would come in and overhear them.

He allowed his father-in-law to walk alone to the boat dock, posed over the river. He saw Eli abruptly take out his cell phone, its faint ringing carrying to him. He felt time rushing by like the river. Things had to be set in motion before Vee and Haley got home. He walked to Eli and caught the last of the conversation.

"No, look Jerry, I appreciate you calling me back at all," Eli said in his old cheery voice, a veteran performer on stage. "You must be going in nine million directions with this thing. I only wanted to let you know, feel free to call on me if you need anything. You or your officers." Pause.

Stevenson realized Eli was talking to the senior Sacramento Police official he had called without success just before they left his office to get some privacy. Eli and the senior cop were friends from the Downtown Rotary Club. They had known each other for years.

"So, the detectives who are working on this damn thing, they're your best? Tell me about them. Great, great. You need the best to find the miserable, you know, who did this. My offer's there for you, Jerry. Anytime, anything, okay? You take care."

Eli ended the call and put his cell phone away. He gazed out onto the river. Stevenson could see that the call disturbed him.

"What did he say?" Stevenson asked, standing beside him.

"The lead detectives are a man named Nye and his partner, a woman, Tafoya. Nishimoto says they're a strong combination. They'll find whoever ran down the cop. Nye's an old school hand, lots of experience and contacts around town and Tafoya's one smart cookie. He says." Eli grinned emptily. "They will find you, Frank."

Stevenson didn't say anything for a moment, picturing the two hunters again.

Eli spoke sadly. "I'm really in it for good, aren't I, after that call?"

"Yes," Stevenson said.

"They'll find us."

Stevenson patted the older man's shoulder. "We're holding some good cards. We know who they are. We know what to expect. They don't have any idea you or I exist. I intend to keep it that way."

They turned from the river and walked a little ways toward the trees. It was a weekday in spring and the park was deserted. It spread out around them in dusty brown patches mixed with ragged green grass.

"You said you had an idea," Eli said quietly. He sounded considerably more alert and sober than he had just a little while ago in his office. "What is it?"

"The problem's my SUV," Stevenson said, his voice soft so it wouldn't carry. "It's the single piece of evidence that connects me to what happened last night. It's obviously been in some kind of collision. I can't fix it and I can't hide it for long. Vee and Haley already noticed that I had to borrow her car for today."

Eli halted. "Burn it," he said with sudden vehemence.

The violence coming from him startled Stevenson.

"I can't. A burned vehicle draws a lot of attention. A burned vehicle involved in this hit-and-run would be put under a microscope. The police would be at my doorstep in ten seconds to find out what happened to my SUV. That's just what we must avoid."

"You can lie, bluff. The damn thing was stolen, you don't know what happened after that."

"Trust me. We do not want to go through that door. There would be too many questions to answer and not enough solid answers." *You are one of them,* he thought.

"Somebody must have seen us in your SUV last night, coming to the event or leaving," Eli said helplessly. "It's already too late."

"No, that's actually a good thing. The real dilemma right now is the opposite. People around the courthouse will start noticing if I don't show up in my SUV as usual. My neighbors will start noticing a change, too. "

"These cops, the A-Team, they'll get some kind of description of the SUV."

"Probably. I'm a little surprised they don't have one yet. The one thing I've got going is that the accident happened late at night downtown and there wasn't anyone around."

Eli stopped and again wiped his sweating face with his damp handkerchief. He smoothed his carefully clipped gray hair. "Well, this is in one fine spot. Can't report the SUV stolen or burn it without drawing attention. Can't get the SUV fixed because you'd get caught. Can't hide it because everybody and their nosy brother will see you're driving something different and as soon as a decent description of the damn SUV gets out, they'll start thinking and wondering about everybody who drives a SUV like it."

"I need to be seen driving my SUV like I've done every day since I got it."

"How the hell can you do that?" Eli shook his head in frustration. "This is hopeless."

Stevenson kicked the dusty ground. The idea had come to him in his father-in-law's office with the force of inevitability and the clarity of its obviousness. It was a moment of risk in return for permanent security.

"Eli, you're going to buy another SUV for me. Just like mine."

TWENTY

THE TENSION IN THE COMMAND center during the viewing of the security camera videos was so thick you could touch it. Nye and Rose stood before the three TV monitors and intently watched the successive videos along with the other detectives who were grouped beside them, making notes, calling out observations in sudden shouts or subdued muttering as shapes moved in gray smears across the screens.

It wasn't just the fact that Nishimoto and Altlander had suddenly popped in right after Nye got Pesce's haul set up and ready to run that exponentially ratcheted up the tension. Everyone in the room wanted answers from the videos. Nishimoto appeared first, casually saying to no one in particular, "I hope you don't mind if I join you."

Nye shook his head, motioned to a seat, and the deputy chief sat down, arms folded stiffly across his thick torso. Rose raised an inquiring eye to Nye and he nodded to indicate he had let Nish know the videos were in the building. A moment later, the door snapped opened again and Altlander marched in without saying a word and took an empty chair a few feet from Nishimoto. It was Nye's turn to glance at Rose and she also nodded. *Swell,* Nye thought, *neither side's got an advantage while we try to keep our eye on the ball, meaning Ensor's hit-and-run and not the dumb fight between two tight-ass wannabe chiefs.*

Nye closed the Venetian blinds at the barred windows and turned off the lights.

"Okay," he said to the people in the room, "first up is the office building directly opposite the crime scene. Got ahead, Pesce."

Pesce advanced the videotape to five minutes before the incident. It would save a lot of time during the review of the videos knowing the time of the event. Unlike many security camera recordings, the detectives knew when and what they were looking for.

"It's so dark," Rose observed quietly.

"Streetlights are out," Nye said aloud. "What time did the city figure that happened, Parkes?" He paused the grainy gray video.

"They were okay from about five P.M. when they automatically come on until someone reported they were out, like eleven thirty about." Parkes said a little self-consciously because both deputy chiefs were staring at him like he had grown a third eye.

"So we've got a street that's a lot darker than normal on a rainy night," Nye began and Altlander broke in coldly.

"I hope you're not saying the driver isn't at fault here, Nye."

"No, sir. I'm just making an observation. Just setting the scene before the accident."

"Good. Let's be clear. The responsibility for Officer Ensor's hit-and-run is solely and completely the driver's of the SUV. There are no mitigating circumstances."

"No, sir," Nye said. "Can we go ahead?"

"Don't wait for me, Nye. I'm simply here as an observer."

Rose rolled her eyes for Nye's benefit. He started the video again.

The image had not been designed to show Capitol Mall. It was from a camera mounted on the far corner of the front of the building and situated to capture whatever happened just in front of the building. The slice of Capitol Mall that appeared on camera was incidental. It did not even show the Wells Fargo construction site at all. Nye and Rose had talked about this problem beforehand. The images from the security cameras would be like a puzzle, each a little piece that might fit together into something useful. The odds were that no single camera would give them what they needed: clear and distinct pictures of the SUV, now known to be a 2013 black Cadillac Escalade, and the driver.

The line of darkened streetlights diminished the likelihood of a clear shot of the driver, Nye knew. Altlander hadn't understood. But he figured Nish, who often kept his own counsel, certainly caught it.

As the running time check in the lower right hand of the video sped on, the command center grew silent. The loud voices and laughter or a stray cry from out in the hallway raucously floated in.

They waited tautly for what none of them wanted to see.

"There it is," Rose said softly. She pointed at the screen.

A dark bulky shape moved rapidly across the gray screen, wraith-like and yet almost a streaking predator against the gray background. It vanished quickly.

Without waiting, Nye rewound and slowed down the replay. They all watched the dark shape again, now slowly stalking forward in jerking movements, along Capitol Mall.

"Anybody make out the make or model?" Nye asked loudly.

"No," Nishimoto said somberly. "You might as well go to the next video."

Rose whispered to him, "What if they're all so dark, Ter?"

"Then they are. We move on," he said.

In the next half hour, their spirits lifted then dropped and lifted again. Videos two, three, and four were clearer, from vantage points on the same side of the street as the Wells Fargo site, and distinctly showed a black SUV hurtling down Capitol Mall and striking the small dark figure half crouched in the street, fumbling an instant before with an overturned traffic cone.

"Kind of like watching the Kennedy assassination," Nye said. "Over and over."

"You can't do anything about it," Rose said to the quiet room, the flickering images going on mindlessly. She only said out loud what everyone had been thinking. There was no way to warn the dark figure of Officer Thomas Ensor as it came into the street, bent over, and then was struck time and time again, flung into the air and sometimes out of camera range. There was no power that could reach out to prevent what had already happened.

"All right, let's stay focused. We don't need this sentimentality.

Officer Ensor certainly doesn't," Altlander called out firmly. For once, Nye agreed with him absolutely.

"Okay, we've got usable side views of the SUV from cameras three and four," Nye said and had the precise times noted by Talman for making photographic blowups that could be circulated around California. "Let's see if we can't get a license number and a look at the driver next."

Rose was unusually solemn and rarely took her eyes off the TV monitor showing the current video. She was willing the image to be what they needed, what would help Ensor. Nye knew the feeling. He had had it once, too. But particularly in Major Crimes where the offenses were irrevocable and often monstrous, you soon settled for being grateful for whatever serviceable evidence might exist, and stopped yearning in vain after ideal proof. Otherwise, you didn't make it all.

The explosion occurred while they were tracking through video six, after finding video five utterly useless, the camera only catching an empty rainy stretch of Capitol Mall. Vu and Parkes swore and the other detectives joined in, everyone forgetting Nishimoto and Altlander until Nishimoto cleared his throat and they quieted down.

Nye said, "We can see that Ensor's not wearing his vest in video six. Same as the earlier ones obviously. Rose, check with Quintana and find out if he remembers when Ensor took off the traffic vest," and Altlander shot up, his chair falling over.

"Tafoya!" he said sharply, "You will not talk to Officer Quintana at this time about that subject. And that goes for the others in this room," he looked pointedly at them as spoke.

"Just a second," Nishimoto's arms had stayed tightly crossed, as if holding himself in, and he did not move or look at Altlander, "these detectives are working on this investigation under my command," and Altlander interrupted angrily.

"Then you better take command, Jerry. When and if"—he went down hard on the last word—"we need to look at Officer Ensor's conduct, that will be Chief Gutierrez's call. It's not Nye's call and it certainly isn't what we've got to do at this point. Our job is to find the damn coward who drove that SUV. Our job is not to make his damn defense for him," and Altlander glared at Nye who stared back at him.

"This is how we do a major crime investigation," Nye said carefully.

"Look, Detective Nye, get it through your head that this is not, all right, repeat, not your usual lunch break, coffee break, smoke break, shift-to-shift investigation. This is flat-out until we get this man and you've got a deadline coming at you like a speeding bullet."

"I know that, sir," Nye said, aware that Rose and the other detectives stood awkwardly caught in the cross fire.

"Damn it, Jerry, how the hell are you running your division?" Altlander demanded, and without waiting for Nishimoto's answer, he stalked from the room, slamming the door.

Nye put his hands in his pockets. He wondered what Altlander might throw at him from IA next. If he and the team moved fast enough, however, he and Rose were untouchable. The gray video images went on shimmering behind him, casting the only light in the room on the faces of the detectives and the deputy chief. "What's the play, Chief?" he asked Nishimoto coolly.

"Concentrate on the driver and the vehicle, Terry."

"Because you don't want reports with anything in them that makes Ensor look bad?"

"There's a time and place for everything," Nishimoto slowly unfolded and stood up, a weary grim smile on his face. "Right now, I agree with Chief Altlander. Our efforts have to be catching the SUV driver."

Nye could tell that Nishimoto was anxious to leave. *He probably figures that Altlander's headed straight for the chief, ready to lay out how the investigation was being screwed up by a short-timer old detective,* Nye reasoned. *Nish wants to get to Chief Gutierrez before the damage is done.*

"Okay by me," Nye said without emotion. "But you should replace me right now with somebody else here."

Nishimoto looked at him silently. The other detectives were silent, too. Rose murmured an uncharacteristic curse under her breath.

Nye didn't blink. Then Nishimoto went to the door. "Tell me you're incompetent, Terry. Tell me you're fumbling this investigation."

"I just don't see how I can do my job," he said.

"Do your job!" Nishimoto snapped at him. "That goes for the rest of you. Let me take care of the sideshow," he said harshly. He left the room.

No one spoke for another few moments. Nye steadied himself because he didn't want to blow up in front of the team. Leave that to desk jockeys like Altlander and even Nish who didn't have people in the field to worry about. Rose spoke up first.

"We've got your back on this, Ter. You're doing okay."

"Definitely okay," Vu said quickly.

"No doubt," Pesce said.

"Yeah, damn straight," Talman chimed in. Parkes nodded beside him.

Nye looked at Rose's so serious expression and felt a small smile creep up on him. "Just okay, you assholes?"

Finally, on video seven that came from the security camera on the front of the State Capitol, Rose saw the driver of the SUV more clearly than any of the previous images. She called out excitedly and pointed, like the first pictures beamed back from the moon or Mars.

"There he is," she said. "Slow it down, Ter, so we can get a good look."

Nye slowed the video play down to a quarter of its normal speed and the small SUV with its even smaller shape visible behind the windshield grew larger as it drew nearer to the camera.

"Call it out," he said.

"White male," Rose said.

"Looks like maybe thirty to forty. Not too old," Vu said.

"No glasses." Parkes added.

"Got all his hair. Looks dark. I can't quite tell," Rose said going closer to the TV.

"No beard, moustache," Pesce said.

"No hat," Talman chimed in.

"I can just see a tie. He's wearing a tie," Rose said, pointing.

Nye said nothing, caught up in what he knew Rose had been fruitlessly doing a few minutes earlier, willing the unknown, unnamed hit-and-run driver to keep coming closer, getting more distinct and describable with each jerked frame of the video.

Then the much sharper image of Tommy Ensor appeared, head down against the rain, unaware of the vehicle swiftly bearing down on him. "Move, Tommy," Nye thought he heard someone softly call out in the darkness. They watched Ensor try to right a fallen traffic cone and clearly saw that he was not wearing the required reflective orange vest for night use in traffic.

"SUV's doing sixty at least," Rose said, eyes fixed on the unchangeable events slowly taking place once again on the TV.

"Seventy easy," Nye corrected from his years on patrol and traffic duty. "Just coming straight down Capitol Mall, no weaving, no lane changes. The guy's not DUI," he said, easily observing that he wasn't driving under the influence of either drugs or alcohol.

"Jesus, Jesus," Vu said involuntarily at the moment of impact, which they all saw more clearly than on any of the other videos.

Nye froze the image immediately after the SUV struck Ensor. The driver was plainly visible, though blurred and oddly inhuman. Nye studied him. He fervently hoped that maybe the tech crew either at the county forensic lab or the state Department of Justice could clean up the picture and get them a better image. Right now the face was anyone's, without the detail stamp of particularity that made it a specific individual.

"His mouth's open," Nye said, gesturing at the TV picture. "Like he's saying something. What is it?"

"It's a warning. Too late. He knows he hit someone," Rose offered.

"I'd be praying," Parkes said soberly.

Nye examined the open-mouthed face, so close to being recognizable and yet so alien. He advanced the video frame by frame, the man's mouth staying open, silent words or a cry, and then he was swerving out of the lane, making a radical left turn off Capitol Mall and out of the video camera's range.

"You're right, Rosie," Nye said, as they prepared to watch the video again, "this guy knows exactly what he did. Right this minute, he knows Ensor's hanging on by a thread. He knows we're looking for him."

She didn't say a word, staring at the TV screen. "I think there's someone else in the SUV."

"Where?"

"Light's really bad, but there's a deeper shadow to the driver's right, like another body." They all stared hard at the video.

"I see a hand," Nye said slowly.

"There are two of the bastards," Rose said angrily.

Nye told Nishimoto.

"I don't want this going outside this building," Nishimoto said. "Nobody says a word. Understood?"

"Definitely." It gave them an edge. It was a critical piece of information against which the truth or falsity of the other information coming at them could be reckoned. It also provided another edge.

"Our guy isn't alone out there," Nishimoto said coldly. "He knows he's got another mouth to worry about."

"That's when it gets scary," Nye agreed.

Thirty frustrating minutes later, they had combed once more through all of the videos, paying special attention to number seven, hoping to catch a more of a glimpse of the second person in the SUV. But aside from the tantalizing hint Rose spotted, there was nothing more, not even the SUV's license plate. Rain, bad lighting, and the haphazard angles of the various cameras made it impossible to see more.

Nye and Pesce laid out segments, the best ones from the videos, so that they could be spliced together by the department's own media staff into a short, punchy package for TV stations. He made arrangements to have all of the videos copied so the department would have a set. Then he called the state Department of Justice. Using the original videos, which would have the best images available, the technicians at the state's mammoth lab on Broadway would employ every computer enhancing trick at their disposal to render a sharp and clean picture of the SUV driver and perhaps bring up something about the passenger. Nye got adamant assurances of priority treatment for the videos.

Feeling exhausted, Nye told Rose and the other detectives he had to go home for a couple of hours sleep. He put them on a rotation, two on, two off, so that none of them would lose an edge by being overtired. "Go see your kid and Luis," he ordered Rose. "Get some rack time yourself. We got another long night coming up."

"I'm okay, old man," she said to him.

"Humor me," he grinned. "I like the idea somebody's seeing their family."

Rose nodded. "Okay, Ter. It's four now. How about we meet back here around eight, start checking SUV dealerships?"

"Done. One condition. You bring your great homemade lumpias for dinner."

"I ain't making lumpias special for your dinner," she protested.

"It's not a deal breaker," Nye pretended to sigh in resignation. "How about whatever you and Luis have for dinner?"

"You are getting too lazy to make your own food," Rose said, turning away with a dismissive wave, as if he had become childish and silly. "All right, I'll bring you a plate, but it won't be fancy."

Nye admitted to himself that he really only wanted to share whatever Rose's family was eating and not feel so alone tonight.

He had half turned his key in the car door when he sensed someone slide up to him under the harsh lights of the department parking lot. Nye straightened. "Do that again, Guth, and I swear I will shoot you."

Guthrie emitted a sound unlike a chuckle but derisive. "Clock's ticking. You haven't given Nish the good news yet."

Nye faced Guthrie. "I'm really tired. And you're more of a wimp than I ever thought, Guth, and I had low expectations."

"Always funny. I'm plowing through twenty years of your garbage and I still keep hitting that family deal in Natomas. Tell me I won't find a lot more if I keep working at that one."

Nye felt a cool twitch along his spine. *Of course, you will,* he thought. But he said, "I'm moving really fast. Try and catch me, you stupid asshole."

He opened the car door and swung inside, slamming it. Guthrie didn't move. He said quietly and distinctly. "I'm right behind you, Nye. Finally. By the way, you told you partner what you did?"

Nye started the car. The cool twitch subsided. He stared ahead as he roughly turned onto the dark street around the police department.

Not yet, he thought miserably. *If I ever can.*

Nye drove with care, because he was more profoundly tired than he wanted Rose or the others to know, and when he got home, he sat in the driveway for a moment before getting out of his car. The encounter with Guthrie disturbed him, rankled. But even more he felt a weight, something ominous and unsettling, pressing on him lately even before the Ensor investigation, and it was hard to move sometimes.

He lived in the same aging brown duplex in East Sacramento he and Marceen had bought right after the kids left. It was a quiet neighborhood, third- and fourth-generation Portuguese mostly, with neat houses and neater lawns, small businesses nearby and a whitewashed tiny Catholic church on the corner. They moved into the duplex when they thought their old house would be too big for them alone. Now, as he opened the front door, stooping to gather up in the mail that had spilled from the slot onto the floor, he dreaded the emptiness of the place, the silence, and how cavernous it seemed with just him in it.

Nye automatically turned on the TV, as he always did first thing when he got home, so there would be voices and other human beings at least electronically in the house. He flipped quickly through the junk mail. His empty house reminded him of his grandfather, who always had the radio on for company after his wife died and it always seemed to be the seventh inning of a Sacramento Solons game. Nye went into the kitchen and got some coffee started. His grandfather retired after thirty-five years as a Sacramento cop. Nye's father was first aghast and then contemptuous when he found out his son intended to apply to the department. Being a cop was a poor way to support a family or have a career. What did you have to show at the end? Too often now, Nye thought his father might have been right after all.

He changed clothes down to his underwear, leaving his holstered service gun on the coffee table, and drank the coffee black in the kitchen. Maybe at the end of a career as a cop he didn't have a business or assets like his father did with his moderately successful restaurant on Freeport Boulevard. But he at least he used to have the irreplaceable electric sensation of connection to people and events. It had gone dead forever until that moment just now back in the command center when he knew he was circling in on the guy who had left Tommy Ensor for dead in the street.

I'm coming, Nye thought, finishing the coffee and rinsing the cup, and he knows I am. It was a cold warning to the unknown, hunted driver.

And to the other bastard out there who knows what happened, too.

The weight pressed hard on him as he went through the untidy living room, a stack of unread and old newspapers and magazines by the dusty green sofa. A lady announcer, casting her eyes around, was speaking rapidly on the TV.

"I thought I just saw Officer Ensor's wife and children go back into the hospital. We'll try to catch up with them. They've been here all night and most of today, but they left just a few hours ago. Now, they've returned suddenly."

Nye's jaw involuntarily tightened.

"I've been told by sources inside Sutter General that Officer Ensor has taken a turn for the worse and has just been rushed back into surgery. There is no immediate word on his condition or what the doctors are trying to do right now. But this latest development isn't good news." She was almost absurdly solemn.

Nye turned off the TV before the announcer could rattle of Ensor's injuries again and went into the bedroom. It was always sepulchrally dim because he never opened the curtains at the windows. He set his clock radio for seven thirty to give him time to get back to the department and meet Rose. The truth was that he could not save Tommy Ensor. No one could do that. Maybe the weight he felt lately was that realization after so many years of denying it, imagining that by working longer harder, by sheer effort, he could change what was set on iron rails. Not true.

Old stuff was rising to the surface of his mind, especially the really bad one and he was unsure whether to unburden himself about it by telling Rose. *Let her know the worst thing you can do,* he thought, *and maybe keep her from doing it, too. Split second, like Maslow said, and your life is different.*

He tried not to think how close that brought him to the driver who hit Tommy.

But he was reluctant about opening up to Rose. Every time it struck him as the solid, right thing to do, an equally powerful voice told him she would think less of him, maybe look down on him. He did not want to leave the department, hell, he did not want to leave her on those terms.

So he remained unsure what to do and it kept bothering him.

All I can do is pick up the pieces, he thought, getting into his unmade bed and pulling the covers up. It was pleasantly cool and dim in the room and when he closed his eyes, he fell asleep quickly.

The noise must be the alarm, he thought at first, fumbling to wake up, a lifelong habit as cop. *Get your bearings fast. Much depended on doing so.*

Nye sat up. It wasn't the radio clock alarm. It was only six P.M. He snatched up the telephone.

"Nye? Nye?" Rose demanded sharply, "Are you awake?"

"Yeah, yeah, I'm awake. What the hell's going on?"

"We've got to move. Get yourself down to the department. I'll meet you outside in twenty, okay?"

"Sure," he said, swinging his legs out of bed, rubbing his eyes. "Tell me something good, Rosie."

"Maybe it's damn good. Talman called me. We've got a solid bite on the witness, Ter. Somebody's got an ID on our possible witness." She couldn't completely restrain her excitement. Even if it turned out to be a dry hole, the promise of a live witness was enough to warrant putting caution aside temporarily.

"I'll see you downtown in twenty minutes, faster if I can do it," he said, catching her enthusiasm.

Nye went into the bathroom and threw cold water on his face and got dressed with practiced efficiency, grabbing his gun on the way out.

He did not want to let his hope overtake reality, but on enough cases he had run, a random spark had lit everything up just when things looked like they would be a hard, tedious slog.

Nye even grinned to himself as he drove downtown. Talman had called Rosie first instead of him. *Let the old man get a couple extra minutes of sleep,* he thought.

Nice.

TWENTY-ONE

STEVENSON DROVE HOME once he dropped Eli off back at his office. "I'll call you tonight," Stevenson told him, "after I get Haley to bed. Take it someplace where you won't be overheard." His father-in-law's reply was quiet, unnerved, but Stevenson knew Eli would cooperate. There were many details still to work out, and yet they both knew the plan Stevenson outlined in the park was the surest, safest, and best way to protect him and the family.

It was a little after four. He had about an hour before he had to pick Haley up at St. Francis and Vee wouldn't be home until later that night. With luck, he figured he could talk to Eli and plot out their next moves about acquiring a new SUV before Vee came home.

Stevenson felt his guts tighten as he pulled into the driveway. The garage door was open. Vee stood at the door, the tan bulk of the covered SUV looming just beyond her. She watched him stop her car. She twisted her wedding ring.

He got out of the car. "You're home early," and it sounded like an accusation even to him. He went to her.

"I couldn't face tonight with the Lenard twins. My secretary

157

dropped me off," Vee said, "so I thought we'd pick Haley up and maybe get a bite out."

"Great," he said with false enthusiasm, "let me change. How about a bit of a dram before we go?" He made a gesture with his thumb and forefinger and pretended he was taking a drink. He didn't like the puzzled, wary way she kept her eyes on him. He was relieved to see that the SUV was covered just as he had left it last night.

"Frank, I took a look at the SUV. I thought I'd get it fixed for you."

Stevenson shook his head angrily. "I told you this morning, I'd take care of it. Why the hell don't you . . ." and she turned back into the garage, yanking at the cover on the SUV.

"What happened, Frank?" Vee said, pulling half of the cover off the SUV so that the ruined front end and cracked windshield were exposed. "What's going on?"

Stevenson jumped forward and grabbed the cover roughly from her hand. The garage was glaringly visible from the sidewalk and the street. "Help me cover this up again," he said abruptly, "then I'll tell you everything inside."

"It was an accident," Stevenson finished, "just a terrible accident."

Vee stood at the kitchen sink, eyes closed, hands gripping the edge of the counter. "We have to talk to the police. Right away."

"You weren't listening, honey," he said with brutal coldness. "It's like I explained to your father, the time for coming forward is long past."

"You shouldn't have involved him. He's not strong now."

"I didn't have a choice. He was with me."

Vee opened her eyes. "I have looked after him my whole life. I can't stop now."

"Everything will work out, Vee. Trust me."

She put her hands on his shoulders. It was reassuring and defiant. "Frank, you're not some ordinary driver who has an accident. You are a Superior Court judge. You are a respected member of the bar and a man people all around this town look up to. That's important. It counts. It all matters." She pulled him toward her, arms around him, head near his face, her grip fierce and determined. "Listen to me," she said several times, insistent, half pleading.

He stared back at her, both of them locked together. He no longer felt like he had last night, lost and frantic. He knew Vee would accept his implacable logic soon. Just as her father had. Because he loved her, he knew she would be with him with utter certainty.

Stevenson kissed her, but she didn't relax her hold. She was talking about how the police would listen to him, to all of the people around Sacramento who would come forward and vouch for him, all of the friends, people he had helped.

He knew none of that mattered.

He was surprised at his own calm. It was relief actually. He had feared being powerless or craven most of his life and, at that moment, he knew he was neither. It was like physically pulling up his climbing partner on Mount Whitney when nature and all reason said they should go back. He gained the summit against the odds, including his own fears.

Stevenson kissed her again. "No, honey," he said gently, "nothing anybody can say now will help me."

"You're giving up!" she said angrily. "You were going to hide this from me!"

"I wanted to make sure you and Haley didn't find out. I don't want either of you to get hurt."

"We're a family, Frank. We're involved no matter what. That's not your choice anymore. Jesus, I don't understand how you're so calm."

"I'm scared to death," he said, not quite truthfully anymore, "but I've got a way to take care of this thing. I am definitely not giving up."

Vee let go of him and he followed her into the living room. Then she turned on him. "I don't know you, Frank. I was always afraid of that and I swear to God, right at this moment, I do not know you."

"I'm just me. No different. No better. No worse."

Vee sat down on a floral upholstered chair near the fireplace they rarely used, even in the damp Sacramento winter. "I always thought," she said, avoiding looking at him, "that if something serious happened to you, you'd come to me. Just like I would go to you first. But you didn't tell me last night. You told my father and I had to find out on my own."

"I'm trying to protect you," he said, standing in the middle of the room, as if he were on trial, and Vee on the bench reckoning his offenses. He knew she was hurt by his decision and angry because Eli was part of the secret before she had anything to say about it.

"I am scared for you," she said with a confused, frightened frown. "I don't know who you are. I don't even know who I am."

He came toward her and bent down, his face brushing her forehead gently. "Vee, we're exactly the same people we were yesterday."

"That's the problem, Frank. Who the hell are we exactly?"

On the way to pick up Haley, Vee retreated into brooding silence. Stevenson left her alone as they drove. She had had a shock and he knew Vee could sort it out. She always did.

Haley noticed the chill in the car from the moment she got in. She gamely told them about practice, what happened in Mrs. Barnabas's class when Joy had to leave because of a stomachache.

"Nobody's listening," Haley said with a low breath. "You're both still mad."

"No, we're just thinking," Vee said without looking back at her. "I heard everything."

"You had quite a day, button. I think we all did. So, Mom and me thought we'd have dinner out, okay?" Stevenson turned and headed along P Street.

"Where would you like to go?" Vee managed a wan smile for Haley. "Your choice."

"Okay," Haley warmed to the prospect. "If I get to pick, I'd like to go to Celeste's."

"Celeste's for Caribbean cuisine, it is," Stevenson said. He knew Haley favored the pulled chicken and rice and it would give Vee a chance to have a mojito or two. There was a great deal to do that evening.

Dinner—chicken and drinks and all—was not a success and Haley ate quietly, glancing at her parents often, then studiously addressing her food as if she had done something wrong. It hurt Stevenson to see her so confused, but there was nothing he could do about it.

Vee drank three mojitos swiftly, picked at her dinner, and then said she had to take a walk. Stevenson and Haley finished together a little later, and when they came out, Vee was standing beside her car, watching the rushing traffic along the street vanish into the hazy Sacramento dusk, ignoring the people ambling to other restaurants along the block.

When they got home, Vee said to Haley, "You've got to go to your room early tonight, hon, all right? You can watch your TV up there."

"But I need to use the computer," Haley protested, "I've got homework." It was part of their family arrangement that she had access to one of the computers in the study after dinner for schoolwork. Neither Stevenson nor Vee wanted her to have a computer in her room just yet.

"You can't tonight," Vee said, a little stiff from the drinks and no food, "Dad and I need the study and that's it."

Haley tried to appeal to him, as she usually did when her mother laid down an edict. Stevenson shook his head. "Nope, that's it, button," he said. "You'll have to do your homework the old-fashioned way tonight. Look on the bright side. You watch TV while you do it."

"That's not a bright side," Haley said grumpily. She eyed them both as Vee went into the kitchen. "I'm sorry if I made you both mad," Haley said to him, part ploy and part desperation. Stevenson heard Vee rummaging around in the refrigerator. It cut him to see Haley's pained, worried expression.

"It's not you at all. Your Mom and I just have a couple of things to sort out and we need to do it tonight."

"Are you getting divorced?" she asked with chilly expectation. Divorce was fairly common among Haley's friends.

"No, we are not getting divorced or even thinking about divorce. Nothing like that."

Haley nodded, not entirely persuaded.

He was not surprised when Vee reappeared a few moments later with a sweating, newly opened bottle of reserve chardonnay they had been saving for their twelfth anniversary in three months. Haley trudged upstairs and he followed Vee into the study, closing the door. She had a glass for one.

"All right, Frank," Vee said from her desk, sipping slowly from her glass, "I've thought about it. We've got to make this work."

"I knew you'd understand as soon," and she went on over him, her eyes a little out of focus from drinking, but her voice rock solid.

"You are a good man, just like I said, but there isn't any way back. I have to look out for my father and you, too. So we'll have to do a lot of things in the next while that we wouldn't ever do otherwise." Vee slowly shook her head and when she looked at him, he saw just three tears on her face. "Afterwards, things won't be the same for you and me. It just won't be because of what we're going to do. You don't trust me."

He had wounded her without intent in the most grievous way. Vee had grown up in a household where love and trust were the rule. "I love you," he said huskily.

She took another drink and turned on her computer. "We better find out what's happening."

Stevenson sat beside her and when he tried to touch her, she shifted wordlessly, as though disturbed by something small and repellent. They watched streaming newscasts on her computer from Sutter General about Officer Ensor's surgery to relieve a blood clot that had developed because of his brain trauma. Then they saw a strange shadow play of a dark SUV soundlessly rushing down a street, always cut off the moment before it struck Officer Ensor, a concession to the sensibilities of the audience.

"That's our SUV," Vee said tonelessly.

"It could be anyone's."

"I don't mean the picture, Frank." And he abruptly grasped her meaning: they were both complicit in the crime now and, by choice, even more so than her father. The burden of what to do next was their shared crime.

Then they watched the reward announcement, grown to nearly seventy-five thousand dollars, and a plea for anyone who had been the area at the time to come forward and contact the Sacramento Police Department. They listened to the vague but threatening description of the black Cadillac Escalade's driver. Vee turned to him as it rolled out, like she was trying to match the words to him. The description was too broad.

"What about my dad?"

"It sounds like the cameras just caught me."

"I wish we'd known that before you told him."

"It wouldn't have made any difference."

He shut off the newscast, leaving a glowing screen waiting for the next commands, when the stories shifted to profiles of Officer Ensor and his family. Vee didn't stop him.

She had gone through almost half the bottle of chardonnay. She put her hands over her eyes for a second. He felt very far from her, unsure how to bring her back.

"I should call your father," he said. "I left it with him that we'd talk about now. There are a lot of nitty-gritty details to sort out."

"My dad isn't the original detail man. You and I'll have to handle them," she said, letting out a breath. "You better call him and tell him to come on over."

Stevenson nodded and called Eli. His mind was sorting out everything he had just heard. The police now had a positive picture of the SUV. That narrowed things down and made his plan imperative. They did not have a good physical description of him, but what they did have was troublesome enough when coupled with the information about the SUV. All around Northern California and beyond, but especially in Sacramento, people were idly sifting through who they knew, who drove black SUVs, who drove that particular model SUV.

On the positive side, the police did not know about Eli. They did not have any description of a second person in the SUV.

Stevenson waited for Eli with Vee. Suddenly he felt the mounting apprehension fight through his calm. He pushed it back with great inner effort. Vee was watching a newscast again and drinking slowly. He had to stay strong.

"Frank?" his father-in-law's voice was tentative and quavered. He sounded almost comic.

"We're waiting for you, Eli," he glanced at Vee.

"I think we should meet someplace first. I'll pick you up in five minutes."

"What's going on?"

"Please, just you. Don't bring Vee."

Stevenson started to say more but the call abruptly ended.

"Frank?" Vee asked, the glass trembling slightly in her hand. "What did Dad want?"

"I really don't know."

Stevenson made a garbled reason for meeting Eli alone, and Vee only nodded, unwilling to probe further, preoccupied with her own thoughts. When the sleek blue Jaguar pulled up, Stevenson had just come out of his front door.

He lurched inside when he saw that Eli was not alone.

"Evening, Judge," said Buzz Fonseca, hands casually draped over the leather covered steering wheel. Eli sat hunched forward in the backseat. "Please join us."

Slowly, Stevenson got in and the car pulled smoothly and powerfully down the street. It smelled of cigar and lime aftershave. He frantically tried to sort out what was going on. Fonseca was a wealthy lobbyist with high-end clients in wine, electronics, and insurance. He was in his late fifties, tending toward fat, but still enough of the graceful athlete who starred on the Sacramento State baseball team decades earlier. His steel-gray hair was swept back and his thick, amber-framed glasses glimmered as they passed under streetlights. He had one cousin in the State Senate and another was mayor of San Diego. He was grooming his oldest son to run for the Assembly because, as the local joke went, there was always a Fonseca in the legislature.

He had been at the fund-raiser the day before, too. Stevenson remembered the hearty laugh, grip on his elbow, and the pledge of a substantial campaign contribution when it was needed.

"This is a bad night, Buzz," Stevenson said, staring ahead at the shadowy street and the long line of gaudy bright franchise businesses and restaurants. "Eli and I have some family matters to work on," and Fonseca nodded, his voice bass and jovial.

"Of course you do. Eli's told me all about it. Let's drive for a few minutes and discuss things."

Stevenson sat back, his back tight and hard. He half turned his head and looked at Eli, shadows splashing over the older man in the dark backseat. What the hell had Eli done?

"A few minutes," Stevenson said tautly.

"I won't impose," Fonseca said genially, "I'm a very big admirer of yours, Judge. You know that. This Third District Court of Appeal appointment's going to come through. I have a sense for things like this," he leaned a little toward Stevenson, who stayed fixed rigidly, "and a few sources in the Governor's Office. Then, you'll have to run for a full term in two years?"

"If I get the appointment, I'll be filling Justice Gallegly's unexpired term."

"Well, when you run, I intend to make a contribution to the legal limit. I know you'll be a superb appellate judge."

"Thank you, Buzz."

Stevenson heard Eli clearing his throat. "I had to call him, Frank. For Vee and Haley's sake. We need help."

Stevenson's jaw tightened and his anger mingled with fear.

Fonseca nodded, gesturing with one hand, the other loosely on the steering wheel. Like he owns the street, Stevenson thought.

"A terrible thing, Judge. It could happen to anyone and I'm so sorry it happened to a man like you." He paused and Stevenson understood the purpose: Do you want me to spell it all out?

"Please make your point."

"I don't have one. Eli's a little confused. I would very much like to help you. Trust me. But if I did anything along those lines, say talk to friends in the police department, or give you assistance with whatever you're planning to do, then haven't I committed some sort of conspiracy?"

"Yes. You've committed obvert acts and you'd be as guilty as me."

"Well, I can't afford that, Judge."

Stevenson closed his eyes briefly. "What do you want?"

"Not one damn thing."

Eli pressed up against the front seat in panic. "I thought you'd help, Buzz. I trusted you."

"I apologize for any misunderstanding, Eli," Fonseca glanced in the rearview mirror at the anguished face. "I can't do anything. I suppose that's not accurate. I won't do anything."

"Be specific," Stevenson snapped. His fear was barely under control.

"I won't inform the police or anybody outside of this car what I know happened. I will be a silent, loyal ally in the shadows, Judge."

"Take me home. Now." Stevenson shook his head in angry confusion.

"Of course," the carelessly draped hand spun the wheel in mid-street, turning them in arc, which would have been dangerous if there had been any traffic. "I do have a case in your courthouse, Judge. A trivial thing. Some former partners in a real estate deal are claiming I hid monies from them, cooked the books," he chuckled, rolling his big shoulders. "It's coming up in Judge Berry's courtroom, but I think you would easily sort through the simple facts of the case, Judge, and realize it has no merit."

Stevenson's frustrated fury at his weak father-in-law receded into the back of his consciousness. A split second had not only put his whole family at risk but also now his very heart and soul.

"It's not possible," he said, low. "Master Calendar makes the assignments and your matter has been assigned."

Fonseca waved a big hand as if brushing away small darting bugs. "There are always wheels. I know. But I'm certain of your ability to bring this simple case into your courtroom."

"Maybe I can't."

"You won't shake my faith in your talents, Judge."

"For the sake of argument, I manage to get your matter transferred to me. You don't expect me to just rule for you?" His voice was suddenly petulant and he barely recognized it.

"You will do what is right," Fonseca said carefully. He slowed the car. "Here we are, back where we started."

Stevenson jumped out of the claustrophobic confines of the expensive car, trailed by his father-in-law. Of course he was back in front of his own house, on his street; he had been on this treadmill since the accident.

I'm going in a great, monstrous circle, he thought.

He heard Fonseca jauntily say good night, felt Eli at his side as he half marched forward. There was no choice. He had to go all the way.

"You're shellacked," Eli said when he saw his daughter. He kissed her forlornly, eyes down when he glanced at Stevenson. "You should leave that to me, honey." He tossed his suit coat onto a chair and paced the study, the door closed.

When he came near, she stroked his face for a moment and murmured to him.

Stevenson stood beside Vee. He fought to control himself. He could not think about Fonseca's precisely implied blackmail. He could not even think about Eli's weakness and folly. Focus on the objective.

The lights were on in the study, the computers running a nature program with the volume up in case Haley crept near the study door.

"Did you check dealerships, Eli?" Stevenson asked. He didn't want them all to sink into maudlin paralysis.

"Yes, I did. There are three within about twenty miles of here that have SUVs like yours. I omitted the one you bought yours from. Seemed too incestuous to go back there."

Vee stirred and stood up, a little unsteadily. She swallowed and blinked to clear her eyes. "Tell me how this works, Frank. Slowly."

"Okay. The problem is to conceal what happened, the damage to my SUV. Normally if you have an accident, you just take the vehicle in, get it repaired. I can't do that."

"Can't go to some good old boy or *vato* with a couple of tools either, you know, get it done, pay cash. Whoever you go to is going to see the reward or figure out there's a damn good reason to turn you in," Eli said. He was lightly braced, but he had not been drinking heavily, Stevenson noted. Just enough to pick up the phone to call an old pal like Buzz Fonseca who had poured millions into the bank.

Stevenson nodded. "I can't avoid driving my SUV either. People will notice. There's a good description and pictures of the SUV out now and a half-assed description of the driver."

"But not the passenger," Vee said distinctly.

"You should feel a little relief," Stevenson said to Eli.

"Not very much, I'm afraid."

"But I'm the driver," Stevenson went on. "Which means it's vital for me to look like nothing's happened. I have to be in my SUV as soon as I can, driving it like I usually do."

"Frank's brilliant idea is for me to go buy an identical SUV tomorrow," Eli said, holding the wine bottle and giving it a quick, critical assessment, "so it's in someone else's name in case the police start checking recent SUV sales."

"I think they're going to look for prior sales, prior to the accident," Stevenson said, "that's how an investigation goes. They'll focus on people who owned SUVs that match the description, not people buying new ones. Besides, it will take some high jumps to link Eli to me. Different names."

Eli said, "Won't those detectives look for something like this?"

"They've never heard of anyone doing this."

"Look at us. Criminal masterminds," Vee said sadly, glancing at her gentle father and her successful husband.

"No," Stevenson said quietly, "that's our problem, Vee. None of us knows anyone to go to. We don't have criminal contacts."

"So we're starting our own gang."

Wearily, Eli sat down heavily in a chair, staring at his hands. "Okay, Frank, I'll buy the SUV tomorrow. We'll work out the time and make the switch. I'll call you."

You owe me that, you stupid old man, Stevenson thought bitterly.

Stevenson stared at the pride of lions roaring over a kill on the computer screen. "Good. Great. We have to figure out someplace you can hide my SUV, Eli. I don't know offhand—"

"What a gang," Vee broke in. "Dad, you can't keep our SUV. Where are you going to put it? Someone sees you in it, we're no better off than we are now."

"Between now and tomorrow, we'll come up with a solution," Stevenson said, trying to rally them. "I've got great faith in the combined brainpower and goodwill in this room."

He meant it to sound pretentious and ironic and true all at once, and he was startled when Vee took him seriously. She didn't appear unsteady anymore, as if the alcohol had burned off. "I know where to put the SUV safe and sound, Frank. Out of sight completely and we control access."

"What do you have in mind?"

"I'll rent a large public storage unit tomorrow. You, me, and Dad will coordinate moving the SUV tomorrow night. Bring the new one here, get ours into a locked storage unit."

"That's a terrific idea, Vee," he said sincerely.

Eli nodded, sitting up. "I like it."

Stevenson kissed her and she did not move away. "Thanks for being so smart," he murmured. She kissed him hard, clinging again as if he was about to be torn away. When she reached for the last of the wine, he could see she was gently crying again.

"Those two detectives, Eli? We'll be one or maybe two steps ahead of them all the time."

The older man nodded a little uncertainly.

"Vee reminded me of one other big advantage we have to work with no matter what the police do," Stevenson continued, smiling achingly. Vee switched off the computer. Eli folded his arms and got up.

"I'd like to hear our ace in the hole."

Stevenson touched Vee's hand tenderly "I'm a judge. I'm a respected judge."

TWENTY-TWO

NYE LEFT HIS CAR IN THE DEPARTMENT parking lot. He met Rose and they drove the rest of the way downtown in her car. The streetlights and store lights were still on in the early dusk, people and shadows intermingling. The traffic along the main streets leading into and out of downtown Sacramento was heavy for a weeknight. A concert by some aging rock band at the convention center on J Street clogged traffic for a mile in every direction.

Rose parked on L Street just across from the noisy Greyhound bus terminal. Exhaust belched from a string of lumbering buses heading south toward Fresno and Los Angeles or north to Oregon. Passengers and other people, with cigarettes or half-eaten McDonald's hamburgers in hand, loitered outside the instant passport photo shop and the liquor store next to the terminal. They all watched with angry, wary eyes when Rose and Nye walked over.

"It's always nice to be noticed," Rose said sourly as they crossed the street. "I bet I could point and find a dozen rap sheets," she gestured.

"My granddad used to make a lot of busts in the restroom

over there," Nye jerked a finger at the bus terminal. "When he had a slow day, he said he and his partner could count on something going on there to liven it up. Drunk rolls, drug sales, and the occasional weird-ass thing like a guy one time passing out counterfeit twenties."

"It's a lack of self-respect, Ter," Rose said, opening the grimy glass door of the rundown Marshall Hotel. "Just because you don't have much money doesn't mean you have to be a puke."

"Indeed," he agreed, not wanting to argue with her. They were both keyed up by the solid prospect of a witness to Ensor's hit-and-run, but likewise afraid that the witness would be worthless. Nye assumed he was hearing Rose's way of blowing off steam, the life philosophy of a poor girl from Cebu City who pulled herself up from despair and demanded that anyone could do the same.

They went past the caged front desk in the lobby to a discolored green elevator. Three men in cheap clothes on a cracked sofa went on arguing about baseball or some personal insult, while observing Nye and Rose carefully. An older skinny man in a sweat-stained Hawaiian shirt rested on his arms inside the cage.

"Need some help?" the man called to them as they waited for the elevator.

"All set," Nye answered without looking at him.

"Seeing someone?"

Rose said, "We're fine. Except you've got the slowest elevator in the city here."

One of the men laughed, said something in Spanish, and gave out a phlegmy cough. Nye noted the green faux-marble ashtray stands, filled with sand and placed throughout the dirty lobby. *You don't see those much anymore,* he thought. *Violates some city or state law, as if anybody cared.*

"It's slow for sure," the man in the cage said. "Maybe whoever you're going to see isn't there."

"We'll take care of it, thanks," Nye said as the elevator finally arrived, the doors opening jerkily and noisily.

In the elevator, Rose wrinkled her nose at the stink from a puddle in one corner. They felt the elevator rising to the fifth floor slowly and with reluctance. "Hey, Ter," she said tensely, "you know the Unabomber?"

"Not personally."

"So funny. He stayed here awhile. When he wasn't living in that shack in the woods between bombings, he stayed here, this dump."

"I bet the shack looked good," Nye said as the elevator door opened onto a corridor of ripped, faded red carpet. At both ends, the fire escape windows were open to the city sounds and let in vagrant night breezes. Shouts and TV sounds came from behind the thickly painted doors. Nye and Rose went to number 516, listened for a moment, Rose's face tight. He knocked loudly. She stood to one side, taut as a stretched wire.

"Mr. Pursley?" Nye said. "You called a little while ago. We'd like to talk to you." Nye and Rose agreed they didn't want to announce they were cops. Besides, Pursley said he'd be waiting for them. Nye knocked again. "Mr. Pursley? You there?"

Rose shook her head slightly. Her mouth tightened. Nye sighed. Emptiness radiated out from the room. An empty room had a resonance all its own and, after encountering it for years, he could recognize it right away. Their tipster was gone.

On the way back down in the elevator, Rose said, "Let me do the talking, Ter."

"Be my guest."

She marched up to the cage, the men on the sofa pausing to watch and be entertained.

"Excuse me," she said. "We're looking for Jerome Pursley in room 516."

"Pursley?" the clerk asked with mild surprise. "What's he done?"

"Where is he?"

"Can you tell me why the police are looking for him? The owners here like to know when guests go south. It hurts our image."

"No, sir, I can't," she said coldly. "If you know where he is, please tell us right now."

The Hawaiian-shirted clerk pursed his lips and pondered. *Something he's seen on TV or in the movies,* Nye thought, wondering when that started. *Rose was certainly right about this guy. His rap sheet would undoubtedly be depressing and mundane. No felonies,* Nye surmised, *probably a bunch of misdemeanors like drunk in public or some drugs.*

"If it helps you think," Nye said mildly, "I can spot about four or five health and safety violations right off," he pointed at the barred windows, "and those ashtrays don't look good either." *He had seen this scene on TV or a movie, too, or something very like it.* The other possible scene, which was not his style, was the one his grandfather gleefully bragged about: using a nightstick freely and merrily on a minor league puke, like this clerk.

"I don't want to put you to any trouble," the clerk said, and someone on the sofa chortled and mutterings in Spanish went back and forth. "Pursley left about twenty minutes ago, right?"

He looked for confirmation at the sofa and one man nodded, *"Si, si,"* he agreed.

"Do you know where he went? When he's coming back?" Rose asked sharply.

"You probably just missed him," the clerk said with mock dismay. "He went across the way to the bus station."

"You should've told us he checked out," Nye wagged a finger at him with a grin. The clerk grinned back. Rose was already heading out the doors.

"He didn't check out," the clerk said. "He said he was taking a trip. He's an old resident. We value his patronage."

Nye smiled again and the clerk's smile faded when he really saw it. He started to apologize, but Nye was half out the glass doors when one of the sofa audience piped up.

"He say, '*Bakersfield,*'" the man wagged his head in feigned fright, "'*I go to Bakersfield.*' Yah. Nice town. Get away."

For some reason, the notion of the dusty sun-fried city in California's central valley as a nice town set the men on the sofa rolling with laughter.

Nye turned around, still smiling, and beckoned to the clerk.

"Come on," Nye said softly, "you better show us what he looks like."

The next bus to Bakersfield was loudly idling in the cavernous terminal, people slowly getting on, wrestling with suitcases and oddly shaped packages. Rose gaped as a man with multiple facial piercings struggled to get on with his large bow and quiver of handmade arrows.

"See Pursley?" she asked the hotel clerk as they scanned people at the bus windows and waiting to board. Nye had done a walk-through with the clerk a few moments before. The bus was scheduled to leave in fifteen minutes.

"No, he's not here. I don't see him," the clerk said, smiling too frequently at Rose, futile efforts to ingratiate himself.

Nye said, "Okay, Rosie, stay here and keep an eye out. Hold the bus if you have to."

"Where you going?"

"Taking my grandad's advice," he winked, pulling the clerk with him.

They did a sweep through the terminal lobby as they headed for the restrooms, the clerk shaking his head as they passed through the throng of people. It was possible that Pursley was grabbing a bite at the McDonald's adjacent to the bus station or that he was waiting outside until the last minute or that he got caught up drinking some-place. Anything was possible, but Nye didn't want to admit that a tipster who'd called boasting that he could produce their eyewitness to the hit-and-run had just slipped away from them.

The large men's restroom was white tile, stank of strong disin-fectant, and had vending machines and old-fashioned coin-weighing machines along the walls. Men stood at the wall of mirrors, combing their hair, adjusting their pants, washing their hands, staring guardedly as Nye and the hotel clerk came in and stood in the doorway. *Nice to be noticed,* Nye thought, remembering Rose's words. He thought his grandfather had probably gotten the identical reception years ago.

Nye spotted the tall man in a stained peacoat before the hotel clerk even raised a hand to point him out. The other men finished whatever they were doing and moved away, leaving the restroom.

Nye went up to a tall man remaining at the sink, tap running. The man didn't look up. He was some age between forty and eighty, wrinkled, unshaven, and balding. He smelled of old tobacco smoke and oranges.

"Mr. Pursley?" Nye said firmly. "We need to talk."

"Who are you?"

"You called us."

"Leave me alone." He tried to move away, head still down, mouth working.

"We're walking out," Nye said, taking his spindly arm tightly, "so you better be ready to tell me what you bragged about when you called."

Pursley's face moved anxiously. "Judas," he spat as he passed the hotel clerk.

They got Pursley settled in the backseat of Rose's car with Nye and a large, heavily sugared coffee from McDonald's. Nye assumed Pursley was a tweaker, a meth addict, and would appreciate the sweetener. The preliminaries with him took long enough that they all watched the Bakersfield bus pull out.

For all of that Pursley seemed right at home in the backseat of a cop car with two cops.

"What's his name?" Rose asked Pursley. "The guy who saw the accident? What's his name?"

"I changed my mind," Pursley said, sipping the coffee and making a happy face.

"Kind of late for that, Jerome," Nye said. He glanced at him and made a quick, and, he was convinced, accurate estimate. "What's the beef?"

"I got a warrant from Texas. Couple years old, nothing big, but they still want me, I guess."

Rose, who sat half turned in the seat so she could watch their informant, made a slight movement of her head. "Stay here, Mr. Pursley, my partner and I need a second."

Pursley nodded and sipped, sitting back. Nye got out and went to Rose beside the car. They spoke low, quickly and intently.

"What do you want to do, Ter?" she asked, plainly not happy.

"We could run him and find out what the warrant's for."

"We could just ask him."

"We could do that, too," Nye admitted, hesitating only long enough to see if Rose was going in the same direction he was. "Then we'd know what it was anyway."

"And we'd have to do something about it," Rose said, shaking her head in disgust. "And maybe lose him and his witness."

"That's the risk.

"I want that witness." She tapped the car roof lightly. "How about we ask him if it's serious, make him stand up that much, then if he swears it's a minor deal, we pass."

"Works for me, Rosie," Nye said, thankful she'd chosen the course he hoped.

"We've made a bunch more deals in the last shift than I did in a couple of years, Ter," she said. "I've got places I won't go, all right? You know that, don't you? Even for this investigation, I'm not going to make any deal that comes along."

"Me, too," he said. "I honestly don't think we've crossed any lines so far. We've just taken care of business because a lot's at stake."

She nodded glumly and they got back in the car. Pursley sat scrunched into a corner of the backseat, clutching his coffee. *Prison reflex,* Nye thought, *so the next guy in the chow line or at your table doesn't steal your dessert.*

"Okay, Jerome," Nye said, "this Texas deal, it's nothing big, right? You're telling us it's nothing we should get all excited about and call them about right now?"

"Just some bullshit years ago. I was dumb. It's dumb," he waved a thin hand at invisible smoke.

Nye looked at Rose, who let out a small breath and nodded slightly. She said, "So what's the name of your friend, the man who witnessed the accident, Mr. Pursley?"

"Doobie. Doobie Rudloff," Pursley said brightly. He finished his coffee in two large slugs. "He came to my place last night, all excited, and he goes, 'I seen this cop get creamed' and he told me all about it and he seen the guy who did it and told me. Then we saw that picture on TV, Doobie's face and you guys looking for him."

Rose made notes. "What's Doobie's true name? Where is he?"

"Doobie. I don't know. That's all I ever heard. He's over at Loaves and Fishes over on 12th, you know where that is?"

Nye nodded. Every city cop was familiar with the Catholic charity that provided housing and free meals for dozens of homeless men and women. While undoubtedly a good and generous enterprise, it generated dozens of police calls every year from fights to stabbings and abandoned children.

"Is he at Loaves and Fishes now?" Rose asked, trying not to let her anticipation show.

Pursley shook his head, "No, they only let him stay when he's on his meds. He's been off for a while so they kicked him out couple days ago. I sneak him into the Marshall, let him bunk with me."

Nye felt his heart fall. Rudloff sounded like a standard-issue street schizophrenic or substance abuser or both. His observations would be tainted from the outset. But we don't know how bad it is until we hear him ourselves, Nye thought.

"Okay, so if Doobie's not at Loaves and Fishes and he ain't with you, where the hell is he, Jerome?" Nye asked peevishly.

Pursley shifted nervously in the backseat and looked for help to Rose, which was pointless. "He's leaving. He said he's going to Tacoma, maybe someplace else up north."

Rose swore involuntarily. "How is he getting there, Mr. Pursley?"

Nye slowly and gently pulled Pursley upright in the seat by his peacoat. "Get it right, Jerome. Because if you give us bullshit, we will come after you and personally deliver you to the fine folks in Austin. And it ain't me you should worry about. My partner's the tough one."

Pursley shook slightly, possibly from the sugar rush or fear. His sunken face was earnest. "Me and Doobie just wanted the reward. Cop getting creamed, it's bad and we wanted to help you," he twisted to look at Rose, "then it didn't feel so great suddenly, and he split and I was splitting." Nye broke in, still holding the peacoat.

"Where, Jerome? Doobie is right now . . ." and he helpfully moved one hand in the air to indicate travel.

"He's getting on the first freight going north, maybe he's gone already," Pursley jabbered. "He's over at the trains, you know, the train yard near the federal courthouse? He went over there couple hours ago."

Nye let go of the coat and sat back. "Get out, Jerome." He slid out the other door as Pursley got out, walked away hurriedly, then turned and came back. Rose had the engine started. Pursley leaned in.

"I'm sorry, okay? I want to help, no bullshit."

"Thank you, Mr. Pursley," Rose said, putting the car in gear.

"Look, when you try to find Doobie, take it easy, okay? He's all wired."

"He got any weapons?" Nye asked.

"Sometimes he's got this Buck knife. I don't know what else."

"Why is he jacked up, Mr. Pursley?" Rose asked.

"He's kind of nervous on freights, okay? He got into some fucked deal with the FTRA and he's pretty sure they're after him."

"FTRA?" Rose looked puzzled at Nye.

"Freight Train Riders of America," Nye said, reaching for the car's radio microphone. "It's a gang that rides the rails. They kill people."

"Yeah, they are bad fuckers," Pursley agreed, walking quickly into the city night.

"We need backup," Rose said, making a left turn and heading across downtown toward the sprawling Southern Pacific rail yard a mile away.

"Oh, to be sure," Nye said sardonically, then to the police dispatcher, "Hey, patch me into the SP cops. See if you can find Rick Solorio, he's their captain." Nye waited for the patched reply. "Solorio's an old bud. He loves my ass."

"Everybody does," Rose said. "You're lovable."

Another spray of gunfire came from Nye's right as he crouched beside the shattered windows and brick front of the enormous empty Locomotive Works. He hunkered lower, trying to see Rose again in the gloom around the deserted buildings of the old rail yard. It was night. The only lights came from the beams over the tracks and around the Amtrak station nearby where cops were hurriedly hustling people off the platforms.

It had been only fifteen minutes ago that he and Rose linked up with Solorio and three other Southern Pacific cops and started trolling the yard for Doobie Rudloff. Solorio was paunchy, salty and in good humor, certain he knew where a street bum like Rudloff would hide. He would wait, off in the shadows, for a freight train to come in, and then jump into an unlocked car or climb onto a flat car.

They clambered over jumbles of rotting rail ties scattered over the yard, through weedy stretches around the abandoned great buildings from the yard's heyday. The ground was soft and muddy from the heavy rain last night. The musk of ancient diesel oil and creosote hung over it all. Close by, separated from them by high new security chain-link fences, was the Amtrak station, passengers gathering on the southbound platform for the *Coast Starlight*'s arrival.

Nye and Rose briefed the SP cops about Rudloff's likely behavior when they spotted him, so everyone was prepared to go gingerly.

Rose saw him first about a hundred yards away near a deserted passenger car, the tall, bearded man still in his poncho, just as Senator Clarke described him. She motioned silently to Nye. He nodded and touched Solorio's shoulder.

"Hey, motherfucker!" Solorio called out to him. Rudloff turned instantly and lit out, disappearing into a warren of old brick buildings, with Solorio, Rose, and a furious Nye in close pursuit. The other SP cops fanned out around the buildings to cut off Rudloff's escape. Nye cursed Solorio's incredible idiocy.

Nye tripped several times as they darted across weed-choked rails. Rose sprinted lithely ahead of him, alongside the surprisingly swift Solorio who had his baton drawn like a sword.

Nye heard the first spatter of gunshots a moment later, off to the left, away from Rudloff's last path. He called out to Rose, and, in the same second, Solorio dropped soundlessly face forward.

Nye saw Rose drop into a crouch and scurry into the shadows of the brick Locomotive Works as more gunshots echoed among the buildings and muddy streets of the yard. He pushed himself against the brick wall, shielded by broken scaffolding, and tried his radio. He couldn't raise the SP cops for some reason and Rose didn't answer either.

Nye cursed. He had only the vaguest idea where he was. He could orient himself a little by the Amtrak station, but, from where he was huddled up, he had no sense of where the unlit streets and buildings lay. He felt his heart heavily and his age, and marveled, for a moment, that he was in the middle of a city he had lived in all of his life, within a mile or so of the State Capitol, and yet he was as lost and vulnerable as if he had been dropped on the surface of the moon.

He tried the radio again. Rose's voice crackled through.

"I can see you, Ter. You okay?"

"Solorio's down. Get some help."

"I'm trying. I've got one of the SP guys here with me. He's talking to their dispatcher and they're sending backup." She didn't sound excited or frightened.

"Where's Rudloff?"

"Somewhere off to your left. In that bunch of—" she hissed and crackled and came back on, "the SP guy says near the old railroad cars. See them? About fifty yards from you."

"I'm heading that way," Nye decided. "How many assholes out there?"

"I count three. Who the hell are they are?"

"Rudloff's buds. Or his enemies. Let's just get him safe and figure it out."

Rose agreed to work her way toward the jumble of rotting old passenger rail cars on an unused siding. They both heard the incoming throb of sheriff's helicopters, ready to blast the entire rail yard with a fierce overhead light. Not far behind would be the news helicopters.

Nye took several deep, steadying breaths. He checked his service weapon, a Sig. Far behind him he heard the call of the incoming *Coast Starlight,* hooting to announce its arrival.

He cursed as he started forward, staying close to the brick wall of the Locomotive Works, his shoes crunching glass from the long shattered high windows. *We should've been more careful,* he thought angrily. *One cop down, Rose under fire, other cops getting shot at, and our witness may get killed in cross fire or by some unseen puke shooting at anything that moved.*

Nye bent low, which hurt his back. He assumed that the shooters were FTRA and the shooting had started when Rudloff had stumbled into them. Or he and Rose, and the other cops, had blundered into some transaction between Rudloff and the Train Riders.

Whatever the case, Nye found himself repeating silently, *Don't kill my witness, don't kill my witness.*

Faint streetlight from the Amtrak station shone through the ragged windows of the rotting rail cars when he got up to them, a little surprised and very grateful that there hadn't been any shots in his direction. He could make out the chipped lettering on the cars, *Union Pacific Railroad.* He stopped, listening. The helicopters were closer, and already he saw the ghostly bright cone of light shafting down, dancing over the grotesque twisted shapes of the rail yard.

At that moment, off to his left a few feet away, came a crackle of dry leaves and weeds as someone moved among them. Nye fervently hoped whoever was up in the helicopters was good and not getting overly anxious. Sometimes the sheriff's snipers rode in the helicopters. *Just don't shoot me or Rose,* he prayed, sliding along the rusted wheel chassis of the rail car toward the sound of movement. In the shadows and jumble below them, the snipers would have to be good to avoid hitting a cop.

Or my witness, Nye thought.

A booming bass voice came from the lead helicopter, ordering everyone to freeze and throw down their weapons, hands up, and then to lie prone on the ground.

Nye lurched and was about to shoot when he suddenly felt someone beside him.

"It's me, Ter," Rose said quietly. He could barely make her out in the shadows.

"I know, I know," he said, lying to hide his relief as much as his tension. "I don't see Rudloff."

Rose started to answer, then stopped. He heard the rustling in the weeds, too. She gestured with one hand to the right and held up one finger, pointing. Nye nodded. One person coming up near them. Presumably unaware that they were hiding against the rail car.

Shots spattered close by and there was the sound of running and someone shouted incoherently. The helicopter light swirled around the landscape crazily and the bass voice above commanded again.

Nye and Rose moved cautiously forward toward the sounds nearest them, guns ready.

The *Coast Starlight* hooted imperiously down the tracks and Nye almost jumped. He wondered why Amtrak hadn't stopped the train before it got this close to the shooting. The answer came to him from a distant part of his mind observing the whole scene: *The goddamn government can't do anything right.*

Rose leapt ahead of him abruptly, tackling a skinny figure in a poncho. Rudloff gabbled in fright and rage, and tried to get free of her iron grip. They were in a small weedy clearing on the siding, between two tilted ancient passenger cars. Nye called out to Rudloff that they were cops, and he was nearly on top of Rudloff with Rose when shots splintered the nearest rail car. Nye threw himself down, over Rose and the upper half of Rudloff. She was busy trying to control him and couldn't shoot. Nye fired three times and another shot tore a chunk of old wood and paint from the rail car beside him.

In a split second, the small clearing was bathed in a cold, white light that jerkily moved around them like a spectral form. There were more shots. Then a volley that seemed to go on forever. Nye was aware of his trembling arms thrown protectively across Rose who, in turn, tried to grab Rudloff's arms, the screaming man beneath him. A voice from somewhere in the dark sky demanded obedience while puffs of dirt sprayed out all around them from invisible high-powered rifle bullets.

TWENTY-THREE

NISHIMOTO CAME BACK into the interview room and put a paper cup of coffee in a cardboard holder on the metal table. He didn't sit down.

"It's from the machine. I wouldn't touch it," he said to Nye.

"Thanks, boss," Nye said, reaching for it. "How's Rose doing?"

"Very nicely. The shooting review's just getting started, of course. You both will be up to your asses in interviews and reports for the next century. But she's solid, Nye."

Nye nodded. He was very tired again and felt almost weightless oddly enough. It was closing on midnight and he and the assistant chief were in one of the interview rooms on the third floor, going over the events of the previous few hours. And going over them again, just as he had with the detectives conducting the postmortem of the events at the rail yard earlier in the evening. It had not been pleasant.

"Anything about Solorio?" Nye asked. He burned his mouth on the bitter coffee and set it down. He could see himself in the one-way mirror across the back wall of the room. *Jesus,* he thought, *I do look like an old jackass.*

"Died an hour ago," Nishimoto said tonelessly. He folded his arms. "Quite a fuck-up."

"He was a good guy," Nye said. He felt too hollow to say more. "Are we about done, boss?"

"I think so. I've just briefed the chief and he's satisfied neither you nor Tafoya were responsible for what happened. Comes to that, Solorio wasn't, either. The pukes would have started shooting as soon as you were out in the open."

Nye tried the coffee again and stood up. Two shooters were in custody, both wanted in Placer County on murder warrants, both suspected of being members of the shadowy and violent Freight Train Riders of America. The third, whom Rose and the SP cops saw, had disappeared. There was a large-scale hunt on for him.

"If we're okay for now, I'd like to get Rose and talk to our witness."

Nye didn't like Nishimoto's cold hesitation. The assistant chief paced to the mirror and studied it. He turned finally.

"By rights I should drop you off this investigation. Tafoya, too. You're both going to be front and center in a shooting review, one officer dead. You can imagine our media crew's going crazy right now between Ensor and you and Tafoya."

"I got that message loud and clear from Guthrie, boss. So I assumed it was coming from Altlander."

Nishimoto stared at Nye. "I want to hear it."

So Nye told him. Nishimoto snorted and paced back and forth, shaking his head. Then he said, "I'll deal with IA and try to keep them off your back. Altlander and I are heading for our rendezvous anyway."

"Think Guth might try to hang Tafoya and me about tonight?"

"He might. You gave him the goddamn rope." Nishimoto swore into empty space.

"Rudloff's our witness. Anything that happens to us down the line, I'm ready, I know Rose is, too. But for right now, he's ours."

Nye was defiant. His own future did not matter to him, but he was fearful for Rose. If she were dropped from the Ensor investigation now, it would be one of those marks that never would be erased from her record. Not the formal record, in files or on the computer screen, but the more important, informal record that shows up in a colleague's casual remark or a superior officer's shake of the head.

There is no process to clear that informal record, but it could swiftly stall or destroy a career.

"For right now, I'll go along with that," Nishimoto finally said, he motioned Nye and opened the door. "You and Tafoya take Rudloff into interview room number five and get his statement. He's a lot quieter than when you brought him in."

"Thanks," Nye said curtly, not so much for himself but for Rose's momentarily saved career. "If he's got the SUV driver's description like we think, we'll get it and we can put it out, maybe catch a break and nail the guy before morning."

"Probably do better than that," Nishimoto said as they headed down the shiny hallway, bustling at that hour with unusual activity. "While you and Tafoya've been cooped up doing the shooting review, we picked up a guy who says he's the driver. He copped to the whole thing. Very credible."

Without changing stride, Nye wondered why Nishimoto sounded less than delighted.

A small knot of excited cops and detectives surrounded interview room number five. Inside, Nye felt the unseen eyes behind the mirror on the far wall, and the others catching everything on the video cameras mounted ostentatiously around the room. Everyone who sat where Doobie Rudloff sat needed to understand that this was for real, it was all for the record. Nothing escaped.

Nye sat down at the end of the small interview table, bolted to the floor. Rudloff and Rose sat across from each other.

The mystery of Nishimoto's coolness was solved when Nye and Rose spoke for a few moments out of earshot from Rudloff.

"Sure he's ticked," she whispered. "Altlander's patrol guys found the suspect, not us. They got him out at Arden Fair Mall about dinnertime."

"You seen him?"

"For a couple minutes. Vu and Parkes are doing the interview. He's no mope like this one, Ter," she nodded toward Rudloff. "He sounds like it's no bullshit."

"He give up the passenger?"

"I didn't have enough time with him."

"Great," Nye said tightly. "Major Crimes gets to shovel, Altlander gets the glory."

"Maybe we found Ensor's hit-and-run, Ter," she said softly.

She was right, of course. That was all that mattered.

They started questioning Rudloff. Nye was pleasantly surprised that he was not entirely incoherent. He knew where he was and why they had brought him in. He even apologized for the trouble at the rail yard. He was trying to sneak out when the FTRA spotted him. "I didn't want anyone to get hurt. Including me," he smiled toothlessly. He was just forty-two years old.

Rose led him carefully through his movements the day before and how he ended up near Capitol Mall after dark. Loaves and Fishes had thrown him out because he was having trouble controlling himself, he said. It was stated without complaint or apology, a fact like the sun rising in the morning. So, Rudloff said, he decided to camp out overnight surrounded by the soothingly protective fortresses of tall buildings just beyond the Capitol. He had done it before and he could expect a hassle-free night since the police rarely spotted him in his makeshift lean-to in the shrubbery around the bank or office buildings.

Nye listened, asked questions, but Rose did most of interview thoroughly and seamlessly. She was someone you wanted to help, and Rudloff obliged.

"Did you actually see the accident, Mr. Rudloff?"

"No," he said slowly, shaking his shaggy head. "But I see the car go by."

"Going by fast, right? In the rain, it's dark," Nye asked, probing a likely weakness. "Not a lot of time for you to see who was driving."

"Lots of time. I got a photographic memory," Rudloff tapped his head. "You ask Dr. Shamansky at County Health Services, he knows me. He'll tell you."

Nye glanced at Rose, then at the mirror. He imagined Altlander smirking behind it, standing alongside a coiled, frustrated Nishimoto. The shooting debacle at the rail yard was bad enough for Major Crimes and Nishimoto, Nye figured. If Rudloff, the object of the hunt, turned out to be useless, then Nishimoto had lost entirely. The game went to Altlander.

But what mattered, as Rose said, was the truth.

Nye pushed his chair back, a luxury Rudloff didn't have. They had decided to leave him uncuffed unless he started to get troublesome, but his chair, like the metal table, was bolted securely to the floor.

Rose continued patiently asking questions, writing them down, Rudloff nodding, speaking conversationally, as Nye went to the door and stuck his head out into the jumble of detectives, trying to hear what was going on inside the interview room.

"Hey, get me a telephone book," he snapped to the nearest detective, a burly new guy in Gangs.

"White pages, Yellow, what?"

"Just a fucking telephone book."

The detective darted away into a nearby office, the others craning to look beyond Nye at Rudloff. Nye ignored their questions and unsolicited suggestions about how to run the interview. He impatiently snatched the city telephone directory from the Gangs detective and closed the interview room door behind him.

Nye flipped open the thick directory. He stood near Rose, who paused midquestion. "Okay, Doobie. You've got thirty seconds to look at page one hundred twenty-six there and then I'm going to ask you about it." He dropped the book in front of Rudloff.

Rudloff nodded with a toothless, open-mouthed smile and then gazed at the page with a frown. Rose watched, intrigued and curious. *She knows it's a do-or-die deal here,* Nye thought, keeping track of the seconds ticking by on his watch. *Rudloff's worthless if he brags about his memory and can't deliver. He could never testify and after all that's happened to bring him in, we're dead. Rose, me, Nish. Dead.*

As if she heard him say something, Rose looked up and then over at the mirror. *Yeah, she knows what's riding on this little parlor trick.* Nye's pulse quickened.

Rudloff, grinning with his empty mouth, sat back. "Okay," he said. "I'm good to go."

Rose took the telephone book from him. "Start at Melton, Andrea S.," she ordered Rudloff. She pointed to Nye, to show him it was halfway down the page. Nye didn't breathe for a moment, watching the unshaven, stinking man pause, then recite in a clear, plain voice.

"Melton, Beverly, Melton, Charles, Mendelsohn, Arthur, Mendoza,

A, Mendoza, Alicia," and on for two minutes until Rose smiled for Nye and closed the telephone book.

"All right, Doobie. That was swell. Now, describe the driver of the SUV you saw," Nye said.

Rudloff squirmed with pleasure and started to talk.

At that moment a buzzer sounded, and Altlander's voice came peremptorily over the speaker just above the mirror. "Hold it, Detective Nye. You and Tafoya report to me immediately."

The room behind the mirror was in semidarkness, the brightly lit square in front of Nye and Rose framing Rudloff, craning his head around, like a very realistic but very strange painting.

Nishimoto, face flushed, stood beside Altlander.

Nye and Tafoya haven't finished their interview yet," he snapped.

"I say it's time to fish or cut bait," Altlander snapped back. "We don't have time to screw around, Jerry."

"Tafoya, what's your call?" Nishimoto demanded.

"I think Rudloff's demonstrated his capacity to recall details, sir," she said, trying to address both assistant chiefs simultaneously. "Ideally, I know my partner and I would like to complete our interview with him before putting a lineup in front of him."

"No lineup," Altlander said firmly. "Plain and simple showup. He takes a look at our suspect and he tells us if we've got the right guy."

"It's premature," Nishimoto snapped again. "Let them finish the interview."

Nye watched, listened, aware he was being ignored, which didn't bother him very much. For some reason Altlander wanted to parade his prize suspect in front of Rudloff before the interview had memorialized his account of the Ensor hit-and-run. *Maybe Rudloff IDs the suspect, and Altlander gets to run to the chief and the media carnival with bragging rights that he wrapped the case,* Nye thought.

Sometimes it was just as simple as that: who was going to get the credit.

Nye cleared his throat while Altlander was speaking. "Excuse me, Chief," he said with stagy modesty, "I got a thought here."

"Yes, Nye?" Altlander asked skeptically. Rose and Nishimoto

waited expectantly for him to unload on the other assistant chief.

"I think it's a swell idea. Let's get Doobie's two cents on your suspect and get the goddamn thing over with."

Nye regretted Nish's shocked, betrayed expression. Rose's mouth tightened.

Altlander was only slightly less startled but he recovered instantly. "Good call, Nye," he said, heading for the door.

"After all these years, I should expect your bullshit, Terry," Nishimoto said quietly. "But you got me."

"I'm thinking of Ensor's family. We owe it to them to get this finished now if we've got the real deal in custody."

It was, for him finally, as simple as that.

The show up was ready in ten minutes, a logistical matter of moving Rudloff to the interview room down the corridor just past Major Crimes where the suspect was sequestered with Parkes and Vu.

Nye and Rose escorted an abruptly sullen Rudloff through the other cops and detectives, who cleared a path for them.

"I don't get you sometimes," Rose said to him.

"Blame yourself, Rosie. You said getting the driver was all that mattered."

"But this is rushing things," she protested. "I didn't mean it that way."

Nye patted Rudloff. "How you making out, Doobie? Okay?"

"Too many people," he muttered.

They went into the darkened room adjacent to the interview room, another one-way mirror showing Parkes and Vu and a third man grouped around a single gray metal table.

Nishimoto and Altlander were already in the darkened room. So was Chief Gutierrez. Nye was surprised he would get so involved. But, as he had come to realize in the last few hours, they were all more caught up in this investigation than they anticipated. The shooting at the rail yard and the shocking death of a cop had hit him more profoundly than he had imagined it would. In some odd, perverse way, Nye felt intensely that a guy as decent as Tommy Ensor, with a family as decent as his, didn't deserve to have more horrors piled on them. If the whole thing could be ended for their sake and Ensor's in the next few minutes, that was what he intended to do. No more surprises.

"Explain it to him," Chief Gutierrez said gruffly to Nye, his gaze fixed on the interview room. Parkes and Vu weren't talking. The third man had his head tilted back, arms folded, eyes closed. He was medium height, with ragged black hair, wearing a worn leather coat and a plaid shirt.

Rose took the cue and said gently to Rudloff, "Take a look in the room, Mr. Rudloff, and if you see someone you recognize, point him out. That's all you have to do."

"They can see me?" Rudloff asked nervously.

Everyone asks that, even in this age of LED TVs and laptops, Nye thought. The magical mirror that lets one side see out while the other can't.

"No," he said aloud, "you can see them, Doobie. Take your time."

Nye stood bedside Rose, bracketing Rudloff. The two assistant chiefs stood as closely as they could to Gutierrez. Only an eternal minute elapsed until Rudloff, plainly twitchy with so many strangers near him, announced to Rose, "That one, the guy at the table," he pointed at the third man near Parkes and Vu, "he's the guy in the car. I see him driving by me last night just before the cop got hit."

Chief Gutierrez swung on Rudloff. "Take another look."

Dutifully, Rudloff stared ahead, his empty mouth working anxiously. "What do you want me to say?"

"Is that the driver?" the chief said tersely.

"I said so. It's him," Rudloff looked nervously and in confusion to Nye, then Rose.

"Did you notice anyone else in the car?" she asked carefully.

"Just this guy. His side of the car."

"I want to see his statement immediately," the chief said to Altlander, and he left the room.

Altlander didn't move for a moment, then he stood stiffly, triumphant. "Okay, Jerry, that's your chore, you and your team. Get this gentleman's statement to me ASAP. Get him settled for the duration. We'll need him for the grand jury. I'm going to call the DA. Grand jury's the fastest way to get this thing moving."

"What about me?" Rudloff said querulously, a little irritated. "I want to get out of here."

Nishimoto remained immobile, too, then said, "Tafoya and Nye, please let Mr. Rudloff know his arrangements for tonight and the next few days. You heard Altlander."

Rose had her head down a little, as she watched the men in the interview room, plainly working the whole thing over in her mind. "He didn't see the passenger," she said softly. "Damn."

Nye thought she understood more of what was going on. *Nish gets some points because we brought in Rudloff, but Altlander's got the guy. Rosie sees we're in the hole.*

But, more than anything else, Nye wanted to assure himself that Rudloff was right. He owed that to Ensor and Jane. Not seeing the passenger was an instant weakness in Rudloff's observations.

"Boss, how about Tafoya and me running through the deal with our suspect," he pointed through the interview room mirror, "and Parkes and Vu can handle Mr. Rudloff here."

"Why?" Nishimoto seemed genuinely puzzled.

"Detective Tafoya and I know the investigation best. We'll be able to get the best statement from the suspect. Fast."

Rose looked up at him, a small, wry smile on her face. *She gets it,* he thought.

So did Nishimoto. He grabbed the opportunity. His detectives would make the case, in the final analysis, either by providing certainty through the suspect's interview or finding holes in his confession.

"Find out what he has to say," Nishimoto ordered sharply.

"What about me?" Rudloff demanded again, whimpering irritatedly to Rose.

She patted his scrawny arm, "Oh, we'll be seeing a lot of each other in the next couple of days, Mr. Rudloff. Tonight we're going to get you the best bed you've had in a long time."

TWENTY-FOUR

"SIT DOWN," NYE SAID AGAIN CALMLY but firmly.

"Where are the other guys?"

"We'll be taking your statement now." Rose pointed to the chair opposite her at the metal table. "So, you need to sit down, sir. Right now."

"I don't blame you guys," the man said, unmoving. "Anybody did to one of mine what I did, I'd shit all over him. Excuse my language."

"If you don't sit down," Nye said, "I will put you into that chair."

The man nodded, as if finally hearing what Rose and Nye had been saying in the five minutes since they entered the interview room. They had spoken to Parkes and Vu to get a sense of the suspect's cooperation and statements so far. Rose handed the suspect's rap sheet to Nye. "Misdemeanors like petty theft, but one decent GTA, stole a Ford Taurus" She pointed to the arrest and conviction from two years earlier. "He's still on probe for that one."

Nye nodded and pointed himself, "And looky here. Three deuces in four years. Last one he did six months at RCCC."

"I told you he looks good, Ter," she said. "He's a drunk driver who likes to steal cars."

Then they went inside, their routine decided. She would beckon. He would punch. Now the man finally sat down, hands on the table.

Rose and Nye now sat down, too. She had on her blank face, a mask that was neither threatening nor sympathetic. It encouraged people, as Nye had discovered, to talk as if they could provoke some reaction. Nye, on the other hand, scowled. He couldn't help himself.

"I'm going to advise you of your rights," Rose said and she coolly recited the Miranda warnings for the benefit of the video recording being made of the interview and for Nishimoto and Altlander, now together again observing from behind the mirror.

It was nearly one thirty on Friday morning. Nye felt an electric tingle keeping him wide awake and tense. It was partly unique to this interview and this circumstance after the shooting at the rail yard, but there was something he couldn't pin down, repellent and infuriating, about the man sitting with Rose and him. Like a witness he escorted into court years earlier in a child-beating case—the guy had known his own brother was beating his three-year-old and didn't do anything about it. Nye remembered the oyster-flat eyes of his witness and the constant desire to punch him in the face.

Just like this guy and what I'd like to do to him, he thought. This was where his years helped. He forced himself to sound a little bored, a little impatient, a little distracted. Like he didn't care so damn much. Rose, to her credit, had the pose down already.

"The other guys already did that. I don't want anybody. I want to tell you what happened because I am so, so sorry."

Nye pretended he was making notes. Rose paused.

"Okay," Nye said finally, "let's start like we're just getting to know one another. First, what's your name?"

"Jack Lucking."

"How old are you, Jack?"

"Twenty-six."

Nye's scowl reappeared. "I figured you were older." He thought about the grainy, blurred images on the videos and hoped again that the state techies would be able to enhance them into something better. The SUV driver had appeared older than this guy, even if Rudloff the Uncanny with his photographic memory had tagged him.

"Do you have your wallet, Mr. Lucking?" Rose asked, leaning forward slightly.

"Yeah. I thought you guys would take it when you arrested me." He reached back into his pants pocket and handed it to her. "I thought I'd be in jail by now."

"We'll see how things go, Mr. Lucking," Rose said, efficiently flipped through his wallet it. "This is your current address on Hilldale Court in Fair Oaks?"

"Yes."

"You live there with anybody?" Nye asked.

"My wife and two kids." He cleared his throat. "She doesn't know."

"When did you last talk to her?"

"About dinnertime. I said I was going out to the bowling lanes we got a couple miles away."

Rose looked up, her face empty still. "Mr. Lucking, your insurance card here says you own a 1999 Chevrolet Cavalier. You were driving that vehicle when you were stopped at Arden Mall earlier tonight."

"I mean, that's the family car. My wife's Andra and she's got a little Honda she uses."

Nye tapped his finger on the metal table. "You don't own a black Cadillac Escalade SUV?"

Lucking shook his head. He wiped his mouth where a thin crust of saliva had formed from nervousness. "I stole that."

"When and where?"

"This is going to get a little tough," he smiled uncertainly. He had a boyish charm that didn't quite match his flat eyes. "Andra and me had a fight, you could say, and I left to kind of cool down. That's what I do, I get out of the house to cool down."

Rose opened her mouth, but immediately realized it would be a mistake to interrupt Lucking, whether he was lying or telling the truth.

"What time was that, Lucking?" Nye broke in, having no compunction about breaking this suspect's conversational flow. They would go over the details again and again before the interview was over.

"Like about eight, maybe eight thirty."

"What were you fighting about?"

"I got fired couple weeks ago. Andra's pissed about that, pissed off I didn't get something right away, really pissed off I bought a little plasma TV. Not for me, for everybody," he sounded aggrieved. Nye and Rose let him ramble on for a few minutes, about his former job as a warehouseman at Sears, how Andra made more than him in the office of a construction union local, how their boy and girl were hard for them to handle. *Shades of Luis Tofoya,* Nye thought, certain the same self-pitying rationalizations were a common feature of Rose's home life.

Lucking squirmed in his chair. "I bet you guys are really pissed at me." He almost seemed to relish the prospect.

"How about just tell us what happened after you left your house last night?" *That's why I'd like to pop him,* Nye thought. *The fucker's enjoying himself.*

"Okay," deep breath, hands clasped, eyes on Rose then Nye alternatively. "I just started driving, I mean I stopped at a place on Belmont near where I live. The Arroyo. I had a couple beers and then I started driving, got on Five and headed for Sacramento."

"Any reason?" Rose asked.

"It's goddamn boring out where we live, like nothing, nothing out there. Excuse my potty mouth. I stopped at a couple places around Exposition," he wagged his head like he was telling bar mates a tale, "and then it gets kind of, you know, confusing. I switched to Jaeger shooters and got into some pool games, I think," he shook his head again. "Next thing I'm out at Arden, you know, kind of cruising the parking lot and I see this kickass SUV, and I was going for a ride."

"You figure you were pretty drunk?" Rose asked.

"Oh, yeah."

"Did you break into the SUV?"

"Got it all set up and I was out of there in a minute flat," he was pleased.

"Not bad for a guy all shitfaced," Nye added.

"I know cars. I grew up taking them apart, worked for a while at this Beemer dealership downtown."

"What time was it when you left Arden Mall?" Rose asked.

"I don't know. Really. Maybe eleven. Maybe twelve. After I did shooters for a while, I kind of got in a zone. Maybe after twelve even."

Nye got up and left the room, going into the adjacent viewing room. Parkes, Vu, and Talman were there with both Nishimoto and Altlander and a few of Altlander's patrol bureau. It was very crowded and stuffy.

"George, get over to Arden and talk to Mosher, the head of security. Go through their videos of the parking lot for Thursday night."

"What a son of a bitch you got in there," Altlander said loudly, looking for agreement around the room.

"Maybe we got him on camera driving out in an SUV," Nye said. Then to Altlander, "Chief, can you get Auto Burg to run through any reports of stolen SUVs for the last twenty-four hours? Like right now?"

"I think we can manage that, Detective." He barked the order to one of the men with him, who left the room with Parkes. "What a son of a bitch," he repeated.

As Nye turned to leave, another detective, one of the shifting crowd outside, gingerly poked his head in. "Hey, Terry, you got a call. Urgent."

"Can't take it now," he said, anxious to get back into the interview room with Rose and Lucking. He felt something tugging at the back of his mind about Lucking, his demeanor and his whole story.

"It's Tommy's wife. She's got to talk to you."

Nye stopped. Nishimoto said quietly, "Go ahead and talk to her."

"I guess so," Nye said.

He followed the detective through the knot of people nearest the interview room, ignoring their importuning comments and questions, and went to a disordered desk just down the hall. There was no privacy, uniform and detectives all around, the graveyard shift going about its business, although definitely not indifferent to him, he noticed.

He turned his back on the rest of the room and the other cops and civilians as much as he could. He took the call.

"How are you, Janey?" he asked gently.

"Not so good tonight, Terry," she said thickly, the faint echoes of hospital's PA behind her. *Probably in some lounge off the ICU,* he thought. "I hear you've got the driver. You arrested him, didn't you?"

"We might have him. Rose and I are talking to him now. We're right in the middle of interviewing him." He hoped she would take the hint and let him go. He inwardly cursed whoever had tipped her off about Lucking's arrest. Atlander, most likely.

"Don't tell me that, don't tell me that," she objected. "This is the bastard who hit Tom. I hear he's the one. Get him to admit it, Terry. I want to hear that he's admitted the thing he did."

"If he's the right guy, I will tell you personally," he said gently again. "Don't think about it now, Janey. Let me go back and do what needs to be done."

"He's the one," she blazed at him over the phone. "He did it. Make him say he's sorry. Make him beg for forgiveness."

"I'll do everything to get answers, believe me. How's Tommy doing?" He wanted to get her off the rising note of vengeance he heard in her voice.

"He's back in Intensive after surgery," her words were flat, thick. "Now they say he's not responding to physical stimulation. He doesn't know I'm with him, or the boys are with him." She was silent and Nye heard a husking, heavy sobbing. "He's just there, Terry. Tom's not with me anymore. Just him lying there. But not him anymore."

"I'm sorry," he said sorrowfully. "Jesus, don't get down yet. He's got great doctors, he's a tough guy. Things will look better tomorrow."

Nye was constantly surprised in these monstrous moments at how easily the sentiments and hope came out. *In the old days we'd sacrifice a goat or something, he thought. Now we just beg.*

"I don't think so, but maybe that's the way to get through the next little while, you think?" Janey's words were slurred enough that Nye knew she had been given powerful sedatives. "I want Tom back."

"Everybody does," he said. "Be strong," he added uselessly.

"I want this man to beg. Make him beg."

It took him several minutes to get himself settled enough to return to the interview room.

Rose took Lucking over the details: his storming out of his house the night before, driving toward Sacramento with stops at several bars, heavier drinking in two bars on Exposition Boulevard, the names of people he spent time with at each bar, then ending up at Arden Fair Mall's vast parking lot where he saw a black SUV, hotwired it, and drove out.

"Where'd you leave your car, the Cavalier?" Rose asked.

Lucking looked down. "Someplace in Arden, I guess. I remember, yeah, I parked it and started looking around for better wheels."

"You intended to steal another car?"

"You know I've done it before," he almost smiled at Nye, then didn't. "I got to grab new wheels sometimes."

"Where did you go from Arden Mall?" Nye asked, trying to ignore Janey Ensor's importunate demand in his head.

Lucking leaned back slightly. He didn't remember much, he said, it was all like through a heavy fog. He remembered going very fast, enjoying the high speed and the wind and then the rain smashing into the powerful SUV. Somehow he got himself on the freeway and ended up downtown. He thought he might have been pointing toward West Sacramento, maybe more bars along Harbor Boulevard. But he liked the surge of power as the SUV tore forward, and he gunned it.

"I have this kind of picture of the Capitol, kind of wavering, and I headed for it, kind of showing off," he grinned ruefully at Rose, who had gone quite tense and somber in the last few minutes. "I was just flying down the street and I remember something hitting me, real hard, but just for a second, and then I was gone."

"You don't remember striking someone near the Capitol?" Rose asked with controlled anger.

"Swear to God, I don't."

"Then how do you know you did?" Nye leaned toward him and his eyes were cold.

Lucking noted the change in both of them and he cleared his throat nervously. "I drove around for another half hour, I don't know, a while. I stopped out by Folsom Dam, I think. It was really dark and the rain had stopped and I was a little sick," he tried to make it sound humorous and failed. "So when I got out, I saw the car was real banged up, fender all tore up, bumper, I mean just looking I could see I'd hit something bad."

"You knew what you'd hit then, right?" Nye said very calmly.

"I guess so. Yeah. What else was there on streets, right? Maybe a dog, but it would be a goddamn big dog, excuse my mouth again."

At that moment, Rose half stood, then got up completely, her hands braced on the metal table. It happened so fast Nye had no time to react.

"You self-centered little son of a bitch," Rose said sharply, "do you have any idea of the pain you've caused? Do you?"

"I said I was sorry," Lucking began.

Rose slapped him hard, his head rocking with the force. Nye didn't move, but he could imagine the commotion going on among the observers. So he said, "That's enough."

"I'm sick of listening to this whining, smug little asshole, Terry. Aren't you?" she demanded to the invisible audience. "Listen, you little puke, you better convince me you're sorry, you're sorrier than you've ever been in your whole life because of the people you've hurt."

Lucking tried to move away and Nye put a hand on his shoulder. "Stay put, Lucking." Then to Rose, "If you need a minute, go outside, okay?"

"I don't need a time out. I need this miserable little puke to tell the truth."

Nye wondered how much of Rose's truly frightening anger sprang from genuine disgust at Lucking's callous crime or her own inability make things with Luis come out right. Or it could be her reaction to the events of the last few hours. Sometimes, Nye knew, a good detective used it all, mixed it up, because what emerged was real.

It shocked Lucking certainly. *Now he doesn't know what's waiting for him and that will keep him talking,* Nye knew.

They went over Thursday night again. More details fell in this time, finding blood on the SUV when he pulled over, driving back toward Sacramento, over a dark levee road.

"I ditched the SUV in the river," Lucking said, eying both Nye and Rose apprehensively. "I mean, I had to get rid of it."

"Where?" Rose asked sharply.

"Oh, jeez, I don't know, I really don't. Someplace north of here, out off a levee. I remember seeing the SUV go down the slope and slide into the water, you know just sink. River was moving really fast because of the storm."

"So, you're out in the middle of no place in the middle of the night and somehow you end up back at home? How did that happen?"

"I got back on the road and got a ride, couple rides."

"From who? What kind of vehicles?" Rose said.

Lucking twisted his face. His hands had started clenching every few moments and now they wouldn't stop. He remembered a trucker hauling seafood, small talkative guy with a big leaping salmon on the truck. Then he thought he got all the way back to Arden Fair Mall with an Hispanic man, fat and suspicious, in a blue or gray minivan who nevertheless dropped him off at the brightly lit, virtually empty huge parking lot. Lucking managed to find his own car and somehow, because everything was very distorted and fragmentary, drive home. He slept downstairs on the couch because he thought Andra would be mad that he came home so late.

"Now, I'm getting confused," Nye said, standing up, blowing a breath, "you got busted tonight back at Arden Mall, right?"

"Yeah, I did."

"You went back there tonight? Why the hell did you do that?"

Lucking didn't answer for a minute and then his voice shook. "I saw all the stuff on TV about this guy who got hit and I go, maybe that was me. The SUV sounded like right and I know I hit something," he dropped his head and raised it again. "I am sorry, just like you said," he told Rose, "more than I've ever been in my life. I know this guy has kids, too. Like me."

"So you went back to Arden to jog your memory maybe?"

"Yeah, look around, see if I could remember where I saw the SUV, you know something. It was really bothering me."

Rose stood up and Lucking cringed, expecting another outburst.

"We need to locate the SUV," she said. "You'll help us find it. We'll take a look along the levee roads and see if you spot something familiar."

"I want to help." His hands shook badly.

Rose stared flatly at him. "Who was with you last night?"

"I gave you names."

"In the car. In the stolen car."

"Nobody. Just me. I mean, I don't remember a lot."

Rose leaned forward and Lucking cringed back. "There was no one else in the SUV with you last night?"

"It's all really confused." He stared at Nye. "Maybe if you tell me what they looked like, I could remember something."

Nye slowly rubbed his eyes. "Excuse us a minute, Lucking. We'll be right back." He motioned to Rose and they left the interview room and joined the others next door watching it all.

"He's lying about something," Nye said to Nishimoto, who somberly sipped bottled water.

"Bullshit," Altlander interrupted. "We've got him. Unless Tafoya's little sideshow screws it up," he glared at her.

"I'm sorry, sir. That's never happened to me before."

"Great time to start, Tafoya."

"We got stuff to work with now, anyway," Nye broke in because he knew there was nothing to be done at that moment about Rose's striking the suspect and he didn't feel like fighting Altlander who was clearly out to score points at Nishimoto's expense.

"Why's he lying, Terry?" Nishimoto asked crisply.

"I don't know for sure. Either he was so drunk he doesn't really remember anything like someone else in the SUV or he knows exactly what happened when he hit Ensor. Going back to the parking lot tonight just sits wrong for me."

"If he hadn't come back, we wouldn't have caught him," Altlander snorted.

"Exactly, Chief. Patrol gets called by mall security that this guy," he pointed at Lucking, sitting forlornly and quietly in the interview room, "is poking around SUVs and generally looking just like a first-time car booster, which this guy is not."

"Point, Nye?"

"He wasn't hard to catch," Nye said simply. Nishimoto nodded, sipped, putting it together. Lucking's capture that night was not chance or even good police work. He essentially turned himself in. Which in turn suggested he was not being wholly truthful about what he did or recalled about the night of Ensor's hit-and-run. It might all be confection or he deliberately ran down a police officer.

"Finish up, squeeze this gentleman bone dry." Nishimoto said. "We'll go brief the chief." He started to leave and Altlander turned to Nye and Rose. His small entourage stood by him.

"Let's be clear. This is the man who ran down Officer Ensor. He's confessed and he's got the record to back it up. He knows details of the crime. He's been unequivocally identified by a witness you vouched for. So, if something goes sour here, and Ensor's attacker walks away, the record's going to show precisely who screwed the pooch."

"We know that there's another person out there with direct knowledge of the hit-and-run," Nishimoto said ponderously. "Another person who knows about this guy. Find the passenger, Nye."

"We'll work the case hard, sir," Nye said, blocking Altlander's exit physically because Nishimoto seemed reluctant to argue with his fellow assistant chief in front of others. "We'll try to find the SUV, corroborate Lucking's story all along the way. I think we keep it wide open who this guy is until then."

Nishimoto surprised him by saying bluntly, "I disagree, Terry. Get this guy into the main jail tonight on attempted murder."

About the highest charge possible, Nye thought. *Shooting for the moon.*

"Right, Jerry, "Altlander said, "what this mope did is at least attempt murder."

They all left, Rose and Nye tiredly getting a moment's respite before tackling Lucking again. Rose said, "I could kick myself for losing it, Ter. I talked to Luis and Annorina awhile ago, just before we went in, and they're both worried as hell about me. But I don't have any good excuses."

"No, I think having your kid and husband scared for your safety is pretty good," he said, grinning and trying to lift her sense of shame a little. He patted her shoulder. Marceen would care about him, some, when she heard about the rail-yard shoot-out, but Nye had no illusions he had anybody close who would lose sleep over his well-being.

Talman came in after knocking. "I got this from Auto Burg," and he handed a printout to Rose. "It's a list of all the reported car thefts in the county since day before yesterday."

Rose and Nye read down the list of times and places vehicles were reported stolen. It was a random collection of new and old, common and expensive.

Rose looked up. "No SUVs stolen around here."

"This is where it gets interesting," Nye said. He stared at Lucking, hands making invisible patterns on the table, alone in the interview room.

TWENTY-FIVE

"GET UP! GET UP, FRANK!" Vee shook him hard and relentlessly.

Stevenson grunted and rolled over in bed toward her. She stood over him, in a pink robe, hair tangled, a fierce, intense expression on her face. "What is it?" he mumbled thickly.

"Come downstairs, you have to see this right now. Be quiet. Hurricane's still asleep."

He struggled up, the windows still curtained against the faint glow just after dawn. Vee impatiently paced nearby, urging him to hurry, then she grabbed his arm, dragging him out of the bedroom. He nearly slipped on two wine bottles and glasses dropped on the rug by the bed. After the stale and unhappy dinner last night, the session with Fonseca, and then Eli afterward, he had brought wine, aged and expensive, something he and Vee could share together. A little peace offering, some penance for what he was putting her through. Their lovemaking was different from the night before, gentle and savored, an echo of their honeymoon on the Big Island. They were both grateful.

"What's going on? Can I get a hint?" he said, his head throbbing painfully from the bottle he had put away himself.

"I got up early and came down," Vee said, pulling him into the study. "I went online and this was the first thing I saw." Her voice rose excitedly. She pushed him toward the computer on her desk, the screen alight with figures and a faint droning voice.

The house was still, poised, it seemed to him, for the threats and unknown dangers of the day. He stared, trying to make sense out of what he was seeing.

Vee kept talking excitedly, "It's not even seven and the police are holding a press conference downtown. Listen, you'll hear it again, this is a replay. They've got the hit-and-run driver." She turned to him, disbelieving, relieved, exultant.

Stevenson thought she must have misunderstood. The police were talking about their investigation to find the driver. It had to be that.

He sat down, Vee pulling a chair near him, her head close, and he savored the familiar smell of her. He sensed her more keenly now, as if she were about to be taken away from him. He realized he was being given a gift. He knew what he could lose.

He recognized Gutierrez, the chief of police. The heavyset man, dark-blue uniform creased sharply with gold stars gleaming on the collar tabs, stood behind a podium with the city's seal on it. An array of gray-haired and serious men in uniform surrounded him in the small space. Gutierrez read slowly from a piece of paper, his glasses perched halfway down his fleshy nose. He looked up every few moments and stumbled at times over the words.

Stevenson listened incredulously.

"The suspect was arrested last night at approximately nine thirty in the Arden Fair Mall parking lot by members of the Sacramento Police Department, working in cooperation with security for the Mall. The suspect's name is Gerald Phillip Lucking. He has admitted driving a vehicle while intoxicated and striking Officer Thomas Ensor early Thursday morning, causing severe injuries to the officer."

The chief shifted, coughed. Stevenson caught glimpses of the dense crowd of photographers and reporters standing, almost on top of each other, in the small room somewhere at police headquarters. The tragic story of the Good Samaritan police officer had attracted growing interest from the national media.

Vee held Stevenson's arm, a tight, desperate grip. "It's like a miracle, isn't it? Like someone's watching out for us."

"Mr. Lucking has been charged with attempted murder, a violation of the Penal Code, and leaving the scene of an accident in which there was injury, a violation of the Vehicle Code. He's presently being held in the Sacramento County Main Jail without bail because he is considered a flight risk. I will be meeting with the district attorney in about an hour so that he can review the results of our investigation and move forward with bringing Mr. Lucking to trial as quickly as possible."

The reporters shouted questions and the chief raised his hands for some order.

Stevenson said, "Attempted murder is a specific intent crime. This guy said he was drunk. It's going to be hard to prove he intended to hit that cop." He was a little stunned, and plotting the thing out coldly like a problem in his court made it almost seem real. Stevenson had trouble believing what he was hearing.

"It doesn't matter, Frank," Vee pulled close to him and embraced him tightly, breathing hard. "It's over. We're free."

Stevenson held her, too, startled that he was so overtaken by relief and joy. He felt Vee shaking and he was afraid she was crying.

But she was laughing. "I feel like I just got wings, I'm flying. Oh, my God."

They clung together, alternately laughing and kissing each other. Behind them, the chief of police raised his voice over clamoring questioners, detailing the arrest but nothing about what the police knew about Lucking or how good their case was. Stevenson heard everything.

Finally, Vee said, "All right, how about we say this is hour one of day one? We'll start over, Frank. Pretend the last couple of days didn't happen at all."

"They didn't happen," he said, caught up in the same exuberant reprieve.

"I was so scared I lost you. Lost both of us."

"Vee, you're never going to lose me," he said with finality. "We are stuck with each other."

They left the computer on and went into the kitchen. She started coffee and switched on the small TV on the counter, shaking her head, chattering aimlessly, like a rescued survivor of a great explosion.

Stevenson took two aspirin, his heart full because Vee was so free abruptly from a terrible burden. He understood, at that instant more deeply than he had during their time together, how much she meant to him and he must mean to her. *It was like dying,* he thought, *that mind-rending fear since Thursday night that we were being separated.*

Now we're free. He wanted to believe it absolutely.

She pulled out eggs and bacon, treats for the weekend usually, ordered him to carve up grapefruit. He kept half an eye on the TV, watching Chief Gutierrez's weary but proud performance.

"I'll get everything on the table, if you go upstairs and drag Hurricane down with you," Vee said. Haley, on Fridays particularly, had used up her steely resolve to be prompt for breakfast. And this breakfast was a little impromptu, earlier, and more elaborate. *A celebration,* Stevenson thought.

"By pike, sword or grappling hook," he vowed, and he passed the TV, leaving the kitchen rich with cheery cooking smells, he caught sight of other people near the chief of police. *The cameras must have moved a little,* he thought detachedly, *because I didn't see them earlier.*

Stevenson leaned to the screen. The same two detectives he had spotted in Yardley's chambers the day before getting search warrants, whispered to each other, an older man, who looked like he was retired military or should be a retired something, and a younger, athletic woman with short black hair.

Then the older man stopped whatever he was whispering, looked directly into the camera, right at Stevenson.

That's impossible, he thought with a sharp stab of panic. *It's a coincidence.*

As if in confirmation, the older man's unblinking gaze shifted to the chief and the camera swung away. *It was a random moment, and foolishly wrong to read anything into it.*

But as he climbed the stairs, knocked on Haley's door, Stevenson felt a premonitory dread welling up inside of himself. *He sees me. The old cop can see me,* he thought against all rational possibility.

Haley took awhile to answer his repeated knocks on her door and, when she admitted him, it was with the growing shyness he had noticed about six months earlier, a vague unease around him and even Vee, too. Stevenson didn't look forward to Hurricane's teenage years. She would be hard to live with.

He told her they were having an early breakfast.

"It's not really fair. You and Mom have your schedules and so do I," she complained and went about getting her school pack and laying out clothes neatly on her bed, which she made up as they talked.

"Look, Haley, how about we all go away for the weekend? A little vacation someplace?" He had to get away now after seeing the TV, out of Sacramento, breathe freely for a day or so anyway. "Your choice. Where would you like to go?"

"Really?" Haley asked a little suspiciously. "I get to choose?"

"Anyplace but Tahoe. Someplace different." She was partial to the lake and they went there often.

"We could go to Disneyland," she tried tentatively, sure it would be vetoed because of the crowds on a weekend and expense.

Stevenson nodded. "Let's do that. We can all have some fun. I think we all deserve a little break, don't you, button?"

"We'll really go to Disneyland?" she asked guardedly.

"You asked for it, you got it."

Stevenson delighted in Haley's smile and the happy way she finished getting ready for the school. He drew so much pleasure from simple acts like her finding the right socks or shoes, meticulously straightening and packing up her homework. Tacked carefully along the walls were posters of revered figure skaters and the *Challenger* astronaut Christa McAuliffe, and, grouped here and there, the stuffed pandas that had started to gather dust as Haley's life moved on.

I'll protect her. Whatever it takes.

He tried to figure out how to say what must happen to Vee. *Like giving her a get-out-of-jail card and yanking it away,* he realized. He prayed she would recognize that they still had to go forward.

He decided to wait until after breakfast. *The condemned ate a hearty meal,* he thought mirthlessly. Fonseca, thanks to his father-in-law, lurked in the wings. But perhaps if he pulled off this deception, Fonseca would have nothing to hold over him.

Vee liked the prospect of leaving the city for the weekend and, as they ate, she and Haley planned out which old rides they would make sure to go on and the newer ones they would hit.

There was still an extra half hour after breakfast before Haley had to get to St. Francis. The little TV on the counter soundlessly went on showing the press conference, interviews, older pictures of the crime scene taken the day before. There were stills and videos of Officer Ensor, on a softball field, getting his Medal of Valor, bowing with his wife and children at the Peace Officers Memorial a year earlier.

Stevenson tried to avoid looking at any of them. He helped Vee clean up.

"Vee, nothing's changed," he said. *Make it inevitable, unavoidable, inarguable.*

"I know," she said, washing, wiping, handing him dishes to put away. "We'll go ahead with the switch today. Just like we talked about."

"It's insurance. We're safe no matter what happens to this guy the cops arrested."

Vee nodded and finished. "You don't have to convince me. After we switch SUVs, nothing can touch us."

Stevenson hung the dishtowel by a rack near the elaborate electric range. Vee's calm, almost clinical assessment was unexpected, but he rejoiced in it. He tested the limit of it.

"I don't care what happens to this guy they arrested," he said flatly. *If someone else took the fall, we're safe.*

"Frank, I thank God someone's been caught and they're parading him around so proudly. Let them lynch the poor slob."

He saw that Vee wasn't calm or clinical at all, but ready to incite a mob and bring the rope herself.

They went into the garage, closing the connecting door to the laundry room, and spoke low in case Haley strayed into the kitchen.

The tan hulk of the covered SUV seemed coiled, ready to be awakened. Vee folded her arms, standing away from it. He and Vee went over the day's battle plan for a final time. They would all leave together as usual, in her car again, to take Haley to school. He would drop Vee off at her firm and then she would meet her father outside of it in his car at ten. Vee and Eli had a fifteen-mile drive north to the

Hardy Cadillac-Pontiac dealership and, by noon, after taking care
of the paperwork, she would follow her father back to his office and
park the new Escalade SUV in his large parking lot, where it would
simply become one SUV among many. It was an SUV he bought.

"Don't get out of his car at the dealership, if you can avoid it.
The fewer people who see you together there, the better." Stevenson
leaned against the garage door. If it came down to someone later
putting pieces together, they had determined the night before, they
shouldn't make it easy.

Vee looked pensively at him. "Remember I told you when I was
little, my mom was in and out of hospitals for a while? She had a lot
of surgeries for a back problem. It was just my father and me at home,
night after night. And the strange thing was that even as a kid I could
see I had to help him get through it, not the other way around."

"We'll all get through this."

"There was a moment," Vee paused, "last night when I was really
afraid I'd have to choose between you and him."

"Forget it."

"You and Haley come first," and she touched his arm, then
stroked it. "But I've still got to take care of him."

You will never have to make that choice for real. "We're all going
to make it," he said soberly.

"I believe that this morning." She kissed him.

He waited and then returned to the mundane chores that would
secure their safety.

"We'll do the actual switch at the public storage place at ten,"
Vee had located a twenty-four-hour facility, People's Storage, about
two miles away. The rental unit, large enough for their SUV, was
already reserved.

"I'll get out of court at four and meet you back here," Stevenson
said. "You drive your car to People's Storage, let them see you coming in, checking out the space. We don't want anything to surprise
us later."

"My dad brings the new SUV over here at ten. It's dark. We
switch the license plates, papers, whatever else needs to come from
our SUV and it goes into the new one. The new one goes here into
our garage. Then my dad and I'll drive our SUV to the storage place,
get it into the rental unit."

Stevenson picked it up. "I'll bring Hurricane and meet you both at the ice cream place across the street. They don't close until eleven. I'll let her know we're getting a jump on the Disneyland trip. Drive Eli home afterward; we come back home in our new SUV. At People's Storage it will look like the same SUV came and went, in case anybody's watching, but I don't think they will be at that hour."

"Presto change-o."

"Ten minutes to make the switch, tops." Stevenson chewed his lip. "What are we forgetting, Vee?"

"Nothing."

"Every time I see a defendant in my courtroom they've always forgotten something."

"We're master criminals," she chuckled archly and touched his face gently. "We're decent people and we're lucky."

Stevenson walked to the covered SUV and gave it a symbolic kick. "What I wouldn't give for five minutes with a trash compactor that could turn this into a little metal cube."

"It was sweet of you to think of Hurricane. Getting out of town will make her feel a lot better. She's worried about us."

Stevenson looked at his watch. It was time for the performance to start. "I want all of our neighbors to see us go off on a weekend vacation in the SUV, Vee," he said. "It's part of the picture."

She looked apprehensive suddenly. "What if this is a trap?"

Stevenson shook his head. "The police don't make gag arrests. It's illegal." He gave her a dark smile and Vee seemed reassured.

After she went inside, he lingered for a moment in the garage. *It's all going to change today,* he thought, staring at the SUV's shapeless bulk. *We are decent and we are lucky.*

He went over to the steel cabinets where he kept his climbing gear and opened them on impulse. He didn't think there would be a climb this year. The neatly coiled nylon ropes, pitons and crampons hanging on hooks, canvas bags made Stevenson feel the stinging acid cold on the last few feet on the last mountain. *The air was bitter, icy, thin and ahead the snow and rock vanished into chilled mist. He heard Doug, the surgeon, panting behind him, struggling to stay up as they strained slowly up to the summit. Stevenson again felt the paradoxical claims of dizzying life-preserving details to master but at the same time there was only one thought: move forward.*

"Frank! Frank! Hold up a second! I've got to catch my breath!"

He didn't answer, just kept moving forward, the nylon rope linking him to Doug taut because the other man was flagging, falling back. Pulling him back, too.

"Goddamn it, Frank, stop for a second! We can't make it!" and the rest of the words were frightened, furious obscenities thrown toward him, into the cold mist.

He moved forward, dragging the other man with him, pulling his weight, too.

Then, suddenly, the rope slackened and Stevenson looked back, certain Doug had cut free. Instead, he saw the cursing, gasping figure stumbling to keep up, close the yards between them. At that instant, Stevenson knew they would make the summit. They would not die.

He fingered the cold metal of the pitons and closed the cabinets. Up on the mountain, in the implacable grip of thin air and cold and fatigue, his life depended on the mountaineering gear just like his life now, all of their lives, depended on that intricate collection of parts and paint and power under the tan cover near him in the garage.

He snorted in irritation suddenly and stalked out of the garage. That was crap. The rope and gear didn't save him and the doctor on the mountain or get them to the summit when two others in their party failed and nearly died.

We did it, he thought. *We pushed and we fought and we were lucky.*

We refused to consider defeat.

I refused.

He thought of Vee this morning and knew together they would make it. She was hard, harder than he suspected, and willing to go the distance.

We will make it.

He dropped Haley off, then Vee, and drove the rest of the way to the courthouse thinking of the eyes on him, not suspicious or hostile, but watchers nonetheless. He couldn't betray any change for the rest of the day. Stevenson thought of the old cop staring out at him from the TV. *Just a damn coincidence,* he thought angrily. *I know your names, Eli got them. Nye and Tafoya.*

But you don't know who I am.

I see you. But you don't see me, Nye and Tafoya.

It gave him great satisfaction and security.

Smitty waved him into the courthouse basement garage with a smile. No mention that Stevenson was driving his wife's car for the second day. Stevenson felt a gripping nervousness creeping outward from his center and he willed it down, away. He grasped at his satisfaction of a few minutes before. He would not show fear or panic. He rode up to the fourth floor with three others judges and they complained about Friday's lunch meeting with the Presiding Judge.

"It's going to be a pep talk about cutting back on using water in your bathroom," an older judge sneered.

"If the damn meeting wasn't mandatory, I had a golf date," another said wistfully. "I'm dark this afternoon."

"What about you, Frank?" the third judge asked. "Anything special going on?"

"Second day of arguments about *voir dire* questions."

"Happy anniversary," the other judges sang out in unison and they all laughed.

After that, Stevenson relaxed. Things were going to be fine. He got to his courtroom, caught up with Joan who prodded him about the meeting with the Presiding Judge at noon upstairs, and joked with Audie, who was excited about going quail hunting with his brothers over the weekend. Stevenson put on his robe, took the bench, and managed to get through the morning for about an hour and a half. The lawyers were arguing as usual every few minutes over pre-trial motions, seeking advantage, and Stevenson listened, ruled, attentively tending to the business of running his contentious courtroom.

Then he noticed a strange thing happening. It was as if the volume of his courtroom was being turned down. He still heard the deputy district attorney and Wallace when they bickered, but they were growing tinny. He also found that he had trouble, imperceptibly, focusing on anyone in the courtroom, even Joan or Audie a few feet away. Their familiar faces grew fuzzy.

All he could see sharply was the time on the stark clock tacked high to the brown paneled wall on his right.

Nearly eleven, he thought. *Vee's getting ready. Eli's telling Georgina's he's going out for lunch, going out with Vee. That will make Georgina happy.*

It went on like that for another half hour as the time crept toward noon. He imagined what Vee was doing or saying at her firm, how she was telling Anson, the rainmaker senior partner that she and her father were going out to lunch.

Stevenson could not stay with the trial. His mind kept filling up, drifting off to whatever he imagined Vee and Eli were doing at that instant. *How do the pros do it,* he wondered, *playing out every second of a burglary or robbery?* It would drive him crazy.

He had to get to his phone for Vee's call. Abruptly, he stood up, announced they would break until two, and strode off the bench.

Joan followed Stevenson into his chambers. "Do you want something from the cafeteria for the meeting, Judge?" she asked.

"Sure. Thanks. Just a ham and cheese sandwich," he fumbled for his wallet as he took off his robe.

Joan waved dismissively. "Pay me later. I took a couple of messages while you were on the bench," and she was gone.

He saw the pink phone message slips, two calls from Buzz Fonseca, please call back. *Probably wants to find out if I've started the machinery to get his damn case transferred to my department,* Stevenson thought, crumpling the message slips, then tearing them up and tossing the fragments into his wastebasket. *Stall the bastard. Move fast enough and everything will come out.*

Stevenson almost grabbed the telephone. Audie was ambling past Joan's desk toward him to chat, and he shut his chambers' door in Audie's face.

He sat down, dialing Vee's cell. He couldn't wait for her to call.

"Where are you?" he said too curtly when she answered.

"We're on our way to the Virgin Sturgeon. I thought sitting out on the river might calm us down."

"How bad is he?" Stevenson said tightly, knowing Eli was a foot away from Vee driving toward the restaurant.

"On a scale of one to ten, I'd say nine and a half." There was rustling, "Dad, Frank says hello."

Stevenson heard a muffled sound. "What's wrong?"

Vee's voice was so quiet he could barely hear it, and apparently she hoped her father could not at all. "Second thoughts. He thinks you both should go to the police. He's been watching the TV."

"Maybe we should do this without him," Stevenson said, leaning back tensely in his chair.

"We can't. I'll handle it. Remember what we said this morning. You need to calm down yourself." She was gentle but direct.

"I'll be fine," he snapped and then apologized. "Look, call me if we need to change things."

"I'll see you at home at four," Vee said firmly.

Joan knocked twice on his door and came in, putting a plastic carton on his desk with a can of diet cola. "I got you a side salad, too. It's going to be a long meeting."

Stevenson managed a bright smile. He took a moment to gather himself. Vee was right. He was too anxious about every moment, things that were not truly under his control. Like the accident. Like a cop standing in the middle of a dark rainy street at midnight.

Or me speeding blindly, not watching how fast I was going, trying to get Eli home, get him off my hands, maybe? Excited because going to the Third District felt a little closer, a little more real, so I didn't see the cop standing in the middle of a dark rainy street. I didn't see him.

He hurried to the elevator and rode up to the sixth floor, where chattering defendants and their friends, families, and lawyers spilled out toward the crowded cafeteria to grab a quick lunch before court went back into session. A brace of lawyers greeted him formally. He nodded and brushed by them as he entered the Presiding Judge's large courtroom near the end of the hall.

Stevenson finally mastered his roiling emotions when he settled in around the conference table with the thirty other judges. Some were eating, some just sat in faintly concealed boredom. In a spasm of nerves, he gave a half wave to Sonia Berry, the dark-haired little woman who held forth in Department 27. He hoped she got the chance to pulverize Buzz Fonseca.

He sat with Yardley, who looked desperate for a smoke, and offered him part of the sandwich he brought. Yardley took it and they chatted around the table while the PJ held forth at the head about housekeeping items before the main meeting. The PJ's father had been a Justice of the United States Supreme Court and the PJ kept his black leather high-backed chair in a place of reverence in his chambers.

Stevenson noted again, with surprising detachment, how the seating pattern in the chamber reflected the haughty disdain that appointed judges, like himself, felt for the elected judges. All the elected judges sat with each other, avoided, by and large, by the appointed ones. Elected judges were shallow, political, showy. Nothing more than jumped-up politicians. A gubernatorial appointment to the bench, however, required running the gauntlet of county and state bar reviewing boards and the Governor's legal appointments secretary. It required demonstrating legal skill, judicial temperament, accomplishment. *I earned this job,* Stevenson thought. *I sweated for it. I'm going to keep it and my integrity.*

Looking around the room, Stevenson realized how much he knew about every man and woman, their weaknesses and habits, who was looked down on, who was respected. At the far end of the table, wearing his usual bemused, empty smile, was an older judge. His son was killed in Iraq a year earlier and, shortly afterward, he had a very noisy breakdown one afternoon in the middle of a trial. Four months in a hospital and now he was back again, soothed with meds and therapy. His last name was Bean. His nickname now, even among sympathetic colleagues, was Loony. Stevenson wondered what the men and women around the table thought of him. He had rivals like dePeralta and Conny Maxwell for the Third District Court of Appeal seat.

But what did they really think of him? What would they think of him if they knew what he had done?

Or what he was about to do?

But at that moment, Stevenson felt safe surrounded by all of these other judges, sitting in the largest chambers on the top floor of the county courthouse. He was also utterly alone. He was among them and alone, apart, and none of them knew it.

He didn't worry about Vee and his father-in-law for the rest of the tedious meeting.

The afternoon went much better than the morning. He resumed the pretrial wrangling at two, and he could look out on the sparsely crowded courtroom with calm. Even the incessant sniping and scrabbling by the rank of attorneys at the counsel table didn't bother him. He only glanced at the clock. *Now Vee and Eli are on the road to the dealership,* he thought evenly. *Now they've arrived. Now Eli's signing the papers for the new SUV, making out a check.*

Everything was orderly, even mechanical, and he let the clock-work run.

The court reporter asked for a break at three thirty and even though he was inclined to go until he recessed for the day at four, she seemed anxious, so he said they would take a five-minute break and then finish up.

Stevenson walked back to his chambers with Joan.

"So it won't be a very exciting weekend," Joan said in his doorway, "just my husband and his cousin cutting down our old oak in the front yard so it doesn't fall on us this winter. After the rain the other day, you can see it's ready to just go."

"You probably don't want to hear that I'm taking Haley to Disneyland."

"Our kids loved Disneyland. Make sure you go on the Matterhorn. I love roller coasters."

"Haley's got our whole itinerary planned out," he grinned.

He sat down alone in his chambers without even bothering to open his robe. Audie popped in a moment later. He shook his head angrily. "Just got the news from the guys downstairs. That city cop who got hit? He died."

Stevenson's mouth tightened. "I'm very sorry." Automatic, unthinking.

"Yeah, it really burns. He would've had a lousy time the way he was messed up," Audie's big shoulders shrugged. "At least they got the bastard and that guy is going to have one hell of a time."

He left. Stevenson rocked very slightly in his chair, eyes forward.

Joan came in, "It's time, judge. Everyone's ready. Oh, I thought of another ride you've got to go on."

Stevenson didn't answer her. He got up and went into his private bathroom to the right of his desk and closed the door. Something was happening in the center of his mind and it kept flowing, shifting, darting away as if in flight.

He closed the seat on the toilet and sat down. The soft light in the ceiling was on. He could see his sink and the chrome framed mirror over it. He looked at his hands, clasped them together, separated, clasped them again. For a second he almost had the dark thing that fluttered hugely and monstrously across the center of his mind.

Stevenson felt something like a shudder go through him. Then again.

The thing stopped. He looked into his own face in the mirror.

I've killed a man.

He's dead.

I killed him.

TWENTY-SIX

NYE SPENT WHAT WAS LEFT of Thursday night on a cot in a small, bare room on the fourth floor reserved for detectives working 'round-the-clock investigations. Or, he knew, a few like him in the past who didn't want to go home drunk.

He sent Rose home, along with half of the team, to get a few hours before the press conference that Altlander had talked Chief Gutierrez into holding early Friday morning. He and Rose had sourly watched the encampment of camera crews and reporters growing outside of the department, spilling into the lobby, which became an obstacle course for other cops and their suspects.

He and Rose had deposited Rudloff for safekeeping at Loaves and Fishes after assuring the skeptical director that Doobie would be well-behaved and, in any case, they would be back for him before close of business Friday. A longer-term residence needed to be found as the Lucking investigation went on.

Lucking was booked and lodged in the main jail, on the third floor, in a new stainless-steel cell with electronically controlled doors and white concrete walls, as bare as the room where Nye was spending his night. Just before he flipped off the light, Nye spotted a small faded blue pen line scratched at eye level beside the cot. *Now I know the joke,* it read. He vaguely remembered scrawling it on the concrete. But he no longer recalled the joke.

He had half remembered dreams during the abbreviated night. He saw Solorio shot again at the rail yard, felt fear for Rose who he could hear but somehow never see. When he opened his eyes in the darkness, he was clammy with cooling sweat.

He was up at six, took a brisk shower down in the locker room in the basement, shaved, got dressed, and joined Vu and Talman in the command center. The others were still out.

"Concerned citizen brought doughnuts," Talman waved a half-eaten bear claw at the pink box in the center of the conference table. "Coffee's pretty fresh."

"Thank God for a healthy breakfast," Nye said, helping himself to something covered with chocolate. He had a stack of phone messages on his desk and he started flipping through them.

"You worried about your cholesterol, Terry?" Vu asked.

"Nope. Remember Lingard? Worked out, ate soda crackers and protein bars or some crap like that. Weighed himself all the time. Kept a chart of his goddamn blood pressure and cholesterol in his car. Took his pulse at the end of every shift."

"Kind of rings some bells. Heart attack got him?"

"Blue Mustang. Hit him when he was directing traffic." Nye chuckled. Well, it wasn't much of a joke, but at least he could still remember fragments of his dim distant past. He stopped at a message from IA. He decided to confront Guthrie.

The TVs all shimmered with morning shows around the room. The phones, for the moment, were mercifully quiet. *Lull before the storm,* Nye thought. *Soon as the word goes out we've arrested Lucking, the lines will be jumping again. Everybody's going to have something to throw in the pot. Real or imaginary, true or false, friends, old girls, guys he helped or hurt, a disjointed raggedy parade. The sad sack life and times of Jerry Lucking would come pouring in through those phones and e-mails in the next few hours.*

Around six thirty, Rose strode in, all energy and purpose. She wrinkled her nose at the doughnuts and helped herself to a chipped mug of black coffee.

"So are we still part of the circus this morning?" she asked.

"Altlander and the gal in media said we're all supposed to be standing around the chief when he tells everyone about Lucking."

"It gripes me to be a damn decoration," Rose said. She sat down at her desk. "How about I drag Pesce and Parkes down here? We shouldn't have all the fun."

Nye looked at his watch, finished his coffee. "Give them until seven thirty. They were here pretty late."

"You never left."

"I'm special."

"Old man," she said, "you are unique."

Talman sputtered into his coffee.

Nye took Rose aside while Talman and Vu ate and wrote up what they had done overnight.

"IA wants to see me at eleven. More shooting review." He assumed there was more, but he didn't say so.

"So I should get my invite anytime," Rose said. "We don't have any apologies or excuses, Ter. You warned Solorio and you and I are both here now."

"Just be ready. These guy sometimes get their own agendas going and I'm too tired out now to figure where they might be coming from."

Rose nodded. "You look tired," and for once she didn't joke.

"I'm fine. How'd it go at home?"

She sucked in a breath and seemed ten years younger. "Luis and I had a little fight. He yelled and scared Annorina. I told her all about the shooting, you know, cleaned up, and how safe I was and she kind of dug it. Luis," Rose shook her head, "wants me to quit."

"Husbands and wives that get unemployment together don't stick together."

"I made that point."

"Well, you can't go anyway. I got a lot more to show you."

The press conference went off well from Nye's perspective. The department's media office had done a good job of herding and tending so many reporters in the main conference room on the third floor. He and Rose were pressed tightly into a scrum along with

Nishimoto, who was hollow-eyed from fatigue or tension, Altlander and other senior police officials, surrounding the chief, all of them blasted by lights.

Rose hissed, "Wasting our time, standing here."

"Major Crimes is about wasting time," he whispered back. "Weeks going after witnesses who crap out, evidence you can't run down. This is good duty compared to that."

"That's what I mean. We've got things to do."

They faced the chief as he introduced Altlander and Nishimoto to fill in more background on the investigation. The shooting at the Southern Pacific rail yard was inconspicuously omitted. As far as anyone outside the department knew, there was no connection. Nye got a little claustrophobic, pressed in around the podium, and hemmed in by so many bodies.

He was glad when it ended, and as he and Rose hurried to get out of the room, Nishimoto blocked them. He wordlessly motioned them to his office down the corridor, away from the roiling nest of reporters and microphones.

"The deadline's still solid," the assistant chief snapped. "Time's running."

"But somebody's in custody," Nye protested.

"We've got a window to redeem ourselves," Nishimoto said. "We've got two days to do it. I want an airtight case against this mope. I want a case that I can turn over to the chief and he can deliver to the DA on a silver platter."

"We've got lines out about Ensor's old cases, we're talking to his old partners, boss. We've got tips about SUVs to run down," Nye pointed out.

Nishimoto was curt and unmistakable. "Drop everything except Lucking. Nail down his story. Get the SUV. Put everybody on the team on it. Make the case," he smiled gruesomely at them, "or bring me evidence that someone in this department jumped too far, too fast and we've arrested the wrong man."

Rose put her hand up. "With all respect, sir, we'll lose valuable momentum, maybe even evidence if we concentrate on one task like that."

Nye liked her forthrightness, but he was certain he was a minority of one.

Nishimoto proved him correct. "Detective Tafoya, you're a very good investigator. I have high hopes for you. Maybe we'll be working together in the future in some different capacity," he grinned for effect, but his tight, anxious face and barely concealed anger made it pointless. "Right now, I'm your superior in both rank and experience, I know Nye will agree."

"You are the boss," Nye said, giving Rose a small sad smile.

Nishimoto went on, "So given those two undeniable facts of life, I expect you to go out now, execute my orders with the skill, diligence, and professionalism I know you possess, and bring me back a goddamn airtight case." His voice was prickly and raw at the end.

Nye took that as a cue to diplomatically draw Rose back to the command center.

Parkes and Pesce had shown up, helped themselves to the dwindling box of doughnuts and were answering calls while they, too, wrote up their activities for the last sixteen hours.

"You could have backed me, Ter," Rose said reproachfully as he rapped on his desk for everyone's attention.

"Rosie, The Shadow has spoken. I'm taking care of you, believe me. I got you out of his office, didn't I?" *Before you said anything more or demonstrated that you don't have the patience for the infighting and internal scrabbling for advantage that are the meat and potatoes of the department, Nye thought. Probably of any department or anyplace that you've got more than two people together.*

Nye firmly and quickly relayed Nishimoto's instructions to the team. He waved down the groans and curses about a rigid deadline. It was an order and that was that. He split the team into pairs. Parkes and Vu would interview the possible witnesses Lucking had named. They would visit his wife and get her story, too. Pesce and Talman were going to Arden Fair Mall to comb through the video surveillance tapes, interview mall security about their procedures, get a warrant for Lucking's car, and go through it inch by inch. They needed to locate any evidence or witness that supported Lucking's confession. Or undermined it.

Like the ghostly passenger might be able to do.

Rose, still annoyed, said, "But we don't have any reported SUV thefts. Lucking's story already has big old holes."

"Maybe the owner doesn't know it's gone yet," Vu said.

"Who doesn't miss their freaking SUV? Cadillac? Escalade?" Talman asked sarcastically.

"Somebody on vacation. Somebody scared," Nye said.

"Ter, I don't think you park your expensive SUV in a shopping mall lot before you go on vacation."

"Look, I'm only saying there are possible reasons we don't have a theft report yet. It could be stuck in our system," Nye grimaced, "contrary to what Chief Altlander got for us. So, Pesce, go back through Auto Burg, go through our incoming complaint reports yourself, check with the sheriff, the other local agencies. They might have a report and it's stuck in their systems."

Rose made notes. The TVs were running bits and pieces of the just-ended press conference. She looked a little embarrassed when the camera caught her appearing angry and sharpish, and the other detectives instantly called her on it.

Nye rapped again on his desk. "Rosie, get hold of main jail's watch commander and set up a pickup for us. I want to swing by there at one and take Lucking out for a field trip. You and I'll work out our route now, but we're going to try to cover as much ground between here and Sutter County as we can this afternoon."

"Along the levee roads?" she asked, "see if he can show us where he ditched the SUV?"

"Yeah, a field trip. We'll need two vehicles and I want to set it up so we don't have a tail when we go, okay? I don't want the damn media on our asses while we drive Lucking around."

Rose went for her telephone. "I'll see what kind of diversion I can come up with."

Nye knew she liked planning and carrying out plans. He thought that was why they made a good partnership. He had trouble organizing breakfast for himself.

Thirty minutes later, while he was going through more contacts to see if anybody knew anything about Lucking, a call came in from the crime lab.

"What's cooking, Cummins?" he asked. "No pun."

"I didn't hear any," the crime lab's diminutive and acerbic director said. "I've got some interesting results on the glass and paint fragments from your hit-and-run."

"I'm listening."

"I think you and your partner should see for yourselves. It will help you describe it to the jury."

Nye looked at his watch again. They could make a run to the crime lab on Broadway and still be back in time for his interview with Internal Affairs. He intended to keep this interview short, and the excuse of picking their suspect up at the main jail would make it work. "I'll bring Tafoya and meet you in about twenty minutes," he said.

He hung up, stood, and tapped Rose on her shoulder. She looked up from her computer.

"Come on. The Julia Child of forensics has something she wants to show us."

TWENTY-SEVEN

"DOES LAST NIGHT GET TO YOU, TER?" Rose asked as they drove to the crime lab. He had the wheel, navigating surely through morning traffic on the city streets, heading through a Japanese-American neighborhood of tiny faded restaurants and rice distributors.

"No. Not really," he said, unwilling to let her know how frightened he had been about her safety.

"I'm thinking I might go see the department counselor," she said. She looked at him to gauge his reaction. "What do you think?"

"Even in these enlightened times, you'll take some grief around the department."

"What do you think?" she persisted.

"I'm in favor of whatever gets you through the day and gets you home."

Rose sat quietly for a moment. They turned left onto Broadway passing the vast old city cemetery, tall cracked stone angels and monuments jutting up among pines and firs. "I don't want to scare my daughter and I sure as heck don't want to give Luis any satisfaction, but I can't get it out of my mind. Solorio going down, the noise. Mostly him getting shot like that."

"It was him, Rosie. Not you. Remember that. He screwed up."

"I do. It doesn't seem to help. You knew him, why doesn't that make it worse for you?"

"Beats me," Nye answered honestly. "My skin's pretty thick by now." He chuckled. "We worked cases over the years, but Solorio and me really *bonded* on a one-eight-seven that was driving him nuts."

"Why?"

"Victim took us four weeks to ID. I mean, ID even as a man or a woman. It was back before a lot of the stuff Cummins has. We found a partial head, not much hair, down the tracks, one in-and-out bullet path, like a .38. But the real problem was the goddamn crime scene. I've never had a crime scene like that and Solorio and I had to really work that one to come up with anything."

Rose frowned, "What was so special about that crime scene?"

"It's the railroad, remember? We had a victim, shot once, thrown off a train sometime, and then we had a bunch of freights and one or two passenger trains come over the victim before what was left got found." He turned past the bulky Department of Motor Vehicles, going under a freeway underpass. "The crime scene was one hundred and sixteen miles long, Rosie. We found physical evidence every mile."

She laughed loudly and he did, too. Then she was quiet for a moment. "I'm pretty sure you saved my life last night."

"They would've stopped shooting," Nye answered. He did not like to think about the number of shots that came perilously close to them.

"But you saved my life, old man. I told that to the shooting review."

"You would've done the same."

"Thanks, Ter," she said, nodding to him. "Just take it, okay? Thank you."

For a brief span, Nye was tempted to tell her his most secret shame and sin, the one he was taunted and threatened with by Guthrie. This was the time, if there ever was to be one. But if he could not forget or forgive himself for his offense, how could he hope or expect that Rose would?

It was too big a chance. He firmly decided he would never tell her what he had done years ago. Guthrie had dug it up to plague him now, but it would be his weight to carry.

Then Nye said, as he saw the modern Sacramento County Forensic Evidence Laboratory come into view on their right, "Look, Rosie, do what you have to do, but if there's anything you need, you let me know. Even after I turn in my papers."

"I appreciate that, Ter." She grinned crookedly. "You are the hardest dope to thank I ever met."

Feeling awkward and unsettled, he pulled into a parking spot under a young Chinese elm. To cover it as they got out, he said brusquely, "Tell you one thing about Nish's new deal this morning, I am really glad we can drop looking into Tommy Ensor's life."

"I wasn't looking forward to that," Rose said. "I don't think there is anything, but you never know. Much better not to find out."

Nye nodded while they walked briskly to the glass doors. *You never know what you'll find. About anyone.*

He knew from personal experience.

Everyone has secrets. Everyone has shadows.

Even Tommy Ensor.

Even Rose.

Much better not to know.

"She's a keeper, Nye. She's saved your bacon on this case. You should be nice to her so she doesn't leave you like they all do."

Nye didn't answer Josie Cummins as they headed for one of the trace evidence laboratories in the new building. He could see Rose grinning. Cummins was barely five feet tall and dressed with expensive taste under the flapping white lab coat. Unmarried, in her late fifties with thick glasses, she was called by friends and enemies "The Lab Nun." The building was a monument to Cummins's long-cultivated talents at winning friends and convincing miserly politicians that a county the size and importance of Sacramento, because it held the capitol after all, required a state-of-the-art crime lab. And she managed to get it.

"You'll hurt my feelings," Nye finally said when they went into the large, airy lab. He sniffed at the vaguely medicinal and strange scents, oil, chemicals, and things he couldn't pin down.

"I've known this one for too many years," Cummins said to Rose chummily. "He's about as tender as a two-dollar steak. Both of you, come over here."

They passed long black-countered tables where technicians worked over microscopes or intently extracted small fragments from clothes or smeared slides with material Nye didn't like to think about. He sometimes wondered, although he wouldn't admit it, even to Rose, how he had contrived to stay squeamish after so many years as a cop or in Major Crimes. *I'm a sensitive soul,* he thought with an inner smirk.

"This is our new ICP-MS," Cummins pointed at a bulky collection of beige and dun-colored machinery that took up most of one wall. "You know my motto, Nye."

"Yeah, 'Traces make cases.'" He sighed for Rose. "Cummins thinks cops are just vacuum cleaners pretty much."

"Not so. I have a great deal of respect for some police officers. Even in this department," Cummins said to Rose. "What Nye means is that I truly believe most crimes are solved by the analysis of trace evidence. Microtrace evidence, the reduction of things to their most basic component parts."

Rose made a wry face. "It doesn't sound like that leaves much for detectives like Terry and me."

"Of course it does. Don't contaminate my samples," Cummins said with a chuckle.

"Okay, so what is this gizmo and what does it do?" Nye pointed at the machinery. Its inert bulk reminded him of a crouching elephant. It hummed slightly.

"This is a research-grade Induced Coupled Particle Mass Spectrometer," Cummins said proudly. "Even Nye remembers the old gas chromatograph intoximeter from his days pulling drunks over, I assume."

"Breathalyzer," he translated for himself but probably not for Rose. "Blow into the tube and get a blood alcohol breakdown of the deep lung air of the drunks. I could pick out an oh-six from a one-oh before the machine did."

"You were probably a permanent one-oh b.a. yourself in those days," Cummins said. Rose frowned at the insult but Nye didn't blink. He had decided he wouldn't respond to Cummins's constant gibes. That was what got under her skin. Besides, they didn't have a lot time to spend at the crime lab.

"And when you put a quarter in, what does this thing do again?" he asked politely.

"The ICP-MS gives us, gives *you*," Cummins nodded to Rose, "a fingerprint of solid trace evidence. It's that good. We don't have to boil or crunch or burn our evidence to get a sensitive multiele- mental result."

Rose translated this time, "The machine tells us the component parts of trace evidence and we still have the evidence? It doesn't get lasered or destroyed?"

"See, Nye? I told she's a keeper. That's right. The ICP-MS is especially good at measuring glass. So good, you can tie evidence from a crime scene to a suspect without question."

"And a suspect to a crime scene?" Rose asked, impressed.

"Now that the ICP-MS has analyzed the glass and paint samples from your crime scene," Cummins said, "once you locate the source, the vehicle, I can testify with what amounts to absolute certainty that your vehicle produced those glass and paint samples."

"Okay. Very nice. We're taking our suspect out today to see if he can remember where he ditched the SUV," Nye said. "So how come this required a personal visit? We could've gotten this good news over the phone."

Cummins winked broadly, which was neither in character or done gracefully. "Look over here," and she brought them to one of the black-countered lab tables where two techs labored beside electronic boxes and microscopes. "Here's your evidence. We took the glass, and, by the way, you've got two different kinds of glass fragments. The first is from a headlight, heat resistant. It's silicon oxide and various other metal oxides. We know it's headlight glass because it's a borosilicate. It's got boron oxide in the mix to withstand heat."

Cummins showed them how the samples were prepared, placed on slides with double adhesive tape, and then introduced into the ICP-MS. She went on, "The other glass you brought in is laminated, pieces of the windshield. There's a layer of plastic between two sheets of glass so if there's an impact, it doesn't shatter, it dices into little pieces or just cracks."

"Even I know this much," Nye said. "I took Forensics 101, Cummins."

"So you probably still think the big deal in matching glass samples is their refractive index?"

Nye fumbled. "Yeah, I do."

Cummins sighed and patted Rose's shoulder sympathetically. "So much work to do. So little time. RI is ancient, Nye. It's like a dial telephone in an iPhone age. We took your glass and ran both kinds through the ICP-MS. So instead of fooling around with RI numbers, I can give you a detailed chemical breakdown of both kinds of glass. When you find the vehicle in your hit-and-run, I can run test samples from its headlights and windshield, and tell you that your crime-scene samples at the atomic level match your vehicle. Yours. No one else's. Let's see one of our knockoff Johnnie Cochrans break that evidence down on cross-examination."

Nye admitted it was satisfying to have another scientific test that could stack up with the public perception of fingerprints for accuracy. DNA evidence was persuasive but hard to explain. In his recent experience on two cases in which murderers successfully challenged it at trial, the jurors had difficulty grasping the science so they ended up just ignoring it. Cummins sounded like her machine was very simple. Everybody knew about the old breath test and everybody, sometimes from cruel personal experience, knew it was accurate.

He liked that idea that Ensor had such an impartial, powerful tool in his favor.

Rose was asking Cummins a welter of questions. The little lab chief answered happily and looked ready to rattle on for hours.

Nye brought them both up. "Look, thanks, Cummins. This is terrific news. We take our guy out this afternoon, we'll bring you the SUV and we've got an airtight case," he raised his eyebrows for Rose's benefit.

"Oh, but I've saved the best for last," Cummins said, winking conspiratorially at Rose.

"Okay, I'm interested," Nye said, wondering what his new partner had done without telling him.

Cummins picked up two small plastic bags of paint fragments. "Your new one here suggested I look for something in particular when we put these into the ICP-MS."

"Did you, Rosie?" sounding a little peevish, which he had not intended. "Look for what?"

Rose, however, was unfazed by his disapproval. "I've been thinking about our other cases, Ter. My legs in the river case. I haven't looked at it since we started this investigation. So, I started thinking about our problem. Like, how far do we have to go to find out where the SUV came from? How many dealerships? Around the state? Around the Southwest, Northwest? The whole country?"

"Lucking says he boosted it from Arden Fair Mall," Nye said.

"But that still doesn't tell us anything about where it came from or who owns it," Rose said. "We need answers fast, right?"

Nye said to Cummins, "We're getting a little bit of a squeeze from upstairs."

"Oh, I can imagine. I can just imagine."

"So, I thought about my legs case. We pulled them out of the Sacramento River." Rose gestured around the trace evidence lab, "These guys were already doing an analysis of the soil on the legs to see what turned up. I suggested to Ms. Cummins that maybe looking at the paint samples for some soil or some of the crap in our air might help us eliminate a lot of places to go hunting around where the SUV came from."

"Very smart," Cummins acknowledged. "We checked samples from the paint fragments against our local air reference samples."

"What the hell is that?" Nye demanded. He felt pig ignorant.

"Sacramento has a specific combination of particulates and chemicals in its air. They change at different times of the year so we started a little library of samples of our air. You characters bring in clothes or tissue samples we can run them against our air samples and determine, with some certainty, whether the clothes or the body in question spent time in Sacramento. And when."

"So how does this tie in to our leg in the river deal?"

Cummins set the plastic bags down and wiped her glasses on her lab coat. "Because we're a river city, our air contains the dried components of riverbanks, the minerals and some particular biological, like grass and tree pollen. Along with our special cocktail of pollutants. So at some point, your SUV got a fresh coat of liquid wax. Keeps the shine up, makes it look sharp."

"I do it myself sometimes," Nye said.

Rose snorted. "Your clunker hasn't been washed since I started working with you. Forget waxed."

Cummins smiled. "Thanks to your new one," she nodded for Nye's benefit at Rose, "the ICP-MS analysis shows that between the SUV paint and in the liquid wax layer there is the same unusual mix of minerals and pollens we find from our ever-popular river soils when they dry and get blown into the air."

Nye nodded gratefully. "Very nice indeed, Rosie. The gizmo here narrows our hunt down to an SUV that spent time in Sacramento. Got washed and waxed here."

"I'd say better than that. I'd say that your SUV was bought near here and has stayed in this area ever since." Cummins started walking toward her small glass-walled office off the main lab floor. They followed.

"Why?" Rose asked.

"One of the biologicals in the liquid wax layer turns out to be the burned remains of rice husks. Burnt rice stubble. Like the farmers out in Yolo County did about a month ago and got the wind wrong so the smoke blew over Sacramento? Some very small pieces of rice ash ended up in your liquid wax in your paint fragments."

"I think we spend our time looking for SUV owners in Sacramento," Nye said with the familiar cool certainty that told him it was right.

"It's a heck of a lot better than hunting around the whole state or the country," Rose said.

Cummins closed the door. She sat down at a very orderly, small desk, almost like that of a young student. Behind her was a wall of diplomas and framed awards. Taking up a row below them were obviously amateur photos in gold-metal frames of a small, dark-haired girl playing on swings, intently eating an egg roll, staring pensively and soberly at whoever took the picture. "How solid is this suspect, Nye?" she asked bluntly.

"I have questions," he said. "But we've got a definite ID."

"We'll have a better handle after this morning. We're checking his statement out, and as Terry said, we're taking him around the area to see if he can show us where he ditched the SUV."

Cummins steepled her small, delicate hands. "I would like you sew this one up. I respect Ensor. He tried hard to help with my adoption. It got quite complicated." She gestured gently at the little girl in the pictures. "That's Margarita. She's from El Salvador."

"I didn't know you adopted," Nye said. "She looks like a sweet kid."

"Yes, she is," Cummins said softly. She looked sternly at Nye and Rose. "But I very much want to go into court and demonstrate how this lab helped you incompetents make the case. I've got a whole henhouse of county supervisors who are talking about cutting our budget this year. A winning high-profile case would shut them up."

"I'll see if we can help out," Nye said. "The trick is going to be finding the damn SUV."

Rose said, "I've got a little one, too. Annorina. How old's yours? I'm guessing five."

"And four months," Cummins said, her voice soft again. She suddenly had a shy quality about her Nye had never seen before. "She's made all difference to me."

"Yeah, Tommy Ensor helps a lot of people," Nye said quietly.

Cummins shook her head. "He tried to set up Margarita's adoption, but he couldn't really do much. I had to go elsewhere. There's a judge in town, Frank Stevenson, and he arranged the whole process. It went very smoothly. I went down to San Salvador, stayed at a hotel for two days until Margarita's mother delivered, three more days taking care of her, and then we flew back here."

"Don't know him," Nye said, after running through the list of judges he had either sparred with or shared drinks with over the years. "Come on, Rosie, we got to hit the road. I've got an appointment," he grimaced at the thought of IA's tedious questioning.

Rose paused as they turned to leave. She pointed at the pictures of Margarita. She said to Cummins, "Call me if you have any questions. I've got a couple answers, not all of them. Sometimes they get things in their heads and you can't get them to do anything, go to bed, eat, get dressed. Don't think about baths."

Nye groaned a little as both Rose and Cummins shared their common perplexities about raising young daughters.

Guthrie was eating his way slowly through a plastic carton of scrambled eggs and chorizo when Nye strolled into his office and slowly and carefully closed the door. Guthrie grunted and went on eating and making notes on a legal pad until Nye came over and with great delicacy took the carton of food from him, closing the lid and dropping it into the recycle wastebasket by Guthrie's desk. The smaller man sighed.

"You're pushing it, Nye," he said calmly. "I'm almost done with a memo for Chief Altlander and you can forget a pension."

"I know, Guth," Nye said softly.

"The more I look at your conduct on that family thing in Natomas, I wonder how the hell you managed to walk away from it."

"You have a theory?"

"Yeah. I believe you got rid of some official evidence."

"Like what?" Nye asked again in his soft voice.

"Quit fucking around. Now I've got this Solorio mess with your name on it, and your partner's, and this," and Nye had slowly put his big hand on Guthrie's throat, just touching it. Guthrie swatted at it and Nye's hand tightened.

"I'm giving you a warning, Guth. Like my grandfather gave pukes when he was feeling generous."

"Get your goddamn hand off me, Nye," Guthrie said sharply. He tried standing and Nye firmly pushed him back into his chair.

"Here's the warning. Tafoya and I are this close to nailing Tommy Ensor's driver. Nobody's going to pull her or me off until that happens, okay? It's not about me or Tafoya, Guth, it's about Ensor and what we owe him. What happened to Solorio was a fuck-up and he's responsible, sorry to say. So, you are to stay away from Tafoya on that one and anything else, okay? When Ensor's driver is locked down, you and me can do whatever we need to do between us. Right now, you sit here quietly and listen to your tapes of guys into whatever sad crap they're into. Occupy yourself. I'm going to do my job."

He slowly opened his hand. Guthrie's eyes had stayed locked on him, his face tense with humiliation and, Nye was not very secretly pleased to note, fear. *It helps to have a reputation, even if a lot of it is bogus,* he thought.

"Get the hell out," Guthrie said, standing up so quickly several

Smart Library

Terminal: GLK 001
Date: 10/04/2021 3:31:58 PM

Member: KELLEY, WILLIAM (Adult)
Membership Number: C11000393-05 D
Current Fine: £0.00

Today's Borrowed Items:

L11000424714
The fifth column
                          Due Date: 11/05/2021

L11000436551
Blackout
                          Due Date: 11/05/2021

L11000435498
Trust
                          Due Date: 11/05/2021

31111055509564
Sudden impact : a novel
                          Due Date: 11/05/2021

Please return all items by the due date.
  Thank you.

files were knocked off his desk and slid to the floor in a jumble of papers.

"One warning, Guth," he said, gently closing the door behind him and smiling grimly for the other detectives he passed.

Nye paused on the stairs, cops and civilians pushing past him. He hoped fervently that he was not making a mistake.

TWENTY-EIGHT

A LITTLE AFTER THREE in the afternoon, Nye signaled and pulled off to the side of a levee road in the middle of farm country. Corn in high green rows filled the land on one side of the levee. On the other, the American River flowed by in a blue-black wide swath.

Rose sat with Lucking in the back of the car. Behind them, an unmarked sheriff's department car also came to a stop.

"Okay, Lucking," Nye said. "How about it? This look any better than the last couple of spots?" He couldn't keep the rising frustration out of his voice.

Lucking awkwardly tried to scratch his nose with his handcuffed hands. Rose tensed, even though he had been cooperative and slightly bewildered since they started out.

"Kind of it does. Can we get out?" he asked. He wore a bright-orange jail jumpsuit and soft-soled slippers. Very hard to go far on foot in them. The outfit always made Nye think of weird loungewear.

"Sure. Why not. Detective Tafoya, please do the honors and help Mr. Lucking exit our vehicle."

The three of them got out and stood for a moment on the empty black asphalt of the levee road. It stretched back toward Sacramento and then out into a haze of more farmland dotted with barns and a line of spidery electrical towers. The river side of the levee was thick with gnarled dusty trees and underbrush. Rose dabbed at her nose and forehead as she held onto one of Lucking's arms. Nye blew out a breath. He was in a race with IA and his own boss.

It was hot suddenly, the sun a high white disk above them in a cloudless blue sky. Two escort detectives from the Sacramento Sheriff's Department got out of their car and came over. They watched Lucking with cool dislike.

Nye felt suspicion growing that either Lucking had no idea where he dumped the stolen SUV or there never was one in the first place. He was soft on whether he had a passenger now, sometimes saying he picked someone up, sometimes saying he was alone, always insisting that he did not remember who it was. A thorough check for a stolen vehicle report on an SUV since Wednesday had come up empty. The video surveillance of Arden Mall only showed Lucking prowling around the night he was arrested, not the night before. Mall security reluctantly admitted that they could have missed him. What did match up were his various stops on Wednesday night. The team had located several witnesses who identified Lucking as doing some serious drinking. No one said he left with a second person. Which left open the possibility that Lucking did pick someone up later.

On their way out the door at the crime lab, Cummins gave them a last piece of good news. She could also narrow down the model years of the SUV from the paint fragments. Nye figured that they would be able to focus in on something between fifty and one hundred black Escalade SUVs and their owners in the area. It was very manageable.

The only positive part of the trek to the river with Lucking was that Rose was able to keep the press off their trail. She floated rumors through the department's media office that Lucking would be making a late-afternoon court appearance in one of the secure courtrooms. That ruse diverted attention away from any vehicles leaving the jail parking garage. No one followed as they headed out with their suspect.

Standing on the empty levee road, Rose said to Lucking, "We're about ten miles outside of Sacramento now. Do you have any recollection why you'd drive all the way out here? Were you going somewhere?"

Lucking shrugged, making his handcuffs jingle a little. "It all looks really familiar. This place. The last place we stopped a couple miles back. I remember the trees and the corn, all that corn at night looks spooky, you know?"

Rose said, "If you got rid of the SUV out here, you still think you got a ride back into the city?" She looked skeptically up the bare stretch of road. It was as if they were the last people left on a baking-hot day in the middle of nowhere.

"You imagine what the traffic's like out here at one in the morning?" Nye said sarcastically. "I bet you had to work hard not to get run over."

"Maybe if we got closer to the river," Lucking said. "I think those trees look familiar," he pointed at a stand of bent birch and elms precariously hanging on the riverbank.

"Sure. Let's take a closer look," Nye said grudgingly. This was the fourth time Lucking had thought some bit of foliage or twist in the road was where he had come early Thursday morning. "We're going for a closer look," Nye said to the other two detectives. One waved. *Knock yourself out, champ,* Nye sourly thought they were saying. Rose didn't show any frustration or trouble with heat. They had been on this thus-far fruitless expedition for about two hours and she was as cool and helpful to Lucking as if they were sitting in an air-conditioned office back in the city.

The three of them trudged to the edge of the asphalt. The steep slope fell abruptly below them, thick with a wild crush of trees and brush, ending in the deceptively slow-moving river with its unseen, lethal currents. Lucking moved his head back and forth. His mouth flickered in a tiny smile. *He does enjoy this,* Nye realized again, *just like last night. He's getting a kick out of everyone running around. Making all of us dance when he calls it.*

"Okay," Nye said, his temper just under control, "you see any broken trees or some sign a big heavy deal like an SUV came down here a day ago, Lucking?"

"No. But something about this place," he looked up, then back down the road, "maybe it's just all the corn. It's got me confused."

"Oh, for Christ sake," Nye said angrily. "Back to the car. Nobody's been down here since Reagan was president."

Rose pointed, "Well, almost," she said. Wrinkled condoms like Christmas-tree icicles hung from a tangle of brush along with a crushed beer can. "Pretty romantic," she smirked at Nye.

They came back along the road. Nye squinted into the haze ahead of them. Where to go next? Turn around? Head further along this levee?

Rose got Lucking into the backseat of the car. Nye went over to the two sheriff's detectives, both heavyset and sweating in their poplin suits. One carried a shotgun loosely, using the upturned barrels as an ashtray for the cigarette he was smoking. Nye vaguely recalled that Casterbridge, the older one wearing nicely tooled boots, had some bad rap for walloping a suspect. Nye thought of Ensor's old partner Maslow and himself. Tommy was good at keeping that kind of thing under control. Maybe not so successfully with Maslow, but it worked with me, Nye thought.

"Okay, guys, I think we'll take bozo a little ways down the line here before we come back. He says he recognizes the corn."

Casterbridge snorted derisively. "Fucker's jerking us around, Nye."

"I think so, too. But maybe not."

"A little attitude adjustment might help out," the smoker said, tapping a length of ash into one shotgun barrel.

"I'm too old for that shit," Nye said and he meant it in every sense. "My partner and I've got IA all over us about the shooting last night anyway. Lucking's going back to jail just like we got him."

Casterbridge shrugged. "I'm just saying it would save us all time. Like instant rehab."

Nye grinned. Instant rehabilitation was shorthand for a dead suspect at the scene of a crime. Early on in his career, Nye remembered a robbery suspect getting shot during a robbery. The tight-faced yet triumphant sergeant dubbed it a perfect case of instant rehabilitation. It had great appeal. Certainty. Finality. Justice.

They drove another two miles along the levee road, Lucking chattering away about his family troubles. His wife had called him, said she wanted a divorce and she would take the kids. "She does that crap all the time. Threats, threats, threats, then she calms down, we work it out. This'll work out."

Rose looked at him as if she thought he was a strange form of alien life. "Mr. Lucking, you're facing attempted murder. This is about as serious as it gets. If this is some kind of sick game you're playing to straighten out your wife or your family problems, you better get real fast."

"God, no," he protested. He repeated that several times. Nye wanted to tell him they got the point so he should shut up. He was such an inconsequential mope, he got under your skin easily. Lucking went on, "But I bet you she's seeing how much she needs me now, okay? She thinks she can hold it all together without me," he bobbed his head angrily, "good fucking luck. Excuse me," he apologized to Rose.

Nye caught her eyes in the rearview mirror. She shook her head slightly.

She thinks he's a phony, too, he thought.

They stopped again when Lucking needed to relieve himself. Nye let the two escort detectives stand watch over Lucking as he urinated down the side of the levee toward the river.

"ID or not, Ter, this is feeling more and more lousy," Rose said, dabbing again at her face.

"Okay, so it is. So that's what we bring back to Nish, okay?" he said curtly, and felt badly for snapping at Rose. "It don't matter whether he's the real thing or some little asshole getting off making his wife crazy and leading us around."

"But what a dumb jerk," she said, apparently unconcerned by his irritability.

"They make our world go round."

Just then, Casterbridge shouted, and Nye and Rose saw the two sheriff's detectives vanish down the side of the levee. Brush crunched and dust shot into the air. There was no sign of Lucking.

Both he and Rose ran over to the side of the road. About ten feet down the levee, just above the river, he saw Casterbridge and his partner grab Lucking and yank him back from the river's edge. Lucking was shouting.

"I see tire tracks! I'm not going anyplace! Tire tracks down here!"

Casterbridge had him by the collar of his jail jumpsuit and forcibly threw him up the levee like a rag doll. His partner, shotgun aimed at Lucking's head, yelled at him to get down.

"Hey, hey," Nye said loudly, "everybody calm down, all right? Rose, go see what's doing with Lucking."

She nimbly got down the remaining few feet of thick brush, her gun pointed at Lucking, who lay on his side. "Do not move. At all."

Lucking froze, gasped, fear tightening his face into a mask. "There's tire tracks down at the river," he said in a croak. He kept saying it.

Nye managed to come down through the brush, catching his pants and cutting his hand when he grabbed for support. Casterbridge's partner, with his shotgun still angled steadily on Lucking, sidestepped up the levee until he was even with Rose.

"Motherfucker," Casterbridge growled when Nye joined him. "The motherfucker tried to run on me." He glared balefully up at the prone figure under the guns of Rose and his partner.

"Well, we got him, okay? Little asshole ain't going anyplace," Nye said reassuringly. "Let's see what he's making noise about."

Casterbridge continued cursing as they went back ten feet down the levee to the river's edge. The smell that close to the water was thick, old river soil and rotted things, and the river made a sibilant mocking as it flowed by the two men.

Nye got down on his haunches to see better. He looked up. There was a depression along the underbrush of the levee and it ended in the dirt and there were tread marks, filled with water and leaves, but still very visible here. Something big for sure. He almost chuckled. There was Lucking, pissing into the water, and, from that vantage point, he can see the trail something made as it came down the levee bank and apparently vanished into the river.

"Hey, Casterbridge," he said, trying to break the other man's unending line of invective, "you see anything in the water?" he pointed ahead of them.

"I don't see a fucking thing. Look at that fucking track, Nye. It's old. It's covered with shit."

"It's still here after the heavy rain we had," Nye said thoughtfully.

"Yeah, but there's a bunch of trees around here, see? All over. Great cover from the rain."

"I'm going to get a dive team out here and see if there's anything out there," he pointed at the impenetrable blue-black river. "Come on, let's go."

They trudged up the levee, almost bent double because of the incline, Casterbridge grunting every step. Rose, Lucking, and Casterbridge's partner waited for them, Lucking safely locked in the backseat of the sheriff's department car.

"I don't think he was trying to escape," Rose said. "He says this is maybe where he dumped the SUV. At least he *thinks* so."

"If he dumped it here, where the hell did he dump his damn passenger?" Nye demanded to no one.

Casterbridge snorted again, catching his breath, hands on his hips.

Nye said to Rose, "You mind calling this in and see if we can get some divers and a tow out here fast? Let's make sure one way or the other," he glanced at Lucking sitting slumped in the sheriff's car. "Let Nish know, too, please." He added the last with a grin, a gag between them, this exaggerated politeness.

Rose went to their car. Nye squinted again into the hot mid-afternoon, the near silence broken by the hum of invisible insects. Casterbridge and his partner talked together, low. Nye felt annoyed at both of them.

"Hey, you guys worried we get bit standing around out here by some mosquitoes and die from West Nile virus?"

"Nah," Casterbridge said. "Mosquitoes hate me. I can stand here buck naked and they won't go near me."

His partner snickered but looked a little worried. He cradled the shotgun. "Not me. I'm like a deli with a sign out, 'Free Meal.'" He swiveled his head around just to make sure there were no kamikaze mosquitoes in his vicinity.

Nye felt better and they all talked for a few minutes until Rose slammed the car door and came over. She was pale.

"You got that look, Rosie," Nye said lightly. "They give you a hard time about getting divers?"

She shook her head. "Tommy Ensor just died, Ter. The chief's putting the word out in a couple minutes."

Nye's smile froze and he found he suddenly had trouble remembering where he was. It was, for an instant, like a very profound drunk when the world seemed to vanish and he was left alone in a void. He heard, as if from a great distance, Casterbridge swearing again, this time very tensely and very softly. His partner stared out down the road.

Nye said plainly enough but oddly detached, "I need to go see Janey. See if she needs anything."

"Yes, we should go to the hospital," Rose said. She lowered her head and then raised it. "A dive team and a tow truck are on their way. Probably thirty minutes. I left word for Nishimoto, too."

Nye nodded. He had momentarily forgotten about Lucking. His mind was someplace else, a welter of old, old memories about Ensor and Janey and their kindness, their home, their kids. It all came in a rush, undifferentiated and unemotional, like a mass of photos dumped onto a kitchen table to be sorted through later. All he felt was something he feared and hated more than anything, the same dread dark enemy that engulfed him when Marceen left, and he realized that his own children were far from him and would be so for the rest of his life.

Loss. Loss. Loss.

"Nye, how about we transport the motherfucker back to Sacramento?" Casterbridge said.

Nye stared, without seeing, at Lucking still slumped in the backseat of the other car, unaware of what had just happened and how much it changed everything for him.

Nye said, "Yeah, all right. That'll work. You guys take him back to the jail, get him inside very quietly, check him back in, and make sure he's in isolation. Keep him away from everyone. He's a famous cop killer now."

"We can handle it," Casterbridge said coldly, motioning for his partner to get into the backseat with Lucking.

"We'll follow back into town as soon as the divers get here and get started," Rose said to Nye. She touched his arm. He felt a little afraid to move and he nodded at her plan. It was sensible. It would work.

Something else worked in the back of his mind as he and Rose watched the sheriff's car squeal its tires and speed away down the levee, back toward the skyline of the state's capital. She turned away. He kept watching. From the rear window, the back of Lucking's head moved abruptly beside Casterbridge's partner as if struck by an unseen force. Nye wondered if he only imagined it. Rose dabbed again and again at her face because she was suddenly sweating, like the rest of them, in the heat and the still air.

Nye went over and leaned against the hood of their car. The sheriff's car was lost out of sight in a far curve of the levee road.

Rose came and leaned against the hood with him.

"Jeez, Ter," she said. "I mean, goddamn, Jesus."

Nye folded his arms. He remembered Casterbridge and his old rap for beating up a suspect in his custody. It was, as best he could recall now in the confusion of his own thoughts, a fairly brutal beating and it was still a wonder how Casterbridge survived the IA and DA's scrutiny. It was before Rose's time and something she wouldn't even have heard about.

Yeah, Nye thought, Rose at his side, only one of them quietly and sadly contemplative in the hot afternoon, *you take the motherfucker back to the jail. You take him.*

Take him.

Nye's thoughts were savage and red.

TWENTY-NINE

STEVENSON DID NOT HAVE MUCH time to think about the cop's death. He muddled through the last minutes of the trial that day, adjourned until Monday at ten, wished Joan and Audie a decent weekend, and tried desperately to remember what he was doing next.

Go home, he thought. *Vee and Eli have the new SUV. She's going to check out the public storage space to make sure nothing goes wrong tonight.*

We're halfway there already.

He managed to get down to the basement garage without talking to anyone, the other courts still in session or already dark for an early start on the weekend. Then his cell phone rang stridently.

"We've got a little crisis," Vee said when he answered. "Don't go home, Frank. You better come to my father's office right now."

"What kind of crisis?" he asked harshly.

"I think we can deal with it together. But you need to get over here."

"I'm coming," he said grimly.

Georgina greeted him again when he strode to his father-in-law's office. The rest of the building, unlike the courthouse, still bustled with people coming and going on a Friday afternoon.

"He in there?" Stevenson demanded without preamble.

"Well, yes," she faltered, startled by his vehemence. "So is Veronica. They came back around two thirty, she left, but she came back herself a little over an hour ago."

"No calls, all right?" he ordered and before she could reply, he pushed into Eli's office and slammed the big doors behind him.

Eli, white-faced, swung away from the big window behind his desk, the curtains partly drawn. Vee stood beside the desk, taut and exasperated, and frightened.

"You're a killer," Eli said, advancing clumsily toward Stevenson, stopping only when Stevenson kept coming toward him unfalteringly. "The cop's dead. You killed a police officer. I was there."

"He wants to go to the police," Vee said.

Before Stevenson could say anything, Eli broke in, "There's no choice now, Frank."

"We had this discussion yesterday. Nothing's changed."

"He's dead." Eli's face contorted. "That's a very big change."

Stevenson's mind flooded with fear and clarity all at the same time. He somehow clearly pictured the last hour since the news of the cop's death had been announced captured in Eli's rising hysteria and Vee's obviously futile efforts to control it. Had Fonseca somehow gotten word even earlier? *Now he must think he can run me like a dog and fetch whenever he calls, jumps whenever he whispers.*

"Did you get the new SUV?" Stevenson asked with great control.

"Did I get the SUV?" Eli almost shouted, swinging to Vee and then back to Stevenson. His face was drawn into a rictus of terror and anger. "I put my name on the paperwork and wrote out the check and watched them call my bank and I drove the thing here, Frank!"

Vee said, "It was fine, Dad. It went very smoothly." She was consoling and maternal.

"Are you both out of your damn minds? My name is all over this horror show. I've got blood on my hands."

Vee came toward her father to touch him reassuringly, but Eli locked onto Stevenson as he said the last words, and moved at him with surprising speed. His right fist was up.

Stevenson was startled, but he blocked his father-in-law's blow easily and, without pausing, grabbed Eli's arm. Eli stopped mid-swing, his face showing pain and shock. Stevenson pushed him, like he was a balky child, to the leather sofa. Eli collapsed onto it, his shirt riding up showing a white, plump belly. His glasses slipped off to the carpet.

"Don't hurt him, Frank!" Vee cried. She sat beside her father on sofa and he leaned his head to her and she cradled it. Eli looked up at her, trying to catch his breath, words forming, lost. "Nobody's going to hurt you, Dad. I'm here," she said, the same certain tone she used on Haley when the unforeseen and frightening loomed. She looked imploringly at Stevenson. "You don't have to hurt him."

"He told someone about it, Vee. He's compromised you and Haley."

She stared and then said to Eli, "Dad? What's that? What did you do?"

Eli tried to sit up, and panted. "I had to get help because this was way beyond Frank," he coughed, "all right, way beyond me."

"You told someone?"

Stevenson nodded to her, "A man named Fonseca. You probably know his family."

Vee was shocked. "Buzz Fonseca? He's on every prosecutor's short wanted list. Jesus, Dad, that's the worst thing you could have done."

"I was thinking of you," Eli pleaded, reaching for her as she stepped back.

"Oh, my God," Vee said, stricken.

Stevenson found himself calm. "Are you all right?" he asked his father-in-law.

Stevenson had not fought since grade school and his reaction to Eli's completely uncharacteristic aggression was automatic. Eli's face was suddenly much older and weak. He lay panting, half sitting, staring at Stevenson. He slowly sat up.

"Would you get my glasses, honey?" he asked Vee slowly. He seemed dazed.

She knelt to retrieve them, and handed them to him and he put them on.

Like he's waking up, Stevenson thought. *Like I woke up. Disbelieving and horrified and trapped. Vee looks the same.*

He felt pity for them, mingled with apprehension.

Stevenson said to Eli, "Things have changed. But they make it completely impossible to go to the police. You've given Fonseca a club he can hold over me and you and now Vee, too. "

Vee sat beside her father and stroked his back. She murmured to him. She stared at Stevenson. Eli looked away from her as if she was not there.

Eli slowly swung his pale gaze to her and his eyes were moist.

He's crying, Stevenson realized with surprise. He wondered if it was for the dead cop or himself. *Not for me,* he thought.

Eli brushed a hand over his eyes. "I heard the news and it all came back, like it was happening at that moment," he swallowed and turned to his daughter. "When she died, you were halfway to Ensenada on the sail race. Remember?"

"Yes," Vee said softly.

"No reason for you to be here, the doctors all agreed the pneumonia was under control, the blood poisoning under control and then the hospital called and things had suddenly gotten much worse and when I got to her, that little doctor, the Pakistani," Eli coughed, "he said there was a short time left. She had just a short time and so I sat there with her, watching her and she went while I sat there in her room, listening to those damn machines."

"Daddy," Vee said and leaned her head to his shoulder and he stroked her. "What are we going to do?" She repeated it.

Eli looked at Stevenson. "I didn't even have a chance to talk to her. She was in a coma. It was just a damn flu. That's all it was supposed to be and then it got worse and worse and I was holding her hand and she lay there. Lurene, Lurene," he said. He lowered his head.

"A life matters, Frank," Eli said, his head down. "I couldn't stand being that helpless again."

"Of course it does," Stevenson said. He could not admit his own initial horror. Someone had to stay on watch and steer things forward. "It's no longer that dead man's life that counts, it's mine and Vee's and your granddaughter. You understand that?"

Eli brushed his eyes again, got up carefully from Vee's now

clutching hand, and, without offering either of them, poured himself a glass of vodka from a bottle in the hidden bar.

Vee came to some inner resolution. Her voice was clear, face composed. She said, "We can't change anything. We can only go forward tonight."

"You've got to bring the new SUV over to our house tonight," Stevenson said.

"I should go to the police. We all know that's the right thing to do." He sat down behind his desk.

"I can't stop you."

"It's what I should do."

"If it helps, I'll tell you again, I'm sorry," Stevenson heard the slight shake in his own voice. "I would undo it if I could. But I can't. Anymore than I can make Buzz Fonseca vanish."

Vee got up and came near Stevenson. He knew she was poised at precisely the awful place she had never wanted to be, caught between him and Haley and her father.

"We have to think past ourselves," she said. "Haley's got her life ahead of her and this would destroy her."

Eli nodded slowly, but without real comprehension.

It was not the older man's fault that his life had been one uninterrupted leisure cruise. He was not bad or malicious, Stevenson thought. *He was caught and he was unprepared and he could never be strong enough.*

"Eli, give me the keys to the SUV," Stevenson said, holding out his hand.

Vee said, "What are you doing?"

"We'll take care of things tonight. He doesn't have to be involved anymore."

Eli said, "I was with you. I signed the sales contract just now. I made call to the police. I told Fonseca. I am involved."

"Give me the keys."

Vee said, "Frank," she began, and he knew she was thinking about Haley, how they could make the switch.

"Trust me," he said to them both, as Eli slowly pushed the new SUV's keys across his desk, past the metal-framed pictures of his granddaughter, his daughter, and son-in-law and the large faded black-and-white picture of him and Lurene coming out of the church where they were married, laughing in an unexpected rainstorm.

Eli said, "This is like dying."

Stevenson understood that faint, final and quarrelsome objection to the way things had gone. Their old lives, including Eli's, were over. It did not mean they were doomed.

Stevenson took the keys. He reached an inescapable conclusion. *Eli was useless from now on. He was an undisputable liability. He could wreck everything. Better to keep him out.*

"No, it's not dying," Stevenson said. "It's exactly the opposite."

They were being born into a unhallowed new existence.

In the parking lot, Stevenson handed Vee the keys to her car.

"I'll drive the SUV home. Show me where it's parked. You take your car."

"I'll stay with him for a while," she said, shaking her head. "He's so scared. I've never seen him frightened like that. I still can't believe he was so reckless."

"You and I'll have to make the switch tonight. We'll have to bring Haley, I guess, can't leave her at home."

"Oh, no. I don't want her anywhere near this," Vee said fiercely. "I'll work something out."

He touched her face gently. "We're together no matter what."

"So far, we're the gang that couldn't shoot straight," she tried a wan smile, and failed. She looked at him wonderingly. "You're not scared, are you?"

"No, I am. It's something else. I don't quite know what it is. Like the old me is shedding."

Vee squeezed her car keys so her hand turned white. "My dad's right. This is like dying."

He kissed her. Vee didn't understand really. How could she? He barely grasped it himself. In the short time since he had heard about the cop's death, Stevenson had run through a wild, terrifying rush from sickness to shock, and then, as if bursting from a darkness into a lighted plain, someplace totally alien. He had struck down another human being, without thinking and certainly without intention. He was being blackmailed.

In his whole life, he had never felt such despair and, like poor Eli, untrammeled helplessness. But if he gave in to it, he was lost. They all were.

"We are going to survive," he said, pulling her close to him, feeling her body against his, arms around him, and her automatic unrestrained shaking.

"Don't cry," he said, kissing her, holding her, "please."

With some astonishment, Stevenson realized he was crying, too. They stood in the parking lot, on a splendid Friday afternoon, locked together, confronting the unfolding chaos of his actions.

THIRTY

"SHE WOULDN'T TALK TO US," Parkes said. Vu nodded. "It's got to be you, the guy in charge of the investigation."

They walked briskly down a corridor in the department to interview room two. Nye and Rose had not spoken much since they came back from the levee. The call over their radio from Parkes caught them by surprise.

"She is pissed," Vu added.

"We'll take it," Rose said not sharply, and the two other detectives nodded as they headed for the command center. No one else knew who they had stashed in the interview room. They had brought her into the department through the still relatively secret rear entrance that had been built for some now-obscure purpose, but which, in the not-so-distant past, had become the entrance and exit for members of the legislature, or even more august personalities, when their presence was required at the police department. The trick was to ensure no one saw them come in or go out.

Nye paused at the interview room door. A single cop stood outside.

"You lead?" Nye asked Rose.

"Sure," she said, opening the door. "It'll just be just girl talk."

Andra Lucking was a large-hipped woman in a dark pantsuit and a blonde pageboy haircut. She looked older than her husband. She stopped pacing beside the table and said to Nye, "I've been trying to see Jerry and I keep getting this runaround that he's not at the jail. Then they tell me you've got him and I want to know what the hell is going on?"

"Do you want to sit down, Mrs. Lucking?" Rose asked politely.

"I can make phone calls. I can make your lives a living hell. Where's my husband?"

Nye sat down, still trying to sort out the reality of Tommy Ensor's death. This was the second time in twenty-four hours someone figured connections around the state capital would translate into pressure on cops. Maybe it did sometimes now. Maybe it used to. Maybe it was just a reflex in a political company town that understood power as ubiquitous as air and not much else.

"He should be back in the jail by now, ma'am," Nye said. He did not think about what might have happened on the way there.

"So I can see him now," and Andra Lucking started for the door.

"Visiting hours are over for the day," Rose said.

"Oh, for Christ sake. I'm hiring a lawyer and you'll regret trying to make Jerry the scapegoat."

She had her hand on the door when Rose said, "Jerry's made a number of statements to us already, Mrs. Lucking."

"What did he say?" she demanded. "You had no right to talk to him without his lawyer."

"He gave up his right to an attorney," Nye said coolly. "It's on the record."

"It should be obvious you're dealing with an immature human being. He doesn't know what he's saying."

Rose pointed at one of the chairs. "It doesn't take much maturity to run someone down, Mrs. Lucking."

"Jerry did not run anyone down. He didn't hit that cop." Her voice shook for the first time and she slowly sat down in the chair.

"I know him."

Nye let Rose run. She began quickly. "You might be able to help us. Would you talk to us?"

Andra Lucking touched her hair unconsciously, then her mouth, her eyes flickering on Rose, then to Nye. All of this happened in a few seconds. "I should wait for a lawyer."

Rose nodded, unconcerned. "It's completely up to you."

"I want to help Jerry. He needs to come home. He didn't hit anybody. I'd know if he did."

"Let's start with Wednesday night," Rose plunged on as if given permission, "were you and your husband together the whole evening? He couldn't have been involved if you were together the whole night."

Nye slowly took out his pad and, without ceremony, began jotting down the questions and answers. He acted as if he was making out his grocery list.

"We weren't together the whole night. Most of it. Almost all of it."

"Did he go somewhere?"

"He went out. But he came back," and she paused.

"Late? A lot later?"

"Late. He didn't say anything to me and he tells me everything."

"Why did he leave earlier in the evening?"

"We had a fight. It's not that unusual. We have fights a lot lately, it seems."

"What did you fight about?"

Andra Lucking stopped again, studying Rose, perhaps seeing something familiar in her expression or attitude because she said boldly, "Money. It's always about who's making money in our house and who isn't. Who's succeeding and who isn't."

"Your husband doesn't think he's succeeding?"

She laughed harshly. "Jerry thinks he's on top of the world. That's the whole trouble. He's had six jobs in the last five years. He's making deals with complete strangers and I have to clean it up afterward. Last month he made some deal with the bum who owns a liquor store down on the corner. Jerry's been hanging around there, doing little chores and errands and he came home and he tells me, and he's got this huge smile on his face, that Eduardo's giving him the chance to invest in a piece of the business and it's only costing ten thousand dollars. He gave this bastard the money and now—and he's still smiling—we're going to be making double our investment in six months."

Rose nodded sympathetically and Nye knew she truly was. "Jerry told us you want a divorce."

Andra Lucking shook her head slowly. "When I talked to him yesterday, I was so mad I could've killed him. If either of you are married, you know that happens sometimes, even if you love someone, there are times when you can't stand their crap, excuse me, and you just want to let them have it. I don't want a divorce. He's my husband. We've got two children. I don't want to lose them. But, for the last fucking time, he has got to stop. Do you understand? He has got to stop."

She took a deep, husky breath. "Excuse my language."

Nye said nothing but nodded.

"When you saw your husband again on Wednesday night, had he been drinking? Was he drunk?" Rose went on.

"I didn't see him exactly Wednesday night. He must've come home and he went to sleep downstairs in this little utility room we've got. That's where he goes, if he's been out," and she looked steadily at Rose.

"If he's been drinking?"

"He know the rules," she said vehemently. "After the intervention, if he starts going out, he stays downstairs, he can't come up to see me or the kids."

Nye looked up. "Intervention?"

"Do you know what it is?" Andra Lucking asked.

"I've heard it," *and, only by the good friendship of Ensor and his wife, avoided it. Maybe what Tommy and Janey did for me qualifies, he thought dully and sadly.*

Andra Lucking said, "A year ago, Jerry's almost out of control. He's drinking. He can't stay at a job, he's got these unrealistic schemes for making money, getting famous. Getting the kids into show business," she stopped and then started more calmly. "So I arranged with some of his friends, me, his sister who lives in Humboldt County, to have a weekend intervention and show him that he was going to lose everything if he kept going the way he was going."

Rose appeared to mull it over. "Did the intervention work?"

"For about five months. Then it started all over again."

"Could you write down the names of some of your husband's friends?"

Andra Lucking nodded. "All I'm trying to do is convince you that Jerry is not the kind of man who could run another person down and not say something to me. It wouldn't happen."

"I can't go into exactly what your husband said, Mrs. Lucking," Rose sat back, "but he did admit he was drunk on Wednesday night and he did strike someone while he was driving."

"He's lying. Or he's confused."

"Kind of a serious thing to lie about," Nye said with quiet anger.

"Tomorrow Jerry will take it all back, believe me." She stood up abruptly. "How can I convince you that this is all wrong? He did not kill that police officer."

"He says he did," Nye caught Rose's disapproving frown. It was not exactly what Lucking said, but the result was the same.

"Then he would have told me," Andra Lucking said loudly to Nye. "Three months ago, after all of the arguments, and we had some winners, Jerry came home really late and he was practically in tears. He was out all night, he was partying with some of those bastards he still likes to be around, like he's a kid and not a man with a family."

"It's not the same," Rose began, but Andra Lucking was on a mission and she kept talking while Nye wrote and watched.

"Jerry was just all broken, in tears as I said. He was coming home and he hit our neighbor's collie, a sweet old dog that wandered all over the block. Nobody minded. Jerry didn't see her in the street until it was too late."

Rose's mouth tightened and Nye laid down his pen.

Andra Lucking said fervently, "Don't you see? If Jerry had done that to a human being, to a police officer, he would've told me. He told me in tears when he hit a dog."

Rose nodded for the last time. "Yes, I see, ma'am."

Andra Lucking straightened a little, spotting Nye's hand tapping the table slowly.

"I guess I better stop," she said.

"That's up to you," Nye said, closing his notepad.

THIRTY-ONE

STEVENSON PARKED THE NEW SUV in the driveway, resigned to the fact that a neighbor might notice that the license plates were different from the other SUV. But it was, he reckoned, a slight risk. The two SUVs were identical and people would see what they expected to see. When Vee drove in about a half hour later, he moved the SUV so she could put her car away in the garage.

She was quieter when they went inside, changing clothes, getting a bottle of chilled sauvignon blanc from the refrigerator, setting out two glasses. When he declined, she poured a large one for herself. Stevenson said he'd go pick up Haley. Vee did not answer him. She seemed somewhere else for the time being, worried about her father.

Haley was still bubbling about the trip to Disneyland the next day, and filled with delighted gloating over how envious several of her classmates were. Stevenson gamely joined in her enthusiasm. He noted that Vee had, in the short time he was gone, run through about half the bottle. She smiled for him and even giggled with Haley about some misstep a teacher made during history class.

Stevenson volunteered to make dinner or send out for pizza,

turning the evening ostensibly into a party, but Vee insisted. She put together odds and ends from the freezer, which he admitted turned out well. She looked at him pensively from time to time as they ate, as if gauging who he was and where she was and what was to come.

When Haley went upstairs to do her homework, they sat alone in the kitchen. The wine bottle was empty.

She looked at the faux old-fashioned wall clock. "Two more hours, Frank."

"It's almost dark outside now."

"You want to move D-Day up a little?" she asked, sitting back in her chair, arms folded.

"No, let's stick to the plan. There'll be fewer people out and less chance anybody will see us at the storage place." He took the bottle from her and dumped it in the bin under the sink. "Are you going to be all right?"

"I will be. Definitely. I'm just trying . . ." she hesitated, avoiding his eyes, and then staring at him brightly, "to get a fix on the new order, Frank. My whole life is kind of making some radical turns lately and it takes me a minute to get my sea legs."

"I know," he said.

They were both quiet for a few minutes.

"While you were out," she went on, "I worked it out for tonight. Hurricane's in the sack by nine thirty and I will make sure she's asleep. We'll do whatever needs to get done to get things from our SUV into the new one. Then we drive the two SUVs to the storage place at ten. I'll drive ours."

Stevenson shook his head. He got up and brought over a new bottle of wine and poured himself and Vee two small glasses as he talked. "I'm driving our SUV. I got us where we are and if anything happens, I get stopped or something unexpected on the way over or while we're making the switch, I don't want you in that vehicle."

Vee held her glass. "Okay. Then I'm against the unexpected. Down with the unexpected. Let's just sit here and be good to each other."

At nine thirty, Stevenson went upstairs and directed Haley to bed. She was watching TV and didn't complain. The alluring promise of the trip to Disneyland made her more obedient than usual. Stevenson wished her good night and said they should be up at six. Early start. He kissed her. From the pit of his newly blazing despair, he knew he would safeguard her from all enemies. He could do that. The two cops who pursued him would never get close to him or his family.

As he walked down the stairs, jacket on, he thought he would anonymously do something generous for the dead police officer's family. It was proper. It was gracious. He would not even tell Vee. It would be his gesture alone. Not penance or atonement, a gift of some kind.

Vee had a flashlight. "I'll hold the light for you," she said.

"How about I get the plates off our SUV and you get them off the new one? We can change them in a couple minutes that way."

"Fine. Let's get this show on the road."

They went into the garage without turning on the light. Vee showed him the way to his toolbox near the climbing equipment cabinets and he quietly got out two screwdrivers. He handed her one. They struggled taking off the tan cover over the SUV, folding it crookedly and stowing it in the backseat. Stevenson could look without flinching at the damaged front end of the SUV. It was something he understood but didn't have the visceral reaction to as he had the first night it happened. It was now just a dented fender and cracked windshield and broken headlight; he had to see it as just a problem to be fixed.

He left Vee to unscrew the license plates on the front and back of the SUV and then he went out through the side door of the garage to the driveway. The streetlights were on, it was a Friday night, and he looked up and down the block to see if anyone was around. Sometimes their neighbors, the Filoys, would be clambering over their twenty-eight foot powerboat in preparation for a weekend on the river. Or the O'Connors across the street had friends over on Fridays and they would stand outside laughing and drinking.

But it was a quiet, empty street tonight. Everyone tucked inside, watching widescreen TV or playing videogames or listening to their iPods. Stevenson laughed to himself as he bent down at the front of the new SUV. *And here are the Stevensons spending a typical Friday night, covering up a killing.*

He quickly unscrewed the license plates. He glanced more appraisingly at the SUV as he got up. It was outwardly indistinguishable from his SUV. He stopped himself. From now on, it had to be his. It had always been his.

He went back inside the garage through the side door again. Vee had gotten her license plates off and she had started pulling maps, papers, insurance, pens, cloth wipes, stray take-out menus, and Haley's drawings from some past trip out of the glove compartment and piling them on the hood.

"We need to keep a close eye on Eli," he said, taking the license plates from her and laying his on the floor. "He's got to make the DMV registration payments. They'll come to him."

"That creep Fonseca? What about him?"

"I don't know right now. He won't do anything as long as he thinks I'm going to do what he wants."

Vee's hands were full of more bits and pieces from the SUV. "You won't, right? Jesus, Frank, you can't."

"One problem at a time," Stevenson said. He wanted to believe he would resist Fonseca's blackmail or figure some way out. "Tonight this is our problem," he gestured at the SUV. "And Eli."

She said nothing for a moment and went on making small piles.

"So in a couple of months, we'll transfer the registration to us," Vee said finally. "I want to take him out of the loop entirely. He deserves that much." She peered inside the SUV. "There. That's the stuff in the front. I'm going through the backseat and the trunk."

Stevenson picked up the clutter from the glove compartment. "I'll be back in a minute."

He stepped outside and froze. The Filoys were outside in their front yard. Harold and Myrna, loud and old and immortal. Each held a glass nestled in an aluminum holder. They were arguing beside the towering pine that straddled Stevenson's yard and theirs.

He briefly thought about retreating back into the garage. Then he stepped forward boldly and called to them. "Ahoy, Filoys," he said cheerfully.

"Hello, Frank," Myrna said, breaking off from snapping at Harold. Both of them were in their late sixties, thin as rails and brown as beef jerky from the sun.

"Hey, look," Harold stepped to Stevenson's driveway, his drink sloshing onto the concrete, "see how the tree's tilting? Another good rain like the other night, it's coming up and *bang*, it lands on your place or ours. How'd that be? Some night you find a damn tree trunk in your bedroom?"

"I hadn't noticed it was having trouble, Harold," Stevenson said, casually putting the license plates, covered by the jumble from the other SUV's glove compartment, into the passenger side of the new SUV. "What do you want to do about it?"

Myrna broke in, "Well, Harold wants to get a chainsaw and cut it down. We lose all that shade."

"How'd you like to wake up with a tree trunk in bed with you, goddamn it?"

"Better than what I got now," she muttered.

Harold lost interest in her suddenly. He drank and peered at Stevenson. "You cleaning the car tonight?" he asked wonderingly.

"Just tidying up. We're taking Haley to Disneyland tomorrow. She's pretty excited about it." He slammed the passenger door.

"Oh, Disneyland, that'll be so nice," Myrna cooed, forgetting her quarrel with Harold. "Wouldn't that be a good idea, get away for the weekend, maybe go down to San Luis Obispo or maybe Santa Barbara?"

Harold snorted. "No, it would not. I've got the patio brick to do, remember?"

Stevenson smiled at them as he always did. They were both retired from the San Juan Union School District and they spent most of their days fixing up their home. "I've got some stuff to do, but you both figure out what you want to do about the tree and I'll go halfway on it with you."

"Yeah, okay, we'll figure it out," Harold said, glowering a little at the tree and then at Myrna. "How long you going to be gone?"

"Just the weekend. I've got a trial to come back to on Monday."

Myrna said, "We'll keep an eye on your place. There have been some odd-looking birds around the neighborhood lately."

"And a bastard running people down," Harold said. "Ran down a police officer the other night. Bastard."

"I heard about it," Stevenson said solemnly. "But they caught the driver. Everyone was talking about it around the courthouse."

"It's your fault," Harold said.

Stevenson faded. "You think so?"

"Sure. Give them some real jail time and you wouldn't see things like that happening. You guys are too soft, Frank."

Stevenson watched Harold Filoy sway slightly, taking a drink, poised to launch into another opinionated argument. He had no time for one. So he replied, "You may be right. Maybe a few tough examples would make some people think twice about committing a crime."

"Damn right," Harold said.

"I'll see you Sunday afternoon, late probably," Stevenson turned and walked with studied calm back to the garage. Myrna called after him that they would keep a very close eye on the house—you couldn't be too careful these days.

Vee just stood up as he came in. She had attached the new SUV's license plates to their SUV.

"The Filoys are at it again," Stevenson said. He touched his forehead. Sweat. Natural nerves and fear. "I didn't get the plates on."

Vee looked at her watch. "We've got a little time. I want to check on Hurricane before we go anyway and make sure she's asleep."

Stevenson could hear the Filoys, voices raised every few moments. He looked at the things Vee had apparently found in the SUV. She had laid them out on the garage floor, several battered traveling cups, CDs, hamburger wrappers, an old newspaper, the tools and sunscreen from the trunk. "Did you get everything?" he pointed at the items on the floor.

"I think so. I went through the car twice. Remember the scratches in the trunk from last winter when we bought that firewood and put it in there? You better make some like that in the other SUV."

Stevenson nodded. "How about you check on Hurricane? I'll put this stuff in the SUV and get the plates on."

"What about—" Vee started and then paused when they both heard Harold say loudly outside, "Oh, *hell,* Myrna," followed by a slamming door.

"Coast should be clear for me now." He grinned and Vee grinned back at him. They were both keyed up, tightly holding together.

She nodded and went back into the house through the laundry room. Stevenson waited a moment longer to make sure neither of the Filoys came banging out of their house again, which they sometimes did after one of their frequent arguments. But this time it was quiet outside.

He moved quickly outside, getting out the SUV license plates and kneeling down and removing the front plates of the new SUV, keeping track of the screws in the dim glow from the streetlights and semidarkness in his driveway. He tensed when a car came cruising down the street, but it never slowed or stopped. Just the normal routine of a normal Friday night.

He got the front plate on, took the new SUV's license plate with him to the rear of the SUV, and gently laid it down on the concrete. He hoped he looked like he was only checking the undercarriage or tires. He worked more surely this second time, screws off, new plate on, one screw back on and tightened. Stevenson reached for the second screw and it skittered off his hand into the darkness. He swore. The license plate hung crookedly, only partly fastened. He felt his hand along the driveway cautiously, the rough surface, bits of weedy grass here and there. Just when he was about to risk going into the garage and getting a screw off the old SUV, his hand brushed the screw and he carefully got hold of it and slowly, like he was polishing a diamond, got into the license plate holder and tightened.

He wiped his mouth with his sleeve. He swallowed, mouth dry. Getting up, he went to the passenger side of the new SUV and opened the door. Keeping his back to the Filoys' house in case they were peering out a window or bored by arguing or TV, he put the glove compartment contents into the new SUV and crumpled the newspaper and garbage. People always cleaned their cars before a road trip. That's all he was doing. No point in putting junk into the new SUV.

He glanced at his watch. Nearly ten. It should be a simple drop-off at the public storage facility at this hour.

He went back into the garage and met Vee coming in. "She's sound asleep. Finally. I had to calm her down a little. She's very jazzed about this trip."

"Almost ready, honey. Just got to get the stuff into the trunk and we're done."

Vee gathered up the sunscreen and the assorted garbage and he took the tools and they both went into the driveway. He popped the new SUV's trunk and they stowed the items in it roughly in the same positions they had been. He knew Vee was right about the firewood scratches, but that could wait until they were somewhere less out in the open.

"Okay, that's it," he said, closing the trunk quietly. He looked up and down the street. He handed the new SUV's keys to Vee. "Are you all right?"

"I've decided that I'm never going to be a master criminal," Vee said with a nervous chuckle. "The tension would kill me."

"We're almost there. I'll give you a minute head start and then follow you to the public storage place. If you're sure everything's clear there, turn off your headlights and wait for me to pull up behind you. I'll follow you in."

"If it's not safe . . . ?" Vee said, looking at him searchingly.

"Like we discussed, we go a block away and wait until it is. We've got to get this thing under cover tonight," he said.

She got into the new SUV and he went back into the garage. He got into the SUV and sat there, anticipating the sound of her engine outside, the signal that it was time to move. He breathed the familiar smells inside the SUV and fancied he could pick out Haley's light deodorant, Vee's perfume, the pleasant reminders of occupancy by people he loved.

Tentatively, Stevenson put his hand on the wheel. Just like that night. Just that simple. Just that insignificant.

Like someone heard my prayer about being able to judge like I do in court, he thought, holding the wheel, letting his hands slide over it. *Pass sentence. Look down and do what must be done.*

He held the wheel with one hand and turned the key in the ignition when Vee's SUV started outside. Stevenson put the SUV in reverse after another moment and backed slowly into the street, lights off. He did not turn them on until he was at the intersection.

There was virtually no traffic. The streets were pools of darkness and shadow and intermittent shafts of light among the trees from the streetlights. He drove slowly and carefully. Vee's red taillights shone ahead of him clearly.

He slowed even more when they approached the public storage lot. It was easy to spot. Against the night's darkness, it stood out like a carnival, high-security lights blasting it with illumination. Stevenson watched Vee pull up to the entrance gate. He didn't like all that bright light and wished she had warned him about it. It was too late now.

He saw her driver's side door open and she stepped out. She looked down the rows of single story cinderblock bunkers and then behind her at the manager's office, dark at this time of night. She got back into the SUV and he saw its headlights, splashing against the nearest gray cinderblock bunker wink out.

He coughed into his hand and drove forward slowly. Vee backed up and let him pass.

He stopped at the entrance gate. Vee leaned out her window. "Hit B as in 'boy' and then 407, Frank. The gate opens. Go through it and make a left and then just follow the numbers on the sides of the buildings. Building B's on your right."

He nodded and punched in the entry code. Vee had arranged all of this during the short time she had left Eli alone that afternoon. He waited as the grilled gate slid back and then he drove forward into the orderly little streets of the facility. He followed Vee's directions and found the right building. It was like a miniature city without variation or color, just rows of identical dun buildings. Stevenson was glad it also seemed deserted.

He stopped in front of the building at unit number 407. It was made up of wide units like its neighbor across the narrow street, where people put small boats or vehicles they did not need for the time being.

Stevenson got out. He slid the unit's door up and saw a space like a garage. The SUV would fit into it easily. He drove in carefully, got out again, and tugged the tan cover from the backseat. As he was hauling it into place around the SUV, Vee drove in and got out, leaving her engine running.

"Come on," she said brusquely, "there's a security guard outside. I didn't see him before."

"Get your side of the cover," he urged, cursing when the cover kept snapping away as he tried to pull it down.

"I can't, it's stuck on something," she said.

He rushed to her side of the SUV and they both tried to hold the cover down, but it seemed to have a life if its own and sprang away, leaving the SUV only partly covered.

"He's in one of those little golf carts, Frank," she said. "He's headed here."

"All right forget this, let's get out now."

They darted out of Unit 407 and Stevenson grabbed the door handle and pulled with such force it closed with a bang. He winced. Vee looked around for the patrolling security guard.

All he has to do is see there's another SUV. Two SUVs, even if he can't see the damage, Stevenson thought. *He'll report it sooner or later.*

He fumbled in his jacket pocket for the sturdy lock Vee had bought. She grabbed his jacket as if she were falling. "Frank," she said in a hoarse, terrible whisper, "he's here. He's coming around the corner now."

Stevenson heard her but did not change his rapid, sure movements. He slipped the lock into the door and snapped it closed, jiggling it once to make certain it was fastened. He turned only when the electric whir of the golf cart, and Vee's pressing against him, made him aware that there was another person with him.

"Hiya, folks," a reedy voice said. "That your vehicle?"

Stevenson faced the security guard. He was fifty and fat and he sat plumply in the golf cart in a too-large gray-and-black uniform.

"Yes, it is," Stevenson said. "We just stopped by to check on our unit."

"You got your card?" the guard asked, a little hardness in his voice.

Vee nodded and handed him a card for the storage facility with the unit's name printed on it in block characters. "We're going out of town and we wanted to get a few things from here."

He handed her back the card. He looked at Stevenson. "I know you, I think."

"It's possible," Stevenson said. The undistinguished face jogged no memory. "I'm a judge downtown."

"Sure. Sure. Look, you won't remember me, but I was in your courtroom a couple years ago. Had a different job then. Worked for Sierra Armored Transport. We got robbed and you did the preliminary hearing against the bums who robbed us."

Stevenson nodded as if he did remember. He could feel Vee trembling a little and he knew she was working hard to stay outwardly calm. "I haven't done prelims for a while. That must have been right after I went on the bench," he chuckled ruefully. "I hope I did the right thing for you."

"Hell, yeah, Your Honor. You were great. I got hit in the rob-bery and I was still wired up," he pulled his mouth open slightly, "See? Busted my jaw with a gun butt. So you made the lawyers all ask their questions slowly and let me answer slowly. It was a big help." He thrust out his hand suddenly. "It's great to see you again."

Stevenson shook his hand. "We've got to be going. As my wife said, we're going out of town early tomorrow."

"Sure, sure. Look, a little piece of advice," the security guard leaned forward over the steering wheel of the golf cart and spoke earnestly to both Stevenson and Vee, "the management won't tell you this, but, even if we got a twenty-four access policy here, you shouldn't come by after closing. Especially after dark."

"Why not?" Vee asked.

"A lot of the bad element, if you know what I mean, hang around here after dark, after we close. We've had break-ins. I've chased a bunch off myself."

"Thanks for the advice," Stevenson said, taking Vee's arm and guiding her back to the waiting SUV. He slid into the driver seat. "Watch out for yourself. Don't get your jaw broken a second time."

The security guard leaned back in the golf cart and patted the black gun in its holster around his thick gut. "Not me, Your Honor. I take no prisoners."

Stevenson waved as he backed out and into the street.

They did not speak for several minutes, the lights and shadows play-ing across them as Stevenson drove.

Then Vee said, "I can't do that ever again. That's worse than the night I thought Haley was coming two months premature."

"We're safe. We did it."

"I guess we did." She ran her hand over the dashboard.

"Were you that scared just now?"

"Yes, I was. I still feel it."

Stevenson nodded. "There's only one cure, Vee." He meant for him as well.

He slowed the SUV as they came around the turn near the Tower Theater. Broadway was lit up but empty and the last showing had not gotten out yet. He looked and spotted the Sacramento Police Department patrol car parked in the shadows, poised if a speeder came around the corner into the residential streets beyond Broadway.

"What are you doing, Frank?" she asked anxiously as he pulled up to the patrol car and rolled down his window.

He looked at her, "This is so you won't be afraid anymore."

The cop in the car warily eyed Stevenson. "Can I help you, sir?"

"Yes, you can," Stevenson said firmly. "I'm Judge Frank Stevenson. I live just a little ways away," he pointed beyond them, "and as my wife and I were coming back now from running a short errand, we thought we saw some men hanging around the back of the Long's Drugs. It might be nothing."

"Judge Stevenson?" the cop asked, now more deferential, leaning out is window. "How many did you see?"

"Vee? What did you say you saw? Three? Four?"

She looked out at the cop and Stevenson saw she was shaky but mastering it moment by moment. He had come to understand that their lives from now on would be packed with hectic emotional fluctuations, like current going on and off from an unstable generator. Right now he had control, power. It might not last. He needed her to understand it, too.

"I think four. Two were standing by the rear door. You can just see it as you drive by," she answered, elaborating the lie confidently.

"Well, I better check it out. Thanks for the tip, Judge," he nodded and reached for his car radio.

"Just a second," Stevenson said, "I heard about the death of that police officer and I was wondering if there's anything being set up for his family, his wife and kids?"

The cop now ran an inquiring eye over Stevenson's SUV as if recognizing finally how closely it matched the description of the hit-and-run vehicle. This was the moment Stevenson had wanted Vee to share, when the cop started making connections and there was a moment's hesitation about what he was seeing and putting it together with who he was talking to. A judge involved? Not possible.

"I believe there is, Judge. It's generous you should ask. There's going to be a scholarship fund probably. Officer Ensor did a lot of charity work and they'll probably be taking donations in his name, too."

"I just wanted to find out. I'd like to do something. My wife and I were talking about it earlier tonight and we'll make a contribution, something to help out."

The cop nodded. "Thanks, Judge. Hey, I really need to call in your tip and take a look over at Long's."

Stevenson slid his hand across the seat to rest on Vee's. She was fevered. He knew the cop was also going to check on the SUV's license and registration.

"You're looking at my SUV," Stevenson said. "It kind of resembles the one that was in the hit-and-run. Gave me a funny feeling, I can tell you."

Vee's hand tightened on his.

"Not kind of resembles, Judge. It's the same make, model, and color. Lucky the guy who did it's in custody already."

"Well, you didn't hear this from me," Stevenson said, mimicking the security guard a few minutes earlier, "but that gentleman better hope to God he doesn't land in my courtroom."

"Got you, Judge," the cop said with blunt agreement. His lights came on and he swung around them swiftly and made a turn back onto Broadway, heading down toward Long's Drugs.

Vee sighed deeply and groaned. "Talk about shock therapy, Frank. I thought you'd lost your mind."

"No," he said evenly, putting the SUV in gear and heading down South Land Park Drive again, "The only way to conquer fear is to jam whatever frightens you right in your face. Like when I'm climbing. It saves your life sometimes."

"I'm a little too stunned to be scared now." She sighed again and marveled. "It's true. It's like the hiccups. I don't have that feeling the sky's falling on me anymore."

"The cop's going to report the tip and he'll run our license plate, too," Stevenson said, "and he'll know that a judge sought him out, alerted him to a possible burglary or disturbing the peace, and that judge and his wife had nothing to hide. Nothing to fear."

"Fearless."

"I think this might make me a better judge," he said flippantly as he thought of the three opaque young men sitting in his courtroom. "Now I've got a real appreciation for the criminal mind."

He wondered what part of him was speaking, because he did not recognize himself.

Vee made the first move after they got back to the house, closed the garage door, and went inside. She grabbed him tightly, suddenly, and with such force he grunted. Her kiss and embrace were enveloping and he let them go on, adding his own desperation and longing.

Then she stopped as suddenly, coughed slightly, mouth parted, her hair disordered and her mouth a little discolored by the ferocity of the kiss. "I'm going to check on Haley, okay? Okay?"

"Sure," he said. "I'll be ready."

She wagged a finger at him, taking his hand and dragging him up the stairs. "You are so wrong, Frank. You are so not ready for me tonight."

The next hours in bed with Vee were a blur of sensation and collision, unlike their lovemaking before or after they got married. Stevenson found himself sometimes breathlessly groaning at Vee, "What are you doing? Jesus," and trying to fit it all into the frame of their lives and failing. This was new and different and remarkable. It was terrifying and explosive.

Near three in the morning, he woke up and rolled over. Vee's arm was across him and she stirred when he moved.

"Oh, Lord," she said.

"Do I know you?" he teased.

"Maybe."

He bent to her breast. "Here's an old friend."

She didn't move or say anything. Then Vee arched her neck. "Where did this come from?"

"I don't know," he said, kissing her. "I don't care."

"So how about we just stay here today, the rest of the day, the rest of the weekend, next week, next month?"

"Remember you wanted to start at Day One?"

"A hundred years ago."

"This is Day One, Vee. We'll never be the way we were."

THIRTY-TWO

NYE MET ROSE AT EIGHT THIRTY Saturday morning in front of the main jail downtown. At that hour on a weekend, the daily mix of lawyers and families, bail bondsmen and cops outside the tall building was much thinner, but still lively.

"You look even lousier than usual, Ter," she offered as they pushed past the other people and into the large lobby flanked by courtrooms. A big empty aquarium, dusty and dry, stood off to the side. The fish were taken out when it became apparent jail visitors liked to drop junk food into it or pound on the sides.

"I'm getting my second wind," he replied defensively. He had slept very little, in fact. He assumed it would sound too whiny if he told her the Three o' Clock Follies. He would toss and turn until four, maybe get back to sleep until five when the fits would start again. He was up for good at six. The last time he hosted the Follies, he was mired deep in self-pity and gloom because Marceen was gone.

This time it was Ensor's death. He had not thought twice about Tommy Ensor in the years since they were partners, but, in the last seventy hours, there seemed to be no one more central to his life. It was wracking to think about his death.

He was also acutely aware of his days as a cop perceptibly trickling away. *Just over a week,* he thought. Retirement had started to make less sense to him. It felt like, no matter how the investigation ended, he had too many loose ends. After Solorio, now Ensor, he was depressed by the irrational thought he was running out on people, quitting. *Almost,* he thought with some surprise, *like I'm running out on Rose.* There was no telling what Guthrie might still do to him, but it seemed insignificant against his feeling he was letting her down.

Rose glanced at him and they both passed through the special security line reserved for cops and lawyers. The civilians, as usual, eyed them with suspicion and envy.

"It's Ensor, right?" she said. "Me, too. I woke up around two this morning and Luis said I was crying. Ter, I never cry. Why the heck am I doing it now?"

"We're both a couple of saps."

She smiled at that. "Long as I can talk to you, I don't need the department's shrink. After that last blast from you know who, maybe I will anyway."

They had both just come from the latest of several recent briefings for Nishimoto and Altlander. They had started yesterday after the interview with Lucking's wife. Now the order coming down from both assistant chiefs was to pin down the passenger, however possible. "Someone else out there knew everything that the department had to know," Nishimoto had barked. "Find them." Nye and Tafoya could only nod in silent, frustrated acknowledgment. The team had uncovered nothing on the passenger in the SUV. They were no closer to identifying him than they had been early Thursday morning. The best hope so far, the enhancements of the surveillance videos, had not been completed yet. Despite hourly threats and exhortations, the state DOJ had not delivered the results. They did not operate according to the Sacramento Police Department's schedule.

As for Friday's other dead end, the divers did not find any black SUV in the river where Lucking had thought he dumped the stolen truck. They did pull out a recently stolen Toyota Corolla. Maybe the mope confused the two, Nye suggested. He and Rose speculated that Lucking had stolen the Corolla four days ago and then gotten all mixed up and lumped it in with the missing SUV. Or maybe, Rose said after listening to what his wife had said, he just made it all up.

Nye also perceived another source for Nishimoto and Altlander's anger. They were shaken obviously by Ensor's sudden death. A police officer's death while on duty was rare in the state's capital and the circumstances around the death of this officer were unique. Flowers had started piling up outside the department on its worn granite steps Friday afternoon. Some had them delivered, while others came in person to honor the fallen officer. The silent citizens who came to stand outside the building were a tribute and yet unnerving, too. This public demonstration of support and grief was hard to fit into the experience of anyone on duty. All levels in the SPD would no doubt feel the unstated pressure coming from this civic support to provide answers to their fellow citizens. The upper ranks would also have that pressure coming on a political level, a fact that did nothing to slow their quick tempers.

So Nye and Rose were left with very clear, pointed instructions from Nishimoto and Altlander: Nail down Lucking's story before the weekend was over.

Nye said they would go immediately to see him and pull every detail from him again. He did not feel any regret that Lucking's trip back to the jail in Casterbridge's custody had probably been a bad one.

The team was gathering at ten for new assignments, including dividing up the Cadillac dealerships in the area and the list of registered Escalade owners around Sacramento in a twenty-mile radius. The circle would be expanded if necessary.

Rose met him on the other side of the security check, two very young sheriff's deputies stared at their badges when they displayed them as if unable to read.

They headed for the elevators. "I'll come to Janey Ensor's with you, Ter," she said as they got into the elevator and hit the button for the watch commander's floor.

"I don't know, Rosie," he said, the doors closing. No one had gotten in with them. "I don't want to hit you with it." In truth, he would welcome her company at the visit that afternoon.

"I sure don't want to intrude. I guess I feel a lot worse about this than I thought I would."

"It's funny, ain't it?" he said as they got to the floor.

"I guess it's because Ensor showed you how it could go. How it should go on the job." She struggled for a moment and then resorted to a cop's sarcasm to get free of an uncomfortable emotion. "That's the trouble with heroes."

They strode to the Plexiglas enclosure from which the watch commander surveyed the pods that made up the modern new jail's inmate holding areas and open spaces. Nye rapped on the glass and showed his badge again, as Rose did.

"Hey, Elvis," Nye said to the slim, hard watch commander with steel-grey hair, "we need to see Lucking. Alone. Can you get him brought to a visiting room now?"

"Nye. Kind of past your bedtime, isn't it?" Elvis Chaney, the watch commander said.

"Yeah, yeah. I'm laughing," Nye replied, annoyed Chaney was resurrecting the old days when indeed his appearance at that morning hour signaled only the end of a long night. "See my partner? Rosie's breaking up, too."

Rose smiled faintly at the same encounter Nye frequently had with older law enforcement personnel around the city. Everyone seemed to know everyone else's sore spots and stuck them deliberately.

"Well, I can get someone to escort him in about twenty minutes, Nye. You should've called ahead," the watch commander picked up the intrajail telephone.

"What kind of shape's he in?"

"Fine. I take good care of all my pukes as long as they respect where they are," he spoke into the phone.

Nye wondered if Casterbridge's knocking around was visible.

Rose said, "I bet he's pretty popular around here."

Elvis Chaney smiled a wintry smile. "Oh, he's going to win the big one on *American Idol*."

Fifteen minutes later, as Rose worked her cell phone to line up appointments at Cadillac dealerships and Nye brooded about what to hit Lucking with to make him more forthcoming than he had been in the first interviews, they both noticed Chaney abruptly leave his command center with two other uniformed deputy sheriffs. Then three more ran by, down the same bright corridor to the right of where Rose and Nye waited.

She said to him, "What's shaking, Ter?"

"Some kind of ruckus probably. Guy tried to shank someone, someone tried to shank someone else. Maybe they're having trouble getting someone out of his cell."

"I hope it isn't Lucking. I don't want to waste time babying him down from a run-in with the guards."

"No," Nye said, scuffing his shoes along the already-cracked tiled floor of the new jail, "I don't want to spend any more time with the sonofabitch than we have to."

At that moment a painful whining siren sounded.

"Jeez, what's that? A fire drill?" Rose asked, grimacing.

"No, they're locking the place down," Nye said. He saw Chaney run back into the command center and he followed at a trot.

"Elvis, what's up?" he demanded.

Chaney ignored him, barking instructions for paramedics and more deputies. Nye listened as he did, in fact, lock down the main jail, sealing all of the outside entrances and moving all of the inmates back into their cells. People waiting downstairs were forced back to the sidewalk.

Then Chaney, mouth tight, eyes hard, said to Nye, "Get your partner, Nye, and come with me."

Lucking's isolation cell was two floors up. Nye and Rose stood in the doorway, the bars electronically rolled back. It smelled of sweat and bleach.

It was a bare, windowless room, concrete and steel. Steel toilet, sink, bedframe that was part of the floor. Simple mattress. And one more thing.

Nye and Rose went inside, careful not to touch any surface. Behind them Chaney was swearing and snapping orders at the half dozen deputies clustered at the cell.

Rose crouched down when she was a few inches from Lucking.

"My first DOA was a hanging, Ter," she said quietly, like they were alone, "a kid, I think he was maybe eighteen. He was bummed out because he didn't make the swim team or something; his note was kind of hard to read. He got two belts and he wrapped them around his neck and tied them to the bar in his closet and he leaned forward," she paused, eyes searching Lucking, "and he just stayed that way. He could've saved himself any time by just standing up. Just a kid."

Nye studied Lucking. He hung limply, feet barely touching the floor, from the sturdy wire protected light in the center of the ceiling. The single sheet from the hard bed was taut around the swollen flesh of his neck and, above it, he glared silently with red eyes at Nye and Rose, his black protruding tongue mocking them.

"Who saw him last?" Nye asked Chaney's back.

"I'm checking." Chaney didn't turn to answer.

"It's real simple, Elvis. Who saw him when he got back here? Who brought him up here? Anybody tuck him in?"

"I don't know, Nye. Fuck off for right now, okay?"

"He didn't have any suicide watch, right? I'm guessing."

Chaney swung from the other deputies. "He didn't have any suicide watch because there wasn't any indication he was suicidal, for Christ sake. You were with him yesterday afternoon. Did you think he was going to do something fucking stupid like this?"

"We didn't bring him in," Nye said. "Ask Casterbridge and his partner."

"What's that mean?"

"They had him after us," Nye gestured at Rose, who nodded. "Maybe he got really depressed on the way back here."

"Look, Terry," Chaney came up to Nye, "you want to tell me something about this? How about you?" he demanded to Rose.

"No, not me. It's a bad way to go out."

Chaney shook his head, cursing low. "Okay, both of you clear this area. I've got to get the investigators in here right away." He grimaced at Lucking, as if daring him to do what he had already done.

Nye and Rose left, passing through the surly knot of families and friends of inmates outside the main jail, many of them demanding to know from harried sheriff's deputies when they would be let back inside. They were both jittery and disturbed.

"You really have to want to go out to do it that way, Ter," Rose said when they got to their cars. "Like that kid I found. You really want to die."

"I saw a guy did it with a hatchet. Hit himself in the head four times."

"Practice makes perfect." She adjusted her gun holster. "I think this nails down Lucking's confession. He knew what he'd done. Ensor died."

"You could certainly look at it that way. Lot of people will do exactly that."

"This guy wanted to die, Ter. Look how he did it."

"What if he had some help?"

"Like who? Someone at the jail?" Rose asked unhappily. She did not like the implications of anything other than suicide.

"Another puke maybe. They get a kick out of knocking off celebrities."

"You don't think Lucking did himself, right?

"Probably he did," Nye said, wondering if Lucking had been so terrified after Casterbridge had at him, that he hanged himself later, alone in his cell. Or if someone not unlike Casterbridge had assisted him in the long, empty dark hours before morning. Or maybe Casterbridge himself. Whatever the sequence of events, from what his wife told them, Lucking was a man who did not face reality very well. His reality, whether based on truth or a lie, was going to be highly unpleasant after Ensor's death.

"Doesn't actually change much for us," Nye said. "We still have to make Lucking's story work. We're on a short fuse. The investigation's still on."

THIRTY-THREE

"THE INVESTIGATION IS OVER," Altlander said firmly. "The suspect hanged himself when he realized he would be facing life in prison."

"Do you want the chief to tell the media that today?" Nishimoto asked Altlander impatiently. "Do you want to put him out there with them and their questions with half a case?"

"Jerry, the main suspect is dead. He was positively identified as being the actual driver. He confessed to the offense. I think the chief would feel damn comfortable taking credit for winding up this investigation, this thoroughly, this fast."

"Nye? Tafoya? You two feel like contributing at some point?" their boss demanded sarcastically. They all sat in his office, jarringly cheerful morning sunshine pouring in on his desk from the window behind him.

Nye carefully folded his hands, glancing at Rose. She straightened in her chair.

"Sir, I think, just from a professional perspective, you know, the department's point of view," she floundered and looked helplessly

289

at Nye for a moment. He was not about to bail her out. Rose's one major weakness was her insecurity, especially around those she mistakenly thought superior or who she had been told were superior. *Time to fly solo, Rosie, you're better than all of them,* Nye thought.

Nishimoto frowned at her garbled reply.

"What are you saying, detective?"

"Sir, I mean, I think we should bring the investigation to a conclusion, just like it was yesterday. We haven't ID'd the passenger and we're still waiting for the video surveillance enhancements. I think the department's going to look better in the long run if we've got a solid case. One the DA could have taken to court." She finished with a faint smile.

Nice going, Rosie, Nye thought, smiling back at her.

"I completely agree with my partner," he said.

Altlander bounced out of his chair. "I'm willing to give Major Crimes ample credit for its part in the finding Ensor's killer. Okay? But it's over."

"We don't have the vehicle," Nishimoto said in exasperation. "We can't tie the suspect to the vehicle."

"He gave it up, Jerry. He said he hit Ensor. The goddamn SUV's a sideshow now."

"Well, not really. Sir." Nye said mildly.

"What are you talking about?" Altlander snapped. He breathed harshly.

"As long as we don't have the SUV, we can't account for Lucking's story. It's got holes. Maybe it works to say he was drunk, but the Arden Mall security tapes don't show him there until the night he got popped. We don't have any stolen or missing black Cadillac Escalades reported. All we turned up was a stolen Corolla where he said he maybe dumped the SUV."

"He copped to it, Nye," Altlander said caustically. "Not many guys cop to a crime like this if they didn't do it."

Nye regarded his superior with genuine amazement. "Excuse me. I can name you a dozen cases I handled personally, up to and including murder, where they did just that."

"Why in the hell would Lucking confess if he didn't do it?" Altlander exploded. He stared angrily at Nishimoto and Nye. Rose, for some reason, escaped his wrath.

"We'll have to go back and interview all of his friends again, spend more time with his wife," Nye said to Nishimoto. "I got the feel yesterday he figured he could get some kind of advantage over his wife by saying he was guilty of a serious crime."

"I did, too, sir," Rose said firmly. "Mr. Lucking wanted his family to see how much they needed him, how much he contributed, how much he was indispensable. They'd find out when he was gone for a while."

Nishimoto sat back. He was halfway in the shadows, only his small hands in the sunlight on his desk. "You think he was going to take it all back at some point?"

"His wife thought so," Nye shrugged. "Most of the time people do things like this, they don't figure it so clearly or cleanly."

"This is idiotic," Altlander snapped again. "Speculation on speculation. We can't prove any of it."

"I think that's Nye's point," Nishimoto's hands did a little tap dance in the sunlight, "we need to find out a lot more before we close down the investigation."

Altlander lapsed into silence, his hard angled face tense and annoyed. "Okay. I'll go this far. Monday morning, we lay it all out. The chief will approve that. He'll hold a press conference, announce the findings of the department's investigation, and we're done."

Nishimoto leaned back into the sunlight. "I do think the longer we go on, the more it looks like we screwed up," he said matter-of-factly to Nye and Rose. "That gives the team today, tomorrow, and we brief the chief Sunday night. Can you get it done?"

Nye raised an eyebrow to Rose and she nodded slightly.

"A couple more days would be good," he ventured.

Nishimoto shook his head. "Assistant Chief Altlander's right. We need to quickly put a cap on the investigation in light of this development. Monday's the new deadline."

"Okay. Monday it is," Nye stood up. He twisted a button on his coat as Altlander grunted either in agreement or annoyance, and gave Nye an inscrutable scowl before stalking from the room. "Boss, I need to talk to you for a minute." He turned to Rose, "Alone."

She got up and looked at him quizzically as if she expected him to explain. There was an awkward momentary void. He didn't look at her. "All right, I'll be in the command center, Ter."

Nishimoto nodded, puzzled as she closed the door.

"It's about the development, boss," Nye hesitated, wondering how to tell Nishimoto.

"What do you want, Nye? A good cry? A pat on the head?" Nishimoto said to him, standing up after he had finished reciting the events at the levee road on Friday. "I haven't heard anything about Lucking being worked over."

"Nobody wants to talk about it," Nye said. "Maybe Casterbridge was careful."

Nishimoto folded his arms. "We should be on our knees thanking God we're not the sheriff or Chaney or anyone connected with Lucking. This is the fourth suicide at the main jail in a year, right? The County Grand Jury's got its nose into the jail and everybody over there."

"Boss, I'm not apologizing. I didn't want you to be blindsided if something comes out that Lucking's got punched up when he got back to the jail."

"He tried to run and he had to be restrained. It got a little rough. You said so. Tafoya would say so, right? He probably does have a couple of shiners and bumps he didn't have. But the important thing here," Nishimoto stared at Nye opposite him, "is that this is not ours, Terry. Not yours or mine or the chief's. We gave Lucking to the sheriff and he is the sheriff's bag of groceries."

Nye nodded, trying to reckon up why he felt so compelled to unburden himself to Nishimoto or what he expected as a consequence. Did he want some comforting words, a professional absolution? He really did not regret turning Lucking over to Casterbridge, that wasn't it. He groped for an answer.

"Boss, what if it's not suicide?"

"What if it's not?" Nishimoto shot back. "It's not on our charge sheet."

"You know the truth," Nye said, the reality breaking on him, "I wanted Casterbridge to take care of this guy. I kind of hoped Lucking never made it back to the jail."

Nishimoto sat down and he looked hard and sympathetic at the same time.

"Terry, you're about the shortest of short-timers. What is it now, two weeks left?"

"Twelve days, boss. I'm not counting."

They both grinned for a moment at the lie.

"Bring this in by Monday and you can just sit back for the last week. You go out with a big win for all of us," he nodded soberly, "and your former partner."

"You think Altlander's going to let it go?"

"He didn't scare you off the case before this happened. He doesn't gain anything now, Nye. In fact, he comes away looking quite successful no matter what you do."

Nye had trouble framing his suddenly conflicting feelings, the odd sense he had back at the jail, even before knowing about Lucking's death, that he was somehow abandoning his responsibilities, his people.

"I just don't feel right, boss," he began, and Nishimoto impatiently and abruptly interrupted him.

"Look, Terry, this will be good for you on your way out and it will do Tafoya a hell of a lot of good going forward. So you better move. The clock's running."

Nye left Nishimoto's office.

The detectives on the team were somber and dispirited in the command center.

"So that's it," Talman said, slumped in his chair.

"Over and out," Pesce added.

Vu, surrounded by the TV monitors showing people with flowers at Sutter General or outside the modest Ensor home, stared out the window, "Like Kennedy's assassination. Ensor's dead and the guy who did him's dead, too. We're left hanging out." He frowned as he faced the room, "Bad joke."

"No joke," Rose retorted. She unwrapped a tinfoil packet of small white cookies and silently offered them around the team. "We're not done."

Nye passed on the cookies. The phones were still ringing constantly, rolling over to recorded messages, the computer screens shimmering with lists of names and addresses the team was checking.

"We've got until Sunday night," he said. "So Vu, you and Pesce get out and talk to Mrs. Lucking again, talk to his kids, talk to the neighbors. Get me a whole profile on this guy and everything he's been doing for the last couple weeks. Like, nail down the story his wife told Rosie and me about running over a dog when he was shit-faced. Sound familiar?"

It was Vu, as usual, Nye noted, who raised the thing they were all thinking.

"What if we come up dry on Lucking? Is that even going to get past first base upstairs?"

"You mean, what if we can't prove he stole an SUV and ran down Ensor?"

"What if we can't?"

Rose carefully folded up the tinfoil, making it in to a perfectly formed sphere and dunked it from five feet into a wastebasket. "Then we can't."

"The wrong guy kills himself? That's not going to sit right upstairs," Talman said. Pesce, always a follower, nodded. Parkes sat glumly and quietly.

"We cross that tollbridge when we get there. If we get there," Nye said. Rose's brusque tone and frosty body language told him she was angry with him. "Maybe at the end of Sunday we still can't connect all the dots, but there's a lot that says Lucking's the guy. So we start from there," he pointed at them. "Talman, go back to the places Lucking stopped, redo the interviews with everyone who had a pop with him, what they talked about, get their times locked down tight."

Rose went to the printer nearest her desk and gathered up several pages. Nye took them from her and she said nothing.

"Tell me again," Nye said roughly to the other detectives, "nobody has anything about the passenger? We got two people, two guys, maybe guy and a woman, and they do a hit-and-run this big and there is not one damn peep out there?"

"We're working it hard," Pesce protested, "like we told you. But it's like the passenger doesn't exist."

"The passenger exists," Rose said forcefully. "The old rule is still good. One puke's bound to start making noise about what he did.

Two pukes take out a full-page ad. Whoever this passenger is, he or she is out there leaving tracks."

"We're having a damn hard time just finding the SUV, for Christ sake," Vu shot in.

"So I've got a chore for everyone, kind of keep you from feeling bored while you keep trying to find our mystery guest," Nye handed the printed out pages to the other detectives. "Start checking out these Escalade owners, by phone but preferably in person."

The team groaned in unison. "Use your judgment," he said. "But by Sunday night you better be able to say you've got a high degree in confidence in whatever these folks tell you. I'm betting we're doing a command briefing Sunday night."

The prospect of facing the chief and the assistant chiefs, and perhaps other city officials, silenced them. Nye could see they were confused, and still shocked by Ensor's death and whatever had happened to their suspect.

Parkes raised his hand. "Okay, what about me?"

Rose replied, "I guess you're the watch commander. Keep on top of everything here and let us know if something breaks."

"Let's get moving," Nye added briskly. Activity, a clear purpose, would put all of the confusions and uncertainties aside, at least for the time being. Nye had always found it so. The enemy was time for reflection and recrimination. The weapon was staying busy.

The other detectives gathered themselves up and left. Nye looked down the slice of the list of Escalade owners for him and Rose. It was not a daunting list. Thanks to Cummins and Rose's inspiration, they had culled the names to a very manageable number. One name gave him a momentary pause. Stevenson. He tried to remember where he'd heard it, and then he recalled that Cummins had said he was a judge, someone who helped her with the adoption of her daughter.

"Hey, Rosie. We lucked out," he pointed at Stevenson's name. "Remember Cummins mentioning this guy? He's a judge. Know him?"

"Nope," she said, checking her computer for answers to inquiries about Lucking's previous DUIs and auto thefts. "How does that make us lucky, Ter?"

He winced inwardly at the iciness. He was ashamed to have hurt her. "Well, a judge has got to be handled carefully, okay? You see Pesce or Vu doing it right?"

"And you're a diplomat?" she asked, cocking her head without looking at him. She said to Parkes, "Give us a minute, would you?"

He nodded. "Sure. I'll get coffee." He left the room, glancing back, curious what he was missing.

"Well, with you," Nye hesitated. "I didn't mean to piss you off back in Nish's office."

She hit a few buttons, printing a page, before looking at him. "It's not a personal deal, Ter. It's not a high school thing. I'm just mad because you're my partner and you go to the assistant chief and shut me out. We don't have long left working together and you don't trust me enough."

"I didn't want to involve you."

Rose stood up and she was angry. "I'm your partner. I'm with you one hundred percent and I expect you're with me one hundred percent right until you walk out the door."

"I am, Rosie," he said defensively, feeling as unmanned and defeated as when Marceen came at him.

"So tell me the big secret," she demanded.

Nye studied her. They were at a crossroads as partners. One misstep now and the last six months together would turn sour and she would think of him with contempt after he was gone. He found that prospect unbearable for reasons even he could not fully lay out. He was not going to tell her the older, more monstrous mark he had reckoned against himself, the old ghosts IA had conjured up. There was no question in his mind how she would react to that. He had sad confidence in his ability to keep it a secret until it didn't matter.

So he told Rose about Casterbridge and what probably happened to Lucking on the way back to the jail. It was the lesser and more immediate transgression.

"Okay," she said quietly when he finished. "I get it." She checked her desk again as he waited impatiently for more of a reaction, something he could grapple with. "We better hit the road," was all she said, heading for the door.

Nye followed her; they passed Parkes going back in, and clusters of cops and detectives in the corridor murmuring about the news of Lucking's death that was flashing through the department.

At his car in the department lot, they got in, two patrol cars nearby swinging out to start a shift.

"You got anything else, Rosie?" he asked finally.

"No, no," she paused. "Ter, I said we were crossing a lot of lines on this investigation. Maybe someone crossed the biggest one of all at the jail and took care of Lucking. I don't know. All I can answer for is myself, and maybe you, when we're working together."

"I'm not asking for anything else."

"They taught me what you did was a sin of omission. When I was a kid in school, the nuns said you could sin by letting a bad thing happen if you could stop it."

Nye could not see where she was going with this line of thinking. He faced her. She sat straight and somber. "You didn't give me a choice," she said. "I'm your partner. I deserve that much respect. I got left out in the cold when I should've been making sure Lucking didn't get punched out by Casterbridge," she stopped. "Or helping Casterbridge beat the shit out of him, if that's what he did."

"Which would it be?" he asked sharply. He needed to know if she felt the same red rage sometimes that he did.

"I don't know. I just know we've lost our perspective, Ter. That's dangerous all the way around."

Nye blurted out, "I want you to be a better cop than me."

He felt instantly embarrassed and wanted to take back the last ten seconds. It was, however, the truth. Nye understood now that he hoped Rose Tafoya would avoid his mistakes and preserve herself and her family and her career. There was a little penance for him in helping her do that. The Church of the Second Chance.

Rose patted his hand, for the first time. "Yeah, well, I couldn't be any worse," she said, and he realized with relief that she had avoided the depths of the moment with cop sarcasm and apparent indifference. But Nye could tell she was touched.

"Okay," he said brusquely, back to business. "Truce, okay?"

"Truce," she said casually. "Who looks good to start with?" She studied their list of SUV owners.

"Let's get the judge out of the way," Nye said, backing out of the department lot the car. "Ease into this chore."

Jerry Nishimoto finished laying out for the chief everything he was able to put together in the last half hour about the suspect's death in the main jail.

Gutierrez listened, grunting in surprise or irritation from time to time, and got another urgent call from the mayor. Nishimoto could tell it was one more in the series of unpleasant calls since Lucking's arrest. It sounded like the mayor wanted another press conference. When the chief turned his high-backed black-leather chair away from Nishimoto, it was their old signal for him to clear out.

No time to grieve for Ensor, Nishimoto thought, *not a second for our dead officer or his family.* He knew that would come, but he resented the clank and clash of the machinery that kept charging forward when all he wanted was to stop and reflect for a moment. *And try to show I care,* he thought as he went back to his office and got a soda from the small refrigerator in the corner. He doubted he would be able to do that with Jane Ensor later that day. It simply wouldn't happen. Nishimoto knew he would be formal, correct, and impeccable in his show of official sorrow, but nothing personal would break the surface.

He sat down, looking at the neat piles of papers arranged around his desk blotter. He sipped from the soda again. He thought about his wife. In the last forty-eight hours he had barely seen Lisa. The idea popped into his head that he should take her to dinner tonight. Things were going to get very busy and tight in the next few days, sorting out the Lucking death, Ensor's funeral, closing down the investigation satisfactorily. Nishimoto made a note on his legal pad. There really was no other time to take her out, to give them both a little breather, except tonight.

He sorted mentally through restaurants. They hadn't been out together for quite a while. He remembered she liked a French cuisine place downtown, lots of white tablecloth, overpriced imported wine, and few tables. People could see you in the place and the food was acceptable. Nishimoto figured he would need to make a reservation right away. On a Saturday night they would probably be crowded.

He pushed niggling, exasperating fragments about Nye, Tafoya, and Altlander to one side in his mind. His detectives were going to pull the investigation together, end it on a triumphant note that linked Lucking irrefutably with the hit-and-run of Officer Ensor. Altlander could only follow now. *I've got the last, best word,* Nishimoto calculated cheerily.

In a way the suspect's death works out best for me, he thought. *No trial to agonize through, no dragged-out preening and crowing from Altlander every day while it went on. It will be my guys who make the case that this man did it. The passenger is a tangent, a nonparticipant in the actual offense, and the DA would have trouble even showing limited complicity in all probability. Whoever was riding with Lucking should have come forward, but there was no duty to do so.*

Except a moral one, he thought. He wondered how whoever it was got to sleep at night.

He dialed information and got the number of the restaurant. He hung up and, in the brief space before he could dial again, his direct line buzzed. He quickly switched mental gears. Whoever called him on the direct line usually had a problem, an insoluble, complex problem.

Nishimoto was surprised at the voice on the other end of the line.

"Good morning, Eli. I don't want to be rude, but I've got a couple of things to take care of right away."

He paused, listening to the other man. He smiled emptily. News travels fast. "No, you heard right, Eli. This guy Lucking was found dead in his cell at the jail a little while ago. Hanged. Right. It's probably suicide, but there's going to be a full-scale investigation. The jail's got a bad rep for losing defendants."

Nishimoto glanced impatiently at the small clock on his desk, embedded in a little mock football, an ornament Lisa had given him some years before, birthday or Christmas, some token when they weren't so distant. He jotted a note on the pad. He'd get her something for tonight. Maybe stop at Grebitus Jewelers and see what they had, nothing big or gaudy; that would look too much like an offering, an apology. A tasteful present was what he would give her at the restaurant, just after the first glass of champagne.

Nishimoto wanted to get Eli Holder off the phone quickly. "Yes, the two detectives you asked about the other day, they're still in charge," he answered. "Nye and Tafoya. They're very good. They're out right now. Yes, the whole thing's been a tragedy, incredible," he doodled on the pad, circles and squares, "it should remind us how fragile everything is. One minute, it all looks rock solid, a guy like Officer Ensor will last forever, and then the next—" he paused, interrupted. "Exactly, Eli. It's all a great mystery."

His face grew perplexed, "Well, sure, Eli. I can accommodate you on that," he made a note of an address and time on the pad. "I'll get in touch with them."

He hung up a few moments later, then dialed the restaurant. There was a burst of baroque music over the telephone. Eli Holder had a wide circle of acquaintances around the city, Nishimoto was aware, and his friends knew people who knew other people, so he was not a man to dismiss or brush off even when his request would cause some modest disruption in Nye and Tafoya's investigation today. He was a good friend to the department and Nishimoto knew he would be an important personal ally when the moment came to make a move past Altlander to become chief. Nishimoto was confident Nye would be on his best behavior and Tafoya showed very supple diplomacy, even if she got tied up in her own nervousness. She also seemed to steady Nye.

He heard a chirpy female voice announce she would be delighted to take his reservation.

He doodled on the pad and wondered why Eli Holder especially wanted to see Nye and Tafoya today.

Like everybody who has heard about this terrible event, he wants to feel he's close to things, Nishimoto surmised. *I can afford to indulge his curiosity and his sympathy. It's a small favor.*

THIRTY-FOUR

ON SATURDAY MORNING, Stevenson, Vee, and Haley got an early start south to Anaheim. They stuffed assorted luggage into the trunk of the SUV, which gave Stevenson an opportunity to score the sides surreptitiously with a piton from his climbing cabinet, so that it roughly resembled the scrapes from the firewood that had been carried in the other SUV's trunk.

It was a chilly, bright new morning and Haley bubbled with enthusiasm, more excited about this family trip, Stevenson realized ruefully again, than he had seen her in a while. Vee, after their strange and exhausting night, was lighthearted, too.

"All righty," Stevenson sang out, getting into the SUV, jingling the keys like they were gold sovereigns he had magically found on the sidewalk, "We're off! Everyone strap in. This is going to be a fun ride on our magic carpet."

He fiercely gazed at Vee. She smiled back at him. "Haley, hon, you get to push the button."

It was one of their oldest family traditions, letting Haley take command.

Solemnly, but with a giggle, Haley said, "Let's set sail."

"Aye, captain," Stevenson acknowledged and backed out. He grinned at Vee. "All shipshape this morning?"

"For the first time in a while," she said, nodding.

Stevenson found I-5 South, little traffic on Saturday at that hour, and they sped along through Stockton, toward Los Angeles and their ultimate destination. Haley wanted music, so they scanned the radio until she ordered a stop, for some reason, on a bouncy, thumping Mexican love song.

Vee, bobbing her head to the music, pretending to mouth the words, nuzzled Haley when she sat forward and planted an unexpected kiss on her cheek.

Stevenson watched the speedometer, listened to his wife and daughter chatting happily, and felt a breathtaking lightness filling him.

Home free, he thought, *home free all the way.*

They made a pit stop and had an early lunch several hours later at a strange oasis made up of gift shops, little toy riding trains for kids, and fruit stands off the highway. The oasis' restaurant was crowded with travelers, mostly families and much older couples, all relaxing for a moment off the road, longingly eyeing racks of homemade pies as they came in.

Stevenson and Vee made a quiet bet that the restaurant's star attraction, a little wizened man in a string tie and white apron who only served the coffee, would forfeit his highly touted, twenty-five-year-old record of flipping one million saucers under cups without breaking one. Haley watched, eyes intent, as the little man nonchalantly pulled a cup and saucer out for Vee, flipped the saucer under the cup, ceremoniously set it down, and repeated the process for Stevenson. Haley's face dropped a little. Certainty and order, however much they were valuable in most things, couldn't compete with the desire for surprise and chaos.

"I lose," Stevenson said after the waitress came by and took their order. "What did I lose anyway?"

"I get to choose the last two rides today," Haley said quickly.

"Was that our bet?" Stevenson looked at Vee.

"I think so. You don't want to go back on a bet."

Stevenson sighed heavily. "Well, never let it be said I'm not a good sport. Okay, button, you decide the rides."

Haley sat back. She smiled and he loved seeing it. She looked around the restaurant, listened to the babble about the quickest routes to various cities and towns, reviews of the coffee, pancakes, omelets.

Vee said, "It is so nice to be out of Sacramento for a little while, isn't it?"

Stevenson felt his cell phone vibrate in his pocket. He took it out and looked at the private number. *Eli? Who would call now?* Vee looked quizzically as he answered.

"You are hard to reach, Judge," Fonseca said.

"This is my private phone. I'm with my family."

"I won't take your time. I know how important time with one's family is. I have a large crew of dependents myself—"

"I'm going to hang up and I don't want you to call me again," Stevenson cut him off.

Because calls can be traced, he thought.

Fonseca's tone was harder, not threatening, merely forceful. "There won't be any more contact, Judge, if you get my case transferred. I understand from my courthouse sources that nothing has happened yet."

"Nothing happens on Friday or the weekend. I'll see what I can do Monday."

Fonseca paused. He breathed and Stevenson, with clarity, understood that he was tense. "Don't let much time go by. These things are easiest when done quickly and cleanly. Give my best regards to Veronica and her father."

Stevenson closed the phone. Vee sat back angrily, knowing who had called by Stevenson's terse conversation. She said, "The bastard."

"Don't let him spoil things. We're clear. We're going to be fine."

"I hate the arrogant bastard and I almost hate my father for letting him into our lives."

"We're smarter, remember? He can't hurt us." Stevenson wasn't sure himself whether he meant Fonseca or Eli. Vee slowly nodded.

Just then, Haley popped in. "The car smells funny."

Vee said, "It's fine. What do you mean?"

"I don't know. It smells different. Like it's brand new."

Stevenson's anger at Fonseca was replaced by the now familiar fear. He tried to sound casual. "We cleaned the car before the trip. Sure it smells new," he stared at her, rolling his eyes a little comically, "it's clean for the first time in a long time."

Haley grinned back at him. "I'm not the one who spilled a whole chicken chow fun dinner in the front seat. Mom."

Vee forced a chuckle. "Well, that wasn't my fault. The car ahead of us stopped suddenly."

"And we had noodles all over the dashboard," Haley finished, delighted at the memory.

Stevenson chuckled emptily, too. Haley was always quite sensitive, picking up nuances in conversation, vibrations in meetings, the smallest alteration in daily routine. *My canary in the mine,* he thought, *the first to sense danger.* He inwardly vowed to get the new-car taint out of the SUV on the trip, leave the windows open, maybe even spill a few things himself when they stopped again. That should give it a more used feeling.

He left Vee and Haley to stock up on some road provisions in the gift shop: bottled water and soda, nuts and pretzels, citrus candy. Stevenson stood in the dusty, busy parking lot, surrounded by strangers, far from Sacramento, heading even farther away. He squinted up into the blue, empty, unthreatening sky.

When Vee and Haley came back to the SUV, he was waiting for them. He helped stow the junk food and drinks and just before Haley clamored into the backseat, he made a clumsy grab at a hug and she tensed, sighed loudly in embarrassment, and closed the door.

Stevenson had noted that just recently she was awkward and unhappy at shows of affection from either him or Vee, particularly in public. Time was pushing her forward relentlessly. He was grateful he would be around to help her through the coming difficult changes as she grew up.

Vee offered him a pretzel and he turned it down in feigned horror, claiming that he had just eaten lunch. "We called Grandpa," she said.

"How did he sound?" Stevenson asked, eyes fixed ahead.

"How did he sound?" Vee turned to Haley.

"He said he was jealous we were on vacation and he wasn't, too."

Vee said to Stevenson, "I wanted him to hear how normal things are."

"How did he sound?" he asked again with more emphasis, worried about the answer.

"Fine, Frank. He was in a very good mood, wasn't he?" she turned again to Haley.

"He said he wished he could've come, but he couldn't."

Vee was reassuring. "I'll call him every so often this weekend. Just to keep the connection. It'll be good for him to hear everything's going so well."

"That's a great idea," he said. From a practical standpoint, it was essential and he wished he had thought of doing it. But Stevenson's high spirits deflated because he was not free, even moving miles from Sacramento every few minutes. They would be tethered to Eli all weekend.

They were tied to him no matter where they were.

Speeding down the freeway, traffic picking up around them as they neared the southern part of California, Stevenson noticed Haley ducking below his sight in the review mirror. She would reappear, face puzzled, flushed.

"What are you doing back there, button?" he asked.

"Nothing," she answered distractedly, eyes moving around the backseat. "Just checking everything."

Vee said, "It's okay, hon. Dad's got the car under control." She turned to him and said, "It's just like on a plane. She has to make sure everything's all right herself."

"And she gets that little trait from whom?" he asked playfully. "Not her pappy."

Haley vanished again, and, when he saw her pop up in the review mirror she was frowning, looking out the window, and then she sat back, trying to work something out.

"Hey, aren't we lucky," Stevenson asked her, to break whatever odd, inexplicable reverie she had slipped into, part of this newly emerging adolescence, "to be traveling with the most beautiful lady in the world, button?"

"Definitely the most beautiful."

Vee smiled, shaking her head. "All these little gratuities. I may have to stay with you two for a while." She stroked Stevenson's arm.

He worked to bring his high spirits back.

"This is the captain. I'm going for warp speed," he warned in a loud, ferocious voice. "Prepare yourselves. Next stop, Disneyland!"

THIRTY-FIVE

ROSE GOT OUT OF THE CAR and looked appreciatively around her. "Nice neighborhood," she said. "I could see this, yeah. Not much traffic, you can watch the kids playing," she nodded as if it were plausible. She observed an older couple with deep-baked suntans next door fussing over a medium-sized boat in their driveway.

"Sure, you and me both," Nye answered, checking the address on his list a final time because it would be extremely awkward to get it wrong, "either of us could take out a really neat loan and maybe make a down payment on a piece of a driveway."

"It can't be that expensive, Ter."

"It ain't. We aren't that rich."

She chuckled and he could see the wheels in her head toting up the benefits of this quiet, upscale older neighborhood near downtown and off a main drag like Broadway but still set off, settled. It would be an improvement on her current borderline neighborhood with its low-rent apartments and nearby street gangs. He wished he had money to give her.

He was glad, though, that their blowup earlier that morning had dissipated and they were back to ordinary business.

"Think we're too early?" she asked as they went up to the front door.

"It's pretty dead. But it's almost ten thirty. Somebody's got to be up."

"I don't want to get on the wrong side of a judge."

Nye paused at the front door. "No, we're okay," he blustered. He didn't like the idea of disturbing a judge on a Saturday morning, particularly over something as bureaucratically procedural and patently ludicrous as checking if the judge was missing an SUV. *Like he forgot where he put it,* Nye thought.

As he rang the doorbell, the woman next door, a wet rag in one hand from wiping down the deck of her boat, said loudly, "Who are you?"

"We're to see Judge Frank Stevenson," Rose said. She walked to the couple on the boat. The man didn't look up, just grunted and went on trying to attach a mirror to one side of the boat's square little cabin.

"Friends?" the man asked.

"Is the judge at home?" Rose asked instead of answering.

"Well, I guess that depends on who you are," the man said, a cigarette wiggling up and down in his mouth. He had the well-cured look of a chronic alcoholic.

Nye joined Rose after getting no response from ringing the doorbell or knocking.

"Sacramento Police," Nye said genially.

The two older people looked at each other.

"Well, if it's official business, they left a little while ago. You missed them," the woman said.

Her husband growled. "Oh, shut up, Myrna. How about showing us your ID before we start opening our big yaps?"

Rose suppressed a grin as she displayed her badge to the man and woman. Nye did the same. The woman shook her head at her husband.

"Thank you," she said with exaggerated politeness. "As I said, the Stevensons left for the weekend awhile ago. Is it urgent?"

"We just need to talk to him," Rose said. "When are they coming back?"

"Late Sunday. They took their daughter to Disneyland. Sweetest little girl you ever met," the woman said.

Nye sighed. First address on their list, the one that was supposed to be the easiest because it would be so routine, and they struck out. He gave the woman one of his business cards. "Thanks for your help. If the judge checks in, would you let him know we stopped by? Here's our phone number. Would you tell him we can take care of what we need to talk to him about over the phone?"

She studied the card. "I'll be glad to, Detective."

Rose asked, "I'm sorry. What are your names?"

"Harold and Myrna Filoy," the man cursed as he dropped his screwdriver. "Want me to spell it?"

"Yeah, please," Nye said. He jotted it down in his notepad as Harold recited it.

"Good luck wherever you're going sailing today," Rose said, a little enviously.

Harold Filoy looked at her steadily. "It's a powerboat. It doesn't have sails."

"Oh, Harold," Myrna said in exasperation.

"*Oh, Harold,*" Rose mimicked as they drove to the next address, about a mile away. "Did you and Marceen sound like that?"

"Not so much. We didn't talk so much after a while."

"I see people like them at restaurants when we go out, old married couples. Just sitting at the table staring at their food or other people. Not talking, not even looking at each other."

"We avoided that. We didn't go out."

Rose laughed slightly. "I hope I never get like that, Ter. Even when Luis drives me nuts, I hope I never just curl up and get sour like that."

He nodded. "Hey, Rosie, you still thinking about talking to a department counselor?"

"Yeah, I am. I feel really funny after everything's that happened in the last couple days. I've never felt like this, nervous, kind of sick inside."

He didn't know exactly how to put it, so he simply said flatly,

"Remember you got me to talk to first. Whatever you say stays here in the car or wherever we are. Just between you and me."

"I don't know, old man."

"Forget it," he said hastily. "Just an offer. No big deal."

She seemed to be weighing it, like he had seen her reckoning the golden days in a new, better neighborhood. "Thanks, Ter. Yeah, maybe I will take you up."

"Sure. Whatever. Like I said, no big deal," he rejoiced because he would be helping her.

Rose took a call from Nishimoto shortly afterward and Nye heard her using her very official voice. She wrote down a time and address. "Assistant chief wants us to swing by and see a guy named Eli Holder at eleven," she gave him the address. "He wants to talk to us about Officer Ensor."

"Who the hell is he?"

Rose said, "Some kind of friend. Important guy, big-noise banker. I'm supposed to make sure you're behaved."

"You'll have your hands full," Nye said, resigned to another political chore from the department's senior management. He figured Rose might just as well get used to doing favors and running errands for assistant chiefs, and even the chief himself, if she wanted to advance. It came with being in Major Crimes.

Nye said, "I want to get a couple of names on our list checked before we go see this chump. You know what he wants, Rosie?"

"Nishimoto didn't say. Sounds like a meet-and-greet."

"It'll be much more," Nye assured her with furious contempt. "I will bet you this chump's got a *theory* about our investigation. He's going to *enlighten* us so we don't fuck things up."

They had no luck with four SUV owners on the list before their appointment. It was Rose, Nye saw, who was on her best behavior when they got to Holder's home in the Arden Hills area of the city, a secluded exclusive neighborhood of large homes behind high white-stone walls and security cameras. The Spanish colonial sat on over an acre of a well-manicured, sloping lawn and decoratively planted pines and plum trees.

Holder waved them inside and noticed her taking inventory. "My late wife did the honors. I can't take credit for how the place looks. She had all the artistic sense."

"It's a lovely home, sir."

"How about something?" Eli Holder asked brightly. He pointed to two exquisite chairs in the large living room and sat in a third one. Rose craned her glance around the room, adding it all up, the floral patterns and carpets, polished heavy furniture and paintings, the sheer drapes moving slightly at the French windows in the morning breeze.

"We're fine, sir," she answered.

"Sure? I can get coffee, tea, bottled water, heck, a couple beers if you'd like," Holder chuckled with forced good humor. He waved away a small East Asian woman in a white-and-lace uniform. "Nothing, I guess, Shinoz. We're going to pass. Except," he half got out of his chair, "maybe you can bring me another ice water, all right?"

The woman nodded and left.

Nye waited. Rose finished her covetous review of the large living room and also sat silently. They both wanted Holder to make the first move.

To Nye's eye, Eli Holder was ill at ease. He was a balding man of medium height, wearing a work shirt that had never seen any manual labor and stiffly ironed blue jeans over heavy, brown, lizard-skin boots. His glasses were small and halfway down his fleshy nose. When he met them at the door, Nye knew Rose also caught the strong minty mouthwash scent rolling from him. The bright-eyed, the slightly too-abrupt gestures and movements, the voice too loud, all added up to a man who had been working away at something in the liquor cabinet for a while that morning. Nye assumed the booze came from a liquor cabinet in a house like this. *Unlike stacked in a corner by my kitchen sink,* he thought of his bygone pleasures.

Holder put his hands on his knees, cleared his throat.

"Well, thanks for stopping by. I know this kind of takes you off your beat," he bore down the word and grinned as if he had said something amusing, "but when I talked to Jerry, you know, your, your," he fumbled.

"Boss," Nye finished.

"Your superior. I wanted to talk to you both and offer any help I can give you."

"Help in what way, sir?" Rose leaned forward slightly.

"I don't know. Whatever you need. Jerry indicated you're still working on the hit-and-run accident."

"That's correct, sir."

"So, do you need anything to finish it up? I know a lot of people. I've got a lot of things going around town." The maid reappeared and handed him a heavy cut glass filled with clear liquid and ice cubes. He took a large gulp. Nye didn't think it was water.

"Well, that's a very generous offer," Rose said, "but I think we've got the resources to complete the investigation."

"Oh, good. Good. I heard about this suicide down at the jail." He shook his head. "I assume that ends the case, doesn't it?"

Nye said, "Not really, Mr. Holder. I don't know how much Assistant Chief Nishimoto shared with you, but we have a ways to go to verify several important aspects of the suspect's story."

"Look, Jerry hasn't told me anything out of school," Holder said hastily. "Not that kind of guy. I have enormous respect for him and you," he gestured with the glass and took another gulp. "But I guess I assumed you'd be done now, you arrested a suspect, he said he did it, and then, Jesus, he kills himself the next day. In my line of work," *gulp, gulp,* "that's the bottom line. End of story."

"It probably works out that way for us, too," Rose said. "But for everyone concerned we need to go the extra mile."

"But it's pretty much paperwork now, isn't it? Formalities?" Holder said, coughing slightly.

Nye wondered why this guy was interested in how the cops closed out a case.

"Excuse me, sir," he asked on a hunch, "did you know Officer Ensor? Work with him on some charity or project?"

"I didn't know him at all, sorry to say. Complete stranger." He wistfully looked at his empty glass, inwardly debating obviously whether to get it refilled. "I'm just a friend of Jerry's, you know, kind of searching around for some way to help him and you guys. I think the world of what you do. Protecting everyone."

Rose smiled emptily. She wanted to leave as well. Duty done, courtesy call paid. Time to get back to real work. She stood up.

"We should be moving on, sir," she said. Nye kept his eyes on Holder, who huffed to his feet, mouth tight.

"We're checking Escalade SUV owners around Sacramento," Nye threw out, curious to see the reaction, a little bored on top of his impatience.

"Yes? Sure. That's the one in the accident."

"You don't own a Cadillac SUV?"

Holder froze and sat down again. He smiled sloppily. "No. Always driven BMWs. I mean," he rubbed his forehead, "I do have one, yes. Just bought it. Need some extra room."

Rose said, "Your name isn't on our list, sir."

"Oh, I *just* bought it," he repeated. "You're checking on SUVs that could've been involved in the accident. I bought mine yesterday. Got the papers, if you want to see."

Rose hesitated and Nye jumped in, "No, that's fine. We are checking on vehicles that could have been used to commit the crime," he deliberately reminded this guy that it was not an accident.

"Well, that's a relief," with a wide grin Holder jokingly put a fluttering hand to his heart. "God, I hope you satisfy yourselves you caught the right man and this tragedy is over. For the officer's family, I mean. Closure." He nodded to each of them.

"So do we," Rose said.

As they headed out of the living room, Rose paused at an old-fashioned family photo album splayed open on the flower-and-laurel-patterned sofa. Holder came up to her and pointed at the pages of blown-up photos of a serious light-haired girl in a turquoise ballet costume, caught in midleap, eyes fixed upward.

"My granddaughter Haley Stevenson," Holder said in a tremulant voice, heavy with pride and loss. "Two years ago at her school. She had the lead. She's a very impressive young lady."

Rose pointed, "May I take a look, sir?"

"Absolutely. I've got all the boastful vices of a grandparent," he reached down and unsteadily handed her the album. "You'll discover as you get older, you like to indulge in nostalgia, hold on to things as they slip away from you. They do slip away when you least expect it."

Nye had caught the name, too, just as he knew Rose had. He let the moment play longer. "They get older no matter what you do, Mr. Holder. Mine did. Seemed like they were leaving toys all over, then next minute, they're driving, next minute they're out of the house."

Rose flipped the pages slowly, studying the faces.

Holder didn't seem to hear Nye. He hungrily watched Rose go through pictures, daring her not to appreciate his grandchild as much as he did.

Holder spoke to Nye while he watched Rose. "Anything I can do, you just let me know. As I said, if you need some doors opened, things expedited, that's what I do. I would love to help you."

Rose pointed at a photograph. "And I assume these are your granddaughter's parents? I can see the resemblance."

"My daughter Veronica," he said warmly, indicating the tall, blonde young woman standing before a minister, sunny vineyards spreading behind them. "My son-in-law, Frank Stevenson. He's a judge here in town. That's their wedding in Napa."

"We just tried to see your son-in-law," Nye spoke, his voice flat. "He is on our list of Cadillac Escalade SUV owners."

"Oh, sure, sure," Holder said in startled burst. "Owned it for a couple years."

Rose set the photo album down on the sofa again. "Is there anything you can tell us about that vehicle? It might save us some time."

Holder shook his head. "Don't think so. No. Frank's out of town this weekend," he said, reaching down and shutting the album with a bang. "Part of your formalities, I guess, see him, check him off."

"We're trying to determine if any Escalade owner's got anything unusual they want to tell us about their vehicle."

"Like what? I thought this man hanged himself, he stole the SUV."

"Well, that's what we're trying to confirm," Nye said, studying Holder's twitchy expression. He and Rose had touched some chord, but he wasn't sure what it was. Rose was poised, alert, too. "Did your son-in-law mention anything about his SUV in the last couple of days? Even in passing?"

Holder sniffed loudly and wiped his nose on his sleeve, a startlingly childlike gesture. He called out, "Shinoz! Fill me up again. *Please.* Thank you." He shook his head and waved them toward the front door. "Nothing I remember. Oh, you know, maybe Frank said something like he needed to get the oil changed or check the tires or the AC wasn't putting out," he barked and blinked rapidly, "but you better ask him. Yeah. You talk to him and ask your questions and get the answers right from the well, so to speak." He grinned harshly at both of them. "But, you remember, my offer stands. Day or night, night or day, you call me if I can help you out."

"While we're talking about SUVs, where did you buy yours, sir?" Rose inquired politely.

"Hardy Cadillac up in Roseville. Nice deal. You interested in one? I could make a call. How about the papers? Now you want to see them?" He was not-so-subtly defensive.

"No, that's not necessary, Mr. Holder," Nye said lightly. "My partner was just curious."

Nye and Rose thanked him and he fixed a hard, waxy smile on them as they left, closing the door behind them with a very gentle, soft click.

"Okay, so there's something really phony." Rose said it first as they pulled away from the house.

"That there is. Something about his grandkid? What do you think?"

"Saturday morning he's sitting around getting all sloppy about her, his daughter, his son-in-law. What the hell's that all about?" Rose said. "I got a negative vibe from him about the judge."

"Yeah. I got that, too," Nye pondered. "So he's got a family thing going, he's feeling sorry for himself, he calls Nish because he's a little plastered. Where does it go for us?"

"I got that he was interested, a lot, in whether we're closing out this case."

"I got that part, too."

"How comes he cares?"

"I wonder, too," Nye echoed.

"This is the second time we've got this judge's name turning up, Ter."

"Cummins don't count," he protested. "Totally different deal."

"I'm only pointing out what you preach. Coincidences are somebody's joke. Something's going on."

"Jesus, if you're going to listen to everything I say," he grumbled, but secretly pleased that Rose accepted a piece of pragmatic wisdom he had acquired very slowly. Connections did exist, obscure and mysterious, often inside mundane coincidences. He had learned painfully to trust his instinct when coincidence appeared. Look deeper at it, pull it apart. Nye sometimes toyed with the unsettling notion that hardly anything he did really mattered; the real world lay underneath everyday surfaces and appearances. It sometimes revealed itself, teasingly, just a little bit. It was a conceit that kept the fear of meaningless motion at bay. The coincidence like the judge's name popping up in different circumstances was just that kind of wink at him and Rose.

"So how about doing a little backgrounder on this judge before we hook up with him tomorrow?" Rose suggested.

"Okay. We get back to the barn, that's your chore, Rosie." He wondered if there was anything to find and, if so, a very light touch would be required. Stevenson was a judge and nothing so unnerved a chief of police and his assistant chiefs as tangling unpleasantly with a judge.

Irritated judges could be vindictive, some of them anyway. Detectives might find evidence consistently being thrown out as improperly seized or receive snide comments from the bench about incompetent police work. *Things like that are bad public relations,* Nye thought uneasily. *Bad all around.*

"I just got a wild, crazy idea," Rose said. She shook her head at whatever it was.

"Yeah?"

"No. I'm jumping ahead. It is wild, though."

"Not going to tell me?"

"Forget it for now. I'm just percolating like you'd say," she chuckled at him.

"Take it easy," he warned.

"You don't know what it is," she protested.

"I can guess it's about this guy Holder and the judge, yeah? So take it easy."

"Relax, old man. I'm not a rookie and I'm not you." She said it not unkindly.

He changed lanes, glancing at her, reckoning what wild notion had bloomed in her mind.

"Cripes, it's getting late," she said, closing the subject for the moment. "We got a boatload of names left," she unhappily ran down their list.

"We also got one stop I really don't want to make."

THIRTY-SIX

IT WAS NEARLY ONE THIRTY when Nye brought them to the Ensor home. They had skipped lunch, contacted almost ten more Escalade owners, and found nothing even remotely unusual. No one had suffered an accident, forgotten to report a missing vehicle, or suggested anything suspicious. Parkes relayed an agitated call from the director of Loaves and Fishes. Doobie Rudloff was disturbing the other residents by acting aggressive. The deal, the director complained, was only to keep him temporarily and he was overstaying his extremely modest welcome.

Nye told Parkes to keep a lid on the director and keep Rudloff calmed down. He was their star, for now. If he couldn't be controlled, Rose suggested getting Rudloff locked up on a seventy-two-hour mental health hold at Sutter Hospital. It would damage his credibility but, since there wasn't going to be a trial now, it didn't matter as much anymore. But they had to make sure he didn't vanish until the investigation was officially ended on Monday.

Rose was quiet and affected by the congregation of people around the Ensor home. The neighbors were easy to pick out, moving across the street or nearby lawns with covered food dishes. Sprinkled among them were obtrusive reporters and cameras. But the glue holding the crowd together were teenagers, lined up to the home's door, forming a silent corridor from the sidewalk. *Somber kids from the soccer teams, homeless shelters, and gang rescue,* Nye thought as he and Rose passed between them, *Tommy's honor guard.*

He felt a tightening in his throat.

The front door was open, more teenagers standing watch inside the house, all of the voices low and constant. It was eerily like a party Nye remembered from some ancient foggy days with Tommy and Janey, except that the noise and color had been leached out, leaving this ghostly, oppressive afterthought.

Jane Ensor, walking slowly and carefully, brought a large foil-covered pan to the dining room table and set it down among other dishes, some with half-eaten food on them. People stood around, eating from plates, putting them down anywhere. The Ensor children must be somewhere in the somber crush of people, but Nye didn't see them.

Two women came up to Jane and hugged her tightly. Nye ached at her gray, stunned look, the common expression of the walking wounded after violence.

Rose touched Jane Ensor's shoulder gently. "How are you?" she asked softly.

"All right."

Nye awkwardly bent forward. "Jesus, Janey. You know."

She smiled at him and patted his shoulder as if he were the one who needed comforting. "Take care of yourself, Terry."

"Can we do anything for you?" Rose asked.

"Thanks, but no. I'm kind of swamped," Jane Ensor smiled again, and it was a ghastly knockoff of genuine contentment Nye had seen too many times before. "There are a zillion things to take care of now. I guess there's going to be a big funeral, lots to do about that." Her smiled wavered and she shook her head.

"It's whatever you want," Nye said gruffly. "Give Tommy the send-off you want. Keep it in the family."

"I don't know. Look at them all," Jane Ensor gestured at the teenagers and the steady flow of people in and out of the house, eyes on her frequently with real sympathy, always curiosity. "Tommy did so much, I don't think I have a choice anymore. So many people want to say goodbye."

Nye bent closer to her. "He's yours. You say goodbye your way."

She nodded emptily and moved around the crowded table, preoccupied as if the party would be a failure if she didn't see to every detail. Rose was as awkward and unsure of herself as Nye felt. The calamity had come, its devastation was apparent, the injured needed to be aided, but it was all disorienting because of Ensor's decency and the patent injustice of what his family would now have to endure forever. Nye felt funny no matter what he did.

More people murmured words to Jane Ensor and she nodded, accepting embraces and fumbled consolation. Nye's stomach growled but he would not touch the food around him. The idea of eating here scared the hell out of him.

He motioned to Rose. They should go. There was nothing more they could do and the relentless deadline imposed on them was rushing down.

Jane Ensor got him away from three gaunt and solemn friends.

"Tommy and I never thought about what it would be like if one of us was left alone," Jane said to Nye, pulling him to a corner. "I'm the last one standing, Terry. I don't know what to do." It was a plea.

"You've got a hell of a lot of friends," he said, taking her cold hand. "I'm here anytime you need me. Anytime."

"I thank God for you. But it's still not enough. Tommy's gone."

Nye nodded, feeling ineffectual and helpless again, just as he had at the hospital a century and more ago, when Ensor lay dying. The bitter, inescapable truth was that Janey was right. She stood on a distant shore with her children now and no one, however caring or helpful, could reach them. Whoever struck Ensor down had made that permanent.

"We should move on, Janey," he found himself murmuring like all the others, as if cringing would placate the cold forces that pitilessly surrounded this woman and her children. "We're still chasing down leads, putting it all together."

"I'm so grateful for that, Terry," she squeezed his hand with almost painful force and gazed at him intently. "Does your partner know what you did?"

"I didn't do anything."

"Okay," she said with sly, horrible intensity, "it's our secret. The last few hours, knowing how you handled it kept me from going crazy," she shuddered with a deep breath, putting a hand protectively over her swelling belly. "I heard he was dead and I knew you had done something so wonderful for me and Tommy."

Nye looked at her with growing sadness and shock. *She thinks I killed Lucking,* he realized. *Like I went into his cell and got that sheet around his neck and hauled him up until he choked to death. She thinks I could do that.* He was dumbfounded. *I must've shown her something those years ago that she'd believe I could do that.*

And maybe, Nye admitted, *there's a part of me that could.* He thought of Casterbridge and Lucking on the drive back to the jail.

"I'll stay close," he told her, moving away, back into the crowded living room, to Rose and the excuse to get away.

Nye let Jane Ensor put her arms around him, her face pressed tightly against his; his hands went to her surprisingly bony shoulders. He wasn't going to tell her it was wrong, it hadn't happened. Because what she desperately needed was the illusion of vengeance exacted.

She held him and whispered fiercely, "Thank you for making the bastard pay."

At five thirty, Rose and Nye returned to the department, the day drifting off into a gauzy wheat-colored sunset. The people outside were down to a small, silent group, surrounded by even more flowers and scrawled condolence signs. Only two camera crews remained, though. Rose looked disapproving. Ensor was dead, his assailant dead, and the news cameras had moved on to the jail for breathless reports about how he died.

Neither of them had said much since leaving the Ensor home. Rose obviously noticed Nye's deep silence after seeing Jane Ensor and let it have its way. They didn't exchange more than ten words after each stop to check on an SUV owner and she never tried to get him to talk.

Parkes, Pesce, and Talman were in the command center and the TVs were running endless stories about the "bizarre turn" in the hit-and-run case, the mysterious death in the county jail of the man arrested for killing Officer Thomas Ensor.

Vu came in shortly after Nye and Rose.

"Anybody strike gold?" Nye asked from his desk.

"Nada," Vu said.

"Something," Pesce broke in, glancing at his partner.

"Yeah, okay. Mrs. Lucking says Jerry tried to do himself twice before. Both times in the last couple of years. Once with tranquilizers, once by drinking antifreeze. "

Rose groaned and made a face.

"Tastes sweet, apparently," Pesce said brightly. "Lucking's wife showed us the hospital records, emergency room, ambulance, docs, the whole shot. He was going out."

Nye nodded. "Makes it more likely he finally got it all together last night in his cell, don't it? Make sure you get that over to Chaney, okay? Should lighten his load a little."

"Not so much," Rose said. "Now he's got five suicides on his watch, Ter. The County Grand Jury's still going to have him and the sheriff for dinner."

"Okay, what else do you have?" he asked sharply.

Talman said, "I've gotten a bunch of supplemental statements from the gang Lucking was with. More details, but the story stays the same. He was shitfaced when he left the last joint and nobody knows what he did after that."

"He leave with anyone?"

"Solo, according to all the wits."

"So he picked up a passenger on the road?" Nye asked.

They all regarded him blankly. Lucking could have made a stop none of them knew about. There was a host of possibilities, which was galling.

Rose said, "The door's still open then for him to snag an Escalade."

"Yeah, and he could've grabbed the damn Corolla we brought up and he was just too drunk to know the difference," Vu groused.

"Do we have any hits from body shops or auto-repair joints?" Nye asked, impatient with the squabbling.

Parkes jumped in, "It's gotten a lot quieter this afternoon so I made the rounds on the phone, shook up a couple of my snitches, and it's all dead out there. Everybody knows about the reward, they all asked how to get it, but nothing so far. No word on someone else in the SUV."

No one else had anything from their snitches or body shops. Reports from law enforcement agencies around the state were also negative. The other members of the team, like Rose and Nye, had worked through a large chunk of the list of registered black Cadillac Escalade SUV owners in and around Sacramento without finding anything very suspicious. Talman wanted to follow up with two owners who had expired registrations and seemed edgy when he talked to them.

"You got it, ace," Nye said. "Rosie and me talked to about twenty of these chumps today and came up dry."

"Which is still weird," she said suddenly.

"How come?" he asked, rubbing his eyes.

"We've got reward money on the table and no one's got even a lousy lead about an SUV getting fixed up after Thursday. We don't have any owners, except maybe Talman's guys, looking out of the ordinary."

"Point, please, Rosie?" Nye asked.

"I'll admit we haven't finished running through the registered owners," she said, standing up and pacing a little, "but with all the media about this case, the reward, it's weird we don't have something, some snitch, some repair yard that looks out of line."

Pesce was grumpy. "I've been jumping around all day. I'm covering all my bases."

"It's not that. We're on the wrong track somehow," Rose said. She repeated it to Nye. He thought for a moment.

"I'm thinking we're going too narrow," Nye said, "focusing on this area. Cummins could be off and we're just looking too close to home for this SUV."

Rose nodded unhappily. "It could be that."

They broke shortly afterward. Nye and Rose went to Nishimoto's office and caught him on his way out.

"I'm taking my bride out to dinner," he blew out a breath, "for the first time in a long time, as she reminded me. So what have you got?"

Nye agreed that Rose should do this evening's briefing. She ended with the frustrating lack of results connecting Lucking further to the hit-and-run and the SUV owners' blank wall.

"We need more time, sir," Rose said. "Terry thinks we're looking too close to home. The absence of any hits about SUVs suggests we need to broaden our area of inquiry."

"In an ideal world," Nishimoto said and then stopped. "Do the best you can until tomorrow. There won't be any extension of the deadline."

"Boss, we just need a little more." Nye spread his hands.

"The preliminary reports on Lucking's death came in," Nishimoto flipped open two files. "He had some bruising on his face, upper torso, maybe a day old. Consistent with his attempted escape earlier yesterday," he glanced at Nye and Rose to see if either of them would dispute him. "There's also reports of threats and harassment from other inmates when he was moved around."

"So everybody's solid that Lucking's the guy," Nye said.

Nishimoto closed the files and stood up. "It's solid, Terry. He was suicidal and he obviously feared what would happen to him in the jail. You and Tafoya and the rest of the team are filling in the blanks, not changing the picture."

Rose was about to protest and then recognized the futility of it. She lowered her head slightly.

"All right, if we're done, my bride's waiting. It's not the best time to be going out to dinner, but we don't get best times in this business," Nishimoto grinned toothily and mirthlessly.

Nye wondered if Rose, who was clearly upset and frustrated, would bring up Nishimoto's friend Holder and the link to a judge who was a matching SUV owner. He shook his head very slightly for her benefit. She and Nye followed the assistant chief out of his office.

Nishimoto said, "Speaking of not the best times, Ensor's funeral is starting to come together. It looks like next Wednesday or Thursday. I'd like you say something, Terry."

Nye froze. "I can't do that. I hate the damn things."

"You're an old partner," Nishimoto said, adamant. "Work up about five minutes. All of Ensor's old partners are going to speak."

It was an order.

Nye and Rose ran into Guthrie in the lobby. He had his coat over his shoulder and sweat stains on his shirt. It seemed everybody was working hard that weekend. Nye and Rose were past him when Guthrie said, "You are the luckiest fuck I ever saw, Nye."

"Say good night, Guth," he said, and they kept walking.

"Tafoya, do you know how lucky your partner is?"

Rose paused and looked back. "Come again, sir?"

"You are hooked up with about the luckiest cop in this whole department, maybe the whole world. He can walk on water. He can make any shit go away."

Rose, Nye saw, thought Guthrie was ribbing him. "He tells me that all the time, Lieutenant."

"Don't encourage him, Rosie," Nye said, still walking toward the door.

"My advice, Tafoya, is stick close to him. He's fucking bulletproof."

Rose smiled and looked puzzled when Nye stopped, lowering his head toward Guthrie.

"If it makes you feel any better, Guth, you can rub it."

Guthrie swore obscenely and stalked to his office.

"Ter, anything you want to add?" she asked as they stepped outside.

"I don't think so," he said.

Rose came back to the table after making a cell phone call home.

"Luis is bitching about taking care of Annorina tonight. I told him I've got to work and he's giving me crap about a couple musicians he's got to meet."

She furiously dug into her cooling bowl of Japanese noodles and chicken.

Nye hadn't touched his spicy beef and rice. The upscale Asian restaurant, angles and bright modular lights, was very busy on an early Saturday night. People around them were having a lively, boisterous time.

"You don't have to work tonight, Rosie. We're going through the motions. We're done."

"A lot has gone down in the last couple days. Going through the motions matters. You think your husband would get that." She chewed rapidly. "I figured you'd get it, Ter."

He had no good comeback. Nye was still spooked by Jane Ensor's conviction he was capable of cold-blooded murder. He was edgy at the prospect of standing before her, their kids, and a couple hundred people who would undoubtedly be at Ensor's funeral.

"What are you going to do?" he asked quietly, poking at his food with chopsticks, as if that would arouse his appetite.

"Check out the judge, like I said. Nothing else stands out. Check out where he was on Thursday. Check out his damn SUV top to bottom, talk to the dealer, okay?"

"Take it easy. Don't go stomping all over the place. He's a judge. He's got friends."

"I'm not cuffing the guy," she snapped. "I'm just going to do my job and find out as much as I can." She wiped her mouth with her napkin. "You want to tell me something else?"

Nye grinned in spite of himself. Seeing Rose's anger, the last thing in the world he would do at that moment was contradict her.

"Just be like a butterfly," he said. "You can't do much tonight anyway."

"I'll do as much as I can. Then we go see him tomorrow. In person."

"Right," Nye said without much enthusiasm. "That's the top of the list."

"If you're lucky, I might tell you my wild idea, too," she said.

"If it's what I think, you might not have to," he lobbed back to her.

They paid soon afterward. On the sidewalk, beside the line of eager young people waiting to get tapped for their table inside, Rose said, "I'll call you if I find anything, okay, Ter?"

"Sure. I'm just going home," he said, tired in many ways.

"I'm pissed at all the attitude tonight," she said loudly, and several people turned to watch the bickering odd couple.

"I got that," Nye said.

He drank two glasses of soda water with a lot of ice and a squeeze of lime, the pale imitation of things long past. He wandered around the house in his shorts and T-shirt, too restless to sleep, too tired to concentrate on anything. He flipped on the TV in the living room, and sat in the semidarkness cast by the glowing pictures, running through dozens of channels without stopping for more than a moment on any of them.

Nye knocked over a stack of old newspapers by the coffee table when he got up and they spilled across the floor like a slow-motion avalanche. It would take him days to get around to picking them up. Nothing ever got cleaned or fixed around the house until days later.

He went back to the kitchen feeling hungry again and made a cheese and tomato sandwich and ate part of it over the sink. Rose was right about the desert of their investigation. Given the notoriety of Ensor's death, he expected more cranks to come out, more claims about the SUV. He wiped his hands with a paper towel, wiped his mouth. Maybe because it was all about a dead cop, none of the usual vultures were willing to get close.

Maybe there wasn't a busted black Cadillac Escalade SUV to find.

Nye sighed wearily and washed his hands. What did it mean if there wasn't a busted SUV? But there had to be. The crime scene indicated damage. Cummins had tested broken fragments. Somewhere there had to be an SUV that bore the marks of that fatal collision. Somewhere there was a driver and, even more elusive, a passenger beside him at the moment of impact.

He wandered back into the living room and pulled aside part of the curtains at the window over the sofa. The street was lit, still and dreamlike. He and Marceen had lived there only about two years before she left. The house where they had spent most of their marriage, raised the kids, and he had come back to every night or early morning from his shift, was miles away. This was a strange place even now to him. He had no personal landmarks here. *No telephone pole Eddie cracked into the first time I showed him how to drive,* Nye thought, remembering his son's frantic mishandling of the family car. *No little piece of slightly raised lawn under the oak where we buried the hamsters when they died.*

In this neighborhood, there were only strangers and empty places.
He let the drape fall back.

He had a week to go before he checked out and drifted into an uncertain life in yet another place near his daughter and her husband, who were not begging for him to come. Before that bright prospect occurred, however, he had the investigation and a phantom busted

SUV and the peculiarity of this Holder guy reaching out to his old buddy Nishimoto. *Reaching out to do what? Blubber about his daughter and grandkid? Act like a kid himself, caught with his hand in the cookie jar? He was nervous and trying to hide something, Rose spotted it right off.*

His son-in-law's a judge downtown who owns a black Cadillac Escalade, right model and right year. Nye shook his head and sat down in a chair, head back. *What's he hiding?*

Nye thought about a judge downtown, sitting in the courthouse, and how close it was to where Tommy was run down. Maybe half a mile, he calculated fuzzily.

He half grinned to himself. There was Rosie's wild idea for sure, a judge tied up in a hit-and-run. He didn't think there would be any pieces of him or Rose or Nish to pick up after the explosion if that bomb ever went off. Handle with extreme caution. Wild.

The jangling phone jerked him awake and it took him a moment to orient himself. He was in his living room, the lights out, the neighborhood sepulchrally quiet. He got up, passing the repulsive mantelpiece clock Marceen's parents had given them. Two forty-five in the morning, he thought with surprise and a little annoyance. Like some old jackass falling asleep. He had been brooding about something, but he couldn't quite touch it at that instant.

He grabbed the phone, expecting to hear Rose.

"Yeah, you're calling late enough," he said, mock angry.

Assistant Chief Altlander was not amused. "Get the hell back to bed if it's too much trouble, Nye," he growled.

"Sorry, sir. I'm wide awake."

"You better be. We've got a hostage situation. Ensor's partner, Quintana. He's got his girlfriend and he's asking for you, so get the fuck down to this address."

THIRTY-SEVEN

NYE WENT INTO THE TIDY HOUSE on Avalon Avenue alone. He felt the lights from a dozen cop cars on his back.

The parquet floor in the living room glistened in the burst of unnatural lights. He noted that the coffee table was overturned, magazines and were glasses scattered, and a small, tufted rug was bunched in a corner, as if someone had run and stumbled on it.

He had knocked, loudly announced who he was, knocked again, and then opened the front door. Behind him, Altlander fumed among his SWAT unit and the startled neighbors kept at bay. *I keep popping up and he hates it,* Nye thought, as if observing himself from a great distance.

Nye stopped and listened. He heard noises outside on the street, the cops stirring and people moving, but it was deadly still in the house. He spotted framed pictures of Quintana and the girlfriend, Beth, sitting on the mostly empty bookshelves. No books, just some little ducks or carvings.

Nye called again.

"Back here," he heard. "We're back here."

Nye said he was coming back there. He had no gun.

He scrunched his hands into his overcoat pockets. It was cold again this early in the morning. He had forgotten until the other night just how deeply cold it could be at a crime scene before dawn. He shivered and pulled the coat more tightly.

Nye walked past a bathroom, the door splintered. He felt a great sadness rushing up in him, sparked by poor Janey Ensor. All these lives smashed off track, hurtling off in new, dark directions because of a split second a few days ago on a rainy street.

Nye came into the bedroom. It was black.

"It's me," he said flatly. "You mind if I turn on a light?"

"No, go ahead," Quintana said from someplace just ahead.

Nye fumbled along the wall until he found a switch. He flipped it and an odd, distorted light filled the bedroom. He realized that two lamps had been knocked over, shades broken, and their tilted, cockeyed light was casting stark, long shadows over the ceiling and wall. Nye bent down and picked up one lamp, setting it down on a dresser near him. Things looked a little better.

He saw Bob Quintana sitting on the end of a large king-sized bed. He had on khaki pants and he was shirtless and barefoot. He had his service weapon in his lap, hand around the grip.

At the other end of the bed, crouched against the headboard, was a young woman, brown haired, in jeans and a white blouse. She trembled a little. She stared at the floor. Nye saw that the covers had been torn from the bed and lay in a heap near Quintana's bare feet.

"Thanks for coming," Quintana said. He was shiny with sweat. "How does it look out there?"

"Pretty good for a Saturday night."

"You want to sit down someplace?"

"Am I staying long?"

"Up to you."

"Okay, maybe I better pull up something." Nye cast his eyes around the room. He found a mirrored bureau with a small stool and sat down.

"Good evening, Beth," he said after a moment.

The young woman nodded. She was scared and furious, trying to avoid glaring at Quintana. "This is ridiculous," she said suddenly.

"Come on, Beth," Quintana said sharply, like they were arguing over dinner or who got the remote for the TV.

Nye studied Quintana and his sadness flowered. The young cop did not want a happy ending tonight.

So Nye said aloud, "Okay, Quintana, what's the deal? I'm a lot older and I need a lot of z's to get me through the day."

"Go back outside and tell them I'm going to kill her."

Beth huddled closer to the headboard. "Bob, for the love of God, cut it out. We'll deal with whatever it is. Please. Please."

Quintana's sweat-slicked face turned to her, anguished and bewildered.

Nye sat up a little straighter. "You know what will happen if I do that, Bob."

"It's the way things are."

"Stop it, honey," Beth cried, "please stop it now. We can handle this."

Nye shook his head. "I don't think so. I think Bob knows it's way beyond any of that. So that's why I'll go back outside and tell Assistant Chief Altlander exactly what you said, Bob, and he'll send his guys in here."

Quintana raised his gun. "Tell them I've got my piece and I've been down on the range practicing."

"You asked for me because you wanted a messenger, right, Bob?"

"Just tell them."

Nye sat back, his eyes thick and heavy. "Okay. I'll do it."

They all sat for a few moments, Quintana breathing fast, looking back at Beth, Nye slumped on the small stool.

Finally, Quintana said, "What are you waiting for?"

"Just catching my breath for a second here. It's really late and I'm feeling pretty beat, I don't mind admitting." He smiled wanly. "All that mess in the house, you guys playing hide-and-seek for a while?"

Beth nodded. "Bob chased me. He started talking crazy, just crazy, and he came after me."

Quintana shook, his hand tightening on his gun, and Nye tensed. Here it comes, he thought in terror and helplessness.

But Quintana relaxed. "Come on," he said softly to Nye, "get out of here and tell them."

Nye nodded, as if he agreed. "You took that course in hostage situations, I bet. Everybody had to sit through intro hostage taking. You've seen all the TV shows and movies, all the hostage negotiation crap. So you know I'm supposed to start talking and keep talking and keep you talking, and then sometime, the SWAT guys come in and it all ends."

Quintana stared at him as if Nye was speaking in a foreign language.

Nye went on, "But, like I said, Bob, I'm not going through that bullshit. I'll just get up and walk out and tell Assistant Chief Altlander what you say you'll do to your fiancé here, and then he'll order his guys in and there'll be a lot of shooting and flash bangs and I don't know what else. I haven't kept up on the latest developments in how to handle hostage situations," he smiled again.

Beth said, "Bob, let us go."

Nye broke in quietly, "Oh, no. We all stay here, Beth. Bob's worked it out and it doesn't make sense any other way, right? So, let me rest here for a few minutes more and then I'll go take care of business."

Quintana's jaw clenched. "I'm sorry to put you through this."

"No apologies. Not now. No, this is the only way to tie the whole thing up tight, end it, solve the problem. You let your partner down," Nye said matter-of-factly, "and he died. Man, that is one heavy load."

"IA's all over me," Quintana murmured, hunching forward a little, "all day yesterday, today. They keep making it that I fucked up and got Tommy killed."

"IA almost always needs someone to blame," Nye said. "Take it from me. You stay in the department long enough, sooner or later they'll try to find someplace you screwed up."

"I can't do it," Quintana said.

"I don't blame you. It's a goddamn joke on top of everything else we have to deal with," Nye shook his head, hands clasped in front of him. "Remember my partner the other day? Good-looking young lady?"

Quintana swallowed.

"Excuse me, Beth," Nye said apologetically. "I know Bob doesn't look at any other women now, but Rose, my partner Detective Tafoya, is a very good-looking police officer." He smiled widely.

She thinks I'm out of my mind, too, Nye thought, assessing the wide-eyed, angry, and still-bewildered expression. *Two crazy cops in her bedroom and one of them has a gun and doesn't want to make it through the next half hour.*

"I kind of do," Quintana said diffidently. "You both were okay."

"See, I'm coming to the end of my season. Lot of bad plays and injuries catch up with you. But, before I say adios to the department, I want to let Rose know the score, give her the benefit of some of my wisdom," he hit the word sarcastically, "so she doesn't make the same screwups I did. That would be a stretch for her anyway, but I worry about her. She's like you. Decent, got her head screwed on, wants to do the right thing, got a future, and the department needs more cops like you both."

"How?" Quintana asked tightly. Nye knew there was everything in the world in that one word.

He paused, let his hands go limp. "Take every day, Bob. One day and then the next. I like to add up all of my screwups and the times I didn't screw up and say, yeah, there are a lot of people I don't know about, families, kids, friends, people at work with them, all doing a little better because I got it right. When you do mess up, and God knows you will," he felt his own sins, as Rose had rightly called them, heavily pressing down, "be goddamn grateful there are guys like Tommy Ensor around to help you out. I learned that much. There are people like that and, if you keep doing your job, you'll run into them and they'll be there when you need them."

Quintana didn't move, his gun cradled in his hands. Beth curled up more, trying to make herself even smaller.

Nye said, "One time, I had this big guy, six feet six inches tall easy, maybe three hundred pounds. He was trying to steal meat from a packing plant out on Power Inn Road and when we got there, he had this half a beef carcass and he was swinging it around like Babe Ruth, just laying guys out, slugging away."

Quintana's eyes raised and he listened.

"So me and my partner jumped on him, this big crazy bastard trying to beat us to death with a half a cow and we just rode him down to the ground. I got a choke on him, my partner emptied a can of Mace in his face, and he was screaming and still trying to swat us when a couple other guys got cuffs on him. That was one pissed-off bastard."

"What was he going to do with that much meat?"

"I have no clue. What's it matter?"

Quintana regarded him, perplexed. "I mean, what's the point?"

"It's a war story. Sometimes there is no point. You know, like

Tommy going out without his gear on, the streetlights out in the storm, it happened. It just was the way things went."

In despair and certainty, Nye looked into Quintana's face and read the dull, deadly resolution that remained untouched. Without even thinking about it, his own unresolved sin filled his mind.

"Here's one I haven't told anybody. I haven't even told my partner. Don't quite have the guts to tell her," Nye began and then the words came more easily and cleanly as the unquiet memory was dragged into the bedroom's crazy light. He saw Quintana watching him closely.

"Just before I got into Major Crimes, I kicked around a couple bureaus for short tours. I spent most of my time in Patrol, so don't run it down, Quintana," he smiled faintly. "I did one short tour, knew I was going to Major Crimes, so I moved the papers, did the chores, minded my business, stayed pretty busy," he paused. "Then one week I got a couple domestic dispute calls out in Natomas, some new housing development. Lady named Sprague. You know what they were, wife afraid husband's acting funny, nothing very specific. I had a lot of experience with these calls, so I figured this lady's overreacting. But I tell Mrs. Sprague, I'm coming out, I'll see for myself. Maybe talk to the husband, and she's okay with that plan."

"You go out there?" Quintana asked.

"See, that was the deal. Something always came up. I just never, never quite got the time to make that trip, which, I knew because I had all this experience, was a domestic beef that was going to blow over. So, no," Nye looked at Beth and then Quintana, "I let those calls slide. Didn't sound so much, the whole beef would sort itself out, and I had, like I said, all of this important stuff to take care of and I knew I was moving on pretty soon."

Nye hunched forward. "Week after the first call, I come on shift one morning and guys are coming out of the building, techs, detectives, cars going by like mad and I say, hey, what's the ruckus? Old detective before your time, named Cantil, he tells me they've got the biggest crime scene in years out in Natomas. Guy killed his wife, his three kids, and then blew his head off with a shotgun. He says to me, 'Don't you hate domestics?' and I'm standing there afraid to ask if the name of the puke was Sprague."

"Was it?" Quintana stared at him.

"Sure. What did you think?"

"Jesus."

"I went out to the crime scene, Bob. I was coming onto Major Crimes, it seemed like a good kickoff, yeah? I can smell that house right now. Nice, new little joint in a brand-new street. You go inside a house where a shotgun's gone off a couple times, and there's blood everyplace, you smell it big time. I would hate if the place you and Beth have here got that smell, because I hear it's a sonofabitch to get rid of."

Quintana's head went down. Beth didn't move and he knew they were imagining the three dead children and the two parents in that house. But imagining was not exactly on the same level as standing in the middle of it and knowing what you had failed to do. It was not at all the same as seeing them at three in the morning again when you had talked yourself into believing they were gone.

Nye looked at them. "My partner calls what I did a sin of omission. I mean, it's not like I wanted it to happen. It's not even like I thought it would happen. I just didn't do what I knew I was supposed to do."

"It's not your fault," Quintana said, head down.

"Of course not."

Nye stopped. He had nothing more. He had come to the finish. He had a thousand stories and they all had come to an end now. He would go outside and the drama would take its inevitable brutal course.

Quintana's head stayed bowed. *He didn't have Rose's inner strength. She might have been born with it,* Nye thought, *or picked it up during the harsh days scrabbling for a living with her family in the Philippines or as a rookie cop like this one here. But Quintana didn't have it.*

Nye was truly surprised when Quintana got up and went to Beth. He put his gun on the small night table beside the bed and touched her tentatively. She drew back for a moment and then pushed forward, holding him.

Nye stood and carefully picked up the gun and put it in his overcoat pocket and then he went through the living room and out the front door, back into the blinding glare of the lights.

"You should have called me. First thing," Rose scolded him.

Nye tried another swallow of his black coffee and it burned acridly. The twenty-four-hour truck stop in the south end of Sacramento was fluorescent, bustling with long haulers stopping in for huge plates of eggs and pancakes.

"I called you, Rosie."

"After. I mean, call me before, Ter. We're partners. We had this discussion a little while ago."

He nodded. She looked less angry than disappointed. He wondered what she told Luis or her daughter when he called and woke them all up and she went rushing out of the house into the predawn night. *We are partners,* he thought, *because you came without hesitation.*

Man, I am a lucky chump.

Nye coughed a little, pushed the thick coffee mug away.

"I don't think I should be a cop anymore," he said.

"You're not going to be," she said with a chuckle.

"You shouldn't be one either."

Rose started to give him a disbelieving smirk and then saw that he meant it.

"Look, Ter, I feel bad about Quintana, too."

"It's not about him. It's you. You're a good one, Rosie. You should move on before something happens."

"I guess I should've realized retiring, Ensor, Solorio, all of it would get you. It's the right time for you to get on with your life, Ter," she said simply and sincerely. "I have a lot more things I want to do in the department."

Nye gripped his thick coffee mug on the table. "You want to know what can happen to you?" he demanded harshly. Before she said anything, he did what he had never been able to bring himself to do before and told her about that neat new house, years ago, that had taken the place of his dreams and about the arrogant veteran cop who knew too much about so many things and so little about anything at all.

THIRTY-EIGHT

STEVENSON GOT HOME EARLIER than planned on Sunday because Haley had an upset stomach when she woke up in the Disneyland Hotel and Vee thought she had a slight fever, too.

The drive north to Sacramento was uneventful and Vee looked restored and happy. She had spoken to Eli several times over the weekend and come away from the calls more relaxed each time. Stevenson felt in control completely; ready to face the trial on Monday. The past few days blurred into receding unpleasantness.

Haley recovered during the drive, but she wasn't as talkative as she had been the day before during the exhausting tramp through the rides and frequent breaks for ice cream or snacks. Stevenson noticed she vanished behind the seat only once, as if hunting for something. She looked out the window for most of the trip, but otherwise seemed very satisfied with the excursion.

He let Vee and Haley out while he pulled the SUV into the garage.

Vee came back a few moments later, her face tighter.

"Myrna just hailed me," she said. "She said two detectives were here yesterday."

Stevenson closed the SUV door carefully. Haley had gone into the house. "Why?"

Vee handed him a card. "They're checking on SUV owners, Frank. People like us."

He smiled. "Well, they should. They've got a description of the SUV that was involved, they should be checking."

"I thought I was over all of this." She trembled.

"We're fine, Vee. We just got back from a relaxing family trip. We'll be glad to talk to the police and help them any way we can."

"Sure, you're right," she said, taking his arm like she had when they dated for the first time and they walked five blocks back to her house and he experienced a wonderment that had never really left him. "I need to feel a little of your self-confidence."

"Don't sell yourself short," he said. "You're the one who's got all the steel."

He called Detective Nye and spoke to a woman, his partner. Vee put their unused bottled water from the trip into the refrigerator. Stevenson hung up.

"They're coming over," he said. "In about an hour."

"Myrna said they just wanted a phone call," Vee replied, uneasy.

"Well, Detective Rose Tafoya was very polite and very insistent. She and her partner Detective Nye are coming over in about an hour to see me because I'm the registered owner of the SUV."

"I drive it sometimes."

"I assume they assume so. We'll both end up talking to them." Stevenson came up behind Vee and pulled a half-full bottle of white wine from the refrigerator and poured himself a small glass. He offered and she shook her head.

"I need a shower," she said. "Make sure they don't forget who you are."

"I'm right behind you." He drank the wine thoughtfully, enjoying it.

When the two detectives showed up, Stevenson recognized them from the brief glimpse in Yardley's chambers and the flash across the TV. The older one, the tattered military man, looked worn out. His partner, brisk and cool, seemed to be in charge. She was a little too formal and ill at ease, though. *No chance of them pulling anything,* he thought, *because Vee's right. They know I'm a judge.*

Vee was elegant and informal, smelling of fragrant soap. Stevenson could see it was indeed all a drill for the two detectives, finishing reports. They had someone in custody. On a late Sunday afternoon they both acted as if they had much better things to do.

He was a little amused when he watched them go through the motions of separating Vee and him, Detective Tafoya taking Vee off to the living room on the pretext of talking about schools while Detective Nye asked to see the SUV.

Nye whistled a faint tune as he examined the SUV's license plates and walked around it.

"I'm sorry to bother both you and your family like this," Nye said.

"No trouble," Stevenson answered, calm and sympathetic. "I'm sorry you and your partner have to come out today. I presume this is a day off."

"Sometimes," the older detective said. "We're trying to finish up on this one, between you and me," he ran a hand over the SUV's driver's door and mirror. "Mind if I look inside?"

"Not at all. We just got back from a trip. It's still pretty messy."

"Nothing like my car, Judge. I got stuff in there even I don't want to find."

Stevenson opened the driver's side door and the detective slid inside, bent down, and then opened the glove compartment and sorted through the registration papers. It was not a very clever way to get a look at them.

"Not a lot of mileage," the detective said, taking in the dashboard.

"I mostly drive it to and from work. Or on trips sometimes. I've only had it a year."

"Jeez, you should see my mileage, Judge. I just drive around town pretty much, but I bet I rack up three times your miles on my car." He chuckled.

"You're probably doing more driving than you think." Stevenson said easily. "We don't notice the routine little jaunts. They add up."

"At my age, I miss a whole lot." He launched into a survey of people they both might know at the courthouse, the cases Stevenson handled, and had anecdotes about three or four names they had in common.

"Finish up your investigation, you said?" Stevenson finally asked, folding his arms.

"Yeah, well, that's unofficial, but that's the deal. Our suspect died in the jail yesterday. He was nine miles from Sunday solid for killing Officer Ensor. So we're really over and out."

The detective chatted on in a heedless, weary voice and he obviously didn't notice Stevenson's slight recoil. After a moment he said, "I didn't know the suspect was dead."

The detective got out of the SUV and slammed the door. "Funny how things that seem so damn important to people like us, Judge," he pointed to Stevenson, "don't mean diddly to people just down the road, so to speak. I guess you missed it on your trip."

He walked around the SUV, crouched down, straightened up, as if sizing it up for a trade-in.

Stevenson asked him more questions about the suspect's death and took it all in as they strolled into the house. He heard Vee and the other detective laughing.

"I'd like to meet your daughter," Detective Tafoya said.

"She's in her room. Haley's at the shy stage. A little nervous around people."

"I suppose I've got that to look forward to. And the teenage stuff."

They both laughed again.

"Well, we're done here," Nye announced. "Right license, model, year. All fine. You want to take a quick look?" Nye asked his partner.

Vee shot a glance at Stevenson but her expression remained pleasant.

The other detective shook her head and then sighed. "Well, I probably better. We both sign the report. I'll be right back." She gestured. "Through here?"

"Just follow through the kitchen, you can't miss it," Stevenson said.

Nye looked around the living room. "We'll get out of your way in just a minute. Again, thank you, Judge and Mrs. Stevenson. You made this very painless."

"It was a pleasure," Vee said, getting up from the sofa where she and Detective Tafoya had been talking. "Frank and I were discussing it the other day and we'd like to do something for the family of the officer who died."

Stevenson nodded and Detective Nye said, "I will pass that along. Your father said almost exactly the same thing when we talked to him yesterday."

Vee asked with a slight, barely discernible catch, "You saw my father?"

"He called us. He wanted to offer to help. Especially after he heard about Officer Ensor's family."

Stevenson said, "He's that kind of man. He does a lot of charitable work."

"Like you, Judge," Detective Nye said. "Actually, you and Officer Ensor crossed paths at least once." He described the adoption of Josie Cummins's daughter.

"It's a very small world," Stevenson said. "I'm sorry I never had a chance to meet Officer Ensor." He appeared distracted.

When Detective Tafoya came back a moment later, the older detective said, "I guess you sold your father-in-law on an SUV. He told us he just bought one, pretty much exactly like yours."

"I suppose so, yes. Hadn't thought about it."

Detective Tafoya said, "He must've driven in yours, I imagine. That's how he got to see what he liked."

"I suppose so, yes," Stevenson said again.

"He ever drive it by himself? Kind of test it out?"

"No, I don't think so," Stevenson looked his wife and she shook her head. "I didn't think so. I imagine that takes care of things."

"You've been very gracious," Detective Tafoya said stiffly as the two of them slowly headed for the door. She turned, still walking and asked, "Do you remember offhand when you and Mr. Holder might have been together recently in your SUV?"

Stevenson frowned. He looked at his wife again. "Must have been sometime last week. One night last week, I think."

"I don't write it down, I can't remember what day it is," Detective Nye said with a grin and small wave and they left.

Vee steadied herself into the kitchen and helped herself to the wine she had turned down earlier. "Why did my dad call them?" she demanded shakily. "He already caused enough trouble with Fonseca."

Stevenson leaned back against the countertop. "Probably in his cups, like we both know he is when he's under stress."

"You're a little too calm," she said. "He called the police this time."

"And they've been and gone. We're home free, hon."

"You didn't have to tell them the two of you were together."

"It won't take much checking to find out Eli and I were together Wednesday night. I don't want to look like I'm hiding anything."

"The questions, Frank. They're wondering."

"Both of them gave the SUV a look. The records match for my SUV and they both saw that it's undamaged. I'm not worried about them. I'm worried about Eli. Didn't he say anything to you when you talked to him?"

Vee shook her head. "I think he was scared to tell me."

"Talk to him. He'll listen to you more than me. He can't do anything like this again. He's got to keep quiet."

She thought for a minute and clinked her glass against his. "I'll take care of him. I know he's frightened."

"Make sure, Vee. He's a dear old guy but he can do all of us a lot of harm."

She nodded, concerned and uncertain. Stevenson thought the best answer now was to focus on the three of them. Remember what they had and could lose.

"Look, the weekend's nearly over," Stevenson said. "Let's have a little party. Why don't you see if Haley's up for pizza?" He finished his glass.

"Where are you going?"

He stopped. "I'm going online to catch up on the dead man who saved us."

He was, in truth, disgusted at his almost-reflexive callousness and the earlier charade with the two detectives. He was seething at what the old man had done. He took the wine bottle with him.

Rose said, "Like I told you on the way over, Ter, this guy's smooth and smart. All those rich clients, the charity stuff, marrying up like he did. The courthouse people I could get hold of last night—"

"I heard you the first time, Rosie. The judge's a swell guy to work for. Works hard. We've got a parking ticket or two, and that's it."

"If he's our guy, how does he live with taking a little trip to Disneyland the day after he kills a man?"

Nye shook his head. "I'm giving up trying to figure people out."

"He's got to be a stone-cold, dead bastard."

They sat in her car on a tree-lined street about a mile from the Stevenson's home.

"I know what I found on him so far is squeaky. I didn't expect anything else," she went on. "But that SUV is wrong. No question."

"Why?"

"You look at the tires? There is no way he's been driving that SUV for a year. There's no treadwear. They're like factory fresh."

"He says he just buzzes around town."

"Crap. You park around Sacramento, you get dings in your doors, you get your bumper dinged, we have the worst drivers around and we bump into every car in every parking lot. I didn't see one ding on that SUV, Ter. It's too clean."

"You're reading too much into it, Rosie," he said quietly.

"I grew up with three brothers and every week we had some car they were taking apart. I had engine blocks in my bedroom until I was twelve. I know cars. You know I do. The judge's SUV is wrong. It's too new."

Rose was arguing and he wasn't responding. Nye stared ahead. A woman in jogging shorts walked her golden lab while another woman pushed a heavily laden shopping cart of crushed soda cans along the street. Two older men in T-shirts, because it was unseasonably warm again, sat on white metal lawn chairs arguing at day's end.

"Ter, we still have this one to finish up right before you pull the pin," she said gruffly. "You think there's something here just like I do and we don't have anything else going on. This is the best lead unless we just hang onto Lucking like everyone else."

Nye nodded. "Well, you're wrong about Stevenson's SUV not having any dings."

"I didn't see any."

"You missed the one I put there," Nye grinned like a kid in spite of himself. "I keyed it just near the left front tire well while he was on the other side. He'll probably never notice it."

"Why the heck did you do that?"

Nye carefully brought out the small baggie in his coat pocket. Tiny black paint bits flecked it. "Something for Cummins to play with. See if she's just bragging about making a match with the SUV that hit Ensor."

"So Cummins puts your paint samples through her machine and it comes back negative, what does that prove exactly? I can tell you that right now."

"We'll know the judge is lying about owning that SUV for a year. You're right, Rosie, it's too out-of-the-box for being driven around this town."

Rose chuckled. "It won't match, Ter. I'll make you a bet."

He put the baggie back in his pocket and looked at his watch. "Name your stakes." They had a final briefing with the department's overlords in three hours. Miles to go before then.

"I'll make you the same deal you made me. If you want to lay anything out like last night, it stays here with us, nobody else hears anything."

Nye was surprised and grateful Rose took his confession, as much as he had told Quintana, the night before and only said, "You sure like to beat yourself up, old man," before telling him he had not broken any commandment. She sounded like she meant it. He wanted to believe her. Now he realized it had not been pretense on her part. Rose truly didn't think he had done something irredeemably wicked. His error was too human and too common for that. Her continuing good opinion mattered more than he had admitted to himself even a day or so ago.

"You're on," Nye said, starting her car. "You feeling dangerous?"

"What do you think?" she replied.

"Holder, the judge's father-in-law. He's got an SUV now, too. Right make and model year. He could be the driver."

"Stevenson's covering for his father-in-law?"

"It works for me just as well as the Judge. We got to do a lot of fast back-checking about where they've both been the last few days."

Rose considered this but Nye knew her wild idea of the day before had encompassed the possibility already.

"Okay, I go with one of them covering for the other," she said. "We got two people in the SUV when it hit Ensor. We got two SUVs."

"I'd like to get a look at Holder's SUV, yeah? I might even like to get a souvenir to go with the ones I got for Cummins."

"We could work him again, ask about all these SUVs in his family. He didn't seem like a guy who'd go the distance."

"I never get my hopes up that some mope will roll over on his buds."

"But it could happen this time."

"Yeah, if we're right to start with about a whole lot of things."

Rose nodded, a smile on her face. "Mr. Holder's not going to like a second visit in one weekend."

Nye kept an eye on the street. "Nope. So we can't ask Nish's permission before we go and we can't tell Altlander if we can't tell Nish."

"I'm dangerous enough for that, Ter," she said.

"I hope to hell," he said with conviction. "We don't have anything close to get a search warrant for Holder's SUV."

"Sometimes it's more fun to do it without protection," Rose replied with unusual crudity.

They were about to do something very risky, probe a man who wasn't an official suspect in a hit-and-run fatality and who had demonstrable high connections in the department. They were also planning to take evidence from this man without his permission and without getting a search warrant first. Nye couldn't think of any of his previous partners, very much including Tommy Ensor, who would do what Rose was ready to do with him in the next few hours. Nye now wished he had told her everything last night about what happened at that little house so garishly decorated inside with random pools of red.

It would test the limits of her understanding and forgiveness.

THIRTY-NINE

STEVENSON JUST MANAGED TO MAKE IT through dinner behind a supporting buzz, the consequence of polishing off the wine himself as he read online about the only suspect's death in county jail and the armed standoff involving the dead cop's partner. Then, with their extra-large pizza, he poured several large glasses of red table wine for Vee and himself, while Haley indulged in iced tea. Nye didn't mention Ensor's partner attempting what was called— Stevenson struggled to find the phrase in his numbed state—suicide by cop. *You would think he'd at least mention something like that as we had our most amiable conversation. Guess he's got reasons for looking hollowed out,* Stevenson thought of Nye with sympathy. *Tough times for city cops.*

Although the pizza's sloppy casualness lent the meal a festive air, it was not a true family moment. Stevenson and Haley ate while Vee repeatedly tried to reach her father over the telephone. They heard her exasperated voice. Stevenson had Haley help him make a green salad, as if that would block out the sound.

"I can't get ahold of him," Vee said, coming in from the living room. "I've tried all the numbers, Frank."

"It's Sunday night. He may have gone out with friends."

"I should've gotten him on his cell." She stood worriedly by the table. Haley looked up at her.

"When did you talk to him last again?" Stevenson asked.

"Just before we left to come home. Wasn't that about eight?" she asked Haley.

"I still had a stomachache."

Stevenson tried to gather his fragmented mind. Vee was growing more agitated and then the phone buzzed softly and she grabbed at it. Stevenson hated Haley's own worried expression.

"Oh, Dad," Vee said breathily. "I just tried to call you and I couldn't get you and it gave me a scare."

Stevenson opened the unwieldy pizza box as he listened. He pointed at a big slice and Haley nodded so he clumsily got it onto her plate. Vee disappeared with the phone into the living room again. *Time to let Eli know he can't indulge himself by calling the police,* Stevenson thought.

Not when cops are trying to kill themselves because of what happened, and he shoved that thought down very deeply.

He heard Vee call him and he got up and went into the living room. She held the cell phone out to him. There was fear and frustration in her brown eyes.

Stevenson spoke quietly, so Haley wouldn't overhear, "Yes, Eli."

"I told Vee I'm out on the boat. I'm going to spend a couple days on the river, clear my mind a little," the voice was defiant, hesitant, and thin at the same time. "So I'm going to stay kind of incommunicado, you understand?"

"Yes, Eli. I do. Vee told you about our visitors this afternoon."

"Nothing happened when they came to see me, Frank," the voice was sharp and frightened.

"You did exactly what we said we'd avoid, Eli," Stevenson felt his resentment boiling. "You gave the police a reason to look at us."

"All right, I was wrong. I made a mistake. But they aren't coming after you."

"No, they are not. They're not going to. No more calls, Eli. Do you understand me?"

"Threats aren't necessary."

"Do you understand me, Eli?" and Stevenson was suddenly aware of Vee's anxious gaze.

"Yes, I do. Yes, I do," and he hung up.

Stevenson handed the phone to Vee. "Case closed."

"It's better for him to be alone and away now. Don't you think so?"

Stevenson put his arm around her. "Sure it is. The police told us they're finishing up, didn't they? In a few days, it will be over. Everything will settle down."

She leaned in to him. "I hope to God it will."

I will be strong, he thought. *There is no alternative.*

Stevenson made a toast to them all when they finished eating, and they fell to recalling the best rides, the longest lines, the worst food from the trip. Vee was distracted again even as she gamely pitched in.

As they sat, full and picking through the remains of the pizza in its husk of a box, Haley put both her hands up in front of her.

Stevenson rocked in a gentle haze, wondering what she was doing.

"Okay, Mom. Dad," Haley said, "I'm just going to say this because I know what you did and I've been thinking about it this afternoon and you're right."

Vee had started to get up, glass in hand, but she settled into her chair again.

"What are you talking about, honey?" she asked.

"While we were driving to Disneyland, you said you'd cleaned the car," Haley went on, her face intent and restrained, "and that's why I realized I couldn't find Bear."

"Who is Bear?" Stevenson asked, mystified.

"One of her pandas," Vee said softly.

Stevenson conjured up the shelf of stuffed bears, what he had presumed were soon-to-be relics of childhood in Haley's bedroom. She never talked about them or asked for more as gifts. They were part of her past, the childhood that was rushing away so fast he sometimes hardly recognized it.

"Since I was little, I took him along and put him in the car, under the backseat where I could know he was there. I put him in the car when you got it, Dad."

Stevenson took another drink. *Oh, God,* he thought. *She knows.*

"I know you found Bear and you figured out why I put him there," she took a breath and lowered her hands, "and I'm too old to be holding onto a little kid's doll. It's not like I need him anymore. I'm too old. So, I understand why you didn't tell me you found him. It's nice of you."

She was suddenly awkward and embarrassed at her revelation, rigid and unclear what to do now. She studied her hands, the crusts on the plates, then both Stevenson and Vee.

Stevenson stared at his daughter's face, stunned that he knew so little of what went on behind her clear, thoughtful eyes.

Vee leaned over and hugged Haley, murmuring. She had tears when she looked up and he saw that she was at least as drunk as he was. "Baby, baby, you are such a marvel," Vee said, taking Haley's hand and grabbing Stevenson's, too. "We are so lucky to have each other right now. This is such a lucky family."

But all Stevenson could think of was his intelligent and guileless child and how she knew, without knowing, that the SUV her father told her was theirs was a fraud. He squeezed Vee's hand too tightly. "I am so lucky to have you both," he said, uncertain how many new lies he would have to keep telling, how much he would have to falsify and conceal from Haley from now on.

Stevenson would have to keep track of Eli as well, warily guarding him, alert to a careless slip or indiscretion, for the rest of his life.

For the rest of our lives, he thought with hideous lucidity.

Night was almost fully over the river, only the last orange strip of the fading sun glittering on the water below a darkening sky. Nye and Rose walked along a gently rocking pier at the Sacramento

Yacht Club with the burly bearded harbormaster. They stopped at an empty slip. It resembled a missing tooth in a row of large white and sleek boats.

"See? He keeps the *Lurene* there," said Gerson, the harbormaster. "Very tidy thirty footer."

Rose made a disapproving sound, her eyes traveling out to the river where a collection of other boats, some quite small, some with engines and few with sails, were making their way into or out of the harbor for the night. "How long ago did he pull out?"

"Couple hours. He set *sail*," Gerson grinned.

"Where did Mr. Holder say he was going?" Nye asked, the cool early evening breeze irritating him under the circumstances. Just as the party at the expansive clubhouse up the green hill made him want to curse.

"Up river. He didn't really say where he was going. I got the idea it was kind of a spur-of-the-moment. People around here do that a lot."

"I bet they do," Rose said. "Was he alone?"

"Just Mr. Holder. He stocked up with some groceries we keep for members and then he set sail," Gerson seemed to think repetition was very funny.

"How long did he say he was going to be on the river?" Nye asked.

"He didn't say."

"Isn't that required or something?"

"Sailing down the Sacramento River isn't like flying somewheres. You don't need to file a flight plan," Gerson said cheerily. "You just go."

"He just went," Rose said to Nye.

"Yes, he did."

Rose was at a loss for the moment. Nye vented his frustration at Gerson by demanding, "Where's the nearest place he could tie up for the night?"

"A dozen places. He could just drop anchor by the riverbank, too."

"If I wanted to follow Mr. Holder," Nye pressed, "where would I go?"

"Not too sure," Gerson scratched his gray-flecked beard. "You know how many islands there are in the delta? Couple hundred."

"He could be anywhere," Rose summed it up. *"Sailing."*

"If it's important, you could raise him on his radio. He's got a radio, like everyone," Gerson swept an arm to embrace the big and small boats clustered on the dark water in the twilight.

Nye glanced at Rose and she shook her head slightly. They did not want to contact Holder except in person and they certainly had no intention of putting him on notice that they were looking for him.

"Let me see if I got this," Nye turned and wobbled back along the pier as it rocked in the river's current, "somebody leaves here, takes their boat for a spin along the river, and, if he doesn't want anybody to find him or talk to him, he's pretty much got that wired, right?"

"I think that's about it," Gerson acknowledged cheerfully. He said to Rose, "Watch your step going up the walkway."

"Show us where Mr. Holder parks," she snapped in response.

They thanked Gerson in the parking lot and repeated for his benefit that they were trying to talk to Mr. Holder about a police charity event he was involved in. The harbormaster grinned and left.

Nye studied the late-model blue Jaguar in front of them, its rounded contours softened and blurred in the falling darkness.

"This sure ain't a new Cadillac SUV." Nye squinted away.

"The housemaid hasn't even seen the new SUV," Rose reminded him of their conversation in the last hour with the woman they spoke to at Eli Holder's home. She had directed them to the Yacht Club. "It wasn't parked in the garage."

"So where the hell is this new SUV?" Nye demanded.

"Pretty obvious, old man. Somewhere nobody can see it."

The briefing was held in the chief's office at nine that night. He sat at his desk, flanked by the flags of California, the United States, and the City of Sacramento, with a battery of family photographs on the walls. The room was crowded and bright. He wore a loose, patterned shirt and old chinos and he absentmindedly picked at dried skin on his cheek.

The two assistant chiefs were at a small table to Chief Gutierrez's right. Nishimoto slouched and had a pad on which he made squares and circles while Altlander sat straight and fixed each detective with a cold, unblinking gaze. A younger woman with acne scars under heavy makeup, the DA's chief deputy, sat by herself against one wall, making endless notes on a yellow legal pad.

The detectives sat at the conference table facing the brass. Nye had each team deliver their briefing, Vu and Parkes, then Pesce and Talman. Nye was proud of them. He saved Rose and him for last. He concealed, he thought pretty well, his tension about losing the chance to talk to Eli Holder again. Or why he and Rose wanted to do it at all.

He was also tense because every time he glanced at her, he admitted he had still not fully revealed everything to Rose. *Sometime soon,* he thought, *I got to tell her the rest of what happened at that house. Guthrie had guessed the pathetic thing he had done. But how the hell do I get the nerve?*

Parkes was rattling off the investigation's statistics, the thousand tips and calls, many still unanswered; Vu described all of the interviews, including the two dozen from patrol. Pesce and Talman laid out Lucking's last journey and his psychological postmortem.

Rose made sure the brass knew what was missing from the case. She and Nye decided to say nothing of their fruitless effort earlier in the evening. She did not get very far with what she could say.

The chief adjusted his glasses. "I want to sum up. We do not have the hit-and-run vehicle."

"That's correct, sir," Rose answered firmly.

"But we do have Lucking's statement and an unequivocal identification. We have a time period in which he could have stolen a Cadillac SUV."

"Yes, sir," she began and the chief turned from her to the chief deputy DA.

"What about the ID witness, Crystal?"

"I'm glad we don't have to put him in front of a jury," the young woman grinned and got nothing back but stony stares, "but after interviewing him today, I think Rudloff's credible and his doctor confirms his unusual talent."

Nye thought of the parlor trick with the telephone book. *Doobie Rudloff sees all, remembers all,* he thought. *He could make a buck in*

Vegas at poker, knowing all the cards. Oh, I forgot, Nye sourly added to himself. *He's nuts.*

Rose didn't wait for the chief to add up the particulars of the case against Lucking. "Another item we're missing, sir, are the enhancements from video cameras along Capitol Mall. They caught the SUV and we have images of the driver and some partial imaging of the passenger and DOJ is trying to enhance them now."

"What's the likelihood we'll get a decent picture of the driver?"

"I'm not a computer expert, sir, but I think we will."

"How about the passenger?"

Rose reluctantly admitted, "There isn't much to work with. I don't think they'll give us anything."

"When do we get a look at these enhancements?" Altlander asked.

Nye, beside Rose and the rest of the team, said, "We've been bugging them. They're having some kind of computer glitches but they swear they'll have them ready tomorrow morning."

The chief said, "I want them by eight."

"By eight," Altlander echoed for Nye's benefit.

"We don't have the passenger," the chief said aloud.

The woman from the DA's office piped in, "At this point, locating the passenger's no longer a high priority. Lucking was the driver. Anybody else in the vehicle might be chargeable as an accomplice, but I have to tell you there are a myriad of ways to defense that. It would be a very tough case to take to trial."

"I came to the same conclusion," Nishimoto didn't look up from his pad. "Our target was the driver who killed Ensor."

Nye and Rose struggled to stay silent.

The chief said to Altlander, "Suppose we don't find the passenger. It's going to leak out there was one, won't it?"

"Probably, sir," Altlander replied. "But the DA's right," and the chief interrupted him.

"What's the department's liability here in terms of public perception if it gets out there was a passenger and we haven't found whoever it is?"

"Minimal," Nishimoto answered laconically, eyes still on his pad, "as long as we emphasize that the actual hit-and-run driver was successfully captured. We say that our search for the passenger is ongoing. It will be, of course."

Everyone in the room knew how low intensity it would be.

"What I'm thinking now," the chief stood up, hands on his hips, a big man restless and frustrated, "is that unless those enhancements are contradictory, I mean they do *not* show Lucking, I'm satisfied we've done our duty. We definitely had Officer Ensor's killer in custody and he managed to get out of our custody the only way possible."

Nishimoto stopped doodling. "Lucking got away from the sheriff, not us."

"Hell of a deal," the chief mused.

Nye spotted Rose's tightly clasped hands. He knew she was aching to blurt out their suspicions, however unformed, about Stevenson and Holder. They both knew too well what kind of reception those speculations would get at this point. *Especially,* he thought, *because Stevenson's a judge across the street.*

Nishimoto, as the deputy chief responsible for Major Crimes, sat back and asked crisply, "Nye? Tafoya? Do either of you have anything else you want to add?"

Nye and Rose traded almost imperceptible glances. He spoke. "I can't add anything to what the team has said, sir. There's nothing more at this point."

Rose's mouth tightened. She might not like withholding Stevenson's or Holder's names, but she understood why it was necessary. If they came up with something, Nye's unnoticed equivocation left the door slightly ajar for reviving the investigation.

The chief sat down again. "Well, I want to thank you all. This has been a tough job and you all did it in spite of extraordinary pressure and personal grief." He bowed his head and then said to Altlander, "Tomorrow I want to see those video enhancements and we'll tentatively schedule a press conference for eleven to announce the investigation's wrapped up. I'll call her myself, but make sure your boss's calendar is clear, Crystal. I want the district attorney right at my side. I'll get the mayor to let us use the City Hall steps."

The chief deputy DA nodded and made a note.

The meeting broke up quickly. The chief spent a few minutes with each detective, shaking hands, complimenting each one. Rose took her turn with a stoical smile. Both Nishimoto and Altlander followed in the chief's wake.

Altlander gave Nye a hard handshake. He said, "You were damn impressive yesterday, Nye. You have guts. I'm rethinking you." He tapped Nishimoto, "Work on this guy, Jerry. We need him."

Nye was surprised by Altlander's dramatic change of mind about him. He and Rose followed the other detectives to the command center. Nishimoto said, "Listen to Altlander, Terry. You might reconsider pulling the pin."

"No chance. Anyway, he'll change his mind in the morning." Guthrie's crudeness the night before made sense. He knew the rules had abruptly changed in Nye's favor even before Quintana's incident.

Nishimoto said, "Altlander's on top. The chief's going for him. That came through loud and clear before the briefing. Take my advice," he said to Rose, "Get close to Altlander. He can do you a lot of good."

"What about you, sir?" Rose asked impetuously, concerned.

"I'm a short-timer like your partner, Detective Tafoya." He vanished toward his office.

"Christ," Nye said sourly. "You imagine what this place's going to be like?"

"Great, old man. Leave me with Altlander," Rose groused. "Always thinking of yourself."

He produced a grin. "I'll always be a phone call away, Rosie."

"Like I need you on my speed dial."

Nye sent his detectives home. They milled around the command center purposelessly for a little while anyway, joking and swapping stories about the strangest tips, the dead ends that proliferated through the case from the outset, the unforeseen sharp turns. Nye didn't rise to their praise when Pesce and Parkes elaborated on his one-man takedown of Quintana, who clearly had gone crazy and was therefore as a rogue cop more dangerous than any street puke. Nye only saw Quintana in the blaze of lights, handcuffed, hauled into a patrol car, Beth weeping.

Finally, he and Rose were alone in the command center, the TVs still flickering pictures from the Ensor home at night with a candlelight vigil outside it, more images of the county jail and Lucking's face or his wife.

Rose went to her desk and started tapping on her computer.

"Look, Ter, maybe the DOJ enhancements will show Stevenson clear as bell. Maybe Holder."

"Or Doobie's right and we see Lucking."

"So it's not over tonight. We missed Holder but we're still pitching until you and me are satisfied," she looked up hard at him, "Not the chief or the DA. You and me."

Nye didn't move for a bit and then went to his desk. "Yeah, that's the way it plays."

"So shake it off, old man. Make your calls. We go after Stevenson. I'm getting the names of people we've got to see who can tell us where the judge's been lately. Clerks, staff at the courthouse, couple bailiffs I know."

She turned away, busily keeping life in the fading Ensor investigation, unwilling to let it go yet.

Nye knew the moment he dreaded had come. They were alone. Rose was prepared to go the full distance for him. He could not let her do that without having all the facts about him.

"Rosie," he said. "I didn't give up everything about my domestic screwup."

She looked up at him, and an annoyed frown creased her mouth. "We've done that one."

"No. I didn't tell you that I came back from the house and I shredded my phone logs. I didn't want a record of the calls she made to me." Nye couldn't even form the poor dead woman's name.

Rose sat back, angry and stern. "You want me to tell you you're an asshole? You want me to tell you that was big-time wrong?"

"I wanted you to have it all."

Rose shook her head. "Ter, in the last six months, hell, in the last couple days, I know the kind of guy you are and the cop you are. Not the one you think, or the jerks at the courthouse think, with their hands out to you and their dirty little trades, but the real one. Okay. You were a major asshole one time and it's a horrible, sickening thing and you should have stood up and taken whatever was coming. But that was one time and it's a long time ago. Tonight we got this case still hanging by its fingernails. You and me, old man, we can make the difference, because no one else around here is going to."

He looked at her hard. "Thanks, Rosie."

"Bullshit," she said crisply. "I need you. You need me."

"Yeah," he said, because he knew she would not say more even if she felt it. "One thing I'll miss here, is you."

"Oh, crap," she said to dismiss the whole episode and move on, lapsing into a torrent of Tagalog, which she only did at times of high stress when she could not help herself. "Okay, Ter? We do this right and you go on your way because we did?"

Nye nodded, relieved beyond words.

He took out his little notebook of phone numbers. The last few days, including Quintana's attempted self-immolation, had torn at him. Rose had helped stitch him together.

He found the home number he was looking for and dialed.

"Cummins? Yeah, I know it's late and I can hear the kid. I didn't mean to wake her." He put the baggie and its tantalizing opaque bits of darkness on his desk. "I got a personal favor I got to ask you." He saw Rose grin.

Stevenson's head burned with an early reaction to the wine as he lay in bed, a faint luminous shadow-play on the ceiling from the streetlights below.

Vee had an arm over him and, even in the near blackness, he knew her eyes were open. He put his face near hers and they spoke in whispers, like children.

"As soon as they say it's over, we've got to get rid of the car, Frank," she said. "It's too dangerous to have around. If the police or anyone looks at it closely, they'll know it's not our SUV."

"I know," he said. "I started thinking about that as soon as Hurricane told us at dinner."

"She's such a smart kid."

Stevenson felt a bubble of anguish. "I don't even think I know her. I don't know how that happened."

"Don't be so hard on yourself."

"I had it in my mind for a long time that the most important thing was what I wanted. Moving up to the Court of Appeal. And then the accident happened and I haven't thought about it at all and it seems so trivial, like I'm at twenty thousand feet straining to see a keychain way down on the ground."

Vee stroked his cheek. "We've got dreams. They're not trivial. They matter. We have to get past what's happened and get our dreams again. Everything will make sense again."

He groaned involuntarily. "Tomorrow I'm going back into my courtroom to start this trial and I'll have three defendants watching me and I'll look down at them. It's not becoming a justice on the Court of Appeal that seems so unreal now; it's tomorrow, Vee. How can I be a judge at all? I'm going to be sitting on the bench, ready to preside over a trial, make rulings, tell the jury when to come in and when to go out, pass sentence on these three men and I do not know at this moment, how I can do any of that now."

"You'll be fine tomorrow. I know you, Frank. You're a good man and a good judge. Trust me, I know all about you," and she pressed closer to him.

Stevenson watched the luminous phantoms above him. He told himself that these roller coasters of emotion were anticipated, but they still gripped and terrified. Tomorrow he would be up again, just like Vee said. *Just hang on until tomorrow, through the night, and the unruly phantoms would be vanquished by the day. Even if,* he thought, *some phantoms are real.*

He pulled Vee closer and realized she had been whispering as he drifted on his own thoughts.

"I can check, but I'm sure the Pensione Lamberti's still in business. We can go back there for a week, maybe a couple of weeks. Haley's old enough to see some of the world. She can miss some school. She'll like Italy, she'll love Rome just like we did on our first vacation. It's time she started seeing the world and getting comfortable with how different it is, learn that so many other people don't live like we do."

Dreams, he thought, holding Vee. *We have our dreams.*

He finally drifted to sleep, but he thought Vee stayed awake in the darkness beside him.

FORTY

NYE AND ROSE MET AT THE MAIN California Department of Justice forensic and technical facility on Broadway a little after seven on Monday morning. A thin, papery layer of clouds hung over the capital, and a prickly breeze nipped at them. The sprawling, red-brick complex was already stirring to life when they went inside.

"I feel like I've got a Mega Millions ticket this morning," Rose said.

"Never get your hopes up too much," Nye advised. "You won't feel so bad when things don't turn out."

But he felt like they had a hot ticket, too.

They went to the imaging section on the third floor. Two earnest techs sat them down at wide flat-screen monitors and carefully, slowly, with many repetitions for Nye, walked them through the various enhancement steps that the Capitol Mall video data had been put through. The techs eagerly talked over each other like excited chipmunks.

Rose stared at the succession of pictures, grainy and then very grainy, as they flipped across the screens. Nye crossed his arms.

"They look worse than when we first saw them," she said to the techs.

"As we've been explaining," the first tech said patiently, "the data just won't support much enhancement. I mean, we could polish it up and do some work on the pixels, but the truth is you'd have our impression of what the cameras got, not what's there."

"It wouldn't be worth a goddamn," Nye said.

"You'd have an interpretation, not a scientifically defensible image."

Rose grimaced. "We didn't win the lottery," she squinted at the computer screen, pointing at the white, indistinct shape floating behind the film of the grainy windshield, "That face could be Lucking, could be a whole lot of people."

"Needless to say," the second techs added, "your passenger's a complete blank."

"Thanks, guys," Nye said. "You can't perform miracles."

He wasn't surprised when one of the techs started to object.

Cummins's face was pinched and fatigued. Two of her criminalists were at work early as well.

"I had to get a neighbor to watch my daughter," she said grumpily to Nye and Rose when they sat down in her office, Nye closing the door. "I'm sure you don't understand it anymore, if you ever did, Nye, but your partner certainly knows what kind of Herculean chore that is on a Sunday night, *late,* so you can do an errand that, for some unknown reason, couldn't wait until regular business hours."

"But you did it," Nye said. "I appreciate it."

Cummins looked to Rose for sympathy and support. Rose shrugged because neither of them should have expected much else from a deteriorating specimen like Nye.

Cummins offered them tiny cups of herbal tea. Rose accepted.

Nye was impatient. The manila envelope of the failed video enhancements sitting in his car still needed to get back to the chief quickly. He would take one look at the unusable, cloudy results and conclude the Ensor investigation, the press conference going ahead as planned later that morning.

So the Julia Child of forensics has the one lifeline we've got left, Nye thought.

And it's one, like Rosie knows, we can't bring to the chief because there was no legal way I was entitled to pull that paint sample off Judge Stevenson's SUV.

Whatever Cummins found wouldn't be an answer. It would simply let Rose and him go on asking questions.

The diminutive lab chief laid his baggie of black paint flecks on her desk. She sipped her tea. "May I ask where this came from?"

"A vehicle we're interested in," Rose said.

"You're turning as annoyingly vague as Nye," Cummins said.

He interrupted. "Does it match your hit-and-run samples?"

"No. You've got the same paint, the same black Escalade SUV model year," Cummins eyed him carefully over her tiny cup, "but there are differences. No clear coat with pollen or burnt rice stubble, for example."

"No question? This sample did not come from the SUV that hit Ensor?"

"It did not."

Nye sighed. "Okay. So much for that." He motioned to Rose and she quickly drained her tea.

"I would have thought a negative finding would be unhelpful," Cummins said. "I was under the impression you're looking for the hit-and-run SUV."

They walked out of her office. He said, "Sometimes a miss works, too, right? Didn't Edison say his five thousand flops with the lightbulb showed him five thousand ways not to make a lightbulb?"

"You surprise me, Nye," Cummins said.

"I'm not as ignorant as I look."

"Don't go there," Rose added.

"When do you need my report on these samples?" Cummins asked with barely contained weariness.

"No report, Cummins. This is unofficial. Just a favor for a friend."

Cummins studied him and then turned her attention to Rose. "Unofficial? You should have made that clear last night."

"Sorry. I was tired. I had a lot on my mind." Nye was cool.

"Is this your understanding as well?" Cummins asked Rose flatly.

"It's a big help and we do appreciate it."

Cummins shook her head slightly and turned back to her office. "I think I get the picture now. Now I really don't want to know where the sample came from. Goodbye to you both."

Driving on their way downtown to the department, Nye said to Rose, "Doesn't look like Cummins will ask you to babysit, Rosie."

"I wasn't holding my breath." Then she said, "Sometimes, Ter, I'm surprised you've got so many friends."

The press conference went on from the marble steps of City Hall promptly at eleven under the thin white clouds, a playful breeze tugging at papers and forcing the chief to smooth his hair with one hand. He read out a statement of mixed condolence and chronology that brought the investigation of the hit-and-run death of Officer Thomas Ensor officially to an end.

Nye and Rose sat alone again in the deserted command center. The other detectives had returned to their regular assignments and cases. All the equipment was scheduled to be shifted back to other offices or storage that afternoon. In a few hours there would be nothing indicating that they had spent three exhausting days in that room.

They watched the press conference on the TVs, each set to a different channel, catching the chief and his cluster of microphones from the front and sides. Senior department officials, along with the District Attorney of Sacramento County and most of the city council, appeared with him in front of a large, solemn audience standing just below the steps, flowing almost to the street.

"What do you want to do, Ter?" she asked, stacking files on her desk.

"You got your folks to check with at the courthouse, get a better fix on what Stevenson's been doing. That sounds like a plan."

Rose tapped her files for a moment and they both silently watched the next speakers at the press conference, everyone trying to maintain a bit of dignity, while the breeze made them flap their arms or hold their hair.

"See, the thing we know now," Nye said, thinking aloud, "is that the SUV we saw yesterday ain't the SUV that hit Ensor but it also ain't an SUV the judge's been driving for a year. So we know he's got a black Cadillac Escalade SUV just like the one we saw because he's been driving it, right? Except it is not in his garage at this moment."

"We don't know where Holder's new SUV is." Rose repeated the information from the night's visits. "I've got an idea."

He waited. Rose enjoyed showing off a little and he thought she deserved center stage.

She sat down next to his desk. She put on a melodramatic expression. "I think I need to put in for a couple of days off. I'm worried Annorina's coming down with that sinus thing she had last year. It lasted almost a month."

"I'm all tired out. I'm an old bastard who's checking out in a couple days. I should take them as CTO," Nye added, going with her scenario. "Everybody says I'm beat. I ain't a growing boy anymore, I guess."

"We both take our days off and we watch the judge and his wife."

"Stevenson's going to drive his old SUV around again?" Nye shook his head. "I don't think so."

Rose was excited and she almost bounced on her feet. "No, look, the chief just made it official. The case is closed. Just what Stevenson's father-in-law was all hot about. People do a lot of things when they know the cops aren't looking."

"Sometimes, Rosie, they don't do anything at all. I've been on too many cases where my guy just goes about his business and we end up with zip."

"Pretty much the same place we are now?" she asked sarcastically. "Come on, Ter. Two days surveillance on our own time. The department's not involved, we don't have to make excuses to Nishimoto or anyone."

Like the fast one I just pulled on Josie Cummins, probably burning her as a resource for Rose, Nye thought.

"Okay, I'll play," he said, pulling his own files into a much smaller stack than hers. "But we got to be like reformed drunks," he warned, "which is something I know a tiny bit about. Two days is it. Nothing happens, we just come quietly back to work, say nothing, get our heads around Ensor's case being closed permanently, and shut the hell up."

"Done."

Nye looked at the press conference, which was apparently ending, the chief wading into the swarm of reporters on the steps below where he had been speaking. *I'm going to miss him,* Nye thought with sudden surprise. *I'm going to miss Nish, too.* It struck him that in fact there was a great deal he would lament losing when he left the department for good in a little over a week.

He flipped the TVs off. "There are two of them and two of us," he said to Rose. "Who do you want to cover, the judge or the wife?"

Rose took out a quarter. "I'll flip you, old man."

"Still feeling lucky?" he asked as she tossed the coin on the desk.

FORTY-ONE

JUST BEFORE COURT RESUMED at ten on Monday morning, Stevenson had Joan bring the lawyers into his chambers.

When the lawyers were sitting before his desk or standing along the walls of gilt-bound court decisions, Stevenson, robe opened, demanded crisply, "I want an estimate how long each side thinks this trial's going to take."

"It's difficult to say, Your Honor," the ponytailed defense attorney answered in querulous tones. "We can't predict what kind of bad evidence the People will try to foist on the court and we'll have to spend time rebutting."

"Oh, Your Honor!" the deputy district attorney hopped to her feet, "I object! Counsel's *ludicrous* accusations—" and Stevenson cut her off before they all joined in. He felt very much in control at that moment.

"I keep reminding you, ladies and gentlemen, there is no jury in my chambers. You don't impress me by making a lot of noise. So, I want all of you to get serious now, and tell me how long this trial's going to last."

367

He sat back, pleased. They huddled in separate bunches for a moment, murmuring. He watched like a lion observing gazelles at a watering hole. Joan had commented how much good the weekend had done him. "You look a hundred percent better this morning, Judge," she said. "It always helps to get away for even a little bit."

Get away, he had thought. *I suppose it matters where you go.* After making it through the night, he had gotten away by dawn from the black fears and remorse and inchoate phantoms. With Vee urging him last night, he decided to confront his patches of despair and doubt head-on this morning. He was still the judge and he was the law in his courtroom.

The lawyers' agitated murmuring continued. Stevenson had endured Audie's noisy recital of the courthouse gossip about the hit-and-run suspect's hanging death, and the unanimous satisfaction that came with it. It was Audie who'd passed along the accurate rumor that the chief of police was going to announce the successful end of the investigation later that morning. *We've got our lives back,* he thought, *Vee and Haley and me. We can have our dreams.*

He vowed never to lie to his daughter again. The loathsome necessity of deceiving her about what had happened made him determined that it would not be repeated for any reason. It was something good that would come out of the last few days.

He reckoned with great clarity that the remorse and violent emotions he still felt were not so much like a roller coaster, as he first imagined, but more like a disease, a chronic fever or malaria. The bouts of sweats, shakes, and terror would come and go for a while.

But he felt certain that he would recover from each episode and each recovery would last longer and longer, until finally, at a point in the not-so-unimaginable future, the disease would have spent itself, burned out. He would be cured. He was embarked on that cure now.

"Does anybody have an answer?" he asked impatiently. They could debate and discuss until the end of time if he let them.

"The People's case will take three days, Your Honor, assuming we can move our witnesses and evidence in cleanly," the deputy DA ventured.

"How many more witnesses do you have?"

"It's difficult to estimate. I can put on our case with six. Perhaps two more if we have to come in rebuttal after the defense."

Stevenson swung to the defense lawyers. "I assume you haven't decided whether or not your clients will testify?"

They all nodded. One said, "The decision has to wait until we see what kind of case the DA puts on."

"Do you have character witnesses?"

Wallace smiled. "Family members possibly."

Stevenson added up the time and the reasonable delays the contentious sides would create and said, "How about two weeks? That sounds like a good estimate for me to pass along to Master Calendar and the sheriff's department." A trial with its defendants in custody had a large logistical side, how long court personnel and the courtroom would be tied up, how many deputy sheriffs would be needed to transport and guard the defendants. Stevenson, because he was going to dispel his own despair through steely control of his courtroom, started there.

He stood up, closing his robe, letting them all know he was going to take the bench. Several of the more audacious lawyers tried to linger and argue, but he called for Audie to escort them out. No one argued for long in Audie's formidable and inexorable presence. Joan came in, her face wreathed in amusement.

"They're mad as hell out there, Judge," she said, pleased.

"I try to oblige," he said.

Audie followed her, also looking pleased. "Man, that is one bunch of ticked-off attorneys. Do it again. It's fun."

Stevenson relished their enjoyment. It was part of his recovery. Just as talking to Yardley and several other judges first thing that morning centered him in his world and his worth. Something very bad had happened, that was unchangeable, but it was time to move on. He had resolved his anguished questions to Vee from last night. He could still be a judge.

"Audie, you've got several pals over in SPD, don't you?" Stevenson asked, pausing at the door from the clerk's office to his courtroom. Joan had already gone ahead, signaling to everyone in court that he was about to take the bench.

"Sure, Judge. Lots of guys."

"I'd like to get some cash to Officer Ensor's wife and family, but anonymously. If I gave it to you, could you make sure someone at SPD passes it along to the family?"

"No problem," Audie said, and Stevenson saw his bailiff's sincere admiration. "I will make sure it happens."

Stevenson patted his shoulder. "Good man."

"What did he say?" Stevenson asked Vee when he called her over the lunch hour, the doors to his chambers closed and locked.

"I think he's having some kind of breakdown. It was very hard to hear him over the phone. I'm even more worried about him than last night, Frank."

"But he'll do it?"

"I finally got him to say yes. He's bringing the boat in now."

"All right," Stevenson said.

"I told him, I'd do all the talking, he just had to stand there at the dealership and nod," Vee's voice was unsteady. "Tell the damn salesman you changed your mind, you're bringing the SUV back and you want your money, less whatever damn fees they say you owe."

Stevenson had never doubted that Vee would compel her father's cooperation in their plan. It seemed the easiest, and most foolproof, way. Simply switch the license plates once more on the SUVs and return the new SUV to Hardy Cadillac. It would not be the first time a customer, on reflection over a weekend, decided that a purchase was unnecessary. *I'll handle the final little chore after that myself,* Stevenson thought, laying out what he would do.

"That's terrific, hon," he said. "I've got to stop at the bank over lunch break and I'll swing by the storage place after work and get our SUV's license plates. You and Eli can return the new one to Hardy's tomorrow."

"But I'm not kidding, Frank. He's having a breakdown or a crackup or something. It's going to be a problem."

"It'll pass," he said, more in hope than certainty. "The important thing now is to get clear of the SUV for good."

"What if it doesn't?" she asked.

"What if what doesn't?"

"He makes more calls to the police."

"There won't be anything for them to find. They're satisfied with the outcome."

"This will get worse. I know my dad. There's some sick, screwed-up part of him that insists on being the center of attention, holding the stage. He'll drag us down sooner or later."

"We'll help him. We'll be a family and that may make it easier. Eli's going to need us."

"Frank, you know if it's ever a choice between you and Haley and my dad, you two come first," Vee said and then hung up.

Stevenson stood, putting on his coat, automatically checking his pockets as his mind whirled around what Vee said and how he pictured their future. He passed Joan eating lunch, as usual during trial, at her desk. He didn't hear her tell him to have a good lunch himself.

Stevenson rode the elevator down to the garage, bemused and trying to comprehend that the world might indeed be coming round again, back to where he had shot it off course. He drove out and stopped at his bank. He gazed up at the sky.

Buzz Fonseca was beside him on the sidewalk. Fonseca's face was gray and tight.

"You're following me," Stevenson said in amazement.

"We just ran into each other, Judge."

"I've got some banking," and Fonseca casually moved to prevent him from going into the building.

"You haven't done anything. You haven't gotten my case into your courtroom as we agreed," the other man's voice shook.

He's scared, Stevenson thought, *truly and deeply scared, because I know what that looks like and feels like. His creditors in the lawsuit must be ready to crush him.* "Let's be clear," Stevenson said, "we didn't agree on anything. You threatened me."

"I wouldn't call it that," Fonseca tried a smile that looked grotesque, "but nothing has changed. This is a warning that you need to get my case transferred immediately."

Stevenson suddenly felt his words to Vee and his night fears coming together. He felt relief and wonderment all at once.

"You're wrong. Everything's changed. The accident's been solved, the police said so. It's finished. They know what happened and how it happened and it's finished."

Fonseca reached out as if to straighten Stevenson's lapel, but Stevenson backed away, hands up. "I'm sure they can be persuaded to change their minds with hard proof otherwise."

"There is no proof, Buzz," Stevenson said, leaning close enough that he could smell the liquor fumes. "Not from Eli, who was drunk, or me. So stay away from me."

He walked toward the bank because he knew he was right. He heard Fonseca say something, but didn't look back.

It was a miracle and all things were new and possible again.

FORTY-TWO

"WHERE ARE YOU NOW?" Nye asked Rose over his cell phone.

"Coming down Fifteenth, heading for home, it looks like."

"Anything in the last hour?"

"She came back to her office after lunch, like I told you, and some funny-looking dude, her boss maybe, had to give her a hand when they crossed the street. More than a hand. He had both arms all over her. Hey, how come we can't get a lunch and a few belts, Ter?"

"It ain't the new way. My granddad used to hit a couple joints on S and T, you know around the old stroll, and he didn't go on any shift for a decade under a point two. Or so he used to brag to this innocent young cop when I first got started."

Nye heard Rose chuckle. S and T was also the notorious center of Sacramento's prostitution activity for years and, he suspected, although his grandfather had never boasted about it, that the liquid lunches also included a nooner now and then with one of the rowdy, sad women on the stroll.

"So Mrs. Judge stayed in her office until twenty minutes ago?"

"Never came out. When she took off from her firm's garage, she must've done thirty or forty down the street. Twenty-mile-per-hour zone. I bet she's still high. I was tempted to pull her over."

"Yeah, and screw up your own surveillance," Nye said, as if he believed Rose would be so bullheaded. "Okay, let me know when she gets home, Rosie. I'm still across the street from the courthouse. The judge hasn't come out yet so I'll stick with him and meet you at their old homestead."

"Roger that," Rose said. He could tell she was having a good time. Even if, as it seemed more likely during the course of the uneventful Monday, nothing came of their off-the-books watch over Judge Frank Stevenson and his lovely wife Veronica, they could at least feel like they were taking care of business. Nye knew that holding on to that meant a lot in a job when so many things went wrong, dissolved in your hands, or simply were not really there in the first place. *Evidence, witnesses, other cops, lawyers and judges,* he thought. *Like holding on to smoke. Nothing you could count on.*

He rolled his stiffening shoulders. The breeze had died down over the course of the afternoon. The clouds were thicker but still vaporous, letting a ghostly whiteness settle over the capital, leaving people and buildings untouched but somehow different.

Except for the short hop Judge Stevenson made at lunch to his Bank of America branch on Alhambra Boulevard, he had stayed in the courthouse. He had chatted briefly with some old acquaintance outside the bank. Nye had checked to make sure the trial Stevenson was running was still underway before coming back out to his car, parked across the street from the jurors' parking lot. There were a lot of thick-branched trees, the street was cool and dim, and it was a perfect place simply to sit, wait, and watch the grilled gate to the courthouse garage.

He checked the time. Nearly five thirty. Court must be done for the day. Most of the judges liked to clear out by five. Nye wryly thought of one memorable exception, a short, very fat, little judge with thick glasses who took inordinate pleasure in scheduling violation of probation hearings at this hour or even later every day, forcing the deputy DAs, public defenders, cops who had to testify, the deputy sheriffs who transported the defendants, and his own bailiff to hang around after hours. *Little jackass loved being king of the hill,* Nye thought. *No one could tell him to go to hell.*

Which was why some people became judges. Or cops for that matter.

He wondered why Stevenson went after it. What did he get out of sitting up there, sorting out other people's lives and fortunes?

Nye gazed at the grilled gate at the courthouse garage, coming up time after time, cars passing out in a steady stream.

How about Stevenson? Rose asked the question that mattered. Is he the kind of man who could run down another human being, a police officer, and leave him in the street?

Nye stopped wondering. Waste of time. Pick anybody, judge, cop or citizen and none of them, much less someone else, could answer that question except at the moment it happened.

Fifteen minutes later, as the daylight was changing to a darkening shimmering sunset, Nye saw Stevenson's black Cadillac SUV roll up out of the garage, pause, and then turn left, joining the sluggish mass of inaptly named rush-hour commuters heading home from downtown.

He slipped several car lengths behind the judge. *Surface streets or freeway?* Nye wondered. If Stevenson chose the short freeway route, it would be harder to stay on top of him. And if Stevenson were not going directly home, Nye knew he could lose him easily.

But instead of getting on the I Street or L Street on-ramps, the judge stayed on Tenth, the traffic a little lighter. Almost simultaneously Nye saw headlights snap on around him as people got the idea it was getting dark quickly. The SUV's black bulk seemed to fade into the growing dimness.

They got held up at a light rail crossing as the commuter train sped by, the three lanes of one-way traffic packed solidly. Nye kept his eye on the SUV four cars ahead of him. There was no assistance to call for, no one else who would pick up the trail if the judge evaded him. Just Rose, and she's sitting on the wife, who was at home by now.

Nye hoped the judge had no surprises.

At the same time, he also hoped for an answer to Rose's question. Not the subjective question, but the pure fact of whether the man in the black SUV ahead of him, who drove on as the light rail crossing guard swung up, hit Tommy Ensor on Thursday morning and set them all on this collision course.

Neither he nor Rose had worked out what was going on with the two black Cadillac SUVs Stevenson and his father-in-law coincidentally owned. Only that it seemed more likely that one of the SUVs had been the hit-and-run vehicle. It was a puzzle at the moment.

Nye had just concluded that the judge was making a straight shot for his home when the SUV, without signaling, abruptly pulled off to the right and headed down a short street of small businesses. *Where the hell was he going,* Nye wondered, peering ahead and trying to make out landmarks.

The SUV slowed and swung into a public storage lot, pausing at the electronic gate. Nye saw Judge Stevenson lean out tapping something, presumably the entry code, and the gate slid back.

Okay, Nye thought, *he's making a detour.* He pulled out his notepad and jotted down the address. This was the first time the public storage place had turned up and it would bear further checking. Nye didn't let himself even jump to the most tantalizing possibility of all. *Too many mistakes happened if you did that. I made them all myself.*

He resisted the almost overwhelming temptation to drive closer to the lot, or even get out and walk up, just to see what Stevenson was doing in there.

After ten anxious minutes, Nye watched the black SUV slowly drive out of the public storage lot and get back on Fifteenth Street. The judge was at last going home.

On impulse, Nye changed his mind and drove to the public storage lot and parked, heading into the manager's office. Rose was in position to spot Stevenson. *We're covered for the next few minutes,* he thought.

He put on his casual cop look and showed his identification and badge to the manager, saying he was from the Sacramento Police Department.

"We're checking local businesses," Nye said to the chunky, white-haired woman who completely filled a black-and-silver Raider's warm-up jacket, "because there've been some burglaries in the area and we want to remind you to keep on the lookout."

"Oh, we do. You should see some of the characters around here," the woman said. "But we've got really good security. Nightly patrols, someone on duty all day."

Nye nodded as if pleased with the precautions. "I'll tell you," he said, letting her in on a trade secret, "a couple of these deals look like a pretty organized gang. They come in, get a job washing dishes, clerking. Place like yours, they'd rent space, get inside and take a look around."

"We keep a good eye on our clients," the manager said tartly.

Nye came to her desk. "How about any recent rentals? Anything in the last couple of days?"

The manager tapped on her computer. "Well, we've had four since Thursday."

Nye stepped beside her, idly looking at the names and the size of the rented storage spaces. Stevenson's wife had rented a large space on Friday.

Which could, of course, mean absolutely nothing.

But Nye saw the date, the footage of the storage space, and felt a tingle of recognition. *Big enough for a boat or car,* he thought. *Like those snarky neighbors, maybe the judge and his wife got a boat we don't know about. Maybe they got something else in there.*

He thanked the manager and promised a patrol unit would stop by in the next day or so, just for show and to make sure everything was all right.

As he got to his car, Nye made a note in his pad to ask patrol to stick their head in.

He wished like hell there was some way to get inside that storage space right then or get a search warrant for it.

There wasn't, not then anyway, so he headed out to rendezvous with Rose. He slowed, after turning off Land Park Drive onto Stevenson's street, when he saw Rose's car parked at the end of the block. He pulled up behind it and got out.

Rose got out to meet him. The dusk was deeper now, the sun almost gone, and the streetlights had not come on, so everything was in purple shadow. He could barely make out Rose.

"They're both home," she said. "How come you're bringing up the back of the parade?"

He told her about the storage space and Stevenson's wife. Rose sighed like she was hovering over a well-done steak, about to tear into it.

"We've got to get in there," she said.

"Not tonight. Not tomorrow. We don't have any PC and nobody's going to sign a warrant."

Rose said something low in frustration. "How about we just break in?"

"I know you're giving me crap, Rosie," he said. "But don't even start thinking like that. It's a dead-end road for your job and you."

"Of course I'm kidding," she said sourly. "But it sure as heck is on my Christmas wish list."

Nye nodded. "We'll come up with something. Look, I'll take the watch tonight. You go home, take care of the kid and you-know-who. Meet me back here around six," he suggested delicately, hoping it was not too early.

"Five, if you want," Rose jumped in.

"No, six. It's going to be a long day. First and last full day of surveillance."

"No extensions?" she suggested, knowing the only possible answer.

"Two days was the deal. Then your kid gets better and I'm all rested up and we go back to our exciting days on the best job in the world."

"Man, you are so bitter tonight," she chuckled. "All right. You okay? You got something to eat?"

"I'm always prepared," he assured her. "Get out of here. I'll see you tomorrow."

He watched her drive away as the streetlights all flashed on, as if in salute, and he felt quite lonely.

Nye sat slumped in his front seat, parked four houses down the block from the Stevenson home. He could watch the lights come on in various rooms, then go out. He wondered what the judge and his wife talked about. He wondered if he and Rose were indulging in a pointless exercise because Lucking had killed Tommy Ensor or, if he hadn't, whoever did was somewhere else, swaddled in the night, going about their own nightly tasks, with their own friends or family.

Morosely, he ate cold Vienna sausages with his fingers from a small can. He had not, contrary to what he told Rose, provisioned himself very much at all. He had a bottle of water from some forgotten excursion, a half-empty cup of 7-Eleven coffee, and the sausages which he learned years before on surveillance duties, somehow went down easily and kept him from feeling hungry better than anything else.

Nye wasn't worried that a neighbor on this quiet street would spot him. If anyone did, he planned to tell the patrol unit that came by to roust him that he was working and get the hell away. He was in his own car, not the department's, and neither he nor Rose was doing anything impermissible. Just watching.

It was a very quiet street and he missed having another detective or cop to talk to.

Somewhere around midnight, he must have dozed off because he had a very vivid vision of spotting Tommy Ensor leaving the department, looking much younger, like the days they had briefly been partners together. Ensor had something like a saddlebag over his shoulder and he moved briskly so that Nye, who was trying to keep up or even get his attention, could not. It was like trotting behind the White Rabbit. He ran after Ensor, who was now in a patrol car and when the saddlebag came sailing out to land in the middle of J Street at lunch hour, Nye didn't know whether to retrieve it or keep trying to get Ensor's attention. He had a question to ask or needed directions. It seemed particularly urgent. At the old Memorial Auditorium, the welter and middleweight fights finishing up, and the excited fans were pouring out in bright daylight. Ensor was there in full uniform and white gloves, vainly trying to control the mob. When Nye finally got near him, Tommy looked at him with a grin and asked, "What the hell do you want, Terry?"

Nye sat up in the car, groaned as he stretched a little, and heard some joint crackle in protest. *What do I want?* he wondered. *Good question, Tommy.*

He groaned again when he looked at his watch and saw how much of the long night remained. He peered down the block. The houses, including Stevenson's, were dark. *What a goddamn waste of time,* he thought.

Near two, he ventured out of the car and took a piss into a tall hedge bordering two homes. He stayed beside his car, savoring the night even if it felt endless. He thought of his dream just now. *Give me a break,* Nye said inwardly. *Saddlebags? I am losing it big time and no question.*

The trick to solo surveillance was making it through the tunnel of solitude without picking at old scabs and scars. It was a perfect time for self-recrimination, doubt, and flagellation. Much better to trot all that garbage out in the glare and bustle of the day, Nye had learned.

More lessons initiated by his grandfather and mastered on his own.

The night ended. At six promptly, Rose drove up. She was sharp and amused at his lived-in demeanor.

"What's the plan this morning, tiger?" she asked brightly and he was quite irritated.

"First thing, you cut out this happy crap, okay? I'll stay with the judge until he gets to the courthouse and then head home for a couple hours. He ain't going anywhere. You stay on the wife and we'll check in around noon."

Rose grinned at him. "After you told me about the storage place, I thought about it all night. You know what they could've done? They could've switched SUVs."

"That would be dumb," he said dismissively, anxious to get back into his own car and sullenly conclude the surveillance. "Who does something like that? You mean, buy a whole fricking SUV?"

"The father-in-law did. He told us. Some coincidence, right? So you get a new SUV, put the one that you hit Ensor with in storage, and drive around in your new one."

Nye was approaching terminal annoyance. "Look, that is so brain-dead it's not even funny. You know what you do? You get home after you hit Ensor, you call the cops and you say, all excited, *My SUV just got stolen. It's gone. I hope nothing's happened to it,* and you leave it someplace, anyplace away from where you live. Cops find it and we start running around looking for the pukes who stole the SUV and hit another cop. Sound familiar?"

"Except the judge and his wife never said their SUV was stolen."

"Lucking stole someone's. Not theirs. Someone's missing an SUV."

"We haven't come across any missing Cadillac Escalades."

"There are a million reasons why we haven't." He snorted angrily. He did not want to debate at that moment. He wanted to go home. Rose dug in stubbornly.

"You just don't want to admit that the judge and his wife, maybe the father, did some kind of Three-Card Monte with SUVs, Ter."

"I don't, I guess," he admitted angrily, "because in the cold light of day here it sounds really dumb. It's a lot riskier than just calling it in stolen. That's what people do."

Rose cocked her head. A car horn sounded down the block as men and women stirred, impatient to get started on whatever they did to pay their taxes. "You're thinking too much like a cop, Ter. That's what hit me last night, you believe it, while I was lying staring awake beside Luis at three in the morning. Your bad habits are catching up with me," she chuckled emptily. "The pukes we run into, that's the thing they would do, report the SUV stolen, leave it, and let us start chasing ourselves around. But the judge, he's not a puke. He doesn't want cops looking at him. Period. He doesn't want us asking questions about his reported stolen Escalade that was used in a big-time hit-and-run," Rose had a tight, implacable frown. "So the judge and his wife and the father, they never want us snooping around so they can't do it your way."

Nye closed his eyes, recognition breaking on him. "Because they're not pukes."

"Because maybe the squirrelly father-in-law is the passenger."

Nye nodded. It made agreeable sense of the mystery.

"For people like them," Rose went on heatedly, "the *worst* thing they can imagine is having a bunch of cops swarming all over them. And, after Ensor gets creamed, there is no doubt we would be swarming all over Judge Stevenson and his wife if their stolen SUV did it, right?"

"No, you're right there, Rosie," he admitted. It would never have occurred to him to think like noncriminals anymore. He immediately assumed, without thinking, that everybody acted in accordance with the rules and bent practices of the assorted crooked and homicidal animals he dealt with all the time.

"We are right on the money about the SUV we want sitting in that storage place down the road." Rose said emphatically.

He crossed his arms. "Only if we're starting with the idea that Stevenson, a judge, ran down Ensor."

"Yes," Rose said gravely, "that's the pitch."

He smiled. "You should try staying up until three more often. That's one hell of a solid idea."

"While you're wasting time at home and I'm wasting time sitting on the judge's wife, I'll keep calling people at the courthouse, lock down what he's been doing in the last week."

"But gently, okay, please? We're tiptoeing, Rosie, not kicking doors down."

"I'm the one who has to hold your leash," she protested.

They went back to their cars and waited. At seven thirty, Nye watched a Lexus come from Stevenson's home. He kept low but saw that the judge was driving. He gave Rose a little wave as he passed her car.

It was the same route as the night before, minus the stop at the storage place. Judge Stevenson rolled right into the courthouse garage and Nye found his old roost across the street. Several deputies, hustling down the street from the sheriff's department, peered at him for a moment, as they hurried to court. One deputy, an old barnacle like him, cocked his finger, aimed it, and fired an imaginary bullet with a grin. Nye waved him off.

He waited for thirty minutes, just to make sure the judge was securely inside the courthouse for the morning, and then drove home. His cell phone went off just as he got inside his door.

"Hey, Ter," Rose said, "guess what? The judge's wife is driving the SUV this morning. We just dropped their daughter off at school and now she's on Five heading north out of town."

"She's not at work?"

"Opposite direction."

"Well," he said, jiggling his door handle as he pondered.

"She looks like she didn't sleep much either."

"We should start a club. A self-help deal for insomniacs."

Rose's voice quickened. "She's turning off, we're over the river. Kind of an office park out here."

Nye tried to picture Rose as she gave her running commentary. She was having the time of her life and he envied her. He was about to tell her to call him back, he was standing in his doorway, when she said, "This is great. The judge's wife, she's picking up someone. I can see the SUV inside the parking lot," silence. "Hey, Ter, she's picking up her father. I guess being on the river didn't agree with him."

"You sure?"

"He's got a suit on this time, he's getting in with her. Yeah, it's him. I'm going to keep following them."

She hung up and he went into his house, taking off his coat and dropping it on a chair in the dining room he never used. He made himself a bowl of cold cereal and tried to figure out what was going on. *It would be great,* he thought, *to have a couple more cars out there tailing these people.*

He started toward the sink, debating whether to wash the bowl or let it join the collection of dishes there when his cell buzzed again.

"Guess where I am?" Rose said and he could hear sibilant freeway sounds around her.

"St. Louis."

"Heading north. Just passed the sign for Roseville." She was gleeful.

"What the hell's in Roseville?" he said aloud as the answer popped into his mind.

"That Cadillac dealership Holder told us about," Rose answered for him. "They're going to Hardy Cadillac, I bet you."

"Call me when you know," he said, and turned off the water in the sink. The dishes were a chore that he would tackle in some future.

Nye went into the bedroom, took off his shoes and pants, and then thought at least something should get washed, so he showered under very hot water. As he dried off, he was still not quite clear about what was happening around him. The judge took the other family car, his wife took the SUV and grabbed her father and headed for the place where the SUV had been bought recently. They were moving around, doing things they did not do ordinarily.

He lay down on the bed, pulling only a sheet over him because the room was warm. What were these people doing?

His cell buzzing woke him up. He had slept for three hours. It was nearly eleven.

"Yeah?" he said tersely.

"Quite a morning," Rose said, and it was quiet around her. "The judge's wife and her father spent about two hours at the dealership. Then they left by Yellow Cab."

"Where's the SUV?" he asked sharply.

"Back where it came from. They left it at the dealership."

"Maybe the brakes didn't work. The seats didn't heat up." It was a bad joke.

"Yeah, yeah. They left it, Ter. Bought it a few days ago and left it. So now they're short one SUV."

"They're short the one we looked at," he added, "the one we

said was A-OK and in the clear." He sat up in bed, rubbing his chin, feeling the stubble. "You know, maybe we're both right. They did a switch like you figured and now they're in the clear, they'll lose the SUV, report it stolen."

"And keep it locked up in that storage place. We have got to get in there," she said hotly. "You and I signed off on the SUV, Ter. We gave the judge and his wife a get-out-of-jail card."

"I know," he said. "Where is the judge's wife now?"

"For the last hour, after she dumped her father back at that office park, she's been at the Zebra Room. You should know it, old-timers bar downtown?"

"She didn't go back to work?" He didn't want to admit that he knew the Zebra, along with a brace of other joints, where it always seemed midnight inside, and you could pour rounds down until you forgot what time it really was or where you were.

"Nope. That monkey who was all over her yesterday, he showed up and went in the bar a couple minutes ago."

"Not exactly the kind of establishment I would choose for the judge's wife, connected up like she is. She looked more like the bar at the Hyatt or Lucca's type when we saw her."

"What about Holder? You want to watch him?"

"I don't think we should change the game plan at this stage. The judge and his wife are in play. They've dumped the new SUV. We stick with them."

"Something's under her skin, she picked a joint where I bet nobody knows her. She's got to come out sometime," Rose said excitedly. "I'll stay with her until she and the monkey come out and get settled and then I'm going to sit on the storage place. I don't want them to take the SUV out and lose it and we're left with nothing."

Nye stood up, pacing. "Okay, do that. Stick with her. Where's the stuff you got together on Stevenson?"

"On my desk. In a folder with my kid's name on it."

Nye thought that was reasonably prudent. You never knew when, idly or purposefully, another detective might take a look at what you were working on. Sometimes you did not want everyone to know what it was. Rose didn't want a snoop seeing that she had collected material on Judge Frank Stevenson. It would start questions.

"I can swing by the courthouse and keep track of the judge," he said. "I'll get over to the barn and grab your notes and see if I can't come up with some PC, some damn thing we can use to take a look inside that storage unit."

"I don't think we've got much time," she said. "I get the feeling they're going to tie up the loose ends quickly."

Nye thought so, too, but he did not want Rose digging in and holding onto the case so that he had no maneuvering room. As she talked, he saw the pattern coming together, what Stevenson had done, how he and his wife concealed it, and what they were doing even now to make the concealment permanent and impenetrable.

"We'll take it as fast as we can," Nye said, hating to lie to her, "because maybe Stevenson and his wife feel safe now. Look, if the SUV is stashed in the storage place they can afford to let it sit there. Years, maybe. I had a guy who left his wife in a large freezer in a storage unit for five years. She wasn't going anyplace."

Rose, he could tell, did not accept his explanation. "You're wrong, Ter. These aren't our usual pukes, remember? They get their own ideas and they feel guilty. Our pukes don't."

"Call me if something happens; otherwise," he looked at the time again, "let's connect up at three, okay?"

"Jeez, I hope you come up with some probable cause," she said.

Nye shaved and then dressed hastily, his tie lopsided. He thought that Rose was probably right about there being little time for them to act. Guthrie and his unrequited vendetta were still real, even if halted. Guthrie wouldn't give up even if Altlander told him to. *He'll come up with some scheme to trip me up,* Nye thought.

Nye knew, with certainty, that he had very little time.

He was running after Ensor, as he had in his dream, and he had to catch up to him because Nye sensed the naked, unavoidable, terrible answer to Ensor's question forming ahead of him. He was running right into it.

He had to act in this small space while no one was watching him. Rose could never be involved if he had to step over the line for Ensor.

That's the only rule I got, he thought. *Whatever happens, whatever I need to do, she stays clear.*

FORTY-THREE

NYE WADED THROUGH FRESH and wilting flowers for Ensor on the cracked stone steps to the Sacramento Police Department. There was a subtle but discernible change in the atmosphere inside. People, he realized, had come to terms with Ensor's death and the finality of Lucking's hanging. Ensor was already turning into a war story, a tale to tell new cops, a heroic foot soldier, worthy of emulation, who was unassuming and who left so many grieving at his passing.

As he mounted the worn marble stairs in the lobby, passing the usual busy Monday-morning gaggle of anxious civilians and uniforms heading out, Nye thought it wouldn't be long before Ensor's plaque joined the dusty ranks of ancient chiefs and fallen cops along the walls, or maybe his photograph, framed and inspiring, turning indistinct and gray as the years went on.

It's okay, Tommy, he thought, *you deserve it. Nothing lasts forever but you should get a little longer at the party than the rest of us.*

He found Rose's file neatly stacked on one side of her desk. He casually picked it up and added it to a few he had snagged from his own desk. Talman and Pesce passed by, going out to interview the victims of a drive-by shooting at a wedding over the weekend. They were trying to catch up on cases that had piled up during Ensor's investigation.

"I bet you every wit's too blitzed to say anything," Talman told Nye, as he buttoned his burgundy sport coat.

Nye wanted them gone, but he couldn't resist. "Nah, you know how it'll go, guys. You'll get five witnesses and you'll get ten stories."

Pesce scowled. "Without a doubt."

"You'll figure them out," Nye called after them. Talman said something obscene over his shoulder.

Nye spent the next twenty minutes reviewing Rose's research, getting to know Judge Frank Stevenson as much as he could from the public record she had collected. His awards and good deeds, his more memorable trials in the last few years. She included a few articles about his father-in-law, the well-placed investment banker and a list of the clients his bank serviced. Nye grinned. He wondered if any of those clients, paying through the nose, had ever seen Eli Holder the way he had over the weekend, twitchy, drunk, and stumbling over his words, the classic civilian dragooned somehow into a war he never realized was going on around him. *A lot of guys like him miss it,* Nye thought. *They think they're safe. They don't know what's really going on until it smashes them in the face.*

Just like the judge's wife, he thought. They all ended up in a place they never thought they would be. He remembered the stunned incredulity of the victims in his first violent armed robbery, husband and wife physicians. The husband, his nose smashed flat and blood covering him, vowed the most extreme brutal retribution. His wife stroked his arm. She would help. She would hold the bastards down while they were slowly cut to pieces.

By the time he closed the file, Nye felt he had a sense of Frank Stevenson. It burned, and he rebelled against it. Stevenson was not a bad man by any means, and he had, like the adoption he arranged for Josie Cummins, done many good things.

Nye was also certain Stevenson had done one terrible, irrevocable thing in the last one hundred hours, and his whole life was now in the balance against it.

This was, as he took Rose's file back to his own desk, what made the job so hard, so unforgiving, and consuming: when he had to

face things that most people could ignore or lie about to themselves
or others.

There were lies he could tell himself, Nye knew, *but not about
the way things are.*

He sat for a moment. He thought of his harsh grandfather and the
illusory simplicity of the old days in the department and he thought
of Rose again. He even felt a little sorry for himself because he could
not put aside what he knew.

He went up the stairs to Nishimoto's office. He didn't really
like coming up to Carpet Row, the lair of the senior managers of
the department, with its gray government carpeting and tan veneer
walls covered with boating and mountain photographs. But he had
an obscure need to do so this morning.

Nishimoto was signing papers mechanically, flipping them to the
signature block, one after the other, because he either didn't bother
reading them or knew exactly what they were after so many years.
He glanced up. "Back in the saddle, Nye?"

"Yeah, boss. Working that arson-homicide."

"Right. I think I remember. Any leads on the victim's identification?"

"Rose's checking a couple, boss," Nye said falsely.

Nishimoto leaned back. "So, how's Tafoya working out? Have
you totally screwed her up?"

"Pretty much," Nye said.

"She did a fine job over the last couple of days. Made a very good
impression on the chief."

"I'm glad. Rosie's a good detective and she'll be good for the
department."

Nye wondered why he had come to see his superior. *I'm probably going to have to do something very cruel,* he thought. Maybe
this viewing was just to reassure himself that he did not look nuts or
bloodthirsty to someone who knew him well. Maybe he just wanted
a little company before he did what had to be done.

Apparently, Nishimoto noticed nothing unusual because he said,
"We might as well face it, Terry. We're heading out. We've had our
turn. I spoke to the chief about an hour ago and he's going to pull
the plug in six months, certainly by the end of the year. Altlander's
definitely getting his support in the city council."

Nye said something suitably sympathetic, but Nishimoto waved it off, and stood up.

"I had a dream. I wanted to be chief. I'm not going to be. My wife's not going to like it. But I can't change things that happened in the last couple of days. Altlander made the catch on Ensor's driver. So the dream's over."

Nye nodded. He understood inevitability.

Nishimoto went on, "I've gotten an offer to come on board as a consultant at Pacific Security. They do police contract work around the world, shape up departments. What would you think about coming along, Terry? You've got a hell of a background."

Nye didn't want to laugh out loud, but he knew Nishimoto would hardly make this invitation if he had even a hint that the Ensor's hit-and-run was still active.

Or how I'm figuring it's got to end, Nye thought.

"I still haven't made up my mind what I'll do when I go," Nye said. "I'm scheduled to move near my youngest. The first grandkid's on the way."

Nishimoto's face fell. "Too bad. But this has been your problem ever since I've known you. You don't have a dream. You're just float along. Now you're at the end and you keep drifting with the current."

"Can't change this late," Nye said, with a self-mocking laugh.

"I guess not," and Nishimoto sighed and sat down. He put a paper clip on the papers he had been working on. "I just signed Quintana's termination papers. Effective immediately."

"Poor bastard," Nye said.

"No question. Poor goddamn bastard. He's in on a psych evaluation to see if he's able to go to trial. The DA's waiting to charge him until the evaluation is done."

Nye saw the pattern here, too, the complete and utter end of Quintana's career as a cop and maybe his conviction, or worse, some commitment to a state hospital. When he was released, that would tag him for the rest of his life, wherever he went.

The man who struck down Tommy Ensor struck down his partner just as fatally. It would simply take Quintana a lot longer to die.

Nye didn't know what else to say and he had no more excuses for his presence. He turned to leave and Nishimoto said, "Ensor's funeral is set for Thursday. Remember you're going to do five minutes about him."

"I haven't forgotten," Nye said.

He went back down to his floor and along the corridor to Auto Burglary/Fugitive Warrants. It was not exactly the hottest assignment in the department and the half dozen detectives in the section had a sedate, well-fed look that came with predictable hours and duties.

He asked for Ernie Lowe and was directed to a supply room at the rear of the section. He found Lowe, a short, heavyset black man in a white short-sleeve shirt and green tie, hitting a photocopy machine with the flat of his hand.

"I need a favor, Ernie," Nye said.

"Yeah, and I need just five damn copies of a report and the damn machine won't give me five."

Nye understood little about photocopiers or cell phones or his TV remote and he thought that Lowe's solution, whacking the side of the machine for encouragement, was about as productive as anything he could suggest. He let Lowe hit the machine a few more times.

"I'm working something and I need any auto theft reports as soon as you get them."

"Any kind of vehicle in particular?"

"Whatever comes in."

Lowe peered at him. "You want reports of every stolen car or truck?"

"As soon as you get them, give me a holler. I'd appreciate it."

"For how long?"

"The next week should do it."

Lowe groaned exaggeratedly. "I got to do a report?"

"Nope. You get me the theft reports and you're done, man."

"All right. You got it, Terry."

"Tell the other guys, too, would you?"

Lowe nodded absentmindedly and gave the photocopy machine another loud, thudding whack with his hand. The machine whirred and pages began flowing smoothly into its tray. He looked up and smiled with satisfaction at Nye.

Nye got lunch from a machine downstairs that dispensed black patties on a bun and bought a coffee from the young lady behind a cart in the lobby. He sat at his desk and opened various files, the legs in the river case, for one, and actually tried to work on them as he waited for Rose's call and reviewed their investigation and what he now believed Judge Stevenson had done.

Nye was trying to locate a space, an interstice so he could get out of the box he found himself in. He wanted an out. What do you want, Terry? Ensor had asked in his dream. *I don't want this responsibility,* he answered now, *I'd like to put all these pieces together and come up with something different from Stevenson running Ensor down on Thursday morning. I would like that one thing very much.*

At three on the dot Rose called. Vu and Parkes were hunched over their computers, oblivious.

"So I'm minding the fort out here, Ter," she said. "The judge's wife and the monkey left in his car around one, drove back to their law office, and that's where I left them. I think they were both tanked. You read my stuff. This is pretty strange behavior for her."

"She's bent out of shape about something. But it could be any damn thing."

"You don't think so."

But he did not want to encourage Rose either. "Hang out there at the public storage joint for a while," he said. "I'll spell you at five."

"Have you come up with something for a warrant?"

"I'm still working on it," he lied. "Just don't leave the place without telling me."

Rose grumbled. "You want to keep an eye on these people for a little longer than we planned?"

"A little longer."

"Terrific. They're going to make a move soon. I know it." She yawned and said, "I talked to a couple folks at the courthouse. I said I was checking up on some suspicious vehicles moving around the place last week, something cooking with one of the prison gangs maybe planning to break out a buddy soon when he's in the courthouse."

"Very inventive, Rosie."

"I got courthouse security to tell me when the last people left the building starting on Tuesday and then up through Friday to cover what I was looking for. Judge Stevenson was inside until six on Wednesday. He told his clerk he was going to meet his father-in-law for dinner then they were going on to some meet-and-greet. The buzz around the courthouse is that Stevenson's going to try to make the move up to the Third District Court of Appeal." She paused, obviously waiting for him ask the next question and draw the ineluctable conclusion.

"You find out when this meet-and-greet wrapped up?"

"I talked to an old pal at Ricci's where they held it. Stevenson and Holder cut out late, basically early Thursday morning."

"How'd he leave?"

"Valet brought around the judge's black Caddy Escalade and he tipped five bucks. He drove, Holder rode shotgun." Rose interpreted his silence wrongly. "That's all we need, Ter."

But Nye did not require further proof or persuasion. He added these facts to his pieces and understood that there was no other picture emerging except that Stevenson was driving the right model and year SUV that struck Ensor and he was in the vicinity at the right time. He had also taken a number of apparently evasive and otherwise inexplicable steps, with his wife and his father-in-law, to hide the fact that he drove that particular SUV. There was good reason to believe he hid it in a public storage unit rented within twenty-four hours of the hit-and-run.

The final piece would be if Stevenson reported his SUV stolen because the judge now believed the pressure was off, the investigation ended.

Then I'm dead in the water, Nye thought, *I have no choices left.*

"Yeah, it is. Nice catch, Rosie. I'll see you at five."

He and Rose hung up. She was obviously more than a little put out that he didn't sound charged up by her news. He paced out of Major Crimes, jostling Vu's chair and getting a snapped reaction. *With luck,* he thought pacing down the hall, *Stevenson will take a little time and I can think this through, come up with alternatives.*

He could hear his grandfather's derisive laughter. *You do what you have to. You don't get to choose.*

Over the next hour, someone from Auto Burg came in with reports of various cars stolen in Sacramento, even a mobile home.

Nye pretended to be interested.

He even began to fantasize that he was home free for the day when he met Rose across the street from the public storage facility and she made noises that it was unfair for him to get the short end of surveillance twice in a row, the long night.

Tomorrow, he told her, they would have to work out a better system. He should, he hoped, have a credible probable cause justification for a search warrant they could use to get into the storage unit by then.

He sent her home. All of it was wishful or simply untrue. He wanted her, for the only time since they became partners, to be away from him.

He was on someone else's clock, a prisoner of their schedule, the thing a cop dreaded, and endured, too often. If Stevenson or his wife waited, like the guy with his wife stashed in the storage freezer, there was nothing Nye could do to prevent it.

He rolled down his car window and took a deep breath of cool night air. But, more important, he could not afford to let the situation degenerate into groveling for a warrant or, worse, serving one and finding the SUV. He was not going to repeat his mistake that cost Mrs. Sprague and her family their lives. He had a duty and he would have to follow it straight through to the end if it became unavoidable.

Rosie just doesn't get it, he thought.

I do not want to find the SUV. I hope to hell it stays right where it is.

Shortly after eight, as Nye counted the security lights around the public storage place again and the surprising number of cars who passed with one or more broken lights, his cell buzzed. He looked at the number. It was not Rose.

"Nye," he said.

"It's Clezio in Auto Burg. Lowe left your contact numbers for after hours. We got two more hot ones just came through."

"Go ahead."

Clezio stumbled through a stolen mini Cooper, blue on white, California plates. Nye tuned out the rest of the details, counting the security lights.

"The other one's an SUV," Clezio said appreciatively. "Nice. Cadillac Escalade," he stumbled again through his narration.

Nye sat back, the cell phone pressed against his head. "Who's the RP?"

"Reporting person is," and Clezio fumbled through pages, "oh, boy. A judge. Some stupid asshole clipped a judge's Cadillac SUV." He started laughing.

"What's the name, please?"

"Frank Stevenson. You want the address?"

"No. That's fine. Tell Lowe thanks."

"Hope this helps whatever you're working on. We maybe get two or three more a night this time of year."

"Keep them coming," Nye said, knowing there were no more as far as he was concerned. He had run out of choices.

FORTY-FOUR

SHORTLY BEFORE TEN ON TUESDAY MORNING, Stevenson saw the old cop Nye enter his courtroom, search around for an empty seat among the spectators, and finally, awkwardly, edge across to one in the rear. He sat down, looking ahead.

Stevenson wondered what Nye was doing there. Another prospective juror droned on in the jury box, questioned by the deputy DA. Stevenson rubbed his eyes. He felt relaxed and at ease for the first time in what seemed a millennium. He and Vee were almost back to normal and he was delighted he had backed Fonseca down. The world had indeed come back to its right order.

He motioned Audie over, whispered to him, and followed his bailiff's path back to the last row in the courtroom. People had to move aside as the bulky young man asked polite questions of Nye, who seemed to answer in one word or two. Audie nodded and came back to the bench. Stevenson got a kick out of so many eyes craning to study Nye, speculate on who he was, whether he was a victim of one of three young defendants, the vengeful parent of a victim, or merely a jaded courtroom spectator like most of them.

Audie came around to the side of the bench. "He's here to take a report on your stolen SUV, Judge," he whispered hoarsely.

"Thanks," Stevenson said, letting go of the involuntary tension he experienced when Nye made his sudden appearance.

Thirty minutes later, Stevenson took the morning break. As he left the bench, pausing to watch the courtroom empty, he saw Nye stand up and wait, like an implacable statue, people having to go clumsily around him.

Stevenson took off his robe, hanging it in his closet, and debated whether to sit or stand, then sat down and waited for Nye. *Just a report, a courtesy from a detective to a judge,* he thought.

He poured water from the carafe. *All right, everything isn't normal just yet,* he thought. Vee was still drinking too much and preoccupied about her father. Stevenson told her he called in the report of the SUV's theft and there was nothing more to worry about. They could leave it anyplace, anytime, and they would be blameless.

Stevenson rubbed his eyes again. A longer vacation was required, he decided, some getaway that put time and distance between Vee and him and Sacramento and anything else that came next. As soon as the trial ended, just as she suggested, they would go away. He made a note to call a travel agent and see what the flights to Rome cost and whether the Lamberti hotel and its memories of promise and happiness was available.

There was a practiced short knock on his door. Joan's head appeared.

"Someone to see you, Judge," she said. She stood slightly aside.

"Detective Nye," Stevenson said, still sitting. "Welcome."

Nye waited until the door was closed. He did not sit down. He carried nothing and his wrinkled tan sport coat was unbuttoned. He had no service weapon.

"We've got fifteen minutes until you go back in there," he said to the judge. "I'll bet you run things by the clock."

"My department's got a reputation for punctuality. I appreciate you coming down to take this report. I know any officer could—"

"I've got pictures from security cameras on Capitol Mall. They caught you driving your SUV and hitting Officer Ensor."

The judge stared at him, and Nye, for a brief span, considered that he and Rose had gone completely off track and he had just committed the worst blunder of his career. *What the hell,* he thought, *that's the beauty of being a short-timer. Who gives a damn?*

The judge said coolly, "That's impossible."

"I've seen them. You're driving and you ran Ensor down."

"Can I see them?"

"No."

The judge shook his head. "That's unacceptable, Detective. If you've got pictures, I demand to see them."

Nye didn't move. "We've only got fifteen minutes and everyone knows you're on time. I've got pictures. I've got samples of paint and glass from your SUV and I know where you've got the SUV."

"It was stolen from outside my wife's office yesterday."

"No. Your wife and your father-in-law drove an SUV back to a dealership in Roseville yesterday morning. It's a cover-up, Judge, and it's over, okay?"

The judge had both hands on the armrests of his high-backed leather chair.

"I don't understand why you're here," he said tightly.

Nye shifted from one foot to the other, as if abruptly ill at ease. He looked down at the judge. "My grandfather was a cop here in town, back when it was kind of Wild West. He was a real piece of work. Back then, everybody'd tell you he was a cop's cop. It kind of meant he took care of business, whatever it took. He was a sweet guy sometimes. He was the best door-to-door salesman for Crystal Dairy after he retired from the department. He could talk anybody into buying a lot of milk and cottage cheese."

The judge's face hardened and turned pale.

Nye went on, "But when he was a cop, my grandfather did some tough things. It was just the way it got done in town in those days. He used to brag about it to me when he knew my dad wasn't around. They didn't get along at all. I guess it was hearing about what cops do, not the hard stuff so much, just how you get to keep things the way they should be, that made me join the department." He frowned. "Every time I start to think like my granddad or act like him, I stop myself. You'd be surprised or maybe you wouldn't, what you'll do if you get the chance."

The judge spoke slowly and with harshness. "What the hell are you talking about?"

Nye looked at him. "One thing my granddad said was, 'No trial for a cop killer.' Back then, a couple of cops were killed on duty and whoever did it never got arrested and sure as hell never went to trial. That was one thing my granddad didn't brag about or tell me about. I don't even know if he was part of whatever went on, except that was the rule."

The judge got up slowly and he trembled a little, either from rage or fear. Nye thought it was a combination. Rose had said this man was not one of their usual suspects but, in fact, it was hard to see a difference now.

"You're actually accusing me of killing this police officer?" the judge said.

"I'm telling you a fact. You hit Tommy Ensor last week and you left him in the street and he died because of it and a lot of lives have been screwed because of what you did."

"Why the hell are you here?" the judge demanded angrily. "You've got all this purported evidence. Who the hell told you to threaten me?"

"No one. I'm here by myself. My partner doesn't even know. I've got her sitting on that storage place just in case you or your wife or your father-in-law or someone tries to move what you've got out there."

"You're going to arrest me," the judge said, shaking, his words bitten out. "I've got access to the best lawyers in California."

"I'm not arresting you."

The judge swallowed. "My bailiff's right outside. I can have twenty armed men in here in ten seconds."

"I don't have a gun. I'm going to walk out in a couple of minutes. I said I'm not like my grandfather, so I came here to tell you what the score is. You get a choice. One thing he believed in, I do, too. No trial for a cop killer."

The judge looked like he was having trouble believing what was happening. "I don't understand. What do you want?"

Nye took a moment because it was hard to say, finally, when it came down to it. "I know a lot about you, Judge. You're a good guy and I know this wasn't your idea at all. It happened. You did things afterward and here you are. You're a good judge. You're the only one who can decide what happens next. Nobody else can judge you now."

"That's the choice?" the judge said carefully, after a few moments of heavy silence. A woman's brief laughter, probably his clerk, floated in.

"Yeah. That's it."

"People don't do that anymore. It's antique."

"Most people wouldn't. I think you're different."

"Assuming for the moment," the judge sat down again, his shoulders slouched, "I made that choice, what about my family?"

"The case's officially over. You heard that. Someone's already paid the price so I'd make sure it stayed that way. Your wife would be clear, same for your father-in-law."

"If it's over, then nothing more is necessary." The wheedling, bargaining impulse to avoid retribution died hard, even for Judge Stevenson, Nye realized.

Nye's face was stony and cold as the moon. "It sure as hell is. You're the guy who killed Tommy Ensor, not that poor jerk Lucking. It won't go away."

The judge's hands splayed on his desk blotter. Nye saw the photos of his family behind him and, for the first time, saw the award plaques and other commendatory pictures around his chambers. He briefly rebelled again at what he had to do.

Then he drove pity out of himself, completely and finally.

The judge breathed deeply several times, eyes down. He spoke slowly, with dreamy longing. "I could go to trial. You and I both know trials can take almost any direction. I have people who can testify where I was when the accident happened. Even with the evidence," he stopped, then resumed, "I could be acquitted."

"Go to trial and everything about your wife and Holder and what you all have done since the hit-and-run will come out and your kid will know all about it and she will live with that, whether you get off or not, for the rest of her life. One more notch, Judge. One more victim. You want that?"

"No," he said quietly. "No," he repeated loudly. He sat back. "When do I have to decide?"

"Twenty-four hours."

"It's not much time."

"It's a hell of a lot longer than you gave Ensor the other night."

He flinched, then didn't move and Nye again thought he had made a mistake, reckoned this man all wrong. Stevenson finally said, "What about the evidence, the pictures?"

"What evidence? I'm the only one who's seen the pictures. There won't be any evidence."

"I suppose I can't get that in writing," the judge said with a weak, twisted grin.

"This is a one-time deal, Judge. Right here. Right now."

Stevenson nodded and breathed out like he was deflating, then rallied. "I'm sorry. Ever since it happened, I wanted to say that to someone."

"Now you did."

Stevenson didn't appear to notice Nye's blunt dismissal. He went on, "I've gotten some money to Officer Ensor's family through my bailiff."

Nye was now fed up with the judge and himself for having to carry this responsibility alone. "So what's it going to be, Your Honor?" he demanded impatiently.

"If you know me," Stevenson said angrily, "you know the answer."

"I want to hear it."

"I'm taking your deal," he almost shouted, half standing. Then he stood, shook his head in an attempt to clear it, and came nearer to Nye.

Okay, Nye thought, *this is the bad part, when you have to look a guy right in face and there is no way you can save him from what's going to happen.* He had seen that in Quintana's anguish and nameless others over the years. He hoped his grandfather had not taken pleasure in these moments. He despised them.

"Do you know what's like, what it feels like to go out there," Stevenson pointed at the courtroom, "and sit on the bench and hold so many people in the palm of your hand? Do you know what it's like to walk into a room and every person, every single one, wants to listen to you, get close to you, and tell you what a superior being you are?"

Nye found himself nodding almost imperceptibly and Judge Stevenson nodded, too.

"Of course you do," Stevenson said. "You're a cop. You know what power feels like every day. We can do things other people don't imagine, change lives, reshape reality. But I learned something the other night, Detective Nye. I pass it along for whatever you want to make of it because we share a very rare and special reality ourselves." He stared at Nye. "It's a con. It's a fraud. It all ends in a moment. We're just like everyone else. We're just as powerless."

Nye stared back at Stevenson. "Bullshit," he said flatly. "Everybody gets to make a choice. You do, you lucky sonofabitch."

"Then that's the only power I've got." He looked slowly around his chambers. "I had dreams."

Nye didn't want to stay any longer in the judge's chambers. He had discharged his responsibility and what happened next was beyond his control. He had told necessary lies about the pictures. He had managed to keep Rose above it, too, and that gladdened him. She'll have plenty of blood to clean up on her own in the future, he thought. She may have her own lies to tell.

Nye turned to go and Stevenson said stumblingly, "I don't know what the protocol is now," he uncertainly put his hand out.

"It sure as hell isn't shaking hands," Nye said scornfully, looking back.

He walked out of the courtroom, into the busy courthouse corridor, trying not to feel that he was leaving the scene of yet another unchangeable, predestined collision.

FORTY-FIVE

"YOU'LL BE BACK TOMORROW?" Vee asked Stevenson. It had an urgent undertone.

"By noon at the latest. It's just a short practice climb and then I'll be on the road again." He continued loading his carefully packed rope, carabineers, and other equipment in the trunk of the Camry he had rented yesterday evening.

Vee insisted on being with him during the final preparations for the hastily arranged trip to Mt. Whitney. She made him a solid breakfast and stood in the garage door to the laundry room, coffee cup in hand.

"Something's wrong," she said and he forced himself to act as though he hadn't heard it. "You've been funny since yesterday."

"Damn right," he blustered, knowing he had to answer her. "Jury selection's moving quickly and I've got to get my head clear before I start hearing evidence. I need a little time off."

It was the same ruse he told Joan and Audie the day before when court resumed, after he had sat desolate in his chambers. He had, remarkably, shaken it off. The whole thing presented itself to him simply and economically, and, if for no other reasons, made final sense to him. Something so direct and plain had to be right. It also, he felt with astounding relief, meant he never had to confront the next horror. He had only deluded himself in thinking neither Eli nor Fonseca would not be a problem sometime in the future. He and Vee would be looking over their shoulders for the rest of their lives, even if the police said the case was now closed. It could be reopened.

Vee said, "I'm still worried about so much. I shouldn't be. I wish I could come with you."

"Not this trip. Look, a little time out for both of us will be good. Everything will look clearer tomorrow." He had no doubt of that.

"I hope so."

She went back into the kitchen and he finished loading the car. He had called his surgeon climbing buddy after recessing court and lightheartedly said they should plan a rock climb this summer. He would need to get some practice in first. Stevenson made a point of stressing his own rustiness. After the call, he told Joan to notify the lawyers on the trial that court would be dark on Wednesday. He called in a favor and on short notice got the permits to climb. It was like checking off boxes before a countdown. It would all make perfect sense when viewed in retrospect.

He went into the kitchen. Haley was eating breakfast and he nearly gave up when he saw her. The old detective was a cruel, ignorant bastard if he didn't know how much it would hurt to sit down to eat with Haley for the last time. *God, this is bad,* he thought. *This is worse than I imagined because I did not imagine it possible.*

But he was able to chat with her like it was any other morning, and while they talked and Vee joined them, he kept the dark away, willed it. If he relented for even a moment and let them see his sorrow and deception unmasked, they would all be finished. He would not allow that to happen.

"What's on tap for today, button?" he asked. He fingered a fork and spoon.

"Nothing very special," Haley said, considering, then nodding. "We're supposed to go on a roller-skating thing this week."

"That should be fun," he said tightly.

"It's supposed to help us *socialize,*" she said with startling sarcasm.

Her mother's superb insight, Stevenson thought. *I will miss how she comes into her own.*

"I want to hear about it. When is it?"

"Friday."

Too late, he thought. His rebellion almost mastered his intentions, but he laid his spoon down carefully to demonstrate to himself that his control was perfect and absolute at this hardest test.

"I took your mom ice-skating for the first time in her life," he said, glancing at Vee, who giggled. It was like chimes on a summer morning.

"I had never been to an ice-skating *rink* and I was so *awful.*"

Stevenson saw his daughter's interest perk up. "What happened?" she asked her mom.

And as they got caught up in laughing at the memory, he slipped out to the garage and left before necessity and resolution failed him.

"You're messing with me," Rose said, sitting down at her desk across from Nye.

"We're partners. I'm supposed to."

"You don't answer my questions," her voice dropped because Pesce and Talman were nearby, loudly arguing over football from the night before, "you won't tell me what's going on with our case."

"I've got it," he said again, feigning annoyance. "I'm working it."

"So tell me."

"What?"

"Nobody's covering the storage place."

Nye rolled his eyes. "I made a deal with the manager. Anybody goes to the unit, I get a call," he poked at his telephone. "I'm sketching out the search warrant affidavit."

"Let me see it," she insisted, like she was demanding his homework.

"You don't have time. We've got witnesses to see on our arson one eighty-seven," and he made it sound inarguable.

Rose got up, unpersuaded. Talman and Pesce shambled by, deep in argument over Minnesota's defense. "The scary thing, Ter, is you are such a good liar. But you know what?"

He continued the pretense, as if he were not watching the clock move with surreal slowness, time elongated to a thin strand, wondering what Stevenson would do. He could not keep Rose's doubts at bay for long. "Do I know *what?*" he repeated.

"You're not as good a liar as you think you are," she said with utter conviction. "I just don't know what you're lying about."

Rose not-so-quietly berated him all the way out of the building and all Nye could think, amid confusion, anger, and betrayal, was that the judge was screwing him.

It was just a goddamn con.

Stevenson drove south for hours and then turned onto Highway 395 into the Sierra Nevada foothills. He made a point of stopping for gas and to get a sandwich along the way, paying with his credit card so there would be a record later of his passage.

He experienced rage, regret, and then resignation in succession, and marveled that none of his apparently ungovernable emotions caused him to change what he was doing. He listened to the radio, passing from rap to country and various hysterical ministers of some sort who seemingly damned him in Spanish.

If he was lost, the day tricked him by its pristine clarity, blue and white sky, the green landscape and finally the mountains themselves, impossibly high and adamantine, the ideal of perfect justice in stone. They loomed over him in cold gray, especially the highest peak, Mt. Whitney. Stevenson understood that the old cop was right. There was something unalterable and necessary at work in all that had happened since he left that police officer in the street.

I'm the only one who can judge what I've done, he thought, pulling into a small motel in Lone Pine, not far from the start of the road's climb into the mountains.

At every step, when he fought against the knowledge that he would never see Vee again or hold Haley or be part of their lives as a living presence, he repeated that one incorruptible certainty.

Stevenson checked in at the motel, paying again by credit card, describing to the clerk his intention to undertake a quick climb partway up the east face of Whitney, come back, and spend the night before returning to Sacramento in the morning. He made it sound like a sudden impulse, not well planned or considered, and that, too, when the motel clerk related it afterward, would underline how foolhardy he had been to go up the mountain alone.

It was cool when he started climbing. He passed several others, but they were not following his route. It turned colder even though the sun flared overhead in a cloudless empty sky.

Stevenson grew tired quickly and realized he was indeed out of shape as a rock climber. His movements became slower and harder and his arms and shoulders ached painfully. Below him the pines were green points and, above him, the flat, unyielding stone face of Mt. Whitney.

He stopped, breathing heavily. He hung by his ropes and harness, suspended between the summit and the land hundreds of feet below. He thought of crawling into bed with Vee last night. It was deep in the night. He carefully pulled next to her, feeling her body mold to his as she slept, and he kissed her neck lightly. Hanging up on the face of the mountain, Stevenson said out loud, "I'm sorry." And then he said it again, quickly unhooked his harness, and closed his eyes.

Arms spread, as though he could fly, he fell backward and fast, and he opened his eyes, the stern and flawless mountain above him observing his fall with indifference.

He panicked for an instant because he believed, briefly, that he could defy gravity and remain as he was, all debts settled, all guilt cleaned away.

But as he continued to fall, Stevenson accepted finally that payments had to be made in full to mean anything.

FORTY-SIX

ROSE CAME BACK WITH ANOTHER ROUND of beers for Talman, Pesce, and their wives, and one for herself, too. Nye helped her navigate around the crowded table in the packed Pine Cove bar. Everyone had to shout to be heard.

"It was a good speech," she said to him. "You surprised me."

Nye sipped tonic water. "What did you think I was going to do?"

"I don't know," she took a long drink. "Something embarrassing. Didn't you think he'd do something and make us all act like we didn't know who the hell he was?"

Talman sputtered in agreement. He was drunk, and his wife, drunker. She stared into the dark, loud bar, steeped in the memory of old cigarettes long stubbed out and stale beer saturating the thin carpet, marveling at the mob of cops in full dress uniforms, all diligently laboring at losing their sobriety. Many were successful.

"It was damn good, Terry," Pesce said, throwing his arm over Nye's shoulder. "I could've cried, man."

Nye good-naturedly shook off the embrace. It was late afternoon, a light drizzle came down as they came in after Tommy Ensor's funeral

411

in the Cathedral of the Blessed Sacrament downtown and the mournful, silent hours afterward with Janey and the kids in their home. In his whole career, which covered more than a few official funerals, Nye had never seen so many uniforms from so many departments in California spread out before him when he got up to speak that morning. It was that sight that pulled him through stabbing stage fright and withering emotion. And, knowing that Tommy's wife and family, all dressed in black, were watching him from the front row—and behind him a large mounted photograph of Ensor, smiling in uniform, with his Medal of Valor on an embroidered cushion set at the foot of the gun-metal gray casket beneath the great suspended gold cross—gave Nye a clear voice and a crisp delivery. Unlike several speakers, he did not quaver or weep.

But I know a few things none of them do, he thought as he made his way back to the pew, and Maslow rolled up in his wheelchair to speak next. *I've got an edge.*

"What about Maslow?" he asked, bringing himself back to the present and changing the subject from himself.

"You know, he was really funny," Pesce shouted over the noise, "and that guy's the most *not* funny asshole around."

"Hey," Talman protested. His wife looked bored.

"Like no one at *this* table," Pesce said, "has ever heard *asshole* or a lot more. *Asshole.*"

"Hey," Talman repeated drunkenly.

Nye glanced around the table and noticed that Rose was looking at him. She had taken up an uncomfortable way of studying Nye since leaving Jane Ensor's house. Like she was doing right now.

"The kid's grown, Rosie," he said to her in an attempt to take her mind off the ill thoughts she was likely harboring of him.

"Yeah, they do that," and she went on studying him and he realized she had gotten a little loaded, too. Rose and Luis, in his best dark-blue suit, and little Annorina in a neat dark dress, had met him at the entrance to the cathedral before the service, in the welter of people and cameras and the low organ music. Luis was a trifle awkward but Annorina smiled and offered her small hand, which Nye took with theatrical formality.

"What's with the look?" he asked Rose now.

"No look. Something bothering you?"

"Not me. It's just a look you've got."

"Really."

"Management alert," someone nearby called out.

At that moment, Nishimoto and his wife appeared, making their way from table to table, pausing briefly. Nye appreciated the interruption. Rose was spoiling to continue the simmering argument from the day before.

Nishimoto introduced his wife to the table. She was a thin woman and, although Nye didn't know her well, she looked pleased with life. He surmised it was a relief for her, in the end, not to be the next chief's wife. Nishimoto complimented him on what he said at the funeral. Nye hoped they didn't want to sit down.

"This guy is a short-timer, too, Lisa," Nishimoto said to his wife, pointing at Nye.

"Well, congratulations," she said. "I hope you like life after the department as much as I do," she caught herself, "as much as we do."

Nye said, "Well, actually boss, I'm going to stay."

Rose slowly formed an inscrutable smile.

Nishimoto said confusedly, "I'm sorry. I guess I got it wrong, Terry. I was under the strong impression you were counting the days."

Rose said, "Some people had the same idea, sir."

"I thought about it. I have a couple more things to do." Nye sipped his tonic water. He longed for whatever the overworked quartet of bartenders was pouring.

Nishimoto and his wife moved on to another group, and then left, much to everyone's relief.

"Like what, Ter?" Rose asked. "What's on your to do list?"

"You."

"You're kidding."

"No, seriously," he leaned forward, pushing aside a wicker basket of stale popcorn, "I can help you. I've got a lot of things to pass along."

Rose finished her beer. "Hey, Pesce," she said. "Hypothetical for you. What about a partner who doesn't tell his partner what's going on?"

"He's an *asshole*."

Rose turned to Nye. "The verdict's in, Ter."

"There's nothing to tell," he said.

"Really. Oh. Really. What about our judge?" she asked in a lowered voice.

"He fell off a mountain."

"You saw his wife and her dad on TV last night. Big tearful hugs, lots of what-the-hell-happened stuff. One big unhappy family from now on. I feel sorry for their kid. She looked pretty bad."

Nye let the noise and chaos swirl around him. The death of Judge Frank Stevenson in a mountain-climbing accident was swiftly crowding out the diminishing media interest in Officer Thomas Ensor's passing.

"It's lousy when a kid loses someone."

"But you won't admit to me right here, this minute, it is one amazing coincidence that our judge takes a dive right when we're on the brink of maybe proving some unpleasant things about him?"

Nye spoke to her, like they were completely alone, and the whole noisy, hectic bar had vanished and it was just them at a table, coming to a final reckoning.

"Tommy Ensor's gone and his family's going to live with it. The guy who hit him's gone, too. It's over, Rosie. It's about as over as anything gets."

"What about Holder?"

"You saw him on TV. He's got a widowed daughter and grandkid to look out for. He's paying."

"You want to forget about that storage unit? Pretend it's empty?"

"Yeah. Exactly."

"Hypothetically again, what happens to anything in it?"

"Sooner or later it disappears."

"What about me? What do I do?" She sat up and studied him.

"You got to do what you think's right. But I think this time you should trust me, Rosie. Nothing gets fixed or better than it is right now."

"This the kind of thing you want to pass along? Your words of wisdom?" she asked.

"Yeah, it is."

"It's crap," she said angrily.

"Ain't it," he agreed.

"I'm getting another round," she announced, and he went with her to the bar. They elbowed through some boisterous detectives from Robbery. Nye noted that a few of them had not worn their dress uniforms in quite awhile, as belts and buttons were straining dangerously.

Rose shouted out her order and the harried bartenders darted around racks of lovely multicolored bottles. Nye felt the pangs of fright and emotion he had conquered in the cathedral. Rose was at a crossroad and she could make a wrong choice. If she made it, he would in fact leave the department. There was no point to stay. He didn't care if Guthrie or a thousand guys like him would be bird-dogging him every second. It was Rose's call this moment that mattered.

He bobbed his head nervously, smiled vacantly at the yelling detectives, and the moments crept by.

She turned to him, leaning on the bar with one arm. She was steady and clear-eyed.

"I don't like it, Ter," Rose said. "It's not the way I want my life to go, or Annorina's or Luis's. Not yours, either."

Nye said nothing, the pain growing.

"It's as messed up as a soup sandwich. But that's the way things work sometimes, yeah?"

"Yeah."

"If you get justice, maybe you have to forget about truth sometimes?"

"That's the deal, best I've seen."

Rose shook her head with resigned, bitter irrevocability. "Christ, old man, what a deal."

Nye's pain flowed away and he smiled. "Don't let it get you down. I'll provide some laughs along the way."

The bartender shoved full glasses at Rose and she struggled to gather them up, pushing away some of the detectives pressed to the bar.

"Undoubtedly," she said, pronouncing every syllable. "Asshole."

"But, like last night, I'm sleeping better."

Nye helped Rose carry the refilled glasses back to the table through the crowd of noisy, drunken cops.